HOUSE AT STEVENTON WHERE
JANE AUSTEN WAS BORN

A SENTIMENTAL JOURNEY
THROUGH FRANCE AND ITALY

BY

LAURENCE STERNE

PRIDE AND PREJUDICE

BY

JANE AUSTEN

EDITED WITH NOTES AND INTRODUCTIONS
BY WILLIAM ALLAN NEILSON Ph D

P F COLLIER & SON COMPANY
NEW YORK

CONTENTS

A SENTIMENTAL JOURNEY THROUGH
FRANCE AND ITALY

BIOGRAPHICAL NOTE

LAURENCE STERNE was born in Clonmel, Tipperary, Ireland, on November 24, 1713. His father, Roger Sterne, was an English soldier who never rose above the rank of lieutenant; and the first ten years of Laurence's life were passed in various garrison towns, the life of the barracks being occasionally varied by periods spent in the houses of compassionate relatives. In 1723 the boy was placed in a school in Halifax, where he stayed till his father's death in 1731. Then, after two years of idleness, the liberality of a cousin enabled him to go to Jesus College, Cambridge, whence he graduated in 1736. Though totally without fitness or inclination for the ministry, he took holy orders, and after a short period as curate of Buckden became vicar of Sutton-in-the-Forest, eight miles from York, in 1738. Here he lived for twenty-two years, his income from the living being supplemented by a prebend in York Cathedral and various other ecclesiastical offices. After a two years' courtship, in his description of which Sterne invented the term "sentimental," he married in 1741 Elizabeth Lumley. The union did not bring great happiness to either party. Sterne found the life of a country parson somewhat dull, and he sought to vary its monotony by dabbling in music and painting, by wide reading, and by social amusements, notable among which were the carousals at Skelton Hall, where a college friend, John Hall-Stevenson, used to gather a roistering company under the name of "The Demoniacks."

Until he was past forty Sterne had apparently no thought of authorship and had published nothing but one or two sermons. About 1748, however, the success of a privately circulated skit on a local ecclesiastical quarrel suggested a new line of activity, the result of which appeared in the first two books of "Tristram Shandy," published at York, January 1, 1760. Their success was great and immediate, and in a few months the author went up to London to enjoy his triumph. He was lionized to his heart's content, his fame bringing him not only the acquaintance of many of the distinguished men of the time, but the more tender attentions of the other sex.

Sterne's relations with women in Yorkshire had been by no means beyond reproach, and now in London he was able to indulge his passion for flirtation on a great scale. The most notorious of his affairs of this kind was with Mrs. Eliza Draper, the young wife of an officer in India. It began in 1765 and led to the composition of "Letters" and the "Journal to Eliza," and to an endless amount of scandal.

In 1760 he was presented to a curacy at Coxwold in Yorkshire, and he moved thither the same year, retaining his other livings. This remained his home for the rest of his life, but he was much in London or abroad. Early in 1762 he was ordered to France for his health, and on crossing to Paris was received with high distinction. When he returned to England in 1764 he left his wife and daughter in the south of France. Meantime he continued to add to "Tristram Shandy," concluding it with a ninth book in 1766. In the previous year he had made the trip to the Continent that formed the basis of "The Sentimental Journey," which he finished in 1767. He went to London to attend to its publication, and when it came out in February, 1768, he had the satisfaction of seeing it raise his reputation still higher. Three weeks later, on March 18, he died.

A defense of Sterne's character is impossible; he had no character, but only a temperament. From childhood he was excessively sensitive, and throughout his life the pleasure that he got out of his feelings was the controlling and almost the sole cause of his actions.

The extraordinary thing is that the writings of such a man should have had so profound an effect throughout Europe, and an effect largely for good. He did, indeed, set a lamentable fashion of mawkish "sensibility"; but, in an age that had tended to cultivate the reason somewhat exclusively, he did much to restore emotion to its place, and by quickening the power of sympathy, helped to make possible the great humanitarian movements which culminated in such achievements as the abolition of slavery.

The sentimentality which brought Sterne immediate popularity is no longer his attraction. Mingled with it there is a delightfully whimsical humor which is entirely his own; and he commanded a style of unsurpassed clarity and ease. The distinctness with which we can picture the successive scenes of his not extraordinary journey and the lastingness of the impressions left on us are the best testimony to his quality as a master of English prose.

W. A. N.

CRITICISMS AND INTERPRETATIONS

I

By Sir Walter Scott

THE style employed by Sterne is fancifully ornamented, but at the same time vigorous and masculine, and full of that animation and force which can only be derived by an intimate acquaintance with the early English prose writers. In the power of approaching and touching the finer feelings of the heart, he has never been excelled, if indeed, he has ever been equaled; and may be at once recorded as one of the most affected, and one of the most simple writers—as one of the greatest plagiarists, and of the most original geniuses whom England has produced.— From "Sterne," in "Lives of the Novelists" (originally in "Ballantyne's Novelists' Library.")

II

By Edmond Scherer

STERNE is at once tender-hearted and sentimental; that is to say, naturally susceptible of sympathetic emotions, and inclined at the same time to invite them for the pleasure that he feels in them, and the credit they gain him. He was very early familiar with the tone of tenderness. See how he describes the solitude in which "his Lumley" has left him. "A solitary plate," he writes to her, "only one knife, one fork, one glass! I bestowed a thousand pensive and penetrating glances on the chair that you have so often adorned with your graceful person in our tranquil and sentimental repasts." He insists that when his time comes, he will die alone, far from home, in some inn.

If you will believe him, the suffering of friends at such a moment, nay, the last offices of affection, would torment his soul and suffice to kill him. "Thank God!" he cries, "for my sensibility; though it has often caused me suffering, I would not give it for all the pleasures of coarse sensualists." We can now understand what Sterne means by a "Sentimental Journey." The traveler *à la* Sterne is a man who troubles himself but little about the goal for which he is making, or the regions which he traverses. He hardly visits remarkable monuments, he says nothing of the beauty of places; his objects of search are sweet and affectionate emotions. Everything becomes to him matter for sympathy: a caged bird, a donkey sinking under ill treatment, a poor child, an old monk. A sort of universal benevolence makes him take his share of all small sorrows, not exactly for the purpose of consolation, but to enter into them, to taste their savor, and, if I may say so, to extract the picturesque from them. Sentimentalism is perfectly compatible with a certain strain of egotism, and the sentimental traveler is at bottom much more his own master than is thought. It is for this reason that he paints so excellently, for this also that he so often exaggerates and strikes into falsetto. The history of Father Lorenzo is an example of these exaggerations. Lorenzo had given Sterne his snuffbox, and some months afterward our traveler, revisiting Calais, learns that the poor monk is dead. He "burst into tears" at the tomb. Well and good, but there are too many of these tears in Sterne. I like him better when his tenderness keeps better measure, or when he contents himself with a simple humane impulse. In this style of touching simplicity, he has told stories which are, and deserve to be, famous, being pure masterpieces, such as the story of Le Fevre, the death of Yorick, the two donkeys, the dead donkey of Naimport, and him of the pastry cook. Did Sterne ever write anything more exquisite than Uncle Toby's fly? Is not the hero of the siege of Namur all in this trait?

To sum up, Sterne is a tale-teller of the first order and excellent in sentimental scenes. But he has the faults of his style: he abuses the trick of interesting the heart in trifles; he enlarges little things too much; he scarcely ever declaims, but he sometimes whimpers. . . .

Without going about to do so, we have just drawn the portrait of Sterne. He had neither ill nature nor egotism; but (which is much more human) he had weakness and levity. His, says M. Stapfer, was a kind of optimism which believed in the good of human nature and the moral government of the world, without denying the evil and the disorders in both—I should add, especially without taking either tragically or troubling himself much about them. He writes, " 'Tis a good little world, the world in which we live. I take Heaven to witness, after all my jesting, my heart is innocent, and the sports of my pen just like those of my infancy when I rode cockhorse on a stick." And elsewhere: "*Vive la bagatelle!* O my humor, never has thou painted in black the objects I met in my way. In danger thou hast gilt my horizon with hope, and when death itself knocked at my door, thou didst tell him to call again with so gay an air of careless indifference that he doubted his mission."

There we have him—a light and easy humor, a man who looks at once with amusement and sympathy at human affairs, who loves the world without forming too high an idea of it. And we have, as the result, a kindly satire, where bitterness is replaced by good-humor, contempt by affection, the spirit of detraction by sensibility, a satire which inspires us with interest and even affection for the very persons of whom it makes fun.—From "Laurence Sterne, or the Humorist," in "Essays on English Literature," translated by George Saintsbury.

III

By Professor Saintsbury

THE way in which his scenes, sometimes corrected and finished as punctiliously as a steel engraving, sometimes shaded off on all sides into a sort of halo of mist, impress themselves on the mind is unique. Dickens had one of not the least of his flashes of genius when he made such an apparently unlikely person as Sam Weller speak of "the gentleman in the black silk smalls as knowed the young 'ooman as kept a goat." This dramatic-pictorial faculty is, in combination, very rare, and its effectiveness depends no doubt to some extent on the want of continuity in Sterne—on the way in which the shapes arise, grow vivid, flicker, faint, and disappear, speaking all the time, when they do speak, in strictest conformity with their presentation. Probably the effectiveness is also due in part to the fact that there is after all very little of it. Although "Tristram" was actually and originally dribbled out over a long series of years, and of cunningly small and widely printed volumes, both it and the "Sentimental Journey" will go, without "diamond" type, into four still smaller— two of moderate size, and even one somewhat but not excessively "squeezed." The stuff which they contain could not, in fact, be hastily produced, and probably could not have been produced at all except in Sterne's actual "twenty years of shooting, fishing, playing the flute," and occasionally performing the light duties of an eighteenth-century parson, followed by nearly half the time of travel, society, and what not. Nor could he, as probably, have produced much more if longer life had been granted him, nor will any wise person wish that he had done so. Of the good strong ale, and generous port, and subtly flavored claret, and wisdom-giving amontillado, and inspiring champagne, and ineffable burgundy of Fielding and Scott and Miss Austen and Dickens and Thackeray and other great novelists, one never can have too much. But Sterne is not a drink or a wine either of barley or grape—he is a liqueur—agreeable, but not perhaps exactly wholesome, artistic but certainly artificial. And it is only a yokel who wants kümmel or goldwasser, chartreuse or curaçoa "in a moog."—From "The Peace of the Augustans" (1916).

LIST OF CHARACTERS

Yorick, the sentimental traveler.
Father Lorenzo; a Franciscan monk.
Monsieur Dessein, master of the hotel at Calais.
Madame de L——
La Fleur, servant to Yorick.
The owner of a dead ass.
The wife of a glove merchant.
An old French officer.
A tall German.
A dwarf.
Marquisina di F——
Madame de Rambouliet.
Fille de chambre to Madame R——
A chevalier of St. Louis.
Marquis d'E——
Count de B——
A Parisian landlord.
A girl selling laces.
A flattering beggar.
Maria, a mad girl.
A French farmer and his family.
A Piedmontese lady.
Her fille de chambre.

A SENTIMENTAL JOURNEY THROUGH FRANCE AND ITALY

—THEY order, said I, this matter better in France.—
—You have been in France? said my gentleman,
turning quick upon me with the most civil triumph
in the world.—Strange! quoth I, debating the matter with myself, that one and twenty miles' sailing, for 't is absolutely
no further from Dover to Calais, should give a man these
rights.—I'll look into them: so giving up the argument—
I went straight to my lodgings, put up half a dozen shirts
and a black pair of silk breeches—"the coat I have on,"
said I, looking at the sleeve, "will do"—took a place in
the Dover stage; and the packet sailing at nine the next
morning—by three I had got sat down to my dinner upon
a fricasseed chicken, so incontestably in France, that had
I died that night of an indigestion, the whole world could
not have suspended the effects of the *droits d'aubaine*[1]—
my shirts, and black pair of silk breeches—portmanteau
and all must have gone to the King of France—even the
little picture which I have so long worn, and so often have
told thee, Eliza, I would carry with me into my grave,
would have been torn from my neck.—Ungenerous!—to
seize upon the wreck of an unwary passenger, whom your
subjects had beckon'd to their coast.—By heaven! SIRE, it
is not well done; and much does it grieve me, 't is the monarch of a people so civilized and courteous, and so re-
nowned for sentiment and fine feelings, that I have to reason with—

But I have scarce set foot in your dominions.—

[1] All the effects of strangers (Swiss and Scotch excepted) dying in
France, are seized by virtue of this law, though the heir be upon the spot—
the profit of these contingencies being farmed, there is no redress.

CALAIS

WHEN I had finish'd my dinner, and drank the King of France's health, to satisfy my mind that I bore him no spleen, but, on the contrary, high honor for the humanity of his temper—I rose up an inch taller for the accommodation.

—No—said I—the Bourbon is by no means a cruel race: they may be misled like other people; but there is a mildness in their blood. As I acknowledged this, I felt a suffusion of a finer kind upon my cheek—more warm and friendly to man, than what Burgundy (at least of two livres a bottle, which was such as I had been drinking) could have produced.

—Just God! said I, kicking my portmanteau aside, what is there in this world's goods which should sharpen our spirits, and make so many kind-hearted brethren of us fall out so cruelly as we do by the way?

When man is at peace with man, how much lighter than a feather is the heaviest of metals in his hands! he pulls out his purse, and holding it airily and uncompress'd, looks round him, as if he sought for an object to share it with.—In doing this, I felt every vessel in my frame dilate—the arteries beat all cheerily together, and every power which sustained life, performed it with so little friction, that 't would have confounded the most *physical précieuse* in France: with all her materialism, she could scarce have called me a machine.—

I'm confident, said I to myself, I should have overset her creed.

The accession of that idea carried nature, at that time, as high as she could go—I was at peace with the world before, and this finish'd the treaty with myself.—

Now, was I a King of France, cried I—what a moment for an orphan to have begg'd his father's portmanteau of me!

THE MONK

CALAIS

I HAD scarce utter'd the words, when a poor monk of the order of St. Francis came into the room to beg something for his convent. No man cares to have his virtues the sport of contingencies—or one man may be generous, as another man is puissant—*sed non quo ad hanc*—or be it as it may—for there is no regular reasoning upon the ebbs and flows of our humors; they may depend upon the same causes, for aught I know, which influence the tides themselves—'t would oft be no discredit to us, to suppose it was so: I'm sure at least for myself, that in many a case I should be more highly satisfied to have it said by the world, "I had had an affair with the moon, in which there was neither sin nor shame," than have it pass altogether as my own act and deed, wherein there was so much of both.

—But be this as it may. The moment I cast my eyes upon him, I was predetermined not to give him a single sou; and accordingly I put my purse into my pocket—button'd it up—set myself a little more upon my center, and advanced up gravely to him: there was something, I fear, forbidding in my look: I have his figure this moment before my eyes, and think there was that in it which deserved better.

The monk, as I judg'd from the break in his tonsure, a few scatter'd white hairs upon his temples being all that remained of it, might be about seventy—but from his eyes, and that sort of fire which was in them, which seem'd more temper'd by courtesy than years, could be no more than sixty—truth might lie between—he was certainly sixty-five; and the general air of his countenance, notwithstanding something seem'd to have been planting wrinkles in it before their time, agreed to the account.

3

It was one of those heads which Guido has often painted —mild, pale—penetrating, free from all commonplace ideas of fat contented ignorance looking downwards upon the earth—it look'd forwards; but look'd, as if it look'd at something beyond this world. How one of his order came by it, heaven above, who let it fall upon a monk's shoulders, best knows; but it would have suited a Brahmin, and had I met it upon the plains of Indostan, I had reverenced it.

The rest of his outline may be given in a few strokes; one might put it into the hands of any one to design, for 't was neither elegant or otherwise, but as character and expression made it so: it was a thin, spare form, something above the common size, if it lost not the distinction by a bend forwards in the figure—but it was the attitude of entreaty; and as it now stands presented to my imagination, it gain'd more than it lost by it.

When he had enter'd the room three paces, he stood still; and laying his left hand upon his breast (a slender white staff with which he journey'd being in his right)—when I had got close up to him, he introduced himself with the little story of the wants of his convent, and the poverty of his order—and did it with so simple a grace—and such an air of deprecation was there in the whole cast of his look and figure—I was bewitch'd not to have been struck with it.—

—A better reason was, I had predetermined not to give him a single sou.

THE MONK

—, 'TIS very true, said I, replying to a cast upwards with his eyes, with which he had concluded his address—'t is very true—and heaven be their resource who have no other but the charity of the world, the stock of which, I fear, is no way sufficient for the many *great claims* which are hourly made upon it.

As I pronounced the words *great claims,* he gave a slight glance with his eye downwards upon the sleeve of his tunic. —I felt the full force of the appeal.—I acknowledge it, said I—a coarse habit, and that but once in three years, with meager diet—are no great matters; and the true point of pity is, as they can be earn'd in the world with so little industry, that your order should wish to procure them by pressing upon a fund which is the property of the lame, the blind, the aged, and the infirm—the captive who lies down counting over and over again the days of his afflictions, languishes also for his share of it; and had you been of the *order of mercy,* instead of the order of St. Francis, poor as I am, continued I, pointing at my portmanteau, full cheerfully should it have been open'd to you, for the ransom of the unfortunate.—The monk made me a bow.—But of all others, resum'd I, the unfortunate of our own country, surely, have the first rights; and I have left thousands in distress upon our own shore.—The monk gave a cordial wave with his head—as much as to say, No doubt, there is misery enough in every corner of the world, as well as within our convent.—But we distinguish, said I, laying my hand upon the sleeve of his tunic, in return for his appeal—we distinguish, my good father! betwixt those who wish only to eat the bread of their own labor—and those who eat the bread of other people's, and have no other plan in life but to get through it in sloth and ignorance, *for the love of God.*

The poor Franciscan made no reply: a hectic of a moment pass'd across his cheek, but could not tarry—Nature seemed to have done with her resentments in him; he showed none—but letting his staff fall within his arm, he press'd both his hands with resignation upon his breast, and retired.

THE MONK

CALAIS

MY heart smote me the moment he shut the door—
Psha! said I, with an air of carelessness, three
several times—but it would not do: every ungracious
syllable I had utter'd, crowded back into my imagination: I
reflected, I had no right over the poor Franciscan, but to
deny him; and that the punishment of that was enough to the
disappointed, without the addition of unkind language: I consider'd his gray hairs—his courteous figure seem'd to reënter
and gently ask me what injury he had done me?—and why I
could use him thus?—I would have given twenty livres for
an advocate.—I have behaved very ill, said I within myself;
but I have only just set out upon my travels; and shall learn
better manners as I get along.

THE DESOBLIGEANT

Calais

WHEN a man is discontented with himself, it has one advantage however, that it puts him into an excellent frame of mind for making a bargain. Now there being no traveling through France and Italy without a chaise—and nature generally prompting us to the thing we are fittest for, I walk'd out into the coachyard to buy or hire something of that kind to my purpose: an old Desobligeant[1] in the furthest corner of the court hit my fancy at first sight, so I instantly got into it, and, finding it in tolerable harmony with my feelings, I ordered the waiter to call Monsieur Dessein, the master of the hotel.—But Monsieur Dessein being gone to vespers, and not caring to face the Franciscan, whom I saw on the opposite side of the court, in conference with a lady just arrived at the inn—I drew the taffeta curtain betwixt us, and being determined to write my journey, I took out my pen and ink, and wrote the preface to it in the *Desobligeant*.

[1] A chaise, so called in France, from its holding but one person.

PREFACE

IT must have been observed by many a peripatetic philosopher, that nature has set up by her own unquestionable authority certain boundaries and fences to circumscribe the discontent of man: she has effected her purpose in the quietest and easiest manner, by laying him under almost insuperable obligations to work out his ease, and to sustain his sufferings at home. It is there only that she has provided him with the most suitable objects to partake of his happiness, and bear a part of that burden, which, in all countries and ages, has ever been too heavy for one pair of shoulders. 'T is true, we are endued with an imperfect power of spreading our happiness sometimes beyond *her* limits, but 't is so order'd, that, from the want of languages, connections, and dependencies, and from the difference in education, customs, and habits, we lie under so many impediments in communicating our sensations out of our own sphere, as often amount to a total impossibility.

It will always follow from hence, that the balance of sentimental commerce is always against the expatriated adventurer: he must buy what he has little occasion for, at their own price—his conversation will seldom be taken in exchange for theirs without a large discount—and this by the by, eternally driving him into the hands of more equitable brokers, for such conversation as he can find it requires no great spirit of divination to guess at his party—

This brings me to my point; and naturally leads me (if the see-saw of this *Desobligeant* will but let me get on) into the efficient as well as the final causes of traveling.—

Your idle people that leave their native country, and go abroad for some reason or reasons which may be derived from one of these general causes—

9

Infirmity of body,
Imbecility of mind, or
Inevitable necessity.

The first two include all those who travel by land or by water, laboring with pride, curiosity, vanity, or spleen, subdivided and combined *in infinitum*.

The third class includes the whole army of peregrine martyrs; more especially those travelers who set out upon their travels with the benefit of the clergy, either as delinquents traveling under the direction of governors recommended by the magistrate—or young gentlemen transported by the cruelty of parents and guardians, and traveling under the direction of governors recommended by Oxford, Aberdeen, and Glasgow.

There is a fourth class, but their number is so small, that they would not deserve a distinction, was it not necessary in a work of this nature to observe the greatest precision and nicety, to avoid a confusion of character. And these men I speak of, are such as cross the seas and sojourn in a land of strangers, with a view of saving money for various reasons and upon various pretenses: but as they might also save themselves and others a great deal of unnecessary trouble by saving their money at home—and as their reasons for traveling are the least complex of any other species of emigrants, I shall distinguish these gentlemen by the name of

Simple Travelers.

Thus the whole circle of travelers may be reduced to the following *heads:*

Idle Travelers,
Inquisitive Travelers,
Lying Travelers,
Proud Travelers,
Vain Travelers,
Splenetic Travelers.

Then follow

The Travelers of Necessity,
The Delinquent and Felonious Traveler,
The Unfortunate and Innocent Traveler,
The Simple Traveler,

And last of all (if you please) The Sentimental Traveler (meaning thereby myself), who have travel'd, and of which I am now sitting down to give an account—as much out of *necessity*, and the *besoin de voyager*, as any one in the class.

I am well aware, at the same time, as both my travels and observations will be altogether of a different cast from any of my forerunners, that I might have insisted upon a whole nitch entirely to myself—but I should break in upon the confines of the *Vain* Traveler, in wishing to draw attention towards me, till I have some better grounds for it, than the mere *novelty of my vehicle*.

It is sufficient for my reader, if he has been a Traveler himself, that with study and reflection hereupon he may be able to determine his own place and rank in the catalogue —it will be one step towards knowing himself, as it is great odds but he retains some tincture and resemblance of what he imbibed or carried out, to the present hour.

The man who first transplanted the grape of Burgundy to the Cape of Good Hope (observe he was a Dutchman) never dreamt of drinking the same wine at the Cape, that the same grape produced upon the French mountains—he was too phlegmatic for that—but undoubtedly he expected to drink some sort of vinous liquor; but whether good, bad, or indifferent—he knew enough of this world to know, that it did not depend upon his choice, but that what is generally called *chance* was to decide his success: however, he hoped for the best: and in these hopes, by an intemperate confidence in the fortitude of his head, and the depth of his discretion, *mynheer* might possible overset both in his new vineyard, and by discovering his nakedness, become a laughing-stock to his people.

Even so it fares with the poor Traveler, sailing and posting through the politer kingdoms of the globe, in pursuit of knowledge and improvements.

Knowledge and improvements are to be got by sailing and posting for that purpose; but whether useful knowledge and real improvements is all a lottery—and even where the adventurer is successful, the acquired stock must be used with caution and sobriety, to turn to any profit—but as the chances run prodigiously the other way, both as to the acquisition and application, I am of opinion, that a man would act wisely, if he could prevail upon himself to live contented without foreign knowledge or foreign improvements especially if he lives in a country that has no absolute want of either—and indeed, much grief of heart has it oft and many a time cost me, when I have observed how many a foul step the Inquisitive Traveler has measured to see sights and look into discoveries, all which, as Sancho Panza said to Don Quixote, they might have seen dry-shod at home. It is an age so full of light, that there is scarce a country or corner of Europe, whose beams are not crossed and interchanged with others.—Knowledge in most of its branches, and in most affairs, is like music in an Italian street, whereof those may partake who pay nothing.—But there is no nation under heaven—and GOD is my record (before whose tribunal I must one day come and give an account of this work)—that I do not speak it vauntingly—but there is no nation under heaven abounding with more variety of learning—where the sciences may be more fitly woo'd, or more surely won, than here—where art is encouraged, and will so soon rise high—where Nature (take her altogether) has so little to answer for—and, to close all, where there is more wit and variety of character to feed the mind with.—Where then, my dear countrymen, are you going—

—We are only looking at this chaise, said they.—Your most obedient servant, said I, skipping out of it, and pulling off my hat.—We were wondering, said one of them, who, I found, was an *Inquisitive Traveler*,—what could occasion its motion.—'T was the agitation, said I coolly, of writing a preface.—I never heard, said the other, who was a *Simple Traveler*, of a preface wrote in a *Desobligeant.*—It would have been better, said I, in a *Vis-à-Vis.*

As an Englishman does not travel to see Englishmen, I retired to my room.

CALAIS

I PERCEIVED that something darken'd the passage more than myself, as I stepp'd along it to my room; it was effectually Monsieur Dessein, the master of the hotel, who had just return'd from vespers, and, with his hat under his arm, was most complaisantly following me, to put me in mind of my wants. I had wrote myself pretty well out of conceit with the *Desobligeant;* and Monsieur Dessein speaking of it with a shrug, as if it would no way suit me, it immediately struck my fancy that it belong'd to some *Innocent Traveler,* who, on his return home, had left it to Monsieur Dessein's honor to make the most of. Four months had elapsed since it had finish'd its career of Europe in the corner of Monsieur Dessein's coach-yard; and having sallied out from thence but a vampt-up business at the first, though it had been twice taken to pieces on Mount Sennis, it had not profited much by its adventures—but by none so little as the standing so many months unpitied in the corner of Monsieur Dessein's coach-yard. Much indeed was not to be said for it—but something might—and when a few words will rescue misery out of her distress, I hate the man who can be a churl of them.

—Now was I the master of this hotel, said I, laying the point of my forefinger on Monsieur Dessein's breast, I would inevitably make a point of getting rid of this unfortunate *Desobligeant*—it stands swinging reproaches at you every time you pass by it.—

Mon Dieu! said Monsieur Dessein—I have no interest—Except the interest, said I, which men of a certain turn of mind take, Monsieur Dessein, in their own sensations.—I'm persuaded, to a man who feels for others as well as for himself, every rainy night, disguise it as you will, must cast a damp upon your spirits.—You suffer, Monsieur Dessein, as much as the machine—

I have always observed, when there is as much *sour* as *sweet* in a compliment, that an Englishman is eternally at a loss within himself, whether to take it or let it alone: a Frenchman never is: Monsieur Dessein made me a bow.

C'est bien vrai, said he—But in this case I should only exchange one disquietude for another, and with loss; figure to yourself, my dear sir, that in giving you a chaise which would fall to pieces before you had got half-way to Paris —figure to yourself how much I should suffer, in giving an ill impression of myself to a man of honor, and lying at the mercy, as I must do, *d'un homme d'esprit.*

The dose was made up exactly after my own prescription; so I could not help taking it—and returning Monsieur Dessein his bow, without more casuistry we walk'd together towards his Remise, to take a view of his magazine of chaises.

IN THE STREET

IT must needs to be a hostile kind of a world, when the
buyer (if it be but of a sorry post-chaise) cannot go
forth with the seller thereof into the street, to ter-
minate the difference betwixt them, but he instantly falls
into the same frame of mind, and views his conventionist
with the same sort of eye, as if he was going along with him
to Hyde Park Corner to fight a duel. For my own part,
being but a poor swordsman, and no way a match for Monsieur *Dessein,* I felt the rotation of all the movements within
me to which the situation is incident.—I looked at Monsieur
Dessein through and through—ey'd him as he walked along
in profile—then, *en face*—thought he look'd like a Jew—then
a Turk—disliked his wig—curs'd him by my gods—wish'd
him at the devil—

—And is all this to be lighted up in the heart for a
beggarly account of three or four louis d'ors, which is the
most I can be overreach'd in?—Base passion! said I, turning
myself about, as a man naturally does upon a sudden reverse
of sentiment—base ungentle passion! thy hand is against
every man, and every man's hand against thee—Heaven forbid! said she, raising her hand up to her forehead, for I
had turned full in front upon the lady whom I had seen in
conference with the monk—she had followed us unperceived.
—Heaven forbid, indeed! said I, offering her my own—
she had a black pair of silk gloves, open only at the thumb
and two forefingers, so accepted it without reserve—and I
led her up to the door of the Remise.

Monsieur *Dessein* had *diabled* the key above fifty times,
before he found out he had come with a wrong one in his
hand: we were as impatient as himself to have it open'd; and
so attentive to the obstacle, that I continued holding her
hand almost without knowing it: so that Monsieur *Dessein*

15

left us together, with her hand in mine, and with our faces turned towards the door of the Remise, and said he would be back in five minutes.

Now a colloquy of five minutes, in such a situation, is worth one of as many ages, with your faces turned towards the street. In the latter case, 't is drawn from the objects and occurrences without—when your eyes are fixed upon a dead blank—you draw purely from yourselves. A silence of a single moment upon Monsieur *Dessein's* leaving us, had been fatal to the situation—she had infallibly turned about—so I begun the conversation instantly.

But what were the temptations (as I write not to apologize for the weaknesses of my heart in this tour,—but to give an account of them) shall be described with the same simplicity with which I felt them.

THE REMISE DOOR

WHEN I told the reader that I did not care to get out of the *Desobligeant,* because I saw the monk in close conference with a lady just arrived at the inn —I told him the truth; but I did not tell him the whole truth; for I was full as much restrained by the appearance and figure of the lady he was talking to. Suspicion crossed my brain, and said, he was telling her what had passed; something jarred upon it within me.—I wished him at his convent.

When the heart flies out before the understanding, it saves the judgment a world of pains.—I was certain she was of a better order of beings—however, I thought no more of her, but went on and wrote my preface.

The impression returned upon my encounter with her in the street; a guarded frankness with which she gave me her hand, showed, I thought, her good education and her good sense; and as I led her on, I felt a pleasurable ductility about her, which spread a calmness over all my spirits—

—Good God! how a man might lead such a creature as this round the world with him!—

I had not yet seen her face—'t was not material; for the drawing was instantly set about, and long before we had got to the door of the Remise, *Fancy* had finish'd the whole head, and pleased herself as much with its fitting her goddess, as if she had dived into the TIBER for it.—But thou art a seduced, and a seducing slut; and albeit thou cheatest us seven times a day with thy pictures and images, yet with so many charms dost thou do it, and thou deckest out thy pictures in the shapes of so many angels of light, 't is a shame to break with thee.

When we had got to the door of the Remise, she withdrew her hand from across her forehead, and let me see the original—it was a face of about six and twenty—of a clear transparent brown, simply set off without rouge or powder—

17

it was not critically handsome, but there was that in it, which, in the frame of mind I was in, attached me much more to it—it was interesting; I fancied it wore the characters of a widow'd look, and in that state of its declension, which had passed the two first paroxysms of sorrow, and was quietly beginning to reconcile itself to its loss—but a thousand other distresses might have traced the same lines; I wish'd to know what they had been—and was ready to inquire (had the same *bon ton* of conversation permitted, as in the days of Esdras)—"*What aileth thee? and why art thou disquieted? and why is thy understanding troubled?*"—In a word, I felt benevolence for her; and resolv'd some way or other to throw in my mite of courtesy—if not of service.

Such were my temptations—and in this disposition to give way to them, was I left alone with the lady with her hand in mine, and with our faces both turned closer to the door of the Remise than what was absolutely necessary.

THE REMISE DOOR

THIS certainly, fair lady! said I, raising her hand up a
a little lightly as I began, must be one of Fortune's
whimsical doings: to take two utter strangers by their
hands—of different sexes, and perhaps from different corners
of the globe, and in one moment place them together in such
a cordial situation as Friendship herself could scarce have
achieved for them, had she projected it for a month.—

—And your reflection upon it, shows how much, Monsieur,
she has embarrassed you by the adventure.—

When the situation is what we would wish, nothing is so
ill-timed as to hint at the circumstances which make it so.
You thank Fortune, continued she—you had reason—the
heart knew it, and was satisfied; and who but an English
philosopher would have sent notices of it to the brain to
reverse the judgment?

In saying this she disengaged her hand with a look which
I thought a sufficient commentary upon the text.

It is a miserable picture which I am going to give of the
weakness of my heart, by owning that it suffered a pain,
which worthier occasions could not have inflicted.—I was
mortified with the loss of her hand, and the manner in which
I had lost it carried neither oil nor wine to the wound: I
never felt the pain of a sheepish inferiority so miserably in
my life.

The triumphs of a true feminine heart are short upon
these discomfitures. In a very few seconds she laid her
hand upon the cuff of my coat, in order to finish her reply;
so some way or other, God knows how, I regained my
situation.

—She had nothing to add.

I forthwith began to model a different conversation for
the lady, thinking from the spirit as well as moral of this,

that I had been mistaken in her character; but upon turning her face towards me, the spirit which had animated the reply was fled—the muscles relaxed, and I beheld the same un-protected look of distress which first won me to her interest.— Melancholy! to see such sprightliness the prey of sorrow.— I pitied her from my soul; and though it may seem ridiculous enough to a torpid heart,—I could have taken her into my arms, and cherished her, though it was in the open street, without blushing.

The pulsations of the arteries along my fingers pressing across hers, told her what was passing within me: she look'd down—a silence of some moments followed.

I fear, in this interval, I must have made some slight efforts towards a closer compression of her hand, from a subtle sensation I felt in the palm of my own—not as if she was going to withdraw hers—but as if she thought about it— and I had infallibly lost it a second time, had not instinct more than reason directed me to the last resource in these dangers—to hold it loosely and in a manner as if I was every moment going to release it of myself; so she let it continue till Monsieur *Dessein* returned with the key; and in the mean time I set myself to consider how I should undo the ill im-pressions which the poor monk's story, in case he had told it her, must have planted in her breast against me.

THE SNUFF-BOX

CALAIS

THE good old monk was within six paces of us, as the idea of him cross'd my mind; and was advancing towards us a little out of the line, as if uncertain whether he should break in upon us or no.—He stopp'd, however, as soon as he came up to us, with a world of frankness: and having a horn snuff-box in his hand, he presented it open to me.—You shall taste mine—said I, pulling out my box (which was a small tortoise one) and putting it into his hand.—'T is most excellent, said the monk. Then do me the favor, I replied, to accept of the box and all, and when you take a pinch out of it, sometimes recollect it was the peace offering of a man who once used you unkindly, but not from his heart.

The poor monk blush'd as red as scarlet. *Mon Dieu!* said he, pressing his hands together—you never used me unkindly. —I should think, said the lady, he is not likely. I blush'd in my turn; but from what movements I leave to the few who feel to analyze.—Excuse me, Madame, replied I—I treated him most unkindly, and from no provocations.—'T is impossible, said the lady.—My God! cried the monk, with a warmth of asseveration which seem'd not to belong to him—the fault was in me, and in the indiscretion of my zeal.—The lady opposed it, and I joined with her in maintaining it was impossible, that a spirit so regulated as his, could give offense to any.

I knew not that contention could be rendered so sweet and pleasurable a thing to the nerves as I then felt it.—We remained silent without any sensation of that foolish pain which takes place, when in such a circle you look for ten minutes in one another's faces without saying a word. Whilst this lasted, the monk rubb'd his horn box upon the sleeve of his tunic; and as soon as it had acquired a little air of bright-

21

ness by the friction—he made a low bow, and said, 't was too late to say whether it was the weakness or goodness of our tempers which had involv'd us in this contest.—But be it as it would—he begg'd we might exchange boxes.—In saying this, he presented his to me with one hand, as he took mine from me in the other; and having kiss'd it—with a stream of good nature in his eyes he put it into his bosom—and took his leave.

I guard this box, as I would the instrumental parts of my religion, to help my mind on to something better: in truth, I seldom go abroad without it: and oft and many a time have I call'd up by it the courteous spirit of its owner to regulate my own, in the justlings of the world; they had found full employment for his, as I learnt from his story, till about the forty-fifth year of his age, when upon some military services ill requited, and meeting at the same time with a disappointment in the tenderest of passions, he abandon'd the sword and the sex together, and took sanctuary, not so much in his convent as in himself.

I feel a damp upon my spirits, as I am going to add, that in my last return through Calais, upon inquiring after Father Lorenzo, I heard he had been dead near three months, and was buried, not in his convent, but, according to his desire, in a little cemetery belonging to it, about two leagues off: I had a strong desire to see where they had laid him—when upon pulling out his little horn box, as I sat by his grave, and plucking up a nettle or two at the head of it, which had no business to grow there, they all struck together so forcibly upon my affections, that I burst into a flood of tears—but I am as weak as a woman; and I beg the world not to smile, but pity me.

THE REMISE DOOR

CALAIS

I HAD never quitted the lady's hand all this time; and had held it so long, that it would have been indecent to have let it go, without first pressing it to my lips: the blood and spirits, which had suffer'd a revulsion from her, crowded back to her, as I did it.

Now the two travelers, who had spoke to me in the coach-yard, happening at that crisis to be passing by, and observing our communications, naturally took it into their heads that we must be *man and wife,* at least; so stopping as soon as they came up to the door of the Remise, the one of them, who was the Inquisitive Traveler, ask'd us, if we set out for Paris the next morning?—I could only answer for myself, I said; and the lady added, she was for Amiens.—We dined there yesterday, said the Simple Traveler.—You go directly through the town, added the other, in your road to Paris. I was going to return a thousand thanks for the intelligence, *that Amiens was in the road to Paris;* but upon pulling out my poor monk's little horn box to take a pinch of snuff— I made them a quiet bow, and wishing them a good passage to Dover—they left us alone.—

—Now where would be the harm, said I to myself, if I was to beg of this distressed lady to accept of half of my chaise? —and what mighty mischief could ensue?

Every dirty passion, and bad propensity in my nature, took the alarm, as I stated the proposition.—It will oblige you to have a third horse, said AVARICE, which will put twenty livres out of your pocket.—You know not who she is, said CAUTION —or what scrapes the affair may draw you into, whisper'd COWARDICE.—

Depend upon it, Yorick! said DISCRETION, 't will be said you went off with a mistress, and came by assignation to Calais for that purpose.—

—You can never after, cried HYPOCRISY aloud, show your face in the world—or rise, quoth MEANNESS, in the church—or be anything in it, said PRIDE, but a lousy prebendary.

—But 't is a civil thing, said I—and as I generally act from the first impulse, and therefore seldom listen to these cabals, which serve no purpose that I know of, but to encompass the heart with adamant—I turn'd instantly about to the lady.

—But she had glided off unperceived, as the cause was pleading, and had made ten or a dozen paces down the street, by the time I had made the determination; so I set off after her with a long stride, to make her the proposal with the best address I was master of; but observing she walk'd with her cheek half resting upon the palm of her hand—with the slow, short, measur'd step of thoughtfulness, and with her eyes, as she went step by step, fix'd upon the ground, it struck me, she was trying the same cause herself.—God help her! said I, she has some mother-in-law, or tartufish aunt, or nonsensical old woman, to consult upon the occasion, as well as myself: so not caring to interrupt the process, and deeming it more gallant to take her at discretion than by surprise, I faced about, and took a short turn or two before the door of the Remise, whilst she walk'd musing on one side.

IN THE STREET

HAVING, on first sight of the lady, settled the affair in my fancy, "that she was of the better order of beings" —and then laid it down as a second axiom, as indisputable as the first, that she was a widow, and wore a character of distress—I went no further; I got ground enough for the situation which pleased me—and had she remained close beside my elbow till midnight, I should have held true to my system, and considered her only under that general idea.

She had scarce got twenty paces distant from me, ere something within me called out for a more particular inquiry —it brought on the idea of a further separation—I might possibly never see her more—the heart is for saving what it can; and I wanted the traces thro' which my wishes might find their way to her, in case I should never rejoin her myself: in a word, I wish'd to know her name—her family's— her condition; and as I knew the place to which she was going, I wanted to know from whence she came: but there was no coming at all this intelligence: a hundred little delicacies stood in the way. I form'd a score different plans— There was no such thing as a man's asking her directly—the thing was impossible.

A little French *débonnaire* captain, who came dancing down the street, showed me, it was the easiest thing in the world; for popping in betwixt us, just as the lady was returning back to the door of the Remise, he introduced himself to my acquaintance, and before he had well got announced, begg'd I would do him the honor to present him to the lady— I had not been presented myself—so turning about to her, he did it just as well by asking her, if she had come from Paris?—No, she was going that route, she said.—*Vous n'êtes pas de Londres?*—She was not, she replied.—Then

Madame must have come thro' Flanders.—*Apparemment vous êtes Flamande?* said the French captain.—The lady answered, she was.—*Peut-être de Lisle?* added he.—She said she was not of Lisle.—Nor Arras?—nor Cambray?—nor Ghent?—nor Brussels? She answered, she was of Brussels.

He had had the honor, he said, to be at the bombardment of it last war—that it was finely situated, *pour cela*—and full of noblesse when the Imperialists were driven out by the French (the lady made a slight curtsy)—so giving her an account of the affair, and of the share he had had in it— he begg'd the honor to know her name—so made his bow.

—*Et Madame a son Mari?*—said he, looking back when he had made two steps—and without staying for an answer— danced down the street.

Had I served seven years' apprenticeship to good breeding, I could not have done as much.

THE REMISE

CALAIS

AS the little French captain left us, Monsieur Dessein
came up with the key of the Remise in his hand, and
forthwith let us into his magazine of chaises.

The first object which caught my eye, as Monsieur Dessein open'd the door of the Remise, was another old tatter'd
Desobligeant, and notwithstanding it was the exact picture
of that which had hit my fancy so much in the coach-yard
but an hour before—the very sight of it stirr'd up a disagreeable sensation within me now; and I thought 't was a churlish
beast into whose heart the idea could first enter, to construct
such a machine; nor had I much more charity for the man
who could think of using it.

I observed the lady was as little taken with it as myself:
so Monsieur Dessein led us on to a couple of chaises which
stood abreast, telling us, as he recommended them, that they
had been purchased by my Lord A. and B. to go the *grand
tour,* but had gone no further than Paris, so were in all
respects as good as new.—They were too good—so I pass'd
on to a third, which stood behind, and forthwith began to
chaffer for the price.—But 't will scarce hold two, said I,
opening the door and getting in.—Have the goodness, Madam,
said Monsieur Dessein, offering his arm, to step in.—The
lady hesitated half a second, and stepp'd in; and the waiter
that moment beckoning to speak to Monsieur Dessein, he shut
the door of the chaise upon us, and left us.

THE REMISE DOOR

Calais

C'EST bien comique, 't is very droll, said the lady smiling, from the reflection that this was the second time we had been left together by a parcel of nonsensical contingencies—*c'est bien comique*, said she.—

—There wants nothing, said I, to make it so, but the comic use which the gallantry of a Frenchman would put it to—to make love the first moment, and an offer of his person the second.

'T is their *fort*, replied the lady.

It is supposed so at least—and how it has come to pass, continued I, I know not : but they have certainly got the credit of understanding more of love, and making it better than any other nation upon earth ; but for my own part, I think them errant bunglers, and in truth the worst set of marksmen that ever tried Cupid's patience.

—To think of making love by *sentiments!*

I should as soon think of making a genteel suit of clothes out of remnants :—and to do it—pop—at first sight by declaration—is submitting the offer and themselves with it, to be sifted with all their *pours* and *contres*, by an unheated mind.

The lady attended as if she expected I should go on.

Consider then, Madam, continued I, laying my hand upon hers—

That grave people hate Love for the name's sake—

That selfish people hate it for their own—

Hypocrites for heaven's—

And that all of us, both old and young, being ten times worse frighten'd than hurt by the very *report*—What a want of knowledge in this branch of commerce a man betrays, who ever lets the word come out of his lips, till an hour or two at least after the time that his silence upon it becomes tormenting. A course of small, quiet attentions, not so

28

pointed as to alarm—nor so vague as to be misunderstood—
with now and then a look of kindness, and little or nothing
said upon it—leaves Nature for your mistress, and she fashions it to her mind—

Then I solemnly declare, said the lady, blushing—you have
been making love to me all this while.

THE REMISE

CALAIS

MONSIEUR *Dessein* came back to let us out of the chaise, and acquaint the lady, the Count de L——, her brother, was just arrived at the hotel. Though I had infinite good will for the lady, I cannot say, that I rejoiced in my heart at the event—and could not help telling her so—for it is fatal to a proposal, Madam, said I, that I was going to make you.—

You need not tell me what the proposal was, said she, laying her hand upon both mine, as she interrupted me.—A man, my good Sir, has seldom an offer of kindness to make to a woman, but she has a presentiment of it some moments before.—

Nature arms her with it, said I, for immediate preservation.—But I think, said she, looking in my face, I had no evil to apprehend—and to deal frankly with you, had determined to accept it.—If I had—(she stopped a moment)—I believe your good will would have drawn a story from me, which would have made pity the only dangerous thing in the journey.

In saying this, she suffered me to kiss her hand twice, and with a look of sensibility mixed with a concern, she got out of the chaise—and bid adieu.

IN THE STREET

CALAIS

I NEVER finished a twelve-guinea bargain so expeditiously in my life: my time seemed heavy upon the loss of the lady, and knowing every moment of it would be as two, till I put myself into motion—I ordered post-horses directly, and walked towards the hotel.

Lord! said I, hearing the town clock strike four, and recollecting that I had been little more than a single hour in Calais—

—What a large volume of adventures may be grasped within this little span of life, by him who interests his heart in everything, and who, having eyes to see what time and chance are perpetually holding out to him as he journeyeth on his way, misses nothing he can *fairly* lay his hands on.—

—If this won't turn out something—another will—no matter—'t is an assay upon human nature—I get my labor for my pains—'t is enough—the pleasure of the experiment has kept my senses and the best part of my blood awake, and laid the gross to sleep.

I pity the man who can travel from *Dan* to *Beersheba,* and cry, 'T is all barren—and so it is; and so is all the world to him, who will not cultivate the fruits it offers. I declare, said I, clapping my hands cheerily together, that was I in a desert, I would find out wherewith in it to call forth my affections.—If I could not do better, I would fasten them upon some sweet myrtle, or seek some melancholy cypress to connect myself to—I would court their shade, and greet them kindly for their protection—I would cut my name upon them, and swear they were the loveliest trees throughout the desert: if their leaves wither'd, I would teach myself to mourn, and when they rejoiced, I would rejoice along with them.

The learned SMELFUNGUS traveled from Boulogne to Paris —from Paris to Rome—and so on—but he set out with the spleen and jaundice, and every object he pass'd by was dis-colored or distorted.—He wrote an account of them, but 't was nothing but the account of his miserable feelings.

I met Smelfungus in the grand portico of the Pantheon —he was just coming out of it.—'T is nothing but a huge cock-pit,[1] said he.—I wish you had said nothing worse of the Venus of Medicis, replied I—for in passing through Flor-ence, I had heard he had fallen foul upon the goddess, and used her worse than a common strumpet, without the least provocation in nature.

I popp'd upon Smelfungus again at Turin, in his return home; and a sad tale of sorrowful adventures had he to tell, "wherein he spoke of moving accidents by flood and field, and of the cannibals which each other eat: the Anthropophagi" —he had been flay'd alive, and bedevil'd, and used worse than St. Bartholomew, at every stage he had come at.—

—I'll tell it, cried Smelfungus, to the world. You had bet-ter tell it, said I, to your physician.

Mundungus, with an immense fortune, made the whole tour; going on from Rome to Naples—from Naples to Venice—from Venice to Vienna—to Dresden, to Berlin, with-out one generous connection or pleasurable anecdote to tell of; but he had travel'd straight on, looking neither to his right hand or his left, lest Love or Pity should seduce him out of his road.

Peace be to them! if it is to be found; but heaven itself, was it possible to get there with such tempers, would want objects to give it.—Every gentle spirit would come flying upon the wings of Love to hail their arrival.—Nothing would the souls of Smelfungus and Mundungus hear of, but fresh anthems of joy, fresh raptures of love, and fresh congratu-lations of their common felicity.—I heartily pity them: they have brought up no faculties for this work; and was the happiest mansion in heaven to be allotted to Smelfungus and Mundungus, they would be so far from being happy, that the souls of Smelfungus and Mundungus would do penance there to all eternity.

[1] Vide S——'s Travels.

MONTRIUL

I HAD once lost my portmanteau from behind my chaise, and twice got out in the rain, and one of the times up to the knees in dirt, to help the postilion to tie it on, without being able to find out what was wanting.—Nor was it till I got to Montriul, upon the landlord's asking me if I wanted not a servant, that it occurred to me, that that was the very thing.

A servant! That I do most sadly, quoth I.—Because, Monsieur, said the landlord, there is a clever young fellow, who would be very proud of the honor to serve an Englishman.—But why an English one, more than any other?—They are so generous, said the landlord.—I'll be shot if this is not a livre out of my pocket, quoth I to myself, this very night.—But they have wherewithal to be so, Monsieur, added he.—Set down one livre more for that, quoth I.—It was but last night, said the landlord, *qu'un my Lord Anglois presentoit un écu à la fille de chambre.—Tant pis, pour Mademoiselle Janatone,* said I.

Now Janatone being the landlord's daughter, and the landlord supposing I was young in French, took the liberty to inform me, I should not have said *tant pis*—but, *tant mieux. Tant mieux, toujours, Monsieur,* said he, when there is anything to be got—*tant pis,* when there is nothing. It comes to the same thing, said I. *Pardonnez moi,* said the landlord.

I cannot take a fitter opportunity to observe, once for all, that *tant pis* and *tant mieux* being two of the great hinges in French conversation, a stranger would do well to set himself right in the use of them, before he gets to Paris.

A prompt French Marquis at our ambassador's table demanded of Mr. H——, if he was H—— the poet? No, said H—— mildly.—*Tant pis,* replied the Marquis.

It is H—— the historian, said another.—*Tant mieux,* said

33

the Marquis. And Mr. H——, who is a man of an excellent heart, return'd thanks for both.

When the landlord had set me right in this matter, he called in La Fleur, which was the name of the young man he had spoke of—saying only first, That as for his talents, he would presume to say nothing—Monsieur was the best judge what would suit him; but for the fidelity of La Fleur, he would stand responsible in all he was worth.

The landlord deliver'd this in a manner which instantly set my mind to the business I was upon—and La Fleur, who stood waiting without, in that breathless expectation which every son of nature of us have felt in our turns, came in.

MONTRIUL

I AM apt to be taken with all kinds of people at first sight; but never more so, than when a poor devil comes to offer his service to so poor a devil as myself; and as I know this weakness, I always suffer my judgment to draw back something on that very account—and this more or less, according to the mood I am in, and the case—and I may add the gender too of the person I am to govern.

When La Fleur enter'd the room, after every discount I could make for my soul, the genuine look and air of the fellow determined the matter at once in his favor; so I hired him first—and then began to inquire what he could do: but I shall find out his talents, quoth I, as I want them—besides, a Frenchman can do everything.

Now poor La Fleur could do nothing in the world but beat a drum, and play a march or two upon the fife. I was determined to make his talents do: and can't say my weakness was ever so insulted by my wisdom, as in the attempt.

La Fleur had set out early in life, as gallantly as most Frenchmen do, with *serving* for a few years: at the end of which, having satisfied the sentiment, and found moreover, that the honor of beating a drum was likely to be its own reward, as it open'd no further track of glory to him—he retir'd *à ses terres*, and lived *comme il plaisoit à Dieu*—that . is to say, upon nothing.

—And so, quoth *Wisdom,* you have hired a drummer to attend you in this tour of yours thro' France and Italy! Psha! said I, and do not one half of our gentry go with a humdrum *compagnon du voyage* the same round, and have the piper and the devil and all to pay besides? When man can extricate himself with an *équivoque* in such an unequal match—he is not ill off.—But you can do something else, La Fleur? said I.—*O qu'oui!*—he could make spatterdashes, and play a little upon the fiddle.—Bravo! said Wisdom.—Why I play a bass myself, said I—we shall do very well.—You can shave, and dress a wig a little, La Fleur?—He had all the dispositions in the world.—It is enough for heaven! said I, interrupting him—and ought to be enough for me.—So supper coming in, and having a frisky English spaniel on one side of my chair, and a French valet, with as much hilarity in his countenance as ever nature painted in one, on the other—I was satisfied to my heart's content with my empire; and if monarchs knew what they would be at, they might be as satisfied as I was.

MONTRIUL

AS La Fleur went the whole tour of France and Italy with me, and will be often upon the stage, I must interest the reader a little further in his behalf, by saying, that I had never less reason to repent of the impulses which generally do determine me, than in regard to this fellow—he was a faithful, affectionate, simple soul as ever trudged after the heels of a philosopher; and notwithstanding his talents of drum-beating and spatterdash-making, which, tho' very good in themselves, happen'd to be of no great service to me, yet was I hourly recompensed by the festivity of his temper—it supplied all defects—I had a constant resource in his looks, in all difficulties and distresses of my own—I was going to have added, of his too; but La Fleur was out of the reach of everything; for whether it was hunger or thirst, or cold or nakedness, or watchings, or whatever stripes of ill luck La Fleur met with in our journeyings, there was no index in his physiognomy to point them out by—he was eternally the same; so that if I am a piece of a philosopher, which Satan now and then puts into my head I am—it always mortifies the pride of the conceit, by reflecting how much I owe to the complexional philosophy of this poor fellow, for shaming me into one of a better kind. With all this, La Fleur had a small cast of the coxcomb—but he seemed at first sight to be more a coxcomb of nature than of art; and before I had been three days in Paris with him— he seemed to be no coxcomb at all.

THE next morning, La Fleur entering upon his employment, I delivered to him the key of my portmanteau,
with an inventory of my half a dozen shirts and silk
pair of breeches; and bid him fasten all upon the chaise—get
the horses put to—and desire the landlord to come in with
his bill.

C'est un garçon de bonne fortune, said the landlord, pointing through the window to half a dozen wenches who had
got round about La Fleur, and were most kindly taking their
leave of him, as the postilion was leading out the horses.
La Fleur kissed all their hands round and round again, and
thrice he wiped his eyes, and thrice he promised he would
bring them all pardons from Rome.

The young fellow, said the landlord, is beloved by all the
town, and there is scarce a corner in Montriul, where the
want of him will not be felt: he has but one misfortune in
the world, continued he, "He is always in love."—I am
heartily glad of it, said I—'t will save me the trouble every
night of putting my breeches under my head. In saying this,
I was making not so much La Fleur's eloge, as my own,
having been in love, with one princess or other, almost all
my life, and I hope I shall go on so till I die, being firmly
persuaded, that if ever I do a mean action, it must be in some
interval betwixt one passion and another: whilst this inter-
regnum lasts, I always perceive my heart locked up—I can
scarce find in it to give Misery a sixpence; and therefore I
always get out of it as fast as I can, and the moment I am
rekindled, I am all generosity and good will again; and would
do anything in the world, either for or with any one, if they
will but satisfy me there is no sin in it.

—But in saying this—surely I am commending the passion
—not myself.

A FRAGMENT

THE town of Abdera, notwithstanding Democritus lived there, trying all the powers of irony and laughter to reclaim it, was the vilest and most profligate town in all Thrace. What for poisons, conspiracies, and assassinations—libels, pasquinades, and tumults, there was no going there by day—'t was worse by night.

Now, when things were at the worst, it came to pass, that the Andromeda of Euripides being represented at Abdera, the whole orchestra was delighted with it: but of all the passages which delighted them, nothing operated more upon their imaginations, than the tender strokes of nature, which the poet had wrought up in that pathetic speech of Perseus, *O Cupid, prince of Gods and men,* &c. Every man almost spoke pure iambics the next day, and talk'd of nothing but Perseus his pathetic address—"O Cupid, prince of Gods and men"—in every street of Abdera, in every house—"O Cupid! Cupid!"—in every mouth, like the natural notes of some sweet melody which drops from it whether it will or no— nothing but "Cupid! Cupid! prince of Gods and men."— The fire caught—and the whole city, like the heart of one man, open'd itself to Love.

No pharmacopolist could sell one grain of hellebore—not a single armorer had a heart to forge one instrument of death. —Friendship and Virtue met together, and kiss'd each other in the street—the golden age return'd, and hung over the town of Abdera—every Abderite took his oaten pipe, and every Abderitish woman left her purple web, and chastely sat her down and listen'd to the song—

'T was only in the power, says the Fragment, of the God whose empire extendeth from heaven to earth, and even to the depths of the sea, to have done this.

MONTRIUL

WHEN all is ready, and every article is disputed and paid for in the inn, unless you are a little sour'd by the adventure, there is always a matter to the compound at the door, before you can get into your chaise, and that is with the sons and daughters of poverty, who surround you. Let no man say, "let them go to the devil"—'t is a cruel journey to send a few miserables, and they have had sufferings enow without it: I always think it better to take a few sous out in my hand; and I would counsel every gentle traveler to do so likewise; he need not be so exact in setting down his motives for giving them.—They will be register'd elsewhere.

For my own part, there is no man gives so little as I do; for few, that I know, have so little to give: but as this was the first public act of my charity in France, I took the more notice of it.

A well-a-way! said I, I have but eight sous in the world, showing them in my hand, and there are eight poor men and eight poor women for 'em.

A poor tatter'd soul, without a shirt on, instantly withdrew his claim, by retiring two steps out of the circle, and making a disqualifying bow on his part. Had the whole parterre cried out, *Place aux dames*, with one voice, it would not have conveyed the sentiment of a deference for the sex with half the effect.

Just Heaven! for what wise reasons hast thou order'd it, that beggary and urbanity, which are at such variance in other countries, should find a way to be at unity in this?

—I insisted upon presenting him with a single sou, merely for his *politesse*.

A poor little dwarfish, brisk fellow, who stood over against me in the circle, putting something first under his arm, which had once been a hat, took his snuff-box out of his pocket, and generously offer'd a pinch on both sides of him: it was a gift of consequence, and modestly declined.—The poor little fellow press'd it upon them with a nod of welcomeness. —*Prenez en—prenez*, said he, looking another way; so they each took a pinch.—Pity thy box should ever want one, said I to myself; so I put a couple of sous into it—taking a small pinch out of his box to enhance their value, as I did it.— He felt the weight of the second obligation more than that of the first—'t was doing him an honor—the other was only doing him a charity—and he made me a bow down to the ground for it.

—Here! said I to an old soldier with one hand, who had been campaign'd and worn out to death in the service— here's a couple of sous for thee. *Vive le Roi!* said the old soldier.

I had then but three sous left: so I gave one, simply *pour l'amour de Dieu*, which was the footing on which it was begg'd.—The poor woman had a dislocated hip; so it could not be well upon any other motive.

Mon cher et très charitable Monsieur—There's no opposing this, said I.

My Lord Anglois—the very sound was worth the money— so I gave *my last sous for it*. But in the eagerness of giving, I had overlooked a *pauvre honteux*, who had no one to ask a sou for him, and who, I believed, would have perish'd ere he could have ask'd one for himself; he stood by the chaise, a little without the circle, and wiped a tear from a face which I thought had seen better days.—Good God! said I—and I have not one single sou left to give him.—But you have a thousand! cried all the powers of nature, stirring within me— so I gave him—no matter what—I am ashamed to say *how much*, now—and was ashamed to think how little, then: so if the reader can form any conjecture of my disposition, as these two fixed points are given him, he may judge within a livre or two what was the precise sum.

I could afford nothing for the rest, but *Dieu vous bénisse— Et le bon Dieu vous bénisse encore*—said the old soldier, the dwarf, &c. The *pauvre honteux* could say nothing—he pull'd out a little handkerchief, and wiped his face as he turned away—and I thought he thank'd me more than them all.

THE BIDET

HAVING settled all these little matters, I got into my post-chaise with more ease than ever I got into a post-chaise in my life; and La Fleur having got one large jack-boot on the far side of a little *bidet*,[1] and another on this (for I count nothing of his legs)—he canter'd away before me as happy and as perpendicular as a prince.—

—But what is happinesss! what is grandeur in this painted scene of life! A dead ass, before we had got a league, put a sudden stop to La Fleur's career—his bidet would not pass by it—a contention arose betwixt them, and the poor fellow was kick'd out of his jack-boots the very first kick.

La Fleur bore his fall like a French Christian, saying neither more or less upon it, than, Diable! so presently got up and came to the charge again astride his bidet, beating him up to it as he would have beat his drum.

The bidet flew from one side of the road to the other, then back again—then this way—then that way, and in short every way but by the dead ass.—La Fleur insisted upon the thing —and the bidet threw him.

What's the matter, La Fleur, said I, with this bidet of thine?—*Monsieur,* said he, *c'est un cheval le plus opiniâtre du monde.*—Nay, if he is a conceited beast, he must go his own way, replied I—so La Fleur got off him, and giving him a good sound lash, the bidet took me at my word, and away he scamper'd back to Montriul.—*Peste!* said La Fleur.

It is not *mal-à-propos* to take notice here, that tho' La Fleur availed himself but of two different terms of exclamation in this encounter—namely, *Diable!* and *Peste!* that there are nevertheless three in the French language, like the positive, comparative, and superlative, one or the other of which serve for every unexpected throw of the dice in life.

Le Diable! which is the first, and positive degree, is generally used upon ordinary emotions of the mind, where small things only fall out contrary to your expectations—

[1] Post-horse.

such as—the throwing once doublets—La Fleur's being kick'd off his horse, and so forth—cuckoldom, for the same reason, is always—*Le Diable!*

But in cases where the cast has something provoking in it, as in that of the bidet's running away after, and leaving La Fleur aground in jack-boots—'t is the second degree.

'T is then *Peste!*

And for the third—

—But here my heart is wrung with pity and fellow-feeling, when I reflect what miseries must have been their lot, and how bitterly so refined a people must have smarted, to have forced them upon the use of it.—

Grant me, O ye powers which touch the tongue with eloquence in distress!—whatever is my *cast*, grant me but decent words to exclaim in, and I will give my nature way.

—But as these were not to be had in France, I resolved to take every evil just as it befell me, without any exclamation at all.

La Fleur, who had made no such covenant with himself, followed the bidet with his eyes till it was got out of sight—and then, you may imagine, if you please, with what word he closed the whole affair.

As there was no hunting down a frighten'd horse in jack-boots, there remained no alternative but taking La Fleur either behind the chaise, or into it.—

I preferred the latter, and in half an hour we got to the post-house at Nampont.

NAMPONT

The Dead Ass

AND this, said he, putting the remains of a crust into his wallet—and this should have been thy portion, said he, hadst thou been alive to have shared it with me. I thought by the accent, it had been an apostrophe to his child; but 't was to his ass, and to the very ass we had seen dead in the road, which had occasioned La Fleur's misadventure. The man seemed to lament it much; and it instantly brought into my mind Sancho's lamentation for his; but he did it with more true touches of nature.

The mourner was sitting upon a stone bench at the door, with the ass's pannel and its bridle on one side, which he took up from time to time—then laid them down—look'd at them and shook his head. He then took his crust of bread out of his wallet again, as if to eat it; held it some time in his hand —then laid it upon the bit of his ass's bridle—looked wistfully at the little arrangement he had made—and then gave a sigh.

The simplicity of his grief drew numbers about him, and La Fleur amongst the rest, whilst the horses were getting ready; as I continued sitting in the post-chaise, I could see and hear over their heads.

—He said he had come last from Spain, where he had been from the furthest borders of Franconia; and had got so far on his return home, when his ass died. Every one seem'd desirous to know what business could have taken so old and poor a man so far a journey from his own home.

It had pleased Heaven, he said, to bless him with three sons, the finest lads in all Germany; but having in one week lost two of the eldest of them by the smallpox, and the youngest falling ill of the same distemper, he was afraid of being bereft of them all; and made a vow, if Heaven would not take him from him also, he would go in gratitude to St. Iago in Spain.

44

When the mourner got thus far on his story, he stopp'd to pay nature his tribute—and wept bitterly.

He said, Heaven had accepted the conditions, and that he had set out from his cottage with this poor creature, who had been a patient partner of his journey—that it had eat the same bread with him all the way, and was unto him as a friend.

Everybody who stood about, heard the poor fellow with concern.—La Fleur offered him money.—The mourner said, he did not want it—it was not the value of the ass—but the loss of him.—The ass, he said, he was assured loved him—and upon this told them a long story of a mischance upon their passage over the Pyrenean mountains, which had separated them from each other three days; during which time the ass had sought him as much as he had sought the ass, and that they had neither scarce eat or drank till they met.

Thou has one comfort, friend, said I, at least, in the loss of thy poor beast; I'm sure thou hast been a merciful master to him.—Alas! said the mourner, I thought so, when he was alive—but now that he is dead I think otherwise.—I fear the weight of myself and my afflictions together have been too much for him—they have shortened the poor creature's days, and I fear I have them to answer for.—Shame on the world! said I to myself—Did we love each other, as this poor soul but loved his ass—'t would be something.—

NAMPONT

T HE concern which the poor fellow's story threw me into required some attention: the postilion paid not the least to it, but set off upon the *pavé* in a full gallop. The thirstiest soul in the most sandy desert of Arabia could not have wished more for a cup of cold water, than mine did for grave and quiet movements; and I should have had an high opinion of the postilion, had he but stolen off with me in something like a pensive pace.—On the contrary, as the mourner finished his lamentation, the fellow gave an unfeeling lash to each of his beasts, and set off clattering like a thousand devils.

I called to him as loud as I could, for heaven's sake to go slower—and the louder I called, the more unmercifully he galloped.—The deuce take him and his galloping too—said I —he'll go on tearing my nerves to pieces till he has worked me into a foolish passion, and then he'll go slow, that I may enjoy the sweets of it.

The postilion managed the point to a miracle: by the time he had got to the foot of a steep hill about half a league from Nampont, he had put me out of temper with him—and then with myself, for being so.

My case then required a different treatment; and a good rattling gallop would have been of real service to me.—

—Then, prithee, get on—get on, my good lad, said I.

The postilion pointed to the hill—I then tried to return back to the story of the poor German and his ass—but I had broke the clue—and could no more get into it again, than the postilion could into a trot.—

—The deuce go, said I, with it all! Here am I sitting as candidly disposed to make the best of the worst, as ever wight was, and all runs counter.

There is one sweet lenitive at least for evils, which Nature holds out to us: so I took it kindly at her hands, and fell asleep; and the first word which roused me was *Amiens*.

—Bless me! said I, rubbing my eyes—this is the very town where my poor lady is to come.

THE words were scarce out of my mouth, when the Count de L——'s post-chaise, with his sister in it, drove hastily by: she had just time to make me a bow of recognition—and of that particular kind of it which told me she had not yet done with me. She was as good as her look; for, before I had quite finished my supper, her brother's servant came into the room with a billet, in which she said she had taken the liberty to charge me with a letter, which I was to present myself to Madame R—— the first morning I had nothing to do at Paris. There was only added, she was sorry, but from what *penchant* she had not considered, that she had been prevented telling me her story—that she still owed it me; and if my route should ever lay through Brussels, and I had not by then forgot the name of Madame de L—— —that Madame de L—— would be glad to discharge her obligation.

Then I will meet thee, said I, fair spirit! at Brussels—'t is only returning from Italy through Germany to Holland, by the route of Flanders, home—'t will scarce be ten posts out of my way; but were it ten thousand! with what a moral delight will it crown my journey, in sharing in the sickening incidents of a tale of misery told to me by such a sufferer! to see her weep! and though I cannot dry up the fountain of her tears, what an exquisite sensation is there still left, in wiping them away from off the cheeks of the first and fairest of women, as I'm sitting with my handkerchief in my hand in silence the whole night besides her?

There was nothing wrong in the sentiment; and yet I instantly reproached my heart with it in the bitterest and most reprobate of expressions.

It had ever, as I told the reader, been one of the singular blessings of my life, to be almost every hour of it miserably in love with some one; and my last flame happening to be blown out by a whiff of jealousy on the sudden turn of a corner, I had lighted it up afresh at the pure taper of Eliza but about three months before—swearing as I did it, that it should last me through the whole journey.—Why should I dissemble the matter? I had sworn to her eternal fidelity— she had a right to my whole heart—to divide my affections was to lessen them—to expose them, was to risk them: where there is risk, there may be loss—and what wilt thou have, Yorick! to answer to a heart so full of trust and confidence —so good, so gentle, and unreproaching!

—I will not go to Brussels, replied I, interrupting myself— but my imagination went on—I recall'd her looks at that crisis of our separation, when neither of us had power to say Adieu! I look'd at the picture she had tied in a black ribband about my neck—and blush'd as I look'd at it.—I would have given the world to have kiss'd it—but was ashamed—and shall this tender flower, said I, pressing it between my hands—shall it be smitten to its very root—and smitten, Yorick! by thee, who hast promised to shelter it in thy breast?

Eternal fountain of happiness! said I, kneeling down upon the ground—be thou my witness—and every pure spirit which tastes it, be my witness also, That I would not travel to Brussels, unless Eliza went along with me, did the road lead me towards heaven.

In transports of this kind, the heart, in spite of the understanding, will always say too much.

THE LETTER

FORTUNE had not smiled upon La Fleur; for he had been unsuccessful in his feats of chivalry—and not one thing had offer'd to signalize his zeal for my service from the time he had enter'd into it, which was almost four and twenty hours. The poor soul burn'd with impatience; and the Count de L——'s servant coming with the letter, being the first practicable occasion which offered, La Fleur had laid hold of it; and in order to do honor to his master, had taken him into a back parlor in the Auberge, and treated him with a cup or two of the best wine in Picardy; and the Count de L——'s servant, in return, and not to be behindhand in politeness with La Fleur, had taken him back with him to the Count's hotel. La Fleur's *prevanancy* (for there was a passport in his very looks) soon set every servant in the kitchen at ease with him; and as a Frenchman, whatever be his talents, has no sort of prudery in showing them, La Fleur, in less than five minutes, had pulled out his fife, and leading off the dance himself with the first note, set the *fille de chambre*, the *maître d'hôtel*, the cook, the scullion, and all the household, dogs and cats, besides an old monkey, a-dancing. I suppose there never was a merrier kitchen since the flood.

Madame de L——, in passing from her brother's apartments to her own, hearing so much jollity below stairs, rung up her *fille de chambre* to ask about it; and hearing it was the English gentleman's servant who had set the whole house merry with his pipe, she order'd him up.

As the poor fellow could not present himself empty, he had loaden'd himself in going up-stairs with a thousand compliments to Madame de L——, on the part of his master —added a long apocrypha of inquiries after Madame de L——'s health—told her, that Monsieur his master was *au désespoir* for her reëstablishment from the fatigues of her journey—and, to close all, that Monsieur had received the letter which Madame had done him the honor—And he has done me the honor, said Madame de L——, interrupting La Fleur, to send a billet in return.

Madame de L—— had said this with such a tone of reliance upon the fact, that La Fleur had not power to disappoint her expectations—he trembled for my honor—and possibly might not altogether be unconcerned for his own, as a man capable of being attach'd to a master who could be a-wanting *en égards vis-à-vis d'une femme!* so that when Madame de L—— asked La Fleur if he had brought a letter—*O qu'oui,* said La Fleur; so laying down his hat upon the ground, and taking hold of the flap of his right side pocket with his left hand, he began to search for the letter with his right — then contrariwise. — *Diable!* — then sought every pocket—pocket by pocket, round, not forgetting his fob—*Peste!*—then La Fleur emptied them upon the floor—pulled out a dirty cravat—a handkerchief—a comb—a whip lash—a night-cap—then gave a peep into his hat—*Quelle étourderie!* He had left the letter upon the table in the Auberge—he would run for it, and be back with it in three minutes.

I had just finished my supper when La Fleur came in to give me an account of his adventure: he told the whole story simply as it was; and only added, that if Monsieur had forgot (*par hazard*) to answer Madame's letter, the arrangement gave him an opportunity to recover the *faux pas*—and if not, that things were only as they were.

Now I was not altogether, sure of my *etiquette,* whether I ought to have wrote or no; but if I had—a devil himself could not have been angry: 't was but the officious zeal of a well-meaning creature for my honor; and however he might have mistook the road—or embarrassed me in so doing—his heart was in no fault—I was under no necessity to write— and what weighed more than all—he did not look as if he had done amiss.

—'T is all very well, La Fleur, said I.—'T was sufficient. La Fleur flew out of the room like lightning, and return'd with pen, ink, and paper, in his hand; and coming up to the table, laid them close before me, with such a delight in his countenance, that I could not help taking up the pen.

I begun and begun again; and though I had nothing to say, and that nothing might have been expressed in half a dozen lines, I made half a dozen different beginnings, and could no way please myself.

In short, I was in no mood to write.

La Fleur stepp'd out and brought a little water in a glass to dilute my ink—then fetch'd sand and seal-wax.—It was all one; I wrote, and blotted, and tore off, and burnt, and wrote again.—*Le diable l'emporte,* said I half to myself—I cannot write this selfsame letter, throwing the pen down despairingly as I said it.

As soon as I had cast down the pen, La Fleur advanced with the most respectful carriage up to the table, and making a thousand apologies for the liberty he was going to take, told me he had a letter in his pocket wrote by a drummer in his regiment to a corporal's wife, which, he durst say, would suit the occasion.

I had a mind to let the poor fellow have his humor.— Then prithee, said I, let me see it.

La Fleur instantly pulled out a little dirty pocket-book cramm'd full of small letters and billet-doux in a sad condition, and laying it upon the table, and then untying the string which held them all together, run them over one by one, till he came to the letter in question.—*La voilà,* said he, clapping his hands: so unfolding it first, he laid it before me, and retired three steps from the table whilst I read it.

THE LETTER

JE suis pénétré de la douleur la plus vive, et réduit en même temps au désespoir par ce retour imprévu du Corporal qui rend notre entrevue de ce soir la chose du monde la plus impossible.

Mais vive la joie! et toute la mienne sera de penser à vous.

L'amour n'est *rien* sans sentiment.

Et le sentiment est encore *moins* sans amour.

On dit qu'on ne doit jamais se désespérer.

On dit aussi que Monsieur le Corporal monte la garde Mercredi: alors ce sera mon tour.

Chacun à son tour.

En attendant—Vive l'amour! et vive la bagatelle!

Je suis, Madame,
Avec toutes les sentiments les
plus respectueux et les plus
tendres, tout à vous,
Jaques Roquf.

It was but changing the Corporal into the Count—and saying nothing about mounting guard on Wednesday—and the letter was neither right or wrong—so to gratify the poor fellow, who stood trembling, for my honor, his own, and the honor of his letter—I took the cream gently off it, and whipping it up in my own way—I seal'd it up and sent him with it to Madame de L—— and the next morning we pursued our journey to Paris.

3—C

PARIS

WHEN a man can contest the point by dint of equipage, and carry all on floundering before him with half a dozen lackeys and a couple of cooks—'t is very well in such a place as Paris—he may drive in at which end of a street he will.

A poor prince who is weak in cavalry, and whose whole infantry does not exceed a single man, had best quit the field; and signalize himself in the cabinet, if he can get up into it—I say *up into it*—for there is no descending perpendicular amongst 'em with a *"Me voici, mes enfans"*—here I am—whatever many may think.

I own my first sensations, as soon as I was left solitary and alone in my own chamber in the hotel, were far from being so flattering as I had prefigured them. I walked up gravely to the window in my dusty black coat, and looking through the glass saw all the world in yellow, blue, and green, running at the ring of pleasure.—The old with broken lances, and in helmets which had lost their vizards—the young in armor bright which shone like gold, beplumed with each gay feather of the east—all—all tilting at it like fascinated knights in tournaments of yore for fame and love.—

Alas, poor Yorick! cried I, what art thou doing here? On the very first onset of all this glittering clatter thou art reduced to an atom.—Seek—seek some winding alley, with a tourniquet at the end of it, where chariot never rolled or flambeau shot its rays—there thou mayest solace thy soul in converse sweet with some kind *grisset* of a barber's wife, and get into such coteries !—

—May I perish ! if I do, said I, pulling out the letter which I had to present to Madame de R——.—I'll wait upon this lady, the very first thing I do. So I call'd La Fleur to go seek me a barber directly—and come back and brush my coat.

THE WIG

PARIS

WHEN the barber came, he absolutely refus'd to have anything to do with my wig: 't was either above or below his art: I had nothing to do, but to take one ready made of his own recommendation.

—But I fear, friend! said I, this buckle won't stand.—You may immerge it, replied he, into the ocean, and it will stand.—

What a great scale is everything upon in this city! thought I.—The utmost stretch of an English periwig-maker's ideas could have gone no further than to have "dipp'd it into a pail of water."—What difference! 't is like time to eternity.

I confess I do hate all cold conceptions, as I do the puny ideas which engender them; and am generally so struck with the great works of nature, that for my own part, if I could help it, I never would make a comparison less than a mountain at least. All that can be said against the French sublime in this instance of it, is this—that the grandeur is *more* in the *word,* and *less* in the *thing.* No doubt the ocean fills the mind with vast ideas; but Paris being so far inland, it was not likely I should run post a hundred miles out of it, to try the experiment.—The Parisian barber meant nothing.—

The pail of water standing besides the great deep, makes certainly but a sorry figure in speech—but 't will be said—it has one advantage—'t is in the next room, and the truth of the buckle may be tried in it, without more ado, in a single moment.

In honest truth, and upon a more candid revision of the matter, *the French expression professes more than it performs.*

I think I can see the precise and distinguishing marks of national characters more in these nonsensical *minutiæ,* than in the most important matters of state; where great men of all nations talk and stalk so much alike, that I would not give ninepence to choose amongst them.

I was so long in getting from under my barber's hands, that it was too late of thinking of going with my letter to Madame R—— that night: but when a man is once dressed at all points for going out, his reflections turn to little account; so taking down the name of the Hotel de Modene, where I lodged, I walked forth without any determination where to go—I shall consider of that, said I, as I walk along.

THE PULSE

HAIL ye small sweet courtesies of life, for smooth do ye make the road of it! like grace and beauty which beget inclinations to love at first sight: 't is ye who open this door and let the stranger in.

—Pray, Madame, said I, have the goodness to tell me which way I must turn to go to the Opera Comique:—Most willingly. Monsieur, said she, laying aside her work.—

I had given a cast with my eye into half a dozen shops as I came along in search of a face not likely to be disorderd by such an interruption; till at last, this hitting my fancy, I had walked in.

She was working a pair of ruffles as she sat in a low chair on the far side of the shop facing the door.

—*Très volontiers;* most willingly, said she, laying her work down upon a chair next her, and rising up from the low chair she was sitting in, with so cheerful a movement and so cheerful a look, that had I been a lying out fifty louis d'ors with her, I should have said—"This woman is grateful."

You must turn, Monsieur, said she, going with me to the door of the shop, and pointing the way down the street I was to take—you must turn first to your left hand—*mais prenez garde*—there are two turns; and be so good as to take the second—then go down a little way and you'll see a church, and when you are past it, give yourself the trouble to turn directly to the right, and that will lead you to the foot of the *Pont Neuf,* which you must cross—and there any one will do himself the pleasure to show you—

She repeated her instructions three times over to me, with the same good-natur'd patience the third time as the first—and if *tones and manners* have a meaning, which certainly they have, unless to hearts which shut them out—she seem'd really interested, that I should not lose myself.

I will not suppose it was the woman's beauty, notwithstanding she was the handsomest grisset, I think, I ever saw, which had much to do with the sense I had of her courtesy; only I remember, when I told her how much I was obliged to her, that I looked very full in her eyes—and that I repeated my thanks as often as she had done her instructions.

I had not got ten paces from the door, before I found I had forgot every tittle of what she had said—so looking back, and seeing her still standing in the door of the shop as if to look whether I went right or not—I returned back, to ask her whether the first turn was to my right or left—for that I had absolutely forgot.—Is it possible? said she, half laughing.—'T is very possible, replied I, when a man is thinking more of a woman, than of her good advice.

As this was the real truth—she took it, as every woman takes a matter of right, with a slight courtesy.

—*Attendez,* said she, laying her hand upon my arm to detain me, whilst she called a lad out of the back shop to get ready a parcel of gloves. I am just going to send him, said she, with a packet into that quarter, and if you will have the complaisance to step in, it will be ready in a moment, and he shall attend you to the place.—So I walk'd in with her to the far side of the shop, and taking up the ruffle in my hand which she laid upon the chair, as if I had a mind to sit, she sat down herself in her low chair, and I instantly sat myself down besides her.

—He will be ready, Monsieur, said she, in a moment.— And in that moment, replied I, most willingly would I say something very civil to you for all these courtesies. Any one may do a casual act of good nature, but a continuation of them shows it is a part of the temperature; and certainly, added I, if it is the same blood which comes from the heart, which descends to the extremes (touching her wrist), I am sure you must have one of the best pulses of any woman in the world.—Feel it, said she, holding out her arm. So laying down my hat, I took hold of her fingers in one hand, and applied the two forefingers of my other to the artery.—

—Would to heaven! my dear Eugenius, thou hadst passed by, and beheld me sitting in my black coat, and in my lack-a-day-sical manner, counting the throbs of it, one by one, with as much true devotion as if I had been watching the critical ebb or flow of her fever.—How wouldst thou have laugh'd and moralized upon my new profession—and thou shouldst have laugh'd and moralized on—Trust me, my dear Eugenius, I should have said, "there are worse occupations in this world *than feeling a woman's pulse*"—But a Grisset's! thou wouldst have said—and in an open shop! Yorick—

—So much the better: for when my views are direct, Eugenius, I care not if all the world saw me feel it.

THE HUSBAND

Paris

I HAD counted twenty pulsations, and was going on fast towards the fortieth, when her husband coming unexpected from a back parlor into the shop, put me a little out of my reckoning.—'T was nobody but her husband, she said—so I began a fresh score.—Monsieur is so good, quoth she, as he pass'd by us, as to give himself the trouble of feeling my pulse.—The husband took off his hat, and making me a bow, said, I did him too much honor—and having said that, he put on his hat and walk'd out.

Good God! said I to myself, as he went out—and can this man be the husband of this woman!

Let it not torment the few who know what must have been the grounds of this exclamation, if I explain it to those who do not.

In London a shopkeeper and a shopkeeper's wife seem to be one bone and one flesh: in the several endowments of mind and body, sometimes the one, sometimes the other has it, so as in general to be upon a par, and to tally with each other as nearly as man and wife need to do.

In Paris, there are scarce two orders of beings more different: for the legislative and executive powers of the shop not resting in the husband, he seldom comes there—in some dark and dismal room behind, he sits commerceless in his thrum nightcap, the same rough son of Nature that Nature left him.

The genius of a people where nothing but the monarchy is *salique,* having ceded this department, with sundry others, totally to the women—by a continual higgling with customers of all ranks and sizes from morning to night, like so many rough pebbles shook long together in a bag, by amicable collisions, they have worn down their asperities and sharp angles, and not only become round and smooth, but will re-

ceive, some of them, a polish like a brilliant.—Monsieur *le
Mari* is little better than the stone under your foot.—

—Surely—surely, man! it is not good for thee to sit alone
—thou wast made for social intercourse and gentle greetings,
and this improvement of our natures from it, I appeal to, as
my evidence.

—And how does it beat, Monsieur? said she.—With all the
benignity, said I, looking quietly in her eyes, that I expected.
—She was going to say something civil in return—but the
lad came into the shop with the gloves.—*A propos,* said I,
I want a couple of pair myself.

THE GLOVES

PARIS

THE beautiful Grisset rose up when I said this, and going behind the counter, reach'd down a parcel and untied it: I advanc'd to the side over against her: they were all too large. The beautiful Grisset measured them one by one across my hand.—It would not alter the dimensions.—She begg'd I would try a single pair, which seemed to be the least.—She held it open—my hand slipp'd into it at once.—It will not do, said I, shaking my head a little.—No, said she, doing the same thing.

There are certain combined looks of simple subtlety—where whim, and sense, and seriousness, and nonsense, are so blended, that all the languages of Babel set loose together could not express them—they are communicated and caught so instantaneously, that you can scarce say which party is the infecter. I leave it to your men of words to swell pages about it—it is enough in the present to say again, the gloves would not do; so folding our hands within our arms, we both loll'd upon the counter—it was narrow, and there was just room for the parcel to lay between us.

The beautiful Grisset look'd sometimes at the gloves, then sideways to the window, then at the gloves—and then at me. I was not disposed to break silence.—I follow'd her example: so I look'd at the gloves, then to the window, then at the gloves, and then at her—and so on alternately.

I found I lost considerably in every attack—she had a quick black eye, and shot through two such long and silken eyelashes with such penetration, that she look'd into my very heart and reins.—It may seem strange, but I could actually feel she did.—

—It is no matter, said I, taking up a couple of the pairs next me, and putting them into my pocket.

I was sensible the beautiful Grisset had not ask'd above a single livre above the price.—I wish'd she had asked a livre more, and was puzzling my brains how to bring the matter about.—Do you think, my dear Sir, said she, mistaking my embarrassment, that I could ask a *sou* too much of a stranger—and of a stranger whose politeness, more than his want of gloves, has done me the honor to lay himself at my mercy? —*M'en croyez capable?*—Faith! not I, said I; and if you were, you are welcome.—So counting the money into her hand, and with a lower bow than one generally makes to a shopkeeper's wife, I went out, and her lad with his parcel followed me.

THE TRANSLATION

Paris

THERE was nobody in the box I was let into but a kindly old French officer. I love the character, not only because I honor the man whose manners are softened by a profession which makes bad men worse; but that I once knew one—for he is no more—and why should I not rescue one page from violation by writing his name in it, and telling the world it was Captain Tobias Shandy, the dearest of my flock and friends, whose philanthropy I never think of at this long distance from his death—but my eyes gush out with tears. For his sake, I have a predilection for the whole corps of veterans; and so I strode over the two back rows of benches, and placed myself beside him.

The old officer was reading attentively a small pamphlet, it might be the book of the opera, with a large pair of spectacles. As soon as I sat down, he took his spectacles off, and putting them into a shagreen case, return'd them and the book into his pocket together. I half rose up, and made him a bow.

Translate this into any civilized language in the world— the sense is this:

"Here's a poor stranger come into the box—he seems as if he knew nobody; and is never likely, was he to be seven years in Paris, if every man he comes near keeps his spectacles upon his nose—'t is shutting the door of conversation absolutely in his face—and using him worse than a German."

The French officer might as well have said it all aloud: and if he had, I should in course have put the bow I made him into French too, and told him, "I was sensible of his attention, and return'd him a thousand thanks for it."

There is not a secret so aiding to the progress of sociality, as to get master of this *shorthand,* and be quick in rendering the several turns of looks and limbs, with all their inflections and delineations, into plain words. For my own part, by long habitude, I do it so mechanically, that when I walk the streets of London, I go translating all the way; and have more than once stood behind in the circle, where not three words have been said, and have brought off twenty different dialogues with me, which I could have fairly wrote down and sworn to.

I was going one evening to Martini's concert at Milan, and was just entering the door of the hall, when the Marquisina di F—— was coming out in a sort of a hurry—she was almost upon me before I saw her; so I gave a spring to one side to let her pass.—She had done the same, and on the same side too: so we ran our heads together: she instantly got to the other side to get out: I was just as unfortunate as she had been; for I had sprung to that side, and opposed her passage again.—We both flew together to the other side, and then back—and so on—it was ridiculous; we both blush'd intolerably; so I did at last the thing I should have done at first —I stood stock-still, and the Marquisina had no more difficulty. I had no power to go into the room, till I had made her so much reparation as to wait and follow her with my eye to the end of the passage.—She look'd back twice, and, walk'd along it rather sideways, as if she would make room for any one coming up-stairs to pass her.—No, said I—that 's a vile translation: the Marquisina has a right to the best apology I can make her; and that opening is left for me to do it in—so I ran and begg'd pardon for the embarrassment I had given her, saying it was my intention to have made her way. She answer'd, she was guided by the same intention towards me—so we reciprocally thank'd each other. She was at the top of the stairs; and seeing no *chichesbee* near her, I begg'd to hand her to her coach—so we went down the stairs, stopping at every third step to talk of the concert and the adventure.—Upon my word, Madame, said I, when I had handed her in, I made six different efforts to let you go out. —And I made six efforts, replied she, to let you enter.—I wish to heaven you would make a seventh, said I.—With all my heart, said she, making room.—Life is too short to be long about the forms of it—so I instantly stepp'd in, and she carried me home with her.—And what became of the concert, St. Cecilia, who, I suppose, was at it, knows more than I.

I will only add, that the connection which arose out of that translation, gave me more pleasure than any one I had the honor to make in Italy.

THE DWARF

I HAD never heard the remark made by any one in my life, except by one; and who that was will probably come out in this chapter; so that being pretty much unprepossessed, there must have been grounds for what struck me the moment I cast my eyes over the *parterre*—and that was the unaccountable sport of nature in forming such numbers of dwarfs.—No doubt she sports at certain times in almost every corner of the world; but in Paris there is no end to her amusements.—The goddess seems almost as merry as she is wise.

As I carried my idea out of the *opera comique* with me, I measured everybody I saw walking in the streets by it.—Melancholy application! especially where the size was extremely little—the face extremely dark—the eyes quick—the nose long—the teeth white—the jaw prominent—to see so many miserables, by force of accidents driven out of their own proper class into the very verge of another, which it gives me pain to write down—every third man a pygmy!—some by rickety heads and hump backs—others by bandy legs—a third set arrested by the hand of Nature in the sixth and seventh years of their growth—a fourth, in their perfect and natural state like dwarf apple-trees; from the first rudiments and stamina of their existence, never meant to grow higher.

A medical traveler might say, 't is owing to undue bandages—a splenetic one, to want of air—and an inquisitive traveler, to fortify the system, may measure the height of their houses—the narrowness of their streets, and in how few feet square in the sixth and seventh stories such numbers of the *Bourgeoisie* eat and sleep together; but I remember, Mr. Shandy the elder, who accounted for nothing like anybody else, in speaking one evening of these matters, averred, that children, like other animals, might be increased almost to any size, provided they came right into the world; but the misery was, the citizens of Paris were so coop'd up, that they had not actually room enough to get them.—I do not call it getting anything, said he—'t is getting nothing.— Nay, continued he, rising in his argument, 't is getting worse than nothing, when all you have got, after twenty or five and twenty years of the tenderest care and most nutritious aliment bestowed upon it, shall not at last be as high as my leg. Now, Mr. Shandy being very short, there could be nothing more said of it.

As this is not a work of reasoning, I leave the solution as I found it, and content myself with the truth only of the re-mark which is verified in every lane and by-lane of Paris. I was walking down that which leads from the Carousal to the Palais Royal, and observing a little boy in some distress at the side of the gutter, which ran down the middle of it, I took hold of his hand, and help'd him over. Upon turning up his face to look at him after, I perceived he was about forty.—Never mind, said I; some good body will do as much for me, when I am ninety.

I feel some little principles within me, which incline me to be merciful towards this poor blighted part of my species, who have neither size or strength to get on in the world—I cannot bear to see one of them trod upon; and had scarce got seated beside my old French officer, ere the digust was exercised, by seeing the very thing happen under the box we sat in.

At the end of the orchestra and betwixt that and the first side-box there is a small esplanade left, where, when the house is full, numbers of all ranks take sanctuary. Though you stand, as in the parterre, you pay the same price as in the orchestra. A poor defenseless being of this order had got thrust, somehow or other, into this luckless place—the night was hot, and he was surrounded by beings two feet and a half higher than himself. The dwarf suffered inexpressibly on all sides; but the thing which incommoded him most, was a tall corpulent German, near seven feet high, who stood directly betwixt him and all possibility of his seeing either the stage or the actors. The poor dwarf did all he could to get a peep

at what was going forwards by seeking for some little opening betwixt the German's arm and his body, trying first one
side, then the other; but the German stood square in the most
unaccommodating posture that can be imagined—the dwarf
might as well have been placed at the bottom of the deepest
draw-well in Paris; so he civilly reach'd up his hand to the
German's sleeve, and told him his distress.—The German
turn'd his head back, look'd down upon him as Goliath did
upon David—and unfeelingly resumed his posture.

I was just then taking a pinch of snuff out of my monk's
little horn box.—And how would thy meek and courteous
spirit, my dear monk! so temper'd to *bear and forbear!*—
how sweetly would it have lent an ear to this poor soul's
complaint!

The old French officer, seeing me lift up my eyes with an
emotion, as I made the apostrophe, took the liberty to ask
me what was the matter.—I told him the story in three words,
and added, how inhuman it was.

By this time the dwarf was driven to extremes, and in his
first transports, which are generally unreasonable, had told
the German he would cut off his long queue with his knife.
—The German look'd back coolly, and told him he was welcome, if he could reach it.

An injury sharpen'd by an insult, be it to whom it will,
makes every man of sentiment a party: I could have leap'd
out of the box to have redressed it.—The old French officer
did it with much less confusion; for leaning a little over, and
nodding to a sentinel, and pointing at the same time with his
finger to the distress—the sentinel made his way up to it.—
There was no occasion to tell the grievance—the thing told
itself; so thrusting back the German instantly with his mus-
ket—he took the poor dwarf by the hand, and placed him
before him.—This is noble! said I, clapping my hands together.—And yet you would not permit this, said the old
officer, in England.

—In England, dear Sir, said I, *we sit all at our ease.*

The old French officer would have set me at unity with
myself, in case I had been at variance,—by saying it was a
bon mot—and as a *bon mot* is always worth something at
Paris, he offered me a pinch of snuff.

THE ROSE

IT was now my turn to ask the old French officer, "what was the matter?" for a cry of *"Haussez les mains, Monsieur l'Abbé,"* reëchoed from a dozen different parts of the parterre, was as unintelligible to me, as my apostrophe to the monk had been to him.

He told me, it was some poor Abbé in one of the upper loges, who he supposed had got planted perdu behind a couple of grissets, in order to see the opera, and that the parterre espying him were insisting upon his holding up both his hands during the representation.—And can it be supposed, said I, that an ecclesiastic would pick the grisset's pockets? The old French officer smiled, and whispering in my ear, open'd a door of knowledge which I had no idea of.—

Good God! said I, turning pale with astonishment—is it possible, that a people so smit with sentiment should at the same time be so unclean, and so unlike themselves.—*Quelle grossierté!* added I.

The French officer told me it was an illiberal sarcasm at the church, which had begun in the theater about the time the Tartuffe was given in it, by Molière—but, like other remains of Gothic manners, was declining.—Every nation, continued he, have their refinements and *grossiertés,* in which they take the lead, and lose it of one another by turns—that he had been in most countries, but never in one where he found not some delicacies, which others seemed to want. *Le* POUR *et le* CONTRE *se trovent en chaque nation;* there is a balance, said he, of good and bad everywhere; and nothing but the knowing it is so, can emancipate one half of the world from the pre-possessions which it holds against the other—that the advantage of travel, as it regarded the *sçavoir vivre,* was by seeing a great deal both of men and manners; it taught us mutual toleration; and mutual toleration, concluded he, making me a bow, taught us mutual love.

The old French officer delivered this with an air of such candor and good sense, as coincided with my first favorable impressions of his character.—I thought I loved the man; but I fear I mistook the object—'t was my own way of thinking—the difference was, I could not have expressed it half so well.

It is alike troublesome to both the rider and his beast—if the latter goes pricking up his ears, and starting all the way at every object which he never saw before.—I have as little torment of this kind as any creature alive; and yet I honestly confess, that many a thing gave me pain, and that I blush'd at many a word the first month—which I found inconsequent and perfectly innocent the second.

Madame de Rambouliet, after an acquaintance of about six weeks with her, had done me the honor to take me in her coach about two leagues out of town.—Of all women, Madame de Rambouliet is the most correct; and I never wish to see one of more virtues and purity of heart.—In our return back, Madame de Rambouliet desired me to pull the cord.—I ask'd her if she wanted anything.—*Rien que pisser,* said Madame de Rambouliet.

Grieve not, gentle traveler, to let Madame de Rambouliet p—ss on.—And, ye fair mystic nymphs! go each one *pluck your rose,* and scatter them in your path—for Madame de Rambouliet did no more.—I handed Madame de Rambouliet out of the coach; and had I been the priest of the chaste CASTALIA, I could not have served at her fountain with a more respectful decorum.

THE FILLE DE CHAMBRE

PARIS

WHAT the old French officer had deliver'd upon traveling, bringing Polonius's advice to his son upon the same subject into my head—and that bringing in Hamlet; and Hamlet the rest of Shakspere's works, I stopp'd at the Quai de Conti in my return home, to purchase the whole set.

The bookseller said he had not a set in the world.—*Comment!* said I; taking one up out of a set which lay upon the counter betwixt us.—He said, they were sent him only to be got bound, and were to be sent back to Versailles in the morning to the Count de B——.

—And does the Count de B——, said I, read Shakspere? *C'est un Esprit fort,* replied the bookseller.—He loves English books; and what is more to his honor, Monsieur, he loves the English too. You speak this so civilly, said I, that it is enough to oblige an Englishman to lay out a Louis d'or or two at your shop.—The bookseller made a bow, and was going to say something, when a young decent girl of about twenty, who by her air and dress seemed to be *fille de chambre* to some devout woman of fashion, came into the shop and asked for *Les Egarements du Cœur & de l'Esprit:* the bookseller gave her the book directly; she pulled out a little green satin purse, run round with a ribband of the same color and putting her finger and thumb into it, she took out the money and paid for it. As I had nothing more to stay me in the shop, we both walk'd out of the door together.

· —And what have you to do, my dear, said I, with *The Wanderings of the Heart,* who scarce know yet you have one; nor, till love has first told you it, or some faithless shepherd has made it ache, canst thou ever be sure it is so?—

Le Dieu m'en garde! said the girl.—With reason, said I—
for if it is a good one, 't is pity it should be stolen; 't is a little
treasure to thee, and gives a better air to your face, than if
it was dress'd out with pearls.

The young girl listened with a submissive attention, holding
her satin purse by its ribband in her hand all the time.—'T is
a very small one, said I, taking hold of the bottom of it—
she held it towards me—and there is very little in it, my dear,
said I; but be but as good as thou art handsome, and heaven
will fill it: I had a parcel of crowns in my hand to pay for
Shakspere; and as she had let go the purse entirely, I put
a single one in; and tying up the ribband in a bow-knot, returned it to her.

The young girl made me more a humble courtesy than a
low one—'t was one of those quiet, thankful sinkings, where
the spirit bows itself down—the body does no more than
tell it. I never gave a girl a crown in my life which gave
me half the pleasure.

My advice, my dear, would not have been worth a pin to
you, said I, if I had not given this along with it: but now,
when you see the crown, you 'll remember it—so don't, my
dear, lay it out in ribbands.

Upon my word, Sir, said the girl, earnestly, I am incapable
—in saying which, as is usual in little bargains of honor, she
gave me her hand.—*En vérité, Monsieur, je mettrai cet argent
apart,* said she.

When a virtuous convention is made betwixt man and
woman, it sanctifies their most private walks; so notwithstanding it was dusky, yet as both our roads lay the same
way, we made no scruple of walking along the Quai de Conti
together.

She made me a second courtesy in setting off, and before
we got twenty yards from the door, as if she had not done
enough before, she made a sort of a little stop to tell me
again—she thank'd me.

It was a small tribute, I told her, which I could not avoid
paying to virtue, and would not be mistaken in the person I
had been rendering it to for the world—but I see innocence,
my dear, in your face—and foul befall the man who ever
lays a snare in its way!

The girl seem'd affected some way or other with what I said—she gave a low sigh—I found I was not impowered to inquire at all after it—so said nothing more till I got to the corner of the Rue de Nevers, where we were to part.

—But is this the way, my dear, said I, to the Hotel de Modene? she told me it was—or, that I might go by the Rue de Guineygaude, which was the next turn.—Then I'll go, my dear, by the Rue de Guineygaude, said I, for two reasons; first I shall please myself, and next I shall give you the protection of my company as far on your way as I can. The girl was sensible I was civil—and said, she wish'd the Hotel de Modene was in the Rue de St. Pierre—You live there? said I.—She told me she was *fille de chambre* to Madame R—— —Good God! said I, 't is the very lady for whom I have brought a letter from Amiens.—The girl told me that Madame R——, she believed, expected a stranger with a letter, and was impatient to see him—so I desired the girl to present my compliments to Madame R——, and say I would certainly wait upon her in the morning.

We stood still at the corner of the Rue de Nevers whilst this pass'd.—We then stopp'd a moment whilst she disposed of her *Egarements du Cœur,* &c., more commodiously than carrying them in her hand—they were two volumes; so I held the second for her whilst she put the first into her pocket; and then she held her pocket, and I put in the other after it.

'T is sweet to feel by what fine-spun threads our affections are drawn together.

We set off afresh, and as she took her third step, the girl put her hand within my arm—I was just bidding her—but she did it of herself with that undeliberating simplicity, which show'd it was out of her head that she had never seen me before. For my own part, I felt the conviction of consanguinity so strongly, that I could not help turning half round to look in her face, and see if I could trace out anything in it of a family likeness.—Tut! said I, are we not all relations?

When we arrived at the turning up of the Rue de Guineygaude, I stopp'd to bid her adieu for good and all: the girl would thank me again for my company and kindness.—She bid me adieu twice—I repeated it as often; and so cordial was the parting between us, that had it happen'd anywhere else, I'm not sure but I should have signed it with a kiss of charity, as warm and holy as an apostle.

But in Paris, as none kiss each other but the men—I did, what amounted to the same thing—

—I bid God bless her.

THE PASSPORT

WHEN I got home to my hotel, La Fleur told me I had been inquired after by the Lieutenant de Police.—The deuce take it! said I—I know the reason. It is time the reader should know it, for in the order of things in which it happened, it was omitted; not that it was out of my head; but that, had I told it then, it might have been forgot now—and now is the time I want it.

I had left London with so much precipitation, that it never enter'd my mind that we were at war with France; and had reach'd Dover, and look'd through my glass at the hills beyond Boulogne, before the idea presented itself; and with this in its train, that there was no getting there without a passport.

Go but to the end of a street, I have a mortal aversion for returning back no wiser than I set out; and as this was one of the greatest efforts I had ever made for knowledge, I could less bear the thoughts of it; so hearing the Count de —— had hired the packet, I begg'd he would take me in his *suite*. The Count had some little knowledge of me, so made little or no difficulty—only said, his inclination to serve me could reach no further than Calais, as he was to return by way of Brussels to Paris; however, when I had once pass'd there, I might get to Paris without interruption; but that in Paris I must make friends and shift for myself.— Let me get to Paris, Monsieur le Count, said I—and I shall do very well. So I embark'd, and never thought more of the matter.

When La Fleur told me the Lieutenant de Police had been inquiring after me—the thing instantly recurred—and by the time La Fleur had well told me, the master of the hotel came into my room to tell me the same thing, with this addition to it, that my passport had been particularly ask'd after: the master of the hotel concluded with saying, He hoped I had one.—Not I, faith! said I.

The master of the hotel retired three steps from me, as from an infected person, as I declared this—and poor La Fleur advanced three steps towards me, and with that sort of movement which a good soul makes to succor a distress'd one—the fellow won my heart by it; and from that single *trait*, I knew his character as perfectly, and could rely upon it as firmly, as if he had served me with fidelity for seven years.

Mon seigneur! cried the master of the hotel—but recollecting himself as he made the exclamation, he instantly changed the tone of it.—If Monsieur, said he, has not a passport, (*apparemment*) in all likelihood he has friends in Paris who can procure him one.—Not that I know of, quoth I, with an air of indifference.—Then, *certes,* replied he, you'll be sent to the Bastille or the Châtelet, *au moins.* Poo! said I, the king of France is a good-natur'd soul—he'll hurt nobody.— *Cela n'empêche pas,* said he—you will certainly be sent to the Bastille to-morrow morning.—But I've taken your lodgings for a month, answer'd I, and I'll not quit them a day before the time for all the kings of France in the world. La Fleur whisper'd in my ear, that nobody could oppose the king of France.

Pardi! said my host, *ces Messieurs Anglois sont des gens très extraordinaires*—and having both said and sworn it—he went out.

THE PASSPORT

I COULD not find in my heart to torture La Fleur's with a serious look upon the subject of my embarrassment, which was the reason I had treated it so cavalierly; and to show him how light it lay upon my mind, I dropt the subject entirely; and whilst he waited upon me at supper, talk'd to him with more than usual gaiety about Paris, and of the opera comique.—La Fleur had been there himself, and had followed me through the streets as far as the bookseller's shop; but seeing me come out with the young *fille de chambre*, and that we walk'd down the Quai de Conti together, La Fleur deem'd it unnecessary to follow me a step further—so making his own reflections upon it, he took a shorter cut—and got to the hotel in time to be inform'd of the affair of the police against my arrival.

As soon as the honest creature had taken away, and gone down to sup himself, I then began to think a little seriously about my situation.—

—And here, I know, Eugenius, thou wilt smile at the remembrance of a short dialogue which pass'd betwixt us the moment I was going to set out—I must tell it here.

Eugenius, knowing that I was as little subject to be overburden'd with money as thought, had drawn me aside to interrogate me how much I had taken care for; upon telling him the exact sum, Eugenius shook his head, and said it would not do; so pull'd out his purse in order to empty it into mine.—I've enough in conscience, Eugenius, said I.—Indeed, Yorick, you have not, replied Eugenius.—I know France and Italy better than you.—But you don't consider, Eugenius, said I, refusing his offer, that before I have been three days in Paris, I shall take care to say or do something or other for which I shall get clapp'd up into the Bastille, and that I shall live there a couple of months entirely at the

78

king of France's expense.—I beg pardon, said Eugenius, dryly: really I had forgot that resource.

Now the event I treated gaily came seriously to my door.

Is it folly, or nonchalance, or philosophy, or pertinacity—or what is it in me, that, after all, when La Fleur had gone down-stairs, and I was quite alone, I could not bring down my mind to think of it otherwise than I had then spoken of it to Eugenius?

—And as for the Bastille; the terror is in the word.—Make the most of it you can, said I to myself, the Bastille is but another word for a tower—and a tower is but another word for a house you can't get out of.—Mercy on the gouty! for they are in it twice a year—but with nine livres a day, and pen and ink and paper and patience, albeit a man can't get out, he may do very well within—at least for a month or six weeks; at the end of which, if he is a harmless fellow, his innocence appears, and he comes out a better and wiser man than he went in.

I had some occasion (I forget what) to step into the court-yard, as I settled this account; and remember I walk'd down-stairs in no small triumph with the conceit of my reasoning. —Beshrew the *somber* pencil! said I vauntingly—for I envy not its powers, which paints the evils of life with so hard and deadly a coloring. The mind sits terrified at the objects she has magnified herself, and blackened: reduce them to their proper size and hue, she overlooks them.—'T is true, said I, correcting the proposition—the Bastille is not an evil to be despised—but strip it of its towers—fill up the fossé—unbarricade the doors—call it simply a confinement, and suppose 't is some tyrant of a distemper—and not of a man, which holds you in it—the evil vanishes, and you bear the other half without complaint.

I was interrupted in the heyday of this soliloquy, with a voice which I took to be of a child, which complained "it could not get out."—I look'd up and down the passage, and seeing neither man, woman, or child, I went out without further attention.

In my return back through the passage, I heard the same words repeated twice over; and looking up, I saw it was a starling hung in a little cage.—"I can't get out—I can't get out," said the starling.

I stood looking at the bird: and to every person who came through the passage it ran fluttering to the side towards which they approach'd it, with the same lamentation of its captivity.—"I can't get out," said the starling.—God help thee! said I, but I'll let thee out, cost what it will; so I turn'd about the cage to get to the door; it was twisted and double twisted so fast with wire, there was no getting it open without pulling the cage to pieces.—I took both hands to it.

The bird flew to the place where I was attempting his deliverance, and thrusting his head through the trellis, press'd his breast against it, as if impatient.—I fear, poor creature! said I, I cannot set thee at liberty.—"No," said the starling— "I can't get out—I can't get out," said the starling.

I vow I never had my affections more tenderly awakened; or do I remember an incident in my life, where the dissipated spirits, to which my reason had been a bubble, were so suddenly call'd home. Mechanical as the notes were, yet so true in tune to nature were they chanted, that in one moment they overthrew all my systematic reasonings upon the Bastille; and I heavily walk'd up-stairs, unsaying every word I had said in going down them.

Disguise thyself as thou wilt, still, slavery! said I—still thou art a bitter draught! and though thousands in all ages have been made to drink of thee, thou art no less bitter on that account.—'T is thou, thrice sweet and gracious goddess, addressing myself to LIBERTY, whom all in public or in private worship, whose taste is grateful, and ever wilt be so, till NATURE herself shall change—no *tint* of words can spot thy snowy mantle, or chymic power turn thy scepter into iron— with thee to smile upon him as he eats his crust, the swain is happier than his monarch, from whose court thou art exiled —Gracious heaven! cried I, kneeling down upon the last step but one in my ascent, grant me but health, thou great Bestower of it, and give me but this fair goddess as my companion—and shower down thy miters, if it seems good unto thy divine providence, upon those heads which are aching for them.

THE CAPTIVE

Paris

THE bird in his cage pursued me into my room; I sat down close to my table, and leaning my head upon my hand, I began to figure to myself the miseries of confinement. I was in a right frame for it, and so I gave full scope to my imagination.

I was going to begin with the millions of my fellow-creatures, born to no inheritance but slavery: but finding, however affecting the picture was, that I could not bring it near me, and that the multitude of sad groups in it did but distract me—

—I took a single captive, and having first shut him up in his dungeon, I then look'd through the twilight of his grated door to take his picture.

I beheld his body half wasted away with long expectation and confinement, and felt what kind of sickness of the heart it was which arises from hope deferr'd. Upon looking nearer I saw him pale and feverish: in thirty years the western breeze had not once fann'd his blood—he had seen no sun, no moon, in all that time—nor had the voice of friend or kinsman breathed through his lattice—his children—

—But here my heart began to bleed—and I was forced to go on with another part of the portrait.

He was sitting upon the ground upon a little straw, in the furthest corner of his dungeon, which was alternately his chair and bed: a little calendar of small sticks were laid at the head, notch'd all over with the dismal days and nights he had pass'd there—he had one of these little sticks in his hand, and with a rusty nail he was etching another day of misery to add to the heap. As I darkened the little light he had, he lifted up a hopeless eye towards the door, then cast it down—shook his head, and went on with his work of affliction. I heard his chains upon his legs, as he turned his body to lay his little stick upon the bundle.—He gave a deep sigh—I saw the iron enter into his soul—I burst into tears—I could not sustain the picture of confinement which my fancy had drawn—I started up from my chair, and calling La Fleur— I bid him bespeak me a *remise,* and have it ready at the door of the hotel by nine in the morning.

—I'll go directly, said I, myself to Monsieur le Duc de Choiseul.

La Fleur would have put me to bed; but not willing he should see anything upon my cheek which would cost the honest fellow a heartache—I told him I would go to bed by myself—and bid him go do the same.

THE STARLING

Road to Versailles

I GOT into my *remise* the hour I proposed: La Fleur got up behind, and I bid the coachman make the best of his way to Versailles.

As there was nothing in this road, or rather nothing which I look for in traveling, I cannot fill up the blank better than with a short history of this selfsame bird, which became the subject of the last chapter.

Whilst the Honorable Mr. —— was waiting for a wind at Dover, it had been caught upon the cliffs before it could well fly, by an English lad who was his groom; who not caring to destroy it, had taken it in his breast into the packet—and by course of feeding it, and taking it once under his protection, in a day or two grew fond of it, and got it safe along with him to Paris.

At Paris the lad had laid out a livre in a little cage for the starling, and as he had little to do better the five months his master stay'd there, he taught it in his mother's tongue the four simple words—(and no more)—to which I own'd myself so much its debtor.

Upon his master's going on for Italy—the lad had given it to the master of the hotel.—But his little song for liberty being in an *unknown* language at Paris—the bird had little or no store set by him—so La Fleur bought both him and his cage for me for a bottle of Burgundy.

In my return from Italy I brought him with me to the country in whose language he had learn'd his notes—and telling the story of him to Lord A——, Lord A begg'd the bird of me—in a week Lord A gave him to Lord B——; Lord B made a present of him to Lord C——; and Lord C's gentleman sold him to Lord D's for a shilling—Lord D gave him to Lord E——, and so on—half round the alphabet.— From that rank he pass'd into the lower house, and pass'd

the hands of as many commoners.—But as all these wanted
to *get in*—and my bird wanted to *get out*—he had almost as
little store set by him in London as in Paris.

It is impossible but many of my readers must have heard
of him; and if any by mere chance have ever seen him,—I beg
leave to inform them, that that bird was my bird—or some
vile copy set up to represent him.

I have nothing further to add upon him, but that from that
time to this, I have borne this poor starling as the crest to
my arms.—Thus:

—And let the heralds' officers twist his neck about if they
dare.

THE ADDRESS

I SHOULD not like to have my enemy take a view of my mind when I am going to ask protection of any man: for which reason I generally endeavor to protect myself; but this going to Monsieur le Duc de C—— was an act of compulsion—had it been an act of choice, I should have done it, I suppose, like other people.

How many mean plans of dirty address, as I went along, did my servile heart form! I deserved the Bastille for every one of them.

Then nothing would serve me, when I got within sight of Versailles, but putting words and sentences together, and conceiving attitudes and tones to wreathe myself into Monsieur le Duc de C——'s good graces.—This will do—said I —Just as well, retorted I again, as a coat carried up to him by an adventurous tailor, without taking his measure.— Fool! continued I—see Monsieur le Duc's face first—observe what character is written in it—take notice in what posture he stands to hear you—mark the turns and expressions of his body and limbs—and for the tone—the first sound which comes from his lips will give it you; and from all these together you'll compound an address at once upon the spot, which cannot disgust the Duke—the ingredients are his own, and most likely to go down.

Well! said I, I wish it well over.—Coward again! as if man to man was not equal throughout the whole surface of the globe; and if in the field—why not face to face in the cabinet too? And trust me, Yorick, whenever it is not so, man is false to himself, and betrays his own succors ten times where nature does it once. Go to the Duc de C—— with the Bastille in thy looks—my life for it, thou wilt be sent back to Paris in half an hour with an escort.

I believe so, said I.—Then I'll go to the Duke, by Heaven! with all the gaiety and debonairness in the world.—

—And there you are wrong again, replied I.—A heart at ease, Yorick, flies into no extremes—'t is ever on its center. —Well! well! cried I, as the coachman turn'd in at the gates —I find I shall do very well: and by the time he had wheel'd round the court, and brought me up to the door, I found myself so much the better for my own lecture, that I neither ascended the steps like a victim to justice, who was to part with life upon the topmost,—nor did I mount them with a skip and a couple of strides, as I do when I fly up, Eliza! to thee, to meet it.

As I enter'd the door of the saloon, I was met by a person who possibly might be the maître d'hôtel, but had more the air of one of the under-secretaries, who told me the Duc de C—— was busy.—I am utterly ignorant, said I, of the forms of obtaining an audience, being an absolute stranger, and what is worse in the present conjuncture of affairs, being an Englishman too.—He replied, that did not increase the difficulty.—I made him a slight bow, and told him, I had something of importance to say to Monsieur le Duc. The secretary look'd towards the stairs, as if he was about to leave me to carry up this account to some one.—But I must not mislead you, said I—for what I have to say is of no manner of importance to Monsieur le Duc de C—— —but of great importance to myself.—*C'est une autre affaire,* replied he.—Not at all, said I, to a man of gallantry. But pray, good Sir, continued I, when can a stranger hope to have *accesse?*—In not less than two hours, said he, looking at his watch. The number of equipages in the courtyard seem'd to justify the calculation, that I could have no nearer a prospect—and as walking backwards and forwards in the saloon, without a soul to commune with, was for the time as bad as being in the Bastille itself, I instantly went back to my *remise,* and bid the coachman to drive me to the *Cordon Bleu,* which was the nearest hotel.

I think there is a fatality in it—I seldom go to the place I set out for.

LE PATISSER

BEFORE I had got half-way down the street I changed my mind: as I am at Versailles, thought I, I might as well take a view of the town; so I pull'd the cord, and ordered the coachman to drive round some of the principal streets.—I suppose the town is not very large, said I.—The coachman begg'd pardon for setting me right, and told me it was very superb, and that numbers of the first dukes and marquises and counts had hotels.—The Count de B——, of whom the bookseller at the Quai de Conti had spoke so handsomely the night before, came instantly into my mind. —And why should I not go, thought I, to the Count de B——, who has so high an idea of English books and Englishmen— and tell him my story? So I changed my mind a second time —in truth it was the third; for I had intended that day for Madame de R—— in the Rue St. Pierre, and had devoutly sent her word by her *fille de chambre* that I would assuredly wait upon her—but I am govern'd by circumstances—I cannot govern them: so seeing a man standing with a basket on the other side of the street, as if he had something to sell, I bid La Fleur go up to him and inquire for the Count's hotel.

La Fleur return'd a little pale: and told me it was a Chevalier de St. Louis selling *pâtés*.—It is impossible, La Fleur, said I.—La Fleur could no more account for the phenomenon than myself; but persisted in his story: he had seen the croix set in gold, with its red ribband, he said, tied to his buttonhole—and had looked into the basket and seen the *pâtés* which the Chevalier was selling; so could not be mistaken in that.

Such a reverse in man's life awakens a better principle than curiosity: I could not help looking for some time at him as I sat in the *remise*—the more I look'd at him, his croix, and his basket, the stronger they wove themselves into my brain—I got out of the *remise,* and went towards him.

He was begirt with a clean linen apron, which fell below his knees, and with a sort of a bib that went half-way up his breast; upon the top of this, but a little below the hem, hung his croix. His basket of little *pâtés* was cover'd over with a white damask napkin: another of the same kind was spread at the bottom; and there was a look of *propreté* and neatness throughout, that one might have bought his *pâtés* of him, as much from appetite as sentiment.

He made an offer of them to neither; but stood still with them at the corner of a hotel, for those to buy who chose it, without solicitation.

He was about forty-eight—of a sedate look, something approaching to gravity. I did not wonder.—I went up rather to the basket than him, and having lifted up the napkin, and taken one of his *pâtés* into my hand—I begg'd he would explain the appearance which affected me.

He told me in a few words, that the best part of his life had pass'd in the service, in which, after spending a small patrimony, he had obtain'd a company and the croix with it; but that, at the conclusion of the last peace, his regiment being reformed, and the whole corps, with those of some other regiments, left without any provision—he found himself in a wide world without friends, without a livre—and indeed, said he, without anything but this—(pointing, as he said it, to his croix).—The poor chevalier won my pity, and he finished the scene with winning my esteem too.

The king, he said, was the most generous of princes, but his generosity could neither relieve or reward every one, and it was only his misfortune to be amongst the number. He had a little wife, he said, whom he loved, who did the *pâtisserie;* and added, he felt no dishonor in defending her and himself from want in this way—unless Providence had offer'd him a better.

It would be wicked to withhold a pleasure from the good, in passing over what happen'd to this poor Chevalier of St. Louis about nine months after.

It seems he usually took his stand near the iron gates which lead up to the palace, and as his croix had caught the eye of numbers, numbers had made the same inquiry which I had done.—He had told the same story, and always with so much modesty and good sense, that it had reach'd at last the king's ears—who hearing the chevalier had been a gallant officer, and respected by the whole regiment as a man of honor and integrity—he broke up his little trade by a pension of fifteen hundred livres a year.

As I have told this to please the reader, I beg he will allow me to relate another, out of its order, to please myself— the two stories reflect light upon each other—and 't is a pity they should be parted.

THE SWORD

WHEN states and empires have their periods of declension, and feel in their turns what distress and poverty is—I stop not to tell the causes which gradually brought the house d'E—— in Brittany into decay. The Marquis d'E—— had fought up against his condition with great firmness; wishing to preserve, and still show to the world some little fragments of what his ancestors had been—their indiscretions had put it out of his power. There was enough left for the little exigencies of *obscurity*—but he had two boys who look'd up to him for *light*—he thought they deserved it. He had tried his sword—it could not open the way—the *mounting* was too expensive—and simple economy was not a match for it—there was no resource but commerce.

In any other province in France, save Brittany, this was smiting the root forever of the little tree his pride and affection wish'd to see reblossom—But in Brittany, there being a provision for this, he avail'd himself of it; and taking an occasion when the states were assembled at Rennes, the Marquis, attended with his two boys, enter'd the court; and having pleaded the right of an ancient law of the duchy, which, though seldom claim'd, he said, was no less in force, he took his sword from his side—Here—said he—take it; and be trusty guardians of it, till better times put me in condition to reclaim it.

The president accepted the Marquis's sword—he stay'd a few minutes to see it deposited in the archives of his house—and departed.

The Marquis and his whole family embarked the next day for Martinico, and in about nineteen or twenty years of successful application to business, with some unlook'd-for bequests from distant branches of his house—return'd home to reclaim his nobility and to support it.

It was an incident of good fortune which will never happen to any traveler, but a sentimental one, that I should be at Rennes at the very time of this solemn requisition: I call it solemn—it was so to me.

The Marquis enter'd the court with his whole family: he supported his lady—his eldest son supported his sister, and his youngest was at the other extreme of the line next his mother—he put his handkerchief to his face twice—

—There was a dead silence. When the Marquis had approach'd within six paces of the tribunal, he gave the Marchioness to his youngest son, and advancing three steps before his family—he reclaim'd his sword. His sword was given him, and the moment he got it into his hand, he drew it almost out of the scabbard—'t was the shining face of a friend he had once given up—he look'd attentively along it, beginning at the hilt, as if to see whether it was the same— when observing a little rust which it had contracted near the point, he brought it near his eye, and bending his head down over it—I think I saw a tear fall upon the place: I could not be deceived by what followed.

"I shall find," said he, "some *other way* to get it off."

When the Marquis had said this, he return'd his sword into its scabbard, made a bow to the guardians of it—and with his wife and daughter, and his two sons following him, walk'd out.

O how I envied him his feelings!

THE PASSPORT

I FOUND no difficulty in getting admittance to Monsieur le Count de B——. The set of Shaksperes was laid upon the table, and he was tumbling them over. I walk'd up close to the table, and giving first such a look at the books as to make him conceive I knew what they were—I told him I had come without any one to present me, knowing I should meet with a friend in his apartment, who, I trusted, would do it for me—it is my countryman the great Shakspere, said I, pointing to his works—*et ayez la bonté, mon cher ami,* apostrophizing his spirit, added I, *de me faire cet honneur-là.*—

The Count smil'd at the singularity of the introduction; and seeing I look'd a little pale and sickly, insisted upon my taking an arm-chair; so I sat down; and to save him conjectures upon a visit so out of all rule, I told him simply of the incident in the bookseller's shop, and how that had impell'd me rather to go to him with the story of a little embarrassment I was under, than to any other man in France.—And what is your embarrassment? let me hear it, said the Count. So I told him the story just as I have told it the reader.—

—And the master of my hotel, said I, as I concluded it, will needs have it, Monsieur le Count, that I should be sent to the Bastille—but I have no apprehensions, continued I—for in falling into the hands of the most polish'd people in the world, and being conscious I was a true man, and not come to spy the nakedness of the land, I scarce thought I laid at their mercy.—It does not suit the gallantry of the French, Monsieur le Count, said I, to show it against invalids.

An animated blush came into the Count de B——'s cheeks as I spoke this.—*Ne craignez rien*—don't fear, said he.—Indeed I don't, replied I again.—Besides, continued I a little sportingly—I have come laughing all the way from London

92

to Paris, and I do not think Monsieur le Duc de Choiseul is such an enemy to mirth, as to send me back crying for my pains.

—My application to you, Monsieur le Comte de B—— (making him a low bow), is to desire he will not.

The Count heard me with great good nature, or I had not said half as much—and once or twice said—*C'est bien dit.* So I rested my cause there—and determined to say no more about it.

The Count led the discourse: we talk'd of indifferent things—of books, and politics, and men—and then of women. —God Bless them all! said I, after much discourse about them—there is not a man upon earth who loves them so much as I do: after all the foibles I have seen, and all the satires I have read against them, still I love them; being firmly persuaded that a man, who has not a sort of an affection for the whole sex, is incapable of ever loving a single one as he ought.

Hèh bien! Monsieur l'Anglois, said the Count, gaily— you are not come to spy the nakedness of the land—I believe you—*ni encore,* I dare say *that* of our women.—But permit me to conjecture—if, *par hazard,* they fell in your way— that the prospect would not affect you.

I have something within me which cannot bear the shock of the least indecent insinuation: in the sportability of chit-chat I have often endeavored to conquer it, and with infinite pain have hazarded a thousand things to a dozen of the sex together—the least of which I could not venture to a single one to gain heaven.

Excuse me, Monsieur le Count, said I—as for the nakedness of your land, if I saw it, I should cast my eyes over it with tears in them—and for that of your women (blushing at the idea he had excited in me), I am so evangelical in this, and have such a fellow-feeling for whatever is *weak* about them, that I would cover it with a garment, if I knew how to throw it on.—But I could wish, continued I, to spy the *nakedness* of their hearts, and through the different disguises of customs, climates, and religion, find out what is good in them to fashion my own by—and therefore am I come.

It is for this reason, Monsieur le Comte, continued I, that I have not seen the Palais Royal—nor the Luxembourg—nor the Façade of the Louvre—nor have attempted to swell the catalogues we have of pictures, statues, and churches—I conceive every fair being as a temple, and would rather enter in, and see the original drawings, and loose sketches hung up in it, than the transfiguration of Raphael itself.

The thirst of this, continued I, as impatient as that which inflames the breast of the connoisseur, has led me from my own home into France—and from France will lead me through Italy—'t is a quiet journey of the heart in pursuit of NATURE, and those affections which rise out of her, which make us love each other—and the world, better than we do.

The Count said a great many civil things to me upon the occasion; and added, very politely, how much he stood obliged to Shakspere for making me known to him.—But, à propos, said he,—Shakspere is full of great things—he forgot a small punctilio of announcing your name—it puts you under a necessity of doing it yourself.

THE PASSPORT

VERSAILLES

THERE is not a more perplexing affair in life to me, than to set about telling any one who I am—for there is scarce anybody I cannot give a better account of than of myself; and I have often wish'd I could do it in a single word—and have an end of it. It was the only time and occasion in my life I could accomplish this to any purpose—for Shakspere lying upon the table, and recollecting I was in his books, I took up Hamlet, and turning immediately to the grave-diggers scene in the fifth act, I laid my finger upon YORICK, and advancing the book to the Count, with my finger all the way over the name—*Me voici!* said I.

Now whether the idea of poor Yorick's skull was put out of the Count's mind by the reality of my own, or by what magic he could drop a period of seven or eight hundred years, makes nothing in this account—'t is certain the French conceive better than they combine—I wonder at nothing in this world, and the less at this; inasmuch as one of the first of our own church, for whose candor and paternal sentiments I have the highest veneration, fell into the same mistake in the very same case.—"He could not bear," he said, "to look into sermons wrote by the king of Denmark's jester."—Good my lord! said I—but there are two Yoricks. The Yorick your lordship thinks of has been dead and buried eight hundred years ago; he flourish'd in Horwendillus's court—the other Yorick is myself, who have flourish'd, my lord, in no court.—He shook his head.—Good God! said I, you might as well confound Alexander the Great with Alexander the Coppersmith, my lord—'T was all one, he replied.—

—If Alexander king of Macedon could have translated your lordship, said I—I'm sure your lordship would not have said so.

The poor Count de B—— fell but into the same *error—* —*Et, Monsieur, est il Yorick?* cried the Count.—*Je le suis,* said I.—*Vous?—Moi—moi qui ai l'honneur de vous parler, Monsieur le Comte.—Mon Dieu!* said he, embracing me—*Vous êtes Yorick!*

The Count instantly put the Shakspere into his pocket— and left me alone in his room.

THE PASSPORT

I COULD not conceive why the Count de B—— had gone so abruptly out of the room, any more than I could conceive why he had put the Shakspere into his pocket.—*Mysteries which must explain themselves are not worth the loss of time which a conjecture about them takes up*: 't was better to read Shakspere; so taking up *"Much Ado about Nothing,"* I transported myself instantly from the chair I sat in to Messina in Sicily, and got so busy with Don Pedro and Benedick and Beatrice, that I thought not of Versailles, the Count, or the Passport.

Sweet pliability of man's spirit, that can at once surrender itself to illusions, which cheat expectation and sorrow of their weary moments!—long—long since had ye number'd out my days, had I not trod so great a part of them upon this enchanted ground; when my way is too rough for my feet, or too steep for my strength, I get off it, to some smooth velvet path which fancy has scattered over with rosebuds of delights; and having taken a few turns in it, come back strengthen'd and refresh'd.—When evils press sore upon me, and there is no retreat from them in this world, then I take a new course—I leave it—and as I have a clearer idea of the elysian fields than I have of heaven, I force myself, like Æneas, into them—I see him meet the pensive shade of his forsaken Dido—and wish to recognize it—I see the injured spirit wave her head, and turn off silent from the author of her miseries and dishonors—I lose the feelings for myself in hers—and in those affections which were wont to make me mourn for her when I was at school.

Surely this is not walking in a vain shadow—nor does man disquiet himself in vain *by it*—he oftener does so in trusting the issue of his commotions to reason only.—I can safely say for myself, I was never able to conquer any one single bad sensation in my heart so decisively, as by beating up as fast as I could for some kindly and gentle sensation to fight it upon its own ground.

When I had got to the end of the third act, the Count de B—— entered with my Passport in his hand. Monsieur le Duc de C——, said the Count, is as good a prophet, I dare say, as he is a statesman—*Un homme qui rit,* said the duke, *ne sera jamais dangereux.*—Had it been for any one but the king's jester, added the Count, I could not have got it these two hours.—*Pardonnez moi,* Monsieur le Comte, said I—I am not the king's jester.—But you are Yorick?—Yes.—*Et vous plaisantez?*—I answered, Indeed I did jest—but was not paid for it—'t was entirely at my own expense.

We had no jester at court, Monsieur le Comte, said I; the last we had was in the licentious reign of Charles the IId—since which time our manners have been so gradually refining, that our court at present is so full of patriots, who wish for *nothing* but the honors and wealth of their country —and our ladies are all so chaste, so spotless, so good, so devout—there is nothing for a jester to make a jest of—

Voilà un persiflage! cried the Count.

THE PASSPORT

AS the Passport was directed to all lieutenant-governors,
governors, and commandants of cities, generals of
armies, justiciaries, and all officers of justice, to let
Mr. Yorick the king's jester, and his baggage, travel quietly
along—I own the triumph of obtaining the Passport was not
a little tarnish'd by the figure I cut in it.—But there is nothing unmixt in this world; and some of the gravest of our
divines have carried it so far as to affirm, that enjoyment
itself was attended even with a sigh—and that the greatest
they knew of terminated *in a general way,* in little better
than a convulsion.

I remembered the grave and learned Bevoriskius, in his
commentary upon the generations from Adam, very naturally breaks off in the middle of a note to give an account to
the world of a couple of sparrows upon the out-edge of his
window, which had incommoded him all the time he wrote,
and at last had entirely taken him off from his genealogy.

—'T is strange! writes Bevoriskius, but the facts are certain, for I have had the curiosity to mark them down one by
one with my pen—but the cock-sparrow, during the little
time that I could have finished the other half this note, has
actually interrupted me with the reiteration of his caresses
three and twenty times and a half.

How merciful, adds Bevoriskius, is heaven to his creatures!

Ill-fated Yorick! that the gravest of thy brethren should
be able to write that to the world, which stains thy face with
crimson, to copy in even thy study.

But this is nothing to my travels.—So I twice—twice beg
pardon for it.

CHARACTER

VERSAILLES

AND how do you find the French? said the Count de B——, after he had given me the Passport.

The reader may suppose, that after so obliging a proof of courtesy, I could not be at a loss to say something handsome to the inquiry.

—*Mais passé, pour cela*—Speak frankly, said he: do you find all the urbanity in the French which the world give us the honor of?—I had found everything, I said, which confirmed it.—*Vraiment,* said the Count.—*Les François sont polis.*—To an excess, replied I.

The Count took notice of the word *excesse;* and would have it I meant more than I said. I defended myself a long time as well as I could against it—he insisted I had a reserve, and that I would speak my opinion frankly.

I believe, Monsieur le Comte, said I, that man has a certain compass, as well as an instrument; and that the social and other calls have occasion by turns for every key in him; so that if you begin a note too high or too low, there must be a want either in the upper or under part, to fill up the system of harmony.—The Count de B—— did not understand music, so desired me to explain it some other way. A polish'd nation, my dear Count, said I, makes every one its debtor; and besides, urbanity itself, like the fair sex, has so many charms, it goes against the heart to say it can do ill: and yet, I believe, there is but a certain line of perfection, that man, take him altogether, is empower'd to arrive at—if he gets beyond, he rather exchanges qualities than gets them. I must not presume to say, how far this has affected the French in the subject we are speaking of—but should it ever be the case of the English, in the progress of their refinements, to arrive at the same polish which distinguishes the French, if we did not lose the *politesse du cœur,* which in-

100

clines men more to human actions, than courteous ones—
we should at least lose that distinct variety and originality
of character, which distinguishes them, not only from each
other, but from all the world besides.

I had a few of King William's shillings as smooth as glass
in my pocket; and foreseeing they would be of use in the
illustration of my hypothesis, I had got them into my hand,
when I had proceeded so far.—

See, Monsieur le Comte, said I, rising up, and laying them
before him upon the table—by jingling and rubbing one
against another for seventy years together in one body's
pocket or another's, they are become so much alike, you can
scarce distinguish one shilling from another.

The English, like ancient medals, kept more apart, and
passing but few people's hands, preserve the first sharpnesses
which the fine hand of nature has given them—they are not
so pleasant to feel—but, in return, the legend is so visible,
that at the first look you see whose image and superscription
they bear.—But the French, Monsieur le Comte, added I,
wishing to soften what I had said, have so many excellences,
they can the better spare this—they are a loyal, a gallant, a
generous, an ingenious, and good-temper'd people as is under
heaven—if they have a fault—they are too *serious*.

Mon Dieu! cried the Count, rising out of his chair.

Mais vous plaisantez, said he, correcting his exclamation.—
I laid my hand upon my breast, and with earnest gravity assured him it was my most settled opinion.

The Count said he was mortified he could not stay to hear
my reasons, being engaged to go that moment to dine with
the Duc de C——.

But if it is not too far to come to Versailles to eat your
soup with me, I beg, before you leave France, I may have
the pleasure of knowing you retract your opinion—or, in
what manner you support it.—But if you do support it,
Monsieur Anglois, said he, you must do it with all your
powers, because you have the whole world against you.—
I promised the Count I would do myself the honor of dining
with him before I set out for Italy—so took my leave.

THE TEMPTATION

WHEN I alighted at the hotel, the porter told me a young woman with a band-box had been that moment inquiring for me.—I do not know, said the porter, whether she is gone away or no. I took the key of my chamber of him, and went up-stairs; and when I had got within ten steps of the top of the landing before my door, I met her coming easily down.

It was the fair *fille de chambre* I had walked along the Quai de Conti with: Madame de R—— had sent her upon some commissions to a *merchante des modes* within a step or two of the Hotel de Modene; and as I had fail'd in waiting upon her, had bid her inquire if I had left Paris; and if so, whether I had not left a letter addressed to her.

As the fair *fille de chambre* was so near my door, she turned back, and went into the room with me for a moment or two whilst I wrote a card.

It was a fine still evening in the latter end of the month of May—the crimson window-curtains (which were of the same color of those of the bed) were drawn close—the sun was setting, and reflected through them so warm a tint into the fair *fille de chambre's* face—I thought she blush'd—the idea of it made me blush myself—we were quite alone; and that superinduced a second blush before the first could get off.

There is a sort of a pleasing half guilty blush, where the blood is more in fault than the man—'t is sent impetuous from the heart, and virtue flies after it—not to call it back, but to make the sensation of it more delicious to the nerves—'t is associated.—

But I'll not describe it.—I felt something at first within me which was not in strict unison with the lesson of virtue I had given her the night before.—I sought five minutes for a card—I knew I had not one.—I took up a pen—I laid it down again—my hand trembled—the devil was in me.

I know as well as any one he is an adversary, whom if we resist he will fly from us—but I seldom resist him at all; from a terror that though I may conquer, I may still get a hurt in the combat—so I give up the triumph for security; and instead of thinking to make him fly, I generally fly myself.

The fair *fille de chambre* came close up to the bureau where I was looking for a card—took up first the pen I cast down, then offer'd to hold me the ink; she offer'd it so sweetly, I was going to accept it—but I durst not.—I have nothing, my dear, said I, to write upon.—Write it, said she, simply, upon anything.—

I was just going to cry out, Then I will write it, fair girl, upon thy lips.—

If I do, said I, I shall perish—so I took her by the hand, and led her to the door, and begg'd she would not forget the lesson I had given her.—She said, indeed she would not—and as she utter'd it with some earnestness, she turn'd about, and gave me both her hands, closed together, into mine—it was impossible not to compress them in that situation—I wish'd to let them go; and all the time I held them, I kept arguing within myself against it—and still I held them on.—In two minutes I found I had all the battle to fight over again—and I felt my legs and every limb about me tremble at the idea.

The foot of the bed was within a yard and a half of the place where we were standing—I had still hold of her hands—and how it happened I can give no account, but I neither ask'd her—nor drew her—nor did I think of the bed—but so it did happen, we both sat down.

I'll just show you, said the fair *fille de chambre,* the little purse I have been making to-day to hold your crown. So she put her hand into her right pocket, which was next me, and felt for it some time—then into the left—"She had lost it."—I never bore expectation more quietly—it was in her right pocket at last—she pull'd it out; it was of green taffeta, lined with a little bit of white quilted satin, and just big enough to hold the crown—she put it into my hand;—it was pretty; and I held it ten minutes with the back of my hand resting upon her lap—looking sometimes at the purse, sometimes on one side of it.

A stitch or two had broke out in the gathers of my stock—the fair *fille de chambre*, without saying a word, took out her little hussive, threaded a small needle, and sew'd it up.—I foresaw it would hazard the glory of the day; and as she pass'd her hand in silence across and across my neck in the manœuver, I felt the laurels shake which fancy had wreath'd about my head.

A strap had given way in her walk, and the buckle of her shoe was just falling off.—See, said the *fille de chambre*, holding up her foot.—I could not for my soul but fasten the buckle in return, and putting in the strap—and lifting up the other foot with it, when I had done, to see both were right—in doing it too suddenly—it unavoidably threw the fair *fille de chambre* off her center—and then—

THE CONQUEST

YES—and then—Ye whose clay-cold heads and luke-warm hearts can argue down or mask your passions—tell me, what trespass is it that man should have them? or how his spirit stands answerable to the Father of spirits but for his conduct under them.

If Nature has so wove her web of kindness that some threads of love and desire are entangled with the piece—must the whole web be rent in drawing them out?—Whip me such stoics, great Governor of nature! said I to myself.—Wherever thy providence shall place me for the trials of my virtue—whatever is my danger—whatever is my situation—let me feel the movements which rise out of it, and which belong to me as a man—and if I govern them as a good one—I will trust the issues to thy justice: for thou hast made us—and not we ourselves.

As I finish'd my address, I raised the fair *fille de chambre* up by the hand, and led her out of the room—she stood by me till I lock'd the door and put the key in my pocket—*and then*—the victory being quite decisive—and not till then, I press'd my lips to her cheek, and taking her by the hand again, led her safe to the gate of the hotel.

THE MYSTERY

IF a man knows the heart, he will know it was impossible
to go back instantly to my chamber—it was touching a
cold key with a flat third to it, upon the close of a piece
of music, which had call'd forth my affections—therefore
when I let go the hand of the *fille de chambre*, I remain'd at
the gate of the hotel for some time, looking at every one who
pass'd by, and forming conjectures upon them, till my attention got fix'd upon a single object which confounded all kind
of reasoning upon him.

It was a tall figure of a philosophic, serious, adust look,
which pass'd and repass'd sedately along the street, making
a turn of about sixty paces on each side of the gate of the
hotel—the man was about fifty-two—had a small cane under
his arm—was dress'd in a dark drab-color'd coat, waistcoat,
and breeches, which seem'd to have seen some years' service
—they were still clean, and there was a little air of frugal
propreté throughout him. By his pulling off his hat, and his
attitude of accosting a good many in his way, I saw he was
asking charity; so I got a sou or two out of my pocket ready
to give him, as he took me in his turn—he pass'd by me without asking anything—and yet did not go five steps further
before he ask'd charity of a little woman—I was much more
likely to have given of the two.—He had scarce done with
the woman, when he pull'd off his hat to another who was
coming the same way.—An ancient gentleman came slowly—
and, after him, a young smart one.—He let them both pass,
and ask'd nothing: I stood observing him half an hour, in
which time he had made a dozen turns backwards and forwards, and found that he invariably pursued the same plan.

There were two things very singular in this, which set my
brain to work, and to no purpose—the first was, why the
man should *only* tell his story to the sex—and secondly—

what kind of story it was, and what species of eloquence it could be, which soften'd the hearts of the women, which he knew 't was to no purpose to practise upon the men.

There were two other circumstances which entangled this mystery—the one was, he told every woman what he had to say in her ear, and in a way which had much more the air of a secret than a petition—the other was, it was always successful—he never stopp'd a woman, but she pull'd out her purse, and immediately gave him something.

I could form no system to explain the phenomenon.

I had got a riddle to amuse me for the rest of the evening, so I walk'd up-stairs to my chamber.

THE CASE OF CONSCIENCE

I WAS immediately followed up by the master of the hotel, who came into my room to tell me I must provide lodgings elsewhere.—How so, friend? said I.—He answer'd, I had had a young woman lock'd up with me two hours that evening in my bedchamber, and 't was against the rules of his house.—Very well, said I, we'll all part friends then—for the girl is no worse—and I am no worse —and you will be just as I found you.—It was enough, he said, to overthrow the credit of his hotel.—*Voyez vous, Monsieur,* said he, pointing to the foot of the bed we had been sitting upon.—I own it had something of the appearance of an evidence; but my pride not suffering me to enter into any detail of the case, I exhorted him to let his soul sleep in peace, as I resolved to let mine do that night, and that I would discharge what I owed him at breakfast.

I should not have minded, *Monsieur,* said he, if you had had twenty girls—'T is a score more, replied I, interrupting him, than I ever reckon'd upon—Provided, added he, it had been but in a morning.—And does the difference of the time of the day at Paris make a difference in the sin?—It made a difference, he said, in the scandal.—I like a good distinction in my heart; and cannot say I was intolerably out of temper with the man. I own it is necessary, reassumed the master of the hotel, that a stranger at Paris should have the opportunities presented to him of buying lace and silk stockings, and ruffles, *et tout cela*—and 't is nothing if a woman comes with a band-box.—O, my conscience, said I, she had one; but I never look'd into it.—Then *Monsieur,* said he, has bought nothing.—Not one earthly thing, replied I.—Because, said he, I could recommend one to you who would use you *en conscience.*—But I must see her this night, said I.—He made me a low bow, and walk'd down.

Now shall I triumph over this *maître d'hôtel*, cried I—and what then?—Then I shall let him see I know he is a dirty fellow.—And what then?—What then!—I was too near myself to say it was for the sake of others.—I had no good answer left—there was more of spleen than principle in my project, and I was sick of it before the execution.

In a few minutes the Grisset came in with her box of lace —I'll buy nothing, however, said I, within myself.

The Grisset would show me everything.—I was hard to please: she would not seem to see it; she open'd her little magazine, and laid all her laces one after another before me —unfolded and folded them up again one by one with the most patient sweetness—I might buy—or not—she would let me have everything at my own price—the poor creature seem'd anxious to get a penny; and laid herself out to win me, and not so much in a manner which seem'd artful, as in one I felt simple and caressing.

If there is not a fund of honest cullibility in man, so much the worse—my heart relented, and I gave up my second resolution as quietly as the first.—Why should I chastise one for the trespass of another? If thou art tributary to this tyrant of an host, thought I, looking up in her face, so much harder is thy bread.

If I had not had more than four *Louis d'ors* in my purse, there was no such thing as rising up and showing her the door, till I had first laid three of them out in a pair of ruffles.

—The master of the hotel will share the profit with her— no matter—then I have only paid as many a poor soul has *paid* before me, for an act he *could* not do, or think of.

THE RIDDLE

PARIS

WHEN La Fleur came up to wait upon me at supper, he told me how sorry the master of the hotel was for his affront to me in bidding me change my lodgings.

A man who values a good night's rest will not lay down with enmity in his heart, if he can help it—so I bid La Fleur tell the master of the hotel, that I was sorry on my side for the occasion I had given him—and you may tell him, if you will, La Fleur, added I, that if the young woman should call again, I shall not see her.

This was a sacrifice not to him, but myself, having resolved, after so narrow an escape, to run no more risks, but to leave Paris, if it was possible, with all the virtue I enter'd in.

C'est déroger à noblesse, Monsieur, said La Fleur, making me a bow down to the ground as he said it.—*Et encore, Monsieur,* said he, may change his sentiments—and if (*par hazard*) he should like to amuse himself—I find no amusement in it, said I, interrupting him—

Mon Dieu! said La Fleur—and took away.

In an hour's time he came to put me to bed, and was more than commonly officious—something hung upon his lips to say to me, or ask me, which he could not get off: I could not conceive what it was, and indeed gave myself little trouble to find it out, as I had another riddle so much more interesting upon my mind, which was that of the man's asking charity before the door of the hotel—I would have given anything to have got to the bottom of it; and that, not out of curiosity—'t is so low a principle of inquiry, in general, I would not purchase the gratification of it with a two-sou piece—but a secret, I thought, which so soon and so certainly soften'd the heart of every woman you came near, was a secret at least equal to the philosopher's stone: had I

110

had both the Indies, I would have given up one to have been master of it.

I toss'd and turn'd it almost all night long in my brains to no manner of purpose; and when I awoke in the morning, I found my spirit as much troubled with my *dreams,* as ever the king of Babylon had been with his; and I will not hesitate to affirm, it would have puzzled all the wise men of Paris as much as those of Chaldea, to have given its interpretation.

LE DIMANCHE

IT was Sunday; and when La Fleur came in, in the morning, with my coffee and roll and butter, he had got himself so gallantly array'd, I scarce knew him.

I had covenanted at Montriul to give him a new hat with a silver button and loop, and four Louis d'ors *pour s'adoniser,* when we got to Paris; and the poor fellow, to do him justice, had done wonders with it.

He had bought a bright, clean, good scarlet coat, and a pair of breeches of the same.—They were not a crown worse, he said, for the wearing—I wish'd him hang'd for telling me—they look'd so fresh, that tho' I know the thing could not be done, yet I would rather have imposed upon my fancy with thinking I had bought them new for the fellow, than that they had come out of the *Rue de Friperie.*

This is a nicety which makes not the heart sore at Paris.

He had purchased moreover a handsome blue satin waistcoat, fancifully enough embroidered—this was indeed something the worse for the service it had done, but 't was clean scour'd—the gold had been touch'd up, and upon the whole was rather showy than otherwise—and as the blue was not violent, it suited with the coat and breeches very well: he had squeez'd out of the money, moreover, a new bag and a solitaire; and had insisted with the *fripier* upon a gold pair of garters to his breeches knees.—He had purchased muslin ruffles *bien brodées,* with four livres of his own money—and a pair of white silk stockings for five more—and, to top all, nature had given him a handsome figure, without costing him a sou.

He entered the room thus set off, with his hair dress'd in the first style, and with a handsome *bouquet* in his breast—in a word, there was that look of festivity in everything about him, which at once put me in mind it was Sunday—and by combining both together, it instantly struck me, that the favor he wish'd to ask of me the night before, was to spend the day as everybody in Pairs spent it besides. I had scarce made the conjecture, when La Fleur, with infinite humility, but with a look of trust, as if I should not refuse him, begg'd I would grant him the day, *pour faire le galant vis-à-vis de sa maîtresse*.

Now it was the very thing I intended to do myself *vis-à-vis* Madame de R———.—I had retain'd the *remise* on purpose for it, and it would not have mortified my vanity to have had a servant so well dress'd as La Fleur was, to have got up behind it: I never could have worse spared him.

But we must *feel*, not argue, in these embarrassments— the sons and daughters of service part with liberty, but not with Nature, in their contracts; they are flesh and blood, and have their little vanities and wishes in the midst of the house of bondage, as well as their taskmasters—no doubt they have set their self-denials at a price—and their expectations are so unreasonable, that I would often disappoint them, but that their condition puts it so much in my power to do it.

Behold!—Behold, I am thy servant—disarms me at once of the powers of a master.—

—Thou shalt go, La Fleur! said I.

—And what mistress, La Fleur, said I, canst thou have pick'd up in so little a time at Paris? La Fleur laid his hand upon his breast, and said 't was a *petite demoiselle,* at Monsieur le Comte de B———'s.—La Fleur had a heart made for society; and, to speak the truth of him, let as few occasions slip him as his master—so that somehow or other—but how —Heaven knows—he had connected himself with the *demoiselle* upon the landing of the staircase, during the time I was taken up with my Passport; and as there was time enough for me to win the Count to my interest, La Fleur had contrived to make it do to win the maid to his.—The family, it seems, was to be at Paris that day, and he had made a party with her, and two or three more of the Count's household, upon the *boulevards*.

Happy people! that once a week at least are sure to lay down all your cares together, and dance and sing, and sport away the weights of grievance, which bow down the spirit of other nations to the earth.

THE FRAGMENT

PARIS

LA FLEUR had left me something to amuse myself with for the day more than I had bargain'd for, or could have enter'd either into his head or mine.

He had brought the little print of butter upon a currant-leaf; and as the morning was warm, he had begg'd a sheet of waste paper to put betwixt the currant-leaf and his hand. —As that was plate sufficient, I bad him lay it upon the table as it was; and as I resolved to stay within all day, I ordered him to call upon the *traiteur*, to bespeak my dinner, and leave me to breakfast by myself.

When I had finish'd the butter, I threw the currant-leaf out of the window, and was going to do the same by the waste paper—but stopping to read a line first, and that drawing me on to a second and third—I thought it better worth; so I shut the window, and drawing a chair up to it, I sat down to read it.

It was in the old French of Rabelais's time, and for aught I know might have been wrote by him—it was moreover in a Gothic letter, and that so faded and gone off by damps and length of time, it cost me infinite trouble to make anything of it.—I threw it down; and then wrote a letter to Eugenius —then I took it up again and embroiled my patience with it afresh—and then to cure that, I wrote a letter to Eliza.— Still it kept hold of me; and the difficulty of understanding it increased but the desire.

I got my dinner; and after I had enlightened my mind with a bottle of Burgundy, I at it again—and after two or three hours' poring upon it, with almost as deep attention as ever Gruter or Jacob Spon did upon a nonsensical inscription, I thought I made sense of it; but to make sure of it, the best way, I imagined, was to turn it into English, and see how it would look then—so I went on leisurely as a trifling man

114

does, sometimes writing a sentence—then taking a turn or two—and then looking how the world went out of the window; so that it was nine o'clock at night before I had done it.—I then begun to read it as follows.

THE FRAGMENT

PARIS

NOW as the notary's wife disputed the point with the notary with too much heat—I wish, said the notary, throwing down the parchment, that there was another notary here only to set down and attest all this.

—And what would you do then, Monsieur? said she, rising hastily up—the notary's wife was a little fume of a woman, and the notary thought it well to avoid a hurricane by a mild reply—I would go, answer'd he, to bed.—You may go to the devil, answer'd the notary's wife.

Now there happening to be but one bed in the house, the other two rooms being unfurnish'd, as is the custom at Paris, and the notary not caring to lie in the same bed with a woman who had but that moment sent him pell-mell to the devil, went forth with his hat and cane and short cloak, the night being very windy, and walk'd out ill at ease towards the *Pont Neuf*.

Of all the bridges which ever were built, the whole world who have pass'd over the *Pont Neuf* must own, that it is the noblest—the finest—the grandest—the lightest—the longest—the broadest that ever conjoin'd land and land together upon the face of the terraqueous globe.—

By this it seems as if the author of the fragment had not been a Frenchman.

The worst fault which divines and the doctors of the Sorbonne can allege against it, is, that if there is but a capful of wind in or about Paris, 't is more blasphemously *sacre Dieu'*d there than in any other aperture of the whole city— and with reason, good and cogent, Messieurs; for it comes against you without crying *garde d'eau,* and with such unpremeditable puffs, that of the few who cross it with their hats on, not one in fifty but hazards two livres and a half which is its full worth.

116

The poor notary, just as he was passing by the sentry, instinctively clapp'd his cane to the side of it, but in raising it up, the point of his cane catching hold of the loop of the sentinel's hat, hoisted it over the spikes of the balustrade clear into the Seine.—

—'T is an ill wind, said a boatsman, who catch'd it, *which blows nobody any good*.

The sentry, being a Gascon, incontinently twirl'd up his whiskers, and level'd his harquebus.

Harquebuses in those days went off with matches; and an old woman's paper lanthorn at the end of the bridge happening to be blown out, she had borrow'd the sentry's match to light it—it gave a moment's time for the Gascon's blood to run cool, and turn the accident better to his advantage.—'T is an ill wind, said he, catching off the notary's castor, and legitimating the capture with the boatman's adage.

The poor notary cross'd the bridge, and passing along the Rue de Dauphine into the fauxbourg of St. Germain, lamented himself as he walk'd along in this manner:

Luckless man that I am! said the notary, to be the sport of hurricanes all my days—to be born to have the storm of ill language level'd against me and my profession wherever I go—to be forced into marriage by the thunder of the church to a tempest of a woman—to be driven forth out of my house by domestic winds, and despoil'd of my castor by pontific ones—to be here, bareheaded, in a windy night at the mercy of the ebbs and flows of accidents—where am I to lay my head?—miserable man! what wind in the two and thirty points of the whole compass can blow unto thee, as it does to the rest of thy fellow-creatures, good!

As the notary was passing on by a dark passage, complaining in this sort, a voice call'd out to a girl, to bid her run for the next notary—now the notary being the next, and availing himself of his situation, walk'd up the passage to the door, and passing through an old sort of a saloon, was usher'd into a large chamber, dismantled of everything but a long military pike—a breastplate—a rusty old sword, and bandoleer, hung up equidistant in four different places against the wall.

An old personage, who had heretofore been a gentleman, and unless decay of fortune taints the blood along with it, was a gentleman at that time, lay supporting his head upon his hand, in his bed; a little table with a taper burning was set close beside it, and close by the table was placed a chair—the notary sat him down in it; and pulling out his inkhorn and a sheet or two of paper which he had in his pocket, he placed them before him, and dipping his pen in his ink, and leaning his breast over the table, he disposed everything to make the gentleman's last will and testament.

Alas! Monsieur le Notaire, said the gentleman, raising himself up a little, I have nothing to bequeath, which will pay the expense of bequeathing, except the history of myself, which I could not die in peace unless I left it as a legacy to the world; the profits arising out of it I bequeath to you for the pains of taking it from me—it is a story so uncommon, it must be read by all mankind—it will make the fortunes of your house—the notary dipp'd his pen into his inkhorn.—Almighty Director of every event in my life! said the old gentleman, looking up earnestly, and raising his hands towards heaven—thou, whose hand hast led me on through such a labyrinth of strange passages down into this scene of desolation, assist the decaying memory of an old, infirm, and broken-hearted man—direct my tongue by the spirit of thy eternal truth, that this stranger may set down naught but what is written in that Book, from whose records, said he, clasping his hands together, I am to be condemn'd or acquitted!—The notary held up the point of his pen betwixt the taper and his eye.—

—It is a story, Monsieur le Notaire, said the gentleman, which will rouse up every affection in nature—it will kill the humane, and touch the heart of cruelty herself with pity.—

—The notary was inflamed with a desire to begin, and put his pen a third time into his inkhorn—and the old gentleman turning a little more towards the notary, began to dictate his story in these words—

—And where is the rest of it, La Fleur? said I, as he just then enter'd the room.

THE FRAGMENT AND THE BOUQUET [1]

PARIS

WHEN La Fleur came up close to the table, and was made to comprehend what I wanted, he told me there were only two other sheets of it, which he had wrapt round the stalks of a *bouquet* to keep it together, which he had presented to the *demoiselle* upon the *boulevards*. —Then prithee, La Fleur, said I, step back to her to the Count de B——'s hotel, and *see if you can get it*—There is no doubt of it, said La Fleur—and away he flew.

In a very little time the poor fellow came back quite out of breath, with deeper marks of disappointment in his looks than could arise from the simple irreparability of the fragment.—*Juste ciel!* in less than two minutes that the poor fellow had taken his last tender farewell of her—his faithless mistress had given his *gage d'amour* to one of the Count's footmen—the footman to a young sempstress—and the sempstress to a fiddler, with my fragment at the end of it.—Our misfortunes were involved together—I gave a sigh—and La Fleur echo'd it back again to my ear.

—How perfidious! cried La Fleur.—How unlucky! said I.—

—I should not have been mortified, Monsieur, quoth La Fleur, if she had lost it.—Nor I, La Fleur, said I, had I found it.

Whether I did or no will be seen hereafter.

[1] Nosegay.

THE ACT OF CHARITY

THE man who either disdains or fears to walk up a dark entry, may be an excellent good man, and fit for a hundred things; but he will not do to make a good sentimental traveler.

I count little of the many things I see pass at broad noonday, in large and open streets.—Nature is shy, and hates to act before spectators; but in such an unobserved corner you sometimes see a single short scene of hers, worth all the sentiments of a dozen French plays compounded together—and yet they are *absolutely* fine;—and whenever I have a more brilliant affair upon my hands than common, as they suit a preacher just as well as a hero, I generally make my sermon out of 'em—and for the text— "Cappadocia, Pontus and Asia, Phrygia and Pamphylia"— is as good as any one in the Bible.

There is a long dark passage issuing out from the Opera Comique into a narrow street; 't is trod by a few who humbly wait for a *fiacre*[1] or wish to get off quietly o' foot when the opera is done. At the end of it, towards the theater, 't is lighted by a small candle, the light of which is almost lost before you get half-way down, but near the door—'t is more for ornament than use: you see it as a fix'd star of the least magnitude; it burns—but does little good to the world, that we know of.

In returning along this passage, I discern'd, as I approach'd within five or six paces of the door, two ladies standing arm in arm with their backs against the wall, waiting, as I imagined, for a *fiacre*—as they were next the door, I thought they had a prior right; so edged myself up within a yard or little more of them, and quietly took my stand—I was in black, and scarce seen.

[1] Hackney-coach.

The lady next me was a tall lean figure of a woman, of about thirty-six; the other of the same size and make, of about forty; there was no mark of wife or widow in any one part of either of them—they seem'd to be two upright vestal sisters, unsapp'd by caresses, unbroke in upon by tender salutations: I could have wish'd to have made them happy—their happiness was destin'd, that night, to come from another quarter.

A low voice, with a good turn of expression, and sweet cadence at the end of it, begg'd for a twelve-sou piece betwixt them, for the love of Heaven. I thought it singular that a beggar should fix the quota of an alms—and that the sum should be twelve times as much as what is usually given in the dark. They both seem'd astonish'd at it as much as myself.—Twelve sous! said one.—A twelve-sou piece! said the other—and made no reply.

The poor man said, he knew not how to ask less of ladies of their rank; and bow'd down his head to the ground.

Poo! said they—we have no money.

The beggar remained silent for a moment or two, and renew'd his supplication.

Do not, my fair young ladies, said he, stop your good ears against me.—Upon my word, honest man! said the younger, we have no change.—Then God bless you, said the poor man, and multiply those joys which you can give to others without change!—I observed the elder sister put her hand into her pocket.—I'll see, said she, if I have a sou.—A sou! give twelve, said the supplicant; Nature has been bountiful to you, be bountiful to a poor man.

I would, friend, with all my heart, said the younger, if I had it.

My fair charitable! said he, addressing himself to the elder—what is it but your goodness and humanity which makes your bright eyes so sweet, that they outshine the morning even in this dark passage? and what was it which made the Marquis de Santerre and his brother say so much of you both as they just pass'd by?

The two ladies seemed much affected; and impulsively at the same time they both put their hands into their pocket, and each took out a twelve-sou piece.

The contest betwixt them and the poor supplicant was no more—it was continued betwixt themselves, which of the two should give the twelve-sou piece in charity—and to end the dispute, they both gave it together, and the man went away.

THE RIDDLE EXPLAINED

I STEPP'D hastily after him: it was the very man whose success in asking charity of the women before the door of the hotel had so puzzled me—and I found at once his secret, or at least the basis of it—'t was flattery.

Delicious essence! how refreshing art thou to nature! how strongly are all its powers and all its weaknesses on thy side! how sweetly dost thou mix with the blood, and help it through the most difficult and tortuous passages to the heart!

The poor man, as he was not straiten'd for time, had given it here in a larger dose: 't is certain he had a way of bringing it into less form, for the many sudden cases he had to do with in the streets; but how he contrived to correct, sweeten, concenter, and qualify it—I vex not my spirit with the inquiry—it is enough, the beggar gain'd two twelve-sou pieces—and they can best tell the rest, who have gain'd much greater matters by it.

WE get forwards in the world, not so much by doing services, as receiving them; you take a withering twig, and put it in the ground; and then you water it because you have planted it.

Monsieur le Comte de B——, merely because he had done me one kindness in the affair of my passport, would go on and do me another, the few days he was at Paris, in making me known to a few people of rank; and they were to present me to others, and so on.

I had got master of my *secret* just in time to turn these honors to some little account; otherwise, as is commonly the case, I should have din'd or supp'd a single time or two round, and then by *translating* French looks and attitudes into plain English, I should presently have seen, that I had got hold of the *couvert*[1] of some more entertaining guest; and in course should have resigned all my places one after another, merely upon the principle that I could not keep them.—As it was, things did not go much amiss.

I had the honor of being introduced to the old Marquis de B——: in days of yore he had signaliz'd himself by some small feats of chivalry in the *Cour d'amour,* and had dress'd himself out to the idea of tilts and tournaments ever since— the Marquis de B—— wish'd to have it thought the affair was somewhere else than in his brain. "He could like to take a trip to England," and ask'd much of the English ladies. Stay where you are, I beseech you Monsieur le Marquis, said I.—Les Messieurs Anglois can scarce get a kind look from them as it is.—The Marquis invited me to supper.

Monsieur P—— the farmer-general was just as inquisitive about our taxes.—They were very considerable, he heard— If we knew but how to collect them, said I, making him a low bow.

I could never have been invited to Monsieur P——'s concerts upon any other terms.

[1] Plate, napkin, knife, fork, and spoon.

I had been misrepresented to Madame de Q—— as an *esprit*.—Madame de Q—— was an *esprit* herself: she burnt with impatience to see me, and hear me talk. I had not taken my seat, before I saw she did not care a sou whether I had any wit or no—I was let in, to be convinced she had.—I call Heaven to witness I never once open'd the door of my lips.

Madame de Q—— vow'd to every creature she met, "she had never had a more improving conversation with a man in her life."

There are three epochas in the empire of a Frenchwoman—She is coquette—then deist—then *dévote:* the empire during these is never lost—she only changes her subjects: when thirty-five years and more have unpeopled her dominions of the slaves of love, she repeoples it with slaves of infidelity—and then with the slaves of the Church.

Madame de V—— was vibrating betwixt the first of these epochas: the color of the rose was shading fast away—she ought to have been a deist five years before the time I had the honor to pay my first visit.

She placed me upon the same sofa with her, for the sake of disputing the point of religion more closely—In short Madame de V—— told me she believed nothing.

I told Madame de V—— it might be her principle; but I was sure it could not be her interest to level the outworks, without which I could not conceive how such a citadel as hers could be defended—that there was not a more dangerous thing in the world than for a beauty to be a deist—that it was a debt I owed my creed, not to conceal it from her—that I had not been five minutes sat upon the sofa besides her, but I had begun to form designs—and what is it but the sentiments of religion, and the persuasion they had existed in her breast, which could have check'd them as they rose up?

We are not adamant, said I, taking hold of her hand—and there is need of all restraints, till age in her own time steals in and lays them on us—but, my dear lady, said I, kissing her hand—'t is too—too soon—

I declare I had the credit all over Paris of unperverting Madame de V——.—She affirmed to Monsieur D—— and the

Abbé M——, that in one half-hour I had said more for revealed religion than all their Encyclopedia had said against it.—I was lifted directly into Madame de V——'s *Coterie*—and she put off the epocha of deism for two years.

I remember it was in this *Coterie*, in the middle of a discourse, in which I was showing the necessity of a *first cause,* that the young Count de Faineant took me by the hand to the furthest corner of the room to tell me my *solitaire* was pinn'd too strait about my neck.—It should be *plus badinant,* said the Count, looking down upon his own—but a word, Monsieur Yorick, *to the wise*—

—And *from the wise,* Monsieur le Comte, replied I, making him a bow—*is enough.*

The Count de Faineant embraced me with more ardor than ever I was embraced by mortal man.

For three weeks together, I was of every man's opinion I met.—*Pardi! ce Monsieur Yorick a autant d'esprit que nous autres.—Il raisonne bien,* said another.—*C'est un bon enfant,* said a third.—And at this price I could have eaten and drank and been merry all the days of my life at Paris; but 't was a dishonest *reckoning*—I grew ashamed of it.—It was the gain of a slave—every sentiment of honor revolted against it—the higher I got, the more was I forced upon my *beggarly system*—the better the *Coterie*—the more children of Art—I languish'd for those of Nature: and one night, after a most vile prostitution of myself to half a dozen different people, I grew sick—went to bed—order'd La Fleur to get me horses in the morning to set out for Italy.

MARIA

MOULINES

I NEVER felt what the distress of plenty was in any one shape till now—to travel it through the Bourbonnois, the sweetest part of France—in the heyday of the vintage, when Nature is pouring her abundance into every one's lap, and every eye is lifted up—a journey through each step of which Music beats time to *Labor,* and all her children are rejoicing as they carry in their clusters—to pass through this with my affections flying out, and kindling at every group before me—and every one of 'em was pregnant with adventures.

Just heaven!—it would fill up twenty volumes—and alas! I have but a few small pages left of this to crowd it into— and half of these must be taken up with the poor Maria my friend Mr. Shandy met with near Moulines.

The story he had told of that disorder'd maid affected me not a little in the reading; but when I got within the neighborhood where she liv'd, it returned so strong into my mind, that I could not resist an impulse which prompted me to go half a league out of the road, to the village where her parents dwelt, to inquire after her.

'T is going, I own, like the Knight of the Woeful Countenance, in quest of melancholy adventures—but I know not how it is, but I am never so perfectly conscious of the existence of a soul within me, as when I am entangled in them.

The old mother came to the door, her looks told me the story before she open'd her mouth.—She had lost her husband; he had died, she said, of anguish, for the loss of Maria's senses, about a month before.—She had feared at first, she added, that it would have plunder'd her poor girl of what little understanding was left—but, on the contrary, it had brought her more to herself—still she could not rest—

her poor daughter, she said, crying, was wandering some-where about the road—

—Why does my pulse beat languid as I write this? and what made La Fleur, whose heart seem'd only to be tun'd to joy, to pass the back of his hand twice across his eyes, as the woman stood and told it? I beckon'd to the postilion to turn back into the road.

When we had got within half a league of Moulines, at a little opening in the road leading to a thicket, I discovered poor Maria sitting under a poplar—she was sitting with her elbow in her lap, and her head leaning on one side within her hand—a small brook ran at the foot of the tree.

I bid the postilion go on with the chaise to Moulines—and La Fleur to bespeak my supper—and that I would walk after him.

She was dress'd in white, and much as my friend described her, except that her hair hung loose, which before was twisted within a silk net.—She had, superadded likewise to her jacket, a pale-green ribband, which fell across her shoulder to the waist; at the end of which hung her pipe.—Her goat had been as faithless as her lover: and she had got a little dog in lieu of him, which she had kept tied by a string to her girdle: as I look'd at her dog, she drew him towards her with the string.—"Thou shalt not leave me, Sylvio," said she. I look'd in Maria's eyes, and saw she was thinking more of her father than of her lover or her little goat, for as she utter'd them, the tears trickled down her cheeks.

I sat down close by her; and Maria let me wipe them away as they fell, with my handkerchief.—I then steep'd it in my own—and then in hers—and then in mine—and then I wip'd hers again—and as I did it, I felt such undescribable emotions within me, as I am sure could not be accounted for from any combinations of matter and motion.

I am positive I have a soul; nor can all the books with which materialists have pester'd the world ever convince me of the contrary.

MARIA

WHEN Maria had come a little to herself, I ask'd her if she remembered a pale thin person of a man, who had sat down betwixt her and her goat about two years before? She said, she was unsettled much at that time, but remember'd it upon two accounts—that ill as she was, she saw the person pitied her; and next, that her goat had stolen his handkerchief, and she had beat him for the theft—she had wash'd it, she said, in the brook, and kept it ever since in her pocket to restore it to him in case she should ever see him again, which, she added, he had half promised her. As she told me this, she took the handkerchief out of her pocket to let me see it; she had folded it up neatly in a couple of vine-leaves, tied round with a tendril—on opening it, I saw an S mark'd in one of the corners.

She had since that, she told me, stray'd as far as Rome, and walk'd round St. Peter's once—and return'd back—that she found her way alone across the Apennines—had travel'd over all Lombardy without money—and through the flinty roads of Savoy without shoes—how she had borne it, and how she had got supported, she could not tell—but *God tempers the wind*, said Maria, to the shorn lamb.

Shorn indeed! and to the quick, said I; and wast thou in my own land, where I have a cottage, I would take thee to it and shelter thee: thou shouldst eat of my own bread and drink of my own cup—I would be kind to thy Sylvio—in all thy weaknesses and wanderings I would seek after thee and bring thee back—when the sun went down I would say my prayers; and when I had done thou shouldst play thy evening song upon thy pipe, nor would the incense of my sacrifice be worse accepted for entering heaven along with that of a broken heart.

Nature melted within me, as I utter'd this; and Maria observing, as I took out my handkerchief, that it was steep'd too much already to be of use, would needs go wash it in

the stream.—And where will you dry it, Maria? said I.—
I'll dry it in my bosom, said she—'t will do me good.

And is your heart still so warm, Maria? said I.

I touch'd upon the string on which hung all her sorrows—
she look'd with wistful disorder for some time in my face;
and then, without saying anything, took her pipe, and play'd
her service to the Virgin.—The string I had touch'd ceased
to vibrate—in a moment or two Maria returned to herself—
let her pipe fall—and rose up.

And where are you going, Maria? said I.—She said, to
Moulines.—Let us go, said I, together.—Maria put her arm
within mine, and lengthening the string, to let the dog follow—in that order we enter'd Moulines.

MARIA

Moulines

THO' I hate salutations and greetings in the market-place, yet when we got into the middle of this, I stopp'd to take my last look and last farewell of Maria. Maria, tho' not tall, was nevertheless of the first order of fine forms—affliction had touch'd her looks with something that was scarce earthly—still she was feminine—and so much was there about her of all that the heart wishes, or the eye looks for in woman, that could the traces be ever worn out of her brain, and those of Eliza's out of mine, she should *not only eat of my bread and drink of my own cup,* but Maria should lay in my bosom, and be unto me as a daughter.

Adieu, poor luckless maiden!—Imbibe the oil and wine which the compassion of a stranger, as he journeyeth on his way, now pours into thy wounds—the being who has twice bruised thee can only bind them up forever.

THE BOURBONNOIS

THERE was nothing from which I had painted out for myself so joyous a riot of the affections, as in this journey in the vintage, through this part of France; but pressing through this gate of sorrow to it, my sufferings have totally unfitted me: in every scene of festivity I saw Maria in the background of the piece, sitting pensive under her poplar; and I had got almost to Lyons before I was able to cast a shade across her.—

—Dear sensibility! source inexhausted of all that's precious in our joys, or costly in our sorrows! thou chainest thy martyr down upon his bed of straw—and 't is thou who lift'st him up to HEAVEN—eternal fountain of our feelings!— 't is here I trace thee—and this is thy divinity which stirs within me—not that in some sad and sickening moments, *"my soul shrinks back upon herself, and startles at destruction"*—mere pomp of words!—but that I feel some generous joys and generous cares beyond myself—all comes from thee, great—great SENSORIUM of the world! which vibrates, if a hair of our heads but falls upon the ground, in the remotest desert of thy creation.—Touch'd with thee, Eugenius draws my curtain when I languish—hears my tale of symptoms, and blames the weather for the disorder of his nerves. Thou giv'st a portion of it sometimes to the roughest peasant who traverses the bleakest mountains—he finds the lacerated lamb of another's flock.—This moment I beheld him leaning with his head against his crook, with piteous inclination looking down upon it.—Oh! had I come one moment sooner!—it bleeds to death—his gentle heart bleeds with it—

Peace to thee, generous swain!—I see thou walkest off with anguish—but thy joys shall balance it—for happy is thy cottage—and happy is the sharer of it—and happy are the lambs which sport about you.

THE SUPPER

A SHOE coming loose from the fore foot of the thill-horse, at the beginning of the ascent of mount Tau-rira, the postilion dismounted, twisted the shoe off, and put it in his pocket; as the ascent was of five or six miles, and that horse our main dependence, I made a point of having the shoe fasten'd on again, as well as we could; but the postilion had thrown away the nails, and the hammer in the chaise-box being of no great use without them, I submitted to go on.

He had not mounted half a mile higher, when coming to a flinty piece of road, the poor devil lost a second shoe, and from off his other fore foot. I then got out of the chaise in good earnest; and seeing a house about a quarter of a mile to the left hand, with a great deal to do I prevailed upon the postilion to turn up to it. The look of the house, and of everything about it, as we drew nearer, soon reconciled me to the disaster.—It was a little farm-house, surrounded with about twenty acres of vineyard, about as much corn—and close to the house, on one side, was a *potagerie* of an acre and a half, full of everything which could make plenty in a French peasant's house—and on the other side was a little wood, which furnish'd wherewithal to dress it. It was about eight in the evening when I got to the house—so I left the postilion to manage his point as he could—and for mine, I walk'd directly into the house.

The family consisted of an old gray-headed man and his wife, with five or six sons and sons-in-law, and their several wives, and a joyous genealogy out of them.

They were all sitting down together to their lentil soup; a large wheaten loaf was in the middle of the table; and a flagon of wine at each end of it, promised joy thro' the stages of the repast—'t was a feast of love.

The old man rose up to meet me, and with a respectful cordiality would have me sit down at the table; my heart was sat down the moment I enter'd the room; so I sat down at once like a son of the family; and to invest myself in the character as speedily as I could, I instantly borrowed the old man's knife, and taking up the loaf, cut myself a hearty luncheon; and as I did it, I saw a testimony in every eye, not only of an honest welcome, but of a welcome mix'd with thanks that I had not seem'd to doubt it.

Was it this; or tell me, Nature, what else it was which made this morsel so sweet—and to what magic I owe it, that the draught I took of their flagon was so delicious with it, that they remain upon my palate to this hour?

If the supper was to my taste—the grace which follow'd it was much more so.

THE GRACE

WHEN supper was over, the old man gave a knock upon the table with the haft of his knife—to bid them prepare for the dance: the moment the signal was given, the women and girls ran all together into a back apartment to tie up their hair—and the young men to the door to wash their faces, and change their sabots; and in three minutes every soul was ready upon a little esplanade before the house to begin.—The old man and his wife came out last, and placing me betwixt them, sat down upon a sofa of turf by the door.

The old man had some fifty years ago been no mean performer upon the vielle—and, at the age he was then of, touch'd it well enough for the purpose. His wife sung now and then a little to the tune—then intermitted—and join'd her old man again as their children and grandchildren danced before them.

It was not till the middle of the second dance, when from some pauses in the movement wherein they all seem'd to look up, I fancied I could distinguish an elevation of spirit different from that which is the cause or the effect of simple jollity.—In a word, I thought I beheld *Religion* mixing in the dance—but as I had never seen her so engaged, I should have look'd upon it now as one of the illusions of an imagination which is eternally misleading me, had not the old man, as soon the dance ended, said that this was their constant way; and that all his life long he had made it a rule, after supper was over, to call out his family to dance and rejoice; believing, he said, that a cheerful and contented mind was the best sort of thanks to heaven that an illiterate peasant could pay—

—Or a learned prelate either, said I.

THE CASE OF DELICACY

WHEN you have gain'd the top of mount Taurira, you run presently down to Lyons—adieu then to all rapid movements! 'T is a journey of caution; and it fares better with sentiments, not to be in a hurry with them; so I contracted with a voiturin to take his time with a couple of mules, and convey me in my own chaise safe to Turin through Savoy.

Poor, patient, quiet, honest people! fear not: your poverty, the treasury of your simple virtues, will not be envied you by the world, nor will your valleys be invaded by it.—Nature! in the midst of thy disorders, thou art still friendly to the scantiness thou hast created—with all thy great works about thee, little hast thou left to give, either to the scythe or to the sickle—but to that little thou grantest safety and protection; and sweet are the dwellings which stand so shelter'd.

Let the wayworn traveler vent his complaints upon the sudden turns and dangers of your roads—your rocks—your precipices—the difficulties of getting up—the horrors of getting down—mountains impracticable—and cataracts, which roll down great stones from their summits, and block his road up.—The peasants had been all day at work in removing a fragment of this kind between St. Michael and Madane; and by the time my voiturin got to the place, it wanted full two hours of completing before a passage could any how be gain'd: there was nothing but to wait with patience—'t was a wet and tempestuous night: so that by the delay, and that together, the voiturin found himself obliged to take up five miles short of his stage at a little decent kind of an inn by the roadside.

I forthwith took possession of my bedchamber—got a good fire—order'd supper; and was thanking heaven it was no worse—when a voiture arrived with a lady in it and her servant-maid.

As there was no other bedchamber in the house, the hostess, without much nicety, led them into mine, telling them, as she usher'd them in, that there was nobody in it but an English gentleman—that there were two good beds in it, and a closet within the room which held another.—The accent in which she spoke of this third bed did not say much for it—however, she said there were three beds, and but three people—and she durst say, the gentleman would do anything to accommodate matters.—I left not the lady a moment to make a conjecture about it—so instantly made a declaration I would do anything in my power.

As this did not amount to an absolute surrender of my bedchamber, I still felt myself so much the proprietor, as to have a right to do the honors of it—so I desired the lady to sit down—pressed her into the warmest seat—call'd for more wood—desir'd the hostess to enlarge the plan of the supper, and to favor us with the very best wine.

The lady had scarce warm'd herself five minutes at the fire before she began to turn her head back, and give a look at the beds; and the oftener she cast her eyes that way, the more they return'd perplex'd.—I felt for her—and for myself; for in a few minutes, what by her looks, and the case itself, I found myself as much embarrassed as it was possible the lady could be herself.

That the beds we were to lay in were in one and the same room, was enough simply by itself to have excited all this— but the position of them, for they stood parallel, and so very close to each other, as only to allow space for a small wicker chair betwixt them, render'd the affair still more oppressive to us—they were fixed up moreover near the fire, and the projection of the chimney on one side, and a large beam which cross'd the room on the other, form'd a kind of recess for them that was no way favorable to the nicety of our sensations—if anything could have added to it, it was that the two beds were both of 'em so very small as to cut us off from every idea of the lady and the maid lying together; which in either of them, could it have been feasible, my lying besides them, tho' a thing not to be wish'd, yet there was nothing in it so terrible which the imagination might not have pass'd over without torment.

As for the little room within, it offer'd little or no consolation to us; 't was a damp cold closet, with a half-dismantled window-shutter, and with a window which had neither glass or oil paper in it to keep out the tempest of the night. I did not endeavor to stifle my cough when the lady gave a peep into it; so it reduced the case in course to this alternative—that the lady should sacrifice her health to her feelings, and take up with the closet herself, and abandon the bed next mine to her maid—or that the girl should take the closet, &c. &c.

The lady was a Piedmontese of about thirty, with a glow of health in her cheeks.—The maid was a Lyonnoise of twenty, and as brisk and lively a French girl as ever moved. —There were difficulties every way—and the obstacle of the stone in the road, which brought us into the distress, great as it appeared whilst the peasants were removing it, was but a pebble to what lay in our ways now.—I have only to add, that it did not lessen the weight which hung upon our spirits, that we were both too delicate to communicate what we felt to each other upon the occasion.

We sat down to supper; and had we not had more generous wine to it than a little inn in Savoy could have furnish'd, our tongues had been tied up, till necessity herself had set them at liberty—but the lady having a few bottles of Burgundy in her voiture, sent down her Fille de Chambre for a couple of them; so that by the time supper was over, and we were left alone, we felt ourselves inspired with a strength of mind sufficient to talk, at least, without reserve upon our situation. We turn'd it every way, and debated and considered it in all kind of lights in the course of a two hours' negotiation; at the end of which the articles were settled finally betwixt us, and stipulated for in form and manner of a treaty of peace—and I believe with as much religion and good faith on both sides, as in any treaty which has yet had the honor of being handed down to posterity.

They were as follows:

First. As the right of the bedchamber is in Monsieur— and he thinking the bed next to the fire to be the warmest, he insists upon the concession on the lady's side of taking up with it.

Granted, on the part of Madame; with a proviso, that as the curtains of that bed are of a flimsy transparent cotton. and appear likewise too scanty to draw close, that the Fille de Chambre shall fasten up the opening, either by corking-pins, or needle and thread, in such manner as shall be deem'd a sufficient barrier on the side of Monsieur.

2dly. It is required on the part of Madame, that Monsieur shall lay the whole night through in his robe de chambre.

Rejected: inasmuch as Monsieur is not worth a robe de chambre; he having nothing in his portmanteau but six shirts and a black silk pair of breeches.

The mentioning the silk pair of breeches made an entire change of the article—for the breeches were accepted as an equivalent for the robe de chambre; and so it was stipulated and agreed upon, that I should lay in my black silk breeches all night.

3dly. It was insisted upon, and stipulated for by the lady, that after Monsieur was got to bed, and the candle and fire extinguished, that Monsieur should not speak one single word the whole night.

Granted; provided Monsieur's saying his prayers might not be deem'd an infraction of the treaty.

There was but one point forgot in this treaty, and that was the manner in which the lady and myself should be obliged to undress and get to bed—there was but one way of doing it, and that I leave to the reader to devise; protesting as I do, that if it is not the most delicate in nature, 't is the fault of his own imagination—against which this is not my first complaint.

Now when we were got to bed, whether it was the novelty of the situation, or what it was, I know not; but so it was, I could not shut my eyes; I tried this side and that, and turn'd and turn'd again, till a full hour after midnight; when Nature and patience both wearing out—O my God! said I—

—You have broke the treaty, Monsieur, said the lady, who had no more slept than myself.—I begg'd a thousand pardons—but insisted it was no more than an ejaculation—she maintain'd 't was an entire infraction of the treaty—I maintain'd it was provided for in the clause of the third article.

The lady would by no means give up her point, tho' she weaken'd her barrier by it; for in the warmth of the dispute, I could hear two or three corking-pins fall out of the curtain to the ground.

Upon my word and honor, Madame, said I—stretching my arm out of bed by way of asseveration—

—(I was going to have added, that I would not have trespass'd against the remotest idea of decorum for the world)—

—But the Fille de Chambre hearing there were words between us, and fearing that hostilities would ensue in course, had crept silently out of her closet, and it being totally dark, had stolen so close to our beds, that she had got herself into the narrow passage which separated them, and had advanc'd so far up as to be in a line betwixt her mistress and me—

So that when I stretch'd out my hand, I caught hold of the Fille de Chambre's——

PRIDE AND PREJUDICE

BY

JANE AUSTEN

CONTENTS

PRIDE AND PREJUDICE

144 CONTENTS

BIOGRAPHICAL NOTE

THE impression of the condition of the Church of England in the eighteenth century which is conveyed by the character and writings of Laurence Sterne receives some necessary modification from a study of the life and works of Jane Austen. Her father, the Reverend George Austen, held the two rectories of Deane and Steventon in Hampshire, having been appointed to them by the favor of a cousin and an uncle. He thus belonged to the gentry, and it seems likely that he entered the church more as a profession than a vocation. He considered that he fulfilled his functions by preaching once a week and administering the sacraments; and though he does not seem to have been a man of spiritual gifts, the decent and dignified performance of these formal duties earned him the reputation of a model pastor. His abundant leisure he occupied in farming the rectory acres, educating his children, and sharing the social life of his class. The environment of refined worldliness and good breeding thus indicated was that in which his daughter lived, and which she pictured in her books.

Jane Austen was born at Steventon on December 16, 1775, the youngest of seven children. She received her education—scanty enough, by modern standards—at home. Besides the usual elementary subjects, she learned French and some Italian, sang a little, and became an expert needlewoman. Her reading extended little beyond the literature of the eighteenth century, and within that period she seems to have cared most for the novels of Richardson and Miss Burney, and the poems of Cowper and Crabbe. Dr. Johnson, too, she admired, and later was delighted with both the poetry and prose of Scott. The first twenty-five years of her life she spent at Steventon; in 1801 she moved with her family to Bath, then a great center of fashion; after the death of her father in 1805, she lived with her mother and sister, first at Southampton and then at Chawton; finally she took lodgings at Winchester to be near a doctor, and there she died on July 18, 1817, and was buried in the cathedral. Apart from a few visits to friends in London and elsewhere, and the vague report of a love affair with a gentleman who died suddenly, there is little else to chronicle in this quiet and uneventful life.

But quiet and uneventful though her life was, it yet supplied her with material for half a dozen novels as perfect of their kind as any in the language. While still a young girl she had experimented with various styles of writing, and when she completed "Pride and Prejudice" at the age of twenty-two, it was clear that she had found her appropriate form. This novel, which in many respects she never surpassed, was followed a year later by "Northanger Abbey," a satire on the "Gothic" romances then in vogue; and in 1809 she finished "Sense and Sensibility," begun a dozen years before. So far she had not succeeded in having any of her works printed; but in 1811 "Sense and Sensibility" appeared in London and won enough recognition to make easy the publication of the others. Success gave stimulus, and between 1811 and 1816, she completed "Mansfield Park," "Emma," and "Persuasion." The last of these and "Northanger Abbey" were published posthumously.

The most remarkable characteristic of Jane Austen as a novelist is her recognition of the limits of her knowledge of life and her determination never to go beyond these limits in her books. She describes her own class, in the part of the country with which she was acquainted; and both the types of character and the events are such as she knew from first-hand observation and experience. But to the portrayal of these she brought an extraordinary power of delicate and subtle delineation, a gift of lively dialogue, and a peculiar detachment. She abounds in humor, but it is always quiet and controlled; and though one feels that she sees through the affectations and petty hypocrisies of her circle, she seldom becomes openly satirical. The fineness of her workmanship, unexcelled in the English novel, makes possible the discrimination of characters who have outwardly little or nothing to distinguish them; and the analysis of the states of mind and feeling of ordinary people is done so faithfully and vividly as to compensate for the lack of passion and adventure. She herself speaks of the "little bit (two inches wide) of ivory on which I work," and, in contrast with the broad canvases of Fielding or Scott, her stories have the exquisiteness of a fine miniature.

W. A. N.

CRITICISMS AND INTERPRETATIONS

I

BY SIR WALTER SCOTT

READ again, and for the third time at least, Miss Austen's very finely written novel of "Pride and Prejudice." That young lady has a talent for describing the involvements and feelings and characters of ordinary life which is to me the most wonderful I ever met with. The big bow-wow strain I can do myself like any now going; but the exquisite touch, which renders ordinary commonplace things and characters interesting, from the truth of the description and the sentiment, is denied to me.—From "The Journal of Sir Walter Scott," March, 1826.

We bestow no mean compliment upon the author of "Emma" when we say that keeping close to common incidents, and to such characters as occupy the ordinary walks of life, she has produced sketches of such spirit and originality that we never miss the excitation which depends upon a narrative of uncommon events, arising from the consideration of minds, manners, and sentiments, greatly above our own. In this class she stands almost alone; for the scenes of Miss Edgeworth are laid in higher life, varied by more romantic incident, and by her remarkable power of embodying and illustrating national character. But the author of "Emma" confines herself chiefly to the middling classes of society; her most distinguished characters do not rise greatly above well-bred country gentlemen and ladies; and those which are sketched with most originality and precision, belong to a class rather below that standard. The narrative of all her novels is composed of such common occurrences as may have fallen under the observation of most folks; and her dramatis personæ conduct themselves

149

6—C

upon the motives and principles which the readers may recognize as ruling their own, and that of most of their own acquaintances.—From "The Quarterly Review," October, 1815.

II

By Lord Macaulay

SHAKESPEARE has had neither equal nor second. But among the writers who, in the point which we have noticed, have approached nearest to the manner of the great master we have no hesitation in placing Jane Austen, a woman of whom England is justly proud. She has given us a multitude of characters, all, in a certain sense, commonplace, all such as we meet every day. Yet they are all as perfectly discriminated from each other as if they were the most eccentric of human beings. There are, for example, four clergymen, none of whom we should be surprised to find in any parsonage in the kingdom— Mr. Edward Ferrars, Mr. Henry Tilney, Mr. Edmund Bertram, and Mr. Elton. They are all specimens of the upper part of the middle class. They have all been liberally educated. They all lie under the restraints of the same sacred profession. They are all young. They are all in love. Not one of them has any hobby-horse, to use the phrase of Sterne. Not one has a ruling passion, such as we read of in Pope. Who would not have expected them to be insipid likenesses of each other? No such thing. Harpagon is not more unlike to Jourdain, Joseph Surface is not more unlike to Sir Lucius O'Trigger, than every one of Miss Austen's young divines to all his reverend brethren. And almost all this is done by touches so delicate that they elude analysis, that they defy the powers of description, and that we know them to exist only by the general effect to which they have contributed.—From essay on "Madame D'Arblay," 1843.

III

By W. F. Pollock

MISS AUSTEN never attempts to describe a scene or a class of society with which she was not herself thoroughly acquainted. The conversations of ladies with ladies, or of ladies and gentlemen together, are given, but no instance occurs of a scene in which men only are present. The uniform quality of her work is one most remarkable point to be observed in it. Let a volume be opened at any place: there is the same good English, the same refined style, the same simplicity and truth. There is never any deviation into the unnatural or exaggerated; and how worthy of all love and respect is the finely disciplined genius which rejects the forcible but transient modes of stimulating interest which can so easily be employed when desired, and which knows how to trust to the never-failing principles of human nature! This very trust has sometimes been made an objection to Miss Austen, and she has been accused of writing dull stories about ordinary people. But her supposed ordinary people are really not such very ordinary people. Let anyone who is inclined to criticise on this score endeavor to construct one character from among the ordinary people of his own acquaintance that shall be capable of interesting any reader for ten minutes. It will then be found how great has been the discrimination of Miss Austen in the selection of her characters, and how skillful is her treatment in the management of them. It is true that the events are for the most part those of daily life, and the feelings are those connected with the usual joys and griefs of familiar existence; but these are the very events and feelings upon which the happiness or misery of most of us depends; and the field which embraces them, to the exclusion of the wonderful, the sentimental, and the historical, is surely large enough, as it certainly admits of the most profitable cultivation. In the end, too, the novel of daily real life is that of which we are least apt to weary: a round of fancy balls would tire the most vigorous admirers of variety in costume, and the return to plain clothes would be hailed with greater delight than their occasional relinquishment ever gives. Miss Austen's personages are always in plain clothes, but no two suits are alike: all are worn with their appropriate differences, and under all human thoughts and feelings are at work.—From "Fraser's Magazine," January, 1860.

IV

By Anne Thackeray Ritchie

NOTWITHSTANDING a certain reticence and self-control which seems to belong to their age, and with all their quaint dresses, and ceremonies, and manners, the ladies and gentlemen in "Pride and Prejudice" and its companion novels seem like living people out of our own acquaintance transported bodily into a bygone age, represented in the half-dozen books that contain Jane Austen's works. Dear books! bright, sparkling with wit and animation, in which the homely heroines charm, the dull hours fly, and the very bores are enchanting. . . .

She has a gift of telling a story in a way that has never been surpassed. She rules her places, times, characters, and marshals them with unerring precision. Her machinery is simple but complete; events group themselves so vividly and naturally in her mind that, in describing imaginary scenes, we seem not only to read them but to live them, to see the people coming and going—the gentlemen courteous and in top-boots, the ladies demure and piquant; we can almost hear them talking to one another. No retrospects; no abrupt flights, as in real life: days and events follow one another. Last Tuesday does not suddenly start into existence all out of place; nor does 1790 appear upon the scene when we are well on in '21. Countries and continents do not fly from hero to hero, nor do long and divergent adventures happen to unimportant members of the company. With Miss Austen, days, hours, minutes, succeed each other like clockwork; one central figure is always present on the scene; that figure is always prepared for company. . . .

Some books and people are delightful, we can scarce tell why; they are not so clever as others that weary and fatigue us. It is a certain effort to read a story, however touching, that is disconnected and badly related. It is like an ill-drawn picture, of which the coloring is good. Jane Austen possessed both gifts of color and drawing. She could see human nature as it was—with near-sighted eyes, it is true; but having seen, she could combine her picture by her art, and color it from life. . . .

It is difficult, reading the novels of succeeding generations, to determine how much each book reflects of the time in which it was written; how much of its character depends upon the mind and mood of the writer. The greatest minds, the most original, have the least stamp of the age, the most of that dominant natural reality which belongs to all great minds. We know how a landscape changes as the day goes on, and how the scene brightens and gains in beauty as the shadows begin to lengthen. The clearest eyes must see by the light of their own hour. Jane Austen's hour must have been a midday hour— bright, unsuggestive, with objects standing clear without relief or shadow. She did not write of herself, but of the manners of her age. This age is essentially an age of men and women of strained emotion, little remains of starch, or powder, or courtly reserve. What we have lost in calm, in happiness, in tranquillity, we have gained in intensity. Our danger is now, not of expressing and feeling too little, but of expressing more than we feel. . . .

Miss Austen's heroines have a stamp of their own. They have a certain gentle self-respect and humor and hardness of heart in which modern heroines are a little wanting. Whatever happens they can for the most part speak of gayly and without bitterness. Love with them does not mean a passion so much as an interest—deep, silent, not quite incompatible with a secondary flirtation. Marianne Dashwood's tears are evidently meant to be dried. Jane Bennet smiles, sighs, and makes excuses for Bingley's neglect. Emma passes one disagreeable morning making up her mind to the unnatural alliance between Mr. Knightley and Harriet Smith. It was the spirit of the age, and perhaps one not to be unenvied. It was not that Jane Austen herself was incapable of understanding a deeper feeling. In the last written page of her last written book there is an expression of the deepest and truest experience. Anne Elliot's talk with Captain Harville is the touching utterance of a good woman's feelings. They are speaking of men and women's affections. "You are always laboring and toiling," she says, "exposed to every risk and hardship. Your home, country, friends, all united; neither time nor life to call your own. It would be hard indeed (with a faltering voice) if a woman's feelings were to be added to all this."

Farther on she says eagerly: "I hope I do justice to all that is felt by you, and by those who resemble you. God forbid that I should undervalue the warm and faithful feelings of any of my fellow-creatures. I should deserve utter contempt if I dared to suppose that true attachment and constancy were known only by woman. No! I believe you capable of everything great and good in your married lives. I believe you equal to every important exertion, and to every domestic forbearance, so long as—if I may be allowed the expression—so long as you have an object; I mean while the woman you love lives, and lives for you. *All the privilege I claim for my own (it is not a very enviable one, you need not court it) is that of loving longest when existence or when hope is gone.*"

She could not immediately have uttered another sentence—her heart was too full, her breath too much oppressed.

Dear Anne Elliot! sweet, impulsive, womanly, tenderhearted!—one can almost hear her voice pleading the cause of all true women. In those days, when perhaps people's nerves were stronger than they are now, sentiment may have existed in a less degree, or have been more ruled by judgment; it may have been calmer and more matter-of-fact; and yet Jane Austen, at the very end of her life, wrote thus. Her words seem to ring in our ears after they have been spoken. Anne Elliot must have been Jane

Austen herself, speaking for the last time. There is something so true, so womanly about her, that it is impossible not to love her. She is the bright-eyed heroine of the earlier novels matured, chastened, cultivated, to whom fidelity has brought only greater depth and sweetness instead of bitterness and pain.—From "The Cornhill Magazine," August, 1871.

V

By GOLDWIN SMITH

AS we should expect from such a life, Jane Austen's view of the world is genial, kindly, and, we repeat, free from anything like cynicism. It is that of a clear-sighted and somewhat satirical onlooker, loving what deserves love, and amusing herself with the foibles, the self-deceptions, the affectations of humanity. Refined almost to fastidiousness, she is hard upon vulgarity; not, however, on good-natured vulgarity, such as that of Mrs. Jennings in "Sense and Sensibility," but on vulgarity like that of Miss Steele, in the same novel, combined at once with effrontery and with meanness of soul. . . .

To sentimentality Jane Austen was a foe. Antipathy to it runs through her works. She had encountered it in the romances of the day, such as the works of Mrs. Radcliffe and in people who had fed on them. What she would have said if she had encountered it in the form of Rousseauism we can only guess. The solid foundation of her own character was good sense, and her type of excellence as displayed in her heroines is a woman full of feeling, but with her feelings thoroughly under control. Genuine sensibility, however, even when too little under control, she can regard as lovable. Marianne in "Sense and Sensibility" is an object of sympathy, because her emotions, though they are ungoverned and lead her into folly, are genuine, and are matched in intensity by her sisterly affection. But affected sentiment gets no quarter. . . .

Jane Austen had, as she was sure to have, a feeling for the beauties of nature. She paints in glowing language the scenery of Lyme. She speaks almost with rapture of a view which she calls thoroughly English, though never having been out of England she could hardly judge of its scenery by contrast. She was deeply impressed by the sea, on which, she says, "all must linger and gaze, on their first return to it, who ever deserves to look on it at all." But admiration of the picturesque had "become a mere jargon," from which Jane Austen recoiled. One of her characters is made to say that he likes a fine prospect, but not on picturesque principles; that he prefers tall and flourishing trees to those which are crooked and blasted; neat to ruined cottages, snug farmhouses to watchtowers, and a troop of tidy, happy villagers to the finest banditti in the world. . . .

Jane Austen held the mirror up to her time, or at least to a certain class of the people of her time; and her time was two generations and more before ours. We are reminded of this as we read her works by a number of little touches of manners and customs belonging to the early part of the century, and anterior to the rush of discovery and development which the century has brought with it. There are no railroads, and no lucifer matches. It takes you two days and a half, even when you are flying on the wings of love or remorse, to get from Somersetshire to London. A young lady who has snuffed her candle out has to go to bed in the dark. The watchman calls the hours of the night. Magnates go about in chariots and four with outriders, their coachmen wearing wigs. People dine at five, and instead of spending the evening in brilliant conversation as we do, they spend it in an unintellectual rubber of whist, or a round game. Life is unelectric, untelegraphic; it is spent more quietly and it is spent at home. If you are capable of enjoying tranquillity, at least by way of occasional contrast to the stir and stress of the present age, you will find in these tales the tranquillity of a rural neighborhood and a little country town in England a century ago. . . .

That Jane Austen held up the mirror to her time must be remembered when she is charged with want of delicacy in dealing with the relations between the sexes, and especially in speaking of the views of women with regard to matrimony. Women in those days evidently did consider a happy marriage as the best thing that destiny could have in store for them. They desired it for themselves and they sought it for their daughters. Other views had not opened out to them; they had not thought of professions or public life, nor had it entered into the mind of any of them that maternity was not the highest duty and the crown of womanhood. Apparently they also confessed their aims to themselves and to each other with a frankness which would be deemed indelicate in our time. The more worldly and ambitious of them sought in marriage rank and money, and avowed that they did, whereas they would not avow it at the present day. Gossip and speculation on these subjects were common and more unrefined than they are now, and they naturally formed a large part of the amusement of the opulent and idle class from which Jane Austen's characters were drawn. Often, too, she is ironical; the love of irony is a feature of her mind, and for this also allowance must be made. She does not approve or reward matchmaking or husband-hunting. Mrs. Jennings, the great matchmaker in "Sense and Sensibilty," is also a paragon of vulgarity. Mrs. Norris's matchmaking in "Mansfield Park" leads to the most calamitous results. Charlotte Lucas in "Pride and Prejudice," who unblushingly avows that her object is a husband with a good income, gets what she sought, but you are made to see that she has bought it dear. . . .

The life which Jane Austen painted retains its leading features, and is recognized by the reader at the present day with little effort of the imagination. It is a life of opulent quiet and rather dull enjoyment, physically and morally healthy compared with that of a French aristocracy, though without much of the salt of duty; a life uneventful, exempt from arduous struggles and devoid of heroism, a life presenting no materials for tragedy and hardly an element of pathos, a life of which matrimony is the chief incident, and the most interesting objects are the hereditary estate and the heir.

Such a life could evidently furnish no material for romance. It could furnish materials only for that class of novel which corresponds to sentimental comedy. To that class all Jane Austen's novels belong.—From "Life of Jane Austen," in "Great Writers," 1890.

VI

By F. W. Cornish

JANE AUSTEN needs no testimonials; her position is at this moment established on a firmer basis than that of any of her contemporaries. She has completely distanced Miss Edgeworth, Miss Ferrier, Fanny Burney, and Hannah More, writers who eclipsed her modest reputation in her own day. The readers of "Evelina," "Ormond," "Marriage," or "Caelebs" are few; but hundreds know intimately every character and every scene in "Pride and Prejudice." She has survived Trollope and Mrs. Gaskell: one may almost say that she is less out of date than Currer Bell and George Eliot. It was not always so. In 1859 a writer in "Blackwood's Magazine" spoke of her as "being still unfamiliar in men's mouths" and "not even now a household word."

The reason for this comparative obscurity in her own time, compared with her fame at the present day, may in some measure be that in writing, as in other arts, finish is now more highly prized than formerly. But conception as well as finish is in it. The miracle in Jane Austen's writing is not only that her presentment of each character is complete and consistent, but also that every fact and particular situation is viewed in comprehensive proportion and relation to the rest. . . . Some facts and expressions which pass almost unnoticed by the reader, and quite unnoticed by the other actors in the story, turn up later to take their proper place. She never drops a stitch. The reason is not so much that she took infinite trouble, though no doubt she did, as that everything was actual to her, as in his larger historical manner everything was actual to Macaulay. . . .

It is easier to feel than to estimate a genius which has no parallel. Jane Austen's faults are obvious. She has no remarkable distinction of style. Her plots, though worked out with microscopic delicacy, are neither original nor striking; incident is almost absent; she repeats situations, and to some extent even characters. She cared for story and situation only as they threw light on character. She has little idealism, little romance, tenderness, poetry, or religion. All this may be conceded, and yet she stands by the side of Molière, unsurpassed among writers of prose and poetry, within the limits which she imposed on herself, for clear and sympathetic vision of human character.

She sees everything in clear outline and perspective. She does not care to analyze by logic what she knows by intuition; she does not search out the grounds of motive like George Eliot, nor illumine them like Meredith by searchlight flashes of insight, nor like Hardy display them by irony, sardonic or pitying, nor like Henry James thread a labyrinth of indications and intimations, repulsions and attractions right and left, all pointing to the central temple, where sits the problem. She has no need to construct her characters, for there they are before her, like Mozart's music, only waiting to be written down.—From "Jane Austen" in "English Men of Letters."

LIST OF CHARACTERS

MR. BENNET, a gentleman in moderate circumstances living in a small town in Hertfordshire.

MRS. BENNET, his wife.

JANE,
ELIZABETH,
MARY, } daughters of Mr. and Mrs. Bennet.
CATHERINE,
LYDIA,

SIR WILLIAM LUCAS, an affable knight, formerly in trade.

LADY LUCAS, his wife.

CHARLOTTE,
MARIA, } children of Sir William and Lady Lucas.
MASTER LUCAS,

MR. CHARLES BINGLEY, a rich and amiable young man of leisure.

MR. HURST, brother-in-law of Mr. Bingley.

MRS. HURST,
MISS CAROLINE BINGLEY, } sisters of Mr. Bingley.

FITZWILLIAM DARCY, a friend of Mr. Bingley and a young man of wealth and high station.

GEORGIANA DARCY, younger sister of Mr. Darcy.

COLONEL FORSTER, of the ——shire Regiment.

MRS. FORSTER, his wife.

MR. PHILIPS, successor to Mrs. Bennet's father in business.

MRS. PHILIPS, his wife, sister to Mrs. Bennet.

MR. GARDINER, in business in London, a brother of Mrs. Bennet.

MRS. GARDINER, his wife.

Several young children of the Gardiners.

REV. WILLIAM COLLINS, a pompous and obsequious clergyman, cousin to the Bennets.

LADY CATHERINE DE BOURGH, a domineering, rich old lady, aunt of Mr. Darcy.

MISS DE BOURGH, invalid daughter of Lady Catherine.

MR. WICKHAM, a worthless young officer in the ——shire Regiment.

MISS KING, courted by Wickham.

MRS. JENKINSON.

COLONEL FITZWILLIAM, a cousin of Mr. Darcy and nephew of Lady Catherine de Bourgh.

MRS. REYNOLDS, Darcy's housekeeper.

PRIDE AND PREJUDICE

CHAPTER I

IT is a truth universally acknowledged, that a single man in possession of a good fortune must be in want of a wife.

However little known the feelings or views of such a man may be on his first entering a neighbourhood, this truth is so well fixed in the minds of the surrounding families, that he is considered as the rightful property of some one or other of their daughters.

'My dear Mr. Bennet,' said his lady to him one day, 'have you heard that Netherfield Park is let at last?'

Mr. Bennet replied that he had not.

'But it is,' returned she; 'for Mrs. Long has just been here, and she told me all about it.'

Mr. Bennet made no answer.

'Do not you want to know who has taken it?' cried his wife, impatiently.

'*You* want to tell me, and I have no objection to hearing it.'

This was invitation enough.

'Why, my dear, you must know, Mrs. Long says that Netherfield is taken by a young man of large fortune from the north of England; that he came down on Monday in a chaise and four to see the place, and was so much delighted with it that he agreed with Mr. Morris immediately; that he is to take possession before Michaelmas, and some of his servants are to be in the house by the end of next week.'

'What is his name?'

'Bingley.'

'Is he married or single?'

'Oh, single, my dear, to be sure! A single man of large fortune; four or five thousand a year. What a fine thing for our girls!'

'How so? how can it affect them?'

'My dear Mr. Bennet,' replied his wife, 'how can you be so tiresome? You must know that I am thinking of his marrying one of them.'

'Is that his design in settling here?'

'Design? nonsense, how can you talk so! But it is very likely that he *may* fall in love with one of them, and therefore you must visit him as soon as he comes.'

'I see no occasion for that. You and the girls may go, or you may send them by themselves, which perhaps will be still better, for, as you are as handsome as any of them, Mr. Bingley might like you the best of the party.'

'My dear, you flatter me. I certainly *have* had my share of beauty, but I do not pretend to be anything extraordinary now. When a woman has five grown-up daughters, she ought to give over thinking of her own beauty.'

'In such cases, a woman has not often much beauty to think of.'

'But, my dear, you must indeed go and see Mr. Bingley when he comes into the neighbourhood.'

'It is more than I engage for, I assure you.'

"But consider your daughters. Only think what an establishment it would be for one of them. Sir William and Lady Lucas are determined to go, merely on that account; for in general, you know, they visit no newcomers. Indeed you must go, for it will be impossible for *us* to visit him, if you do not.'

'You are over scrupulous, surely. I daresay Mr. Bingley will be very glad to see you; and I will send a few lines by you to assure him of my hearty consent to his marrying whichever he chooses of the girls; though I must throw in a good word for my little Lizzy.'

'I desire you will do no such thing. Lizzy is not a bit better than the others: and I am sure she is not half so handsome as Jane, nor half so good-humoured as Lydia. But you are always giving *her* the preference.'

'They have none of them much to recommend them,' replied he: 'they are all silly and ignorant like other girls; but Lizzy has something more of quickness than her sisters.'

'Mr. Bennet, how can you abuse your own children in such a way? You take delight in vexing me. You have no compassion on my poor nerves.'

'You mistake me, my dear. I have a high respect for your nerves. They are my old friends. I have heard you mention them with consideration these twenty years at least.'

'Ah, you do not know what I suffer.'

'But I hope you will get over it, and live to see many young men of four thousand a year come into the neighbourhood.'

'It will be no use to us, if twenty such should come, since you will not visit them.'

'Depend upon it, my dear, that when there are twenty, I will visit them all.'

Mr. Bennet was so odd a mixture of quick parts, sarcastic humour, reserve, and caprice, that the experience of three-and-twenty years had been insufficient to make his wife understand his character. *Her* mind was less difficult to develop. She was a woman of mean understanding, little information, and uncertain temper. When she was discontented, she fancied herself nervous. The business of her life was to get her daughters married: its solace was visiting and news.

CHAPTER II

MR. BENNET was among the earliest of those who waited on Mr. Bingley. He had always intended to visit him, though to the last always assuring his wife that he should not go; and till the evening after the visit was paid she had no knowledge of it. It was then disclosed in the following manner. Observing his second daughter employed in trimming a hat, he suddenly addressed her with,—

'I hope Mr. Bingley will like it, Lizzy.'

'We are not in a way to know *what* Mr. Bingley likes,' said her mother, resentfully, 'since we are not to visit.'

'But you forget, mamma,' said Elizabeth, 'that we shall meet him at the assemblies, and that Mrs. Long has promised to introduce him.'

'I do not believe Mrs. Long will do any such thing. She has two nieces of her own. She is a selfish, hypocritical woman, and I have no opinion of her.'

'No more have I,' said Mr. Bennet; 'and I am glad to find that you do not depend on her serving you.'

Mrs. Bennet deigned not to make any reply; but, unable to contain herself, began scolding one of her daughters.

'Don't keep coughing so, Kitty, for heaven's sake! Have a little compassion on my nerves. You tear them to pieces.'

'Kitty has no discretion in her coughs,' said her father; 'she times them ill.'

'I do not cough for my own amusement,' replied Kitty, fretfully. 'When is your next ball to be, Lizzy?'

'To-morrow fortnight.'

'Ay, so it is,' cried her mother, 'and Mrs. Long does not come back till the day before; so, it will be impossible for her to introduce him, for she will not know him herself.'

'Then, my dear, you may have the advantage of your friend, and introduce Mr. Bingley to *her?*'

'Impossible, Mr. Bennet, impossible, when I am not acquainted with him myself; how can you be so teasing?'

'I honour your circumspection. A fortnight's acquaintance is certainly very little. One cannot know what a man
really is by the end of a fortnight. But if *we* do not venture,
somebody else will; and after all, Mrs. Long and her nieces
must stand their chance; and, therefore, as she will think it
an act of kindness, if you decline the office, I will take it on
myself.'

The girls stared at their father. Mrs. Bennet said only,
'Nonsense, nonsense!'

'What can be the meaning of that emphatic exclamation?'
cried he. 'Do you consider the forms of introduction, and
the stress that is laid on them, as nonsense? I cannot quite
agree with you *there*. What say you, Mary? for you are a
young lady of deep reflection, I know, and read great books,
and make extracts.'

Mary wished to say something very sensible, but knew not
how.

'While Mary is adjusting her ideas,' he continued, 'let us
return to Mr. Bingley.'

'I am sick of Mr. Bingley,' cried his wife.

'I am sorry to hear *that;* but why did not you tell me so
before? If I had known as much this morning, I certainly
would not have called on him. It is very unlucky; but as I
have actually paid the visit, we cannot escape the acquaintance now.'

The astonishment of the ladies was just what he wished;
that of Mrs. Bennet perhaps surpassing the rest; though
when the first tumult of joy was over, she began to declare
that it was what she had expected all the while.

'How good it was in you, my dear Mr. Bennet. But I
knew I should persuade you at last. I was sure you loved
your girls too well to neglect such an acquaintance. Well,
how pleased I am! and it is such a good joke, too, that you
should have gone this morning, and never said a word about
it till now.'

'Now, Kitty, you may cough as much as you choose,' said
Mr. Bennet; and, as he spoke, he left the room, fatigued
with the raptures of his wife.

'What an excellent father you have, girls,' said she, when
the door was shut. 'I do not know how you will ever make

him amends for his kindness; or me either, for that matter. At our time of life, it is not so pleasant, I can tell you, to be making new acquaintance every day; but for your sakes we would do anything. Lydia, my love, though you *are* the youngest, I daresay Mr. Bingley will dance with you at the next ball.'

'Oh,' said Lydia, stoutly, 'I am not afraid; for though I *am* the youngest, I'm the tallest.'

The rest of the evening was spent in conjecturing how soon he would return Mr. Bennet's visit, and determining when they should ask him to dinner.

CHAPTER III

NOT all that Mrs. Bennet, however, with the assistance of her five daughters, could ask on the subject, was sufficient to draw from her husband any satisfactory description of Mr. Bingley. They attacked him in various ways; with barefaced questions, ingenious suppositions, and distant surmises; but he eluded the skill of them all; and they were at last obliged to accept the second-hand intelligence of their neighbour, Lady Lucas. Her report was highly favourable. Sir William had been delighted with him. He was quite young, wonderfully handsome, extremely agreeable, and, to crown the whole, he meant to be at the next assembly with a large party. Nothing could be more delightful! To be fond of dancing was a certain step towards falling in love; and very lively hopes of Mr. Bingley's heart were entertained.

'If I can but see one of my daughters happily settled at Netherfield,' said Mrs. Bennet to her husband, 'and all the others equally well married, I shall have nothing to wish for.'

In a few days Mr. Bingley returned Mr. Bennet's visit, and sat about ten minutes with him in his library. He had entertained hopes of being admitted to a sight of the young ladies, of whose beauty he had heard much; but he saw only the father. The ladies were somewhat more fortunate, for they had the advantage of ascertaining, from an upper window, that he wore a blue coat and rode a black horse.

An invitation to dinner was soon afterwards despatched; and already had Mrs. Bennet planned the courses that were to do credit to her housekeeping, when an answer arrived which deferred it all. Mr. Bingley was obliged to be in town the following day, and consequently unable to accept the honour of their invitation, etc. Mrs. Bennet was quite disconcerted. She could not imagine what business he could have in town so soon after his arrival in Hertfordshire; and she began to fear that he might always be flying about from

169

one place to another, and never settled at Netherfield as he ought to be. Lady Lucas quieted her fears a little by starting the idea of his being gone to London only to get a large party for the ball; and a report soon followed that Mr. Bingley was to bring twelve ladies and seven gentlemen with him to the assembly. The girls grieved over such a number of ladies; but were comforted the day before the ball by hearing that, instead of twelve, he had brought only six with him from London, his five sisters and a cousin. And when the party entered the assembly-room, it consisted of only five altogether: Mr. Bingley, his two sisters, the husband of the eldest, and another young man.

Mr. Bingley was good-looking and gentlemanlike: he had a pleasant countenance, and easy, unaffected manners. His sisters were fine women, with an air of decided fashion. His brother-in-law, Mr. Hurst, merely looked the gentleman; but his friend Mr. Darcy soon drew the attention of the room by his fine, tall person, handsome features, noble mien, and the report, which was in general circulation within five minutes after his entrance, of his having ten thousand a year. The gentlemen pronounced him to be a fine figure of a man, the ladies declared he was much handsomer than Mr. Bingley, and he was looked at with great admiration for about half the evening, till his manners gave a disgust which turned the tide of his popularity; for he was discovered to be proud, to be above his company, and above being pleased; and not all his large estate in Derbyshire could then save him from having a most forbidding, disagreeable countenance, and being unworthy to be compared with his friend.

Mr. Bingley had soon made himself acquainted with all the principal people in the room: he was lively and unreserved, danced every dance, was angry that the ball closed so early, and talked of giving one himself at Netherfield. Such amiable qualities must speak for themselves. What a contrast between him and his friend! Mr. Darcy danced only once with Mrs. Hurst and once with Miss Bingley, declined being introduced to any other lady, and spent the rest of the evening in walking about the room, speaking occasionally to one of his own party. His character was decided. He was the proudest, most disagreeable man in the world, and everybody hoped that he would never come there again. Amongst the most violent against him was Mrs. Bennet, whose dislike of his general behaviour was sharpened into particular resentment by his having slighted one of her daughters.

Elizabeth Bennet had been obliged, by the scarcity of gentlemen, to sit down for two dances; and during part of that time, Mr. Darcy had been standing near enough for her to overhear a conversation between him and Mr. Bingley, who came from the dance for a few minutes to press his friend to join it.

'Come, Darcy,' said he, 'I must have you dance. I hate to see you standing about by yourself in this stupid manner. You had much better dance.'

'I certainly shall not. You know how I detest it, unless I am particularly acquainted with my partner. At such an assembly as this, it would be insupportable. Your sisters are engaged, and there is not another woman in the room whom it would not be a punishment to me to stand up with.'

'I would not be so fastidious as you are,' cried Bingley, 'for a kingdom! Upon my honour, I never met with so many pleasant girls in my life as I have this evening; and there are several of them, you see, uncommonly pretty.'

'*You* are dancing with the only handsome girl in the room,' said Mr. Darcy, looking at the eldest Miss Bennet.

'Oh, she is the most beautiful creature I ever beheld! But there is one of her sisters sitting down just behind you, who is very pretty, and I daresay very agreeable. Do let me ask my partner to introduce you.'

'Which do you mean?' and turning round, he looked for a moment at Elizabeth, till, catching her eye, he withdrew his own, and coldly said, 'She is tolerable; but not handsome enough to tempt *me;* and I am in no humour at present to give consequence to young ladies who are slighted by other men. You had better return to your partner and enjoy her smiles, for you are wasting your time with me.'

Mr. Bingley followed his advice. Mr. Darcy walked off; and Elizabeth remained with no very cordial feelings towards him. She told the story, however, with great spirit among her friends; for she had a lively, playful disposition, which delighted in anything ridiculous.

The evening altogether passed off pleasantly to the whole family. Mrs. Bennet had seen her eldest daughter much admired by the Netherfield party. Mr. Bingley had danced with her twice, and she had been distinguished by his sisters. Jane was as much gratified by this as her mother could be, though in a quieter way. Elizabeth felt Jane's pleasure. Mary had heard herself mentioned to Miss Bingley as the most accomplished girl in the neighbourhood; and Catherine and Lydia had been fortunate enough to be never without partners, which was all that they had yet learned to care for at a ball.

They returned, therefore, in good spirits to Longbourn, the village where they lived, and of which they were the principal inhabitants. They found Mr. Bennet still up. With a book, he was regardless of time; and on the present occasion he had a good deal of curiosity as to the event of an evening which had raised such splendid expectations. He had rather hoped that all his wife's views on the stranger would be disappointed; but he soon found that he had a very different story to hear.

'Oh, my dear Mr. Bennet,' as she entered the room, 'we have had a most delightful evening, a most excellent ball. I wish you had been there. Jane was so admired, nothing could be like it. Everybody said how well she looked; and Mr. Bingley thought her quite beautiful, and danced with her twice. Only think of *that*, my dear; he actually danced with her twice; and she was the only creature in the room that he asked a second time. First of all, he asked Miss Lucas. I was so vexed to see him stand up with her; but, however, he did not admire her at all; indeed, nobody can, you know; and he seemed quite struck with Jane as she was going down the dance. So he inquired who she was, and got introduced, and asked her for the two next. Then, the two third he danced with Miss King, and the two fourth with Maria Lucas, and the two fifth with Jane again, and the two sixth with Lizzy, and the *Boulanger*——'

'If he had had any compassion for *me*,' cried her husband impatiently, 'he would not have danced half so much! For God's sake, say no more of his partners. Oh that he had sprained his ankle in the first dance!'

'Oh, my dear,' continued Mrs. Bennet, 'I am quite delighted with him. He is so excessively handsome! and his sisters are charming women. I never in my life saw anything more elegant than their dresses. I daresay the lace upon Mrs. Hurst's gown——'

Here she was interrupted again. Mr. Bennet protested against any description of finery. She was therefore obliged to seek another branch of the subject, and related, with much bitterness of spirit, and some exaggeration, the shocking rudeness of Mr. Darcy.

'But I can assure you,' she added, 'that Lizzy does not lose much by not suiting *his* fancy; for he is a most disagreeable, horrid man, not at all worth pleasing. So high and so conceited, that there was no enduring him! He walked here, and he walked there, fancying himself so very great! Not handsome enough to dance with! I wish you had been there, my dear, to have given him one of your set-downs. I quite detest the man.'

CHAPTER IV

WHEN Jane and Elizabeth were alone, the former, who had been cautious in her praise of Mr. Bingley before, expressed to her sister how very much she admired him.

'He is just what a young man ought to be,' said she, 'sensible, good-humoured, lively; and I never saw such happy manners! so much ease, with such perfect good breeding!'

'He is also handsome,' replied Elizabeth, 'which a young man ought likewise to be if he possibly can. His character is thereby complete.'

'I was very much flattered by his asking me to dance a second time. I did not expect such a compliment.'

'Did not you? *I* did for you. But that is one great difference between us. Compliments always take *you* by surprise, and *me* never. What could be more natural than his asking you again? He could not help seeing that you were about five times as pretty as every other woman in the room. No thanks to his gallantry for that. Well, he certainly is very agreeable, and I give you leave to like him. You have liked many a stupider person.'

'Dear Lizzy!'

'Oh, you are a great deal too apt, you know, to like people in general. You never see a fault in anybody. All the world are good and agreeable in your eyes. I never heard you speak ill of a human being in my life.'

'I would wish not to be hasty in censuring any one; but I always speak what I think.'

'I know you do; and it is *that* which makes the wonder. With *your* good sense, to be so honestly blind to the follies and nonsense of others! Affectation of candour is common enough; one meets with it everywhere. But to be candid without ostentation or design,—to take the good of everybody's character and make it still better, and say nothing of the bad,—belongs to you alone. And so, you like this man's sisters, too, do you? Their manners are not equal to his.'

174

'Certainly not, at first; but they are very pleasing women when you converse with them. Miss Bingley is to live with her brother, and keep his house; and I am much mistaken if we shall not find a very charming neighbour in her.'

Elizabeth listened in silence, but was not convinced: their behaviour at the assembly had not been calculated to please in general; and with more quickness of observation and less pliancy of temper than her sister, and with a judgment, too, unassailed by any attention to herself, she was very little disposed to approve them. They were, in fact, very fine ladies; not deficient in good-humour when they were pleased, nor in the power of being agreeable where they chose it; but proud and conceited. They were rather handsome; had been educated in one of the first private seminaries in town; had a fortune of twenty thousand pounds; were in the habit of spending more than they ought, and of associating with people of rank; and were, therefore, in every respect entitled to think well of themselves and meanly of others. They were of a respectable family in the north of England; a circumstance more deeply impressed on their memories than that their brother's fortune and their own had been acquired by trade.

Mr. Bingley inherited property to the amount of nearly a hundred thousand pounds from his father, who had intended to purchase an estate, but did not live to do it. Mr. Bingley intended it likewise, and sometimes made choice of his county; but, as he was now provided with a good house and the liberty of a manor, it was doubtful to many of those who best knew the easiness of his temper, whether he might not spend the remainder of his days at Netherfield, and leave the next generation to purchase.

His sisters were very anxious for his having an estate of his own; but though he was now established only as a tenant, Miss Bingley was by no means unwilling to preside at his table; nor was Mrs. Hurst, who had married a man of more fashion than fortune, less disposed to consider his house as her home when it suited her. Mr. Bingley had not been of age two years when he was tempted, by an accidental recommendation, to look at Netherfield House. He did look at it, and into it, for half an hour; was pleased with the situation and the principal rooms, satisfied with what the owner said in its praise, and took it immediately.

Between him and Darcy there was a very steady friendship, in spite of a great opposition of character. Bingley was endeared to Darcy by the easiness, openness, and ductility of his temper, though no disposition could offer a greater contrast to his own, and though with his own he never appeared dissatisfied. On the strength of Darcy's regard Bingley had the firmest reliance, and of his judgment the highest opinion. In understanding, Darcy was the superior. Bingley was by no means deficient; but Darcy was clever. He was at the same time haughty, reserved, and fastidious; and his manners, though well bred, were not inviting. In that respect his friend had greatly the advantage. Bingley was sure of being liked wherever he appeared; Darcy was continually giving offence.

The manner in which they spoke of the Meryton assembly was sufficiently characteristic. Bingley had never met with pleasanter people or prettier girls in his life; everybody had been most kind and attentive to him; there had been no formality, no stiffness; he had soon felt acquainted with all the room; and as to Miss Bennet, he could not conceive an angel more beautiful. Darcy, on the contrary, had seen a collection of people in whom there was little beauty and no fashion, for none of whom he had felt the smallest interest, and from none received either attention or pleasure. Miss Bennet he acknowledged to be pretty; but she smiled too much.

Mrs. Hurst and her sister allowed it to be so; but still they admired her and liked her, and pronounced her to be a sweet girl, and one whom they should not object to know more of. Miss Bennet was therefore established as a sweet girl; and their brother felt authorised by such commendation to think of her as he chose.

CHAPTER V

WITHIN a short walk of Longbourn lived a family with whom the Bennets were particularly intimate. Sir William Lucas had been formerly in trade in Meryton, where he had made a tolerable fortune, and risen to the honour of knighthood by an address to the king during his mayoralty. The distinction had, perhaps, been felt too strongly. It had given him a disgust to his business and to his residence in a small market town; and, quitting them both, he had removed with his family to a house about a mile from Meryton, denominated from that period Lucas Lodge; where he could think with pleasure of his own importance and, unshackled by business, occupy himself solely in being civil to all the world. For, though elated by his rank, it did not render him supercilious; on the contrary, he was all attention to everybody. By nature inoffensive, friendly, and obliging, his presentation at St. James's had made him courteous.

Lady Lucas was a very good kind of woman, not too clever to be a valuable neighbour to Mrs. Bennet. They had several children. The eldest of them, a sensible, intelligent young woman, about twenty-seven, was Elizabeth's intimate friend.

That the Miss Lucases and the Miss Bennets should meet to talk over a ball was absolutely necessary; and the morning after the assembly brought the former to Longbourn to hear and to communicate.

'*You* began the evening well, Charlotte,' said Mrs. Bennet, with civil self-command, to Miss Lucas. '*You* were Mr. Bingley's first choice.'

'Yes; but he seemed to like his second better.'

'Oh, you mean Jane, I suppose, because he danced with her twice. To be sure that *did* seem as if he admired her—indeed, I rather believe he *did*—I heard something about it—but I hardly know what—something about Mr. Robinson.'

'Perhaps you mean what I overheard between him and Mr. Robinson: did not I mention it to you? Mr. Robinson's asking him how he liked our Meryton assemblies, and whether he did not think there were a great many pretty women in the room, and *which* he thought the prettiest? and his answering immediately to the last question, Oh, the eldest Miss Bennet, beyond a doubt: there cannot be two opinions on that point.'

'Upon my word! Well, that was very decided, indeed— that does seem as if—but, however, it may all come to nothing, you know.'

'*My* overhearings were more to the purpose than *yours*, Eliza,' said Charlotte. 'Mr. Darcy is not so well worth listening to as his friend, is he? Poor Eliza! to be only just *tolerable*.'

'I beg you will not put it into Lizzy's head to be vexed by his ill-treatment, for he is such a disagreeable man that it would be quite a misfortune to be liked by him. Mrs. Long told me last night that he sat close to her for half an hour without once opening his lips.'

'Are you quite sure ma'am? Is not there a little mistake?' said Jane. 'I certainly saw Mr. Darcy speaking to her.'

'Ay, because she asked him at last how he liked Netherfield, and he could not help answering her; but she said he seemed very angry at being spoken to."

'Miss Bingley told me,' said Jane, 'that he never speaks much unless among his intimate acquaintance. With *them* he is remarkably agreeable.'

'I do not believe a word of it, my dear. If he had been so very agreeable, he would have talked to Mrs. Long. But I can guess how it was; everybody says that he is eat up with pride, and I daresay he had heard somehow that Mrs. Long does not keep a carriage, and had to come to the ball in a hack chaise.'

'I do not mind his not talking to Mrs. Long,' said Miss Lucas, 'but I wish he had danced with Eliza.'

'Another time, Lizzy,' said her mother, 'I would not dance with *him*, if I were you.'

'I believe, ma'am, I may safely promise you *never* to dance with him.'

'His pride,' said Miss Lucas, 'does not offend *me* so much as pride often does, because there is an excuse for it. One cannot wonder that so very fine a young man, with family, fortune, everything in his favour, should think highly of himself. If I may so express it, he has a *right* to be proud.'

'That is very true,' replied Elizabeth, 'and I could easily forgive *his* pride, if he had not mortified *mine*.'

'Pride,' observed Mary, who piqued herself upon the solidity of her reflections, 'is a very common failing, I believe. By all that I have ever read, I am convinced that it is very common indeed; that human nature is particularly prone to it, and that there are very few of us who do not cherish a feeling of self-complacency on the score of some quality or other, real or imaginary. Vanity and pride are different things, though the words are often used synonymously. A person may be proud without being vain. Pride relates more to our opinion of ourselves; vanity to what we would have others think of us.'

'If I were as rich as Mr. Darcy,' cried a young Lucas, who came with his sisters, 'I should not care how proud I was. I would keep a pack of foxhounds, and drink a bottle of wine every day.'

'Then you would drink a great deal more than you ought,' said Mrs. Bennet; 'and if I were to see you at it, I should take away your bottle directly.'

The boy protested that she should not; she continued to declare that she would; and the argument ended only with the visit.

CHAPTER VI

THE ladies of Longbourn soon waited on those of Netherfield. The visit was returned in due form. Miss Bennet's pleasing manners grew on the goodwill of Mrs. Hurst and Miss Bingley; and though the mother was found to be intolerable, and the younger sisters not worth speaking to, a wish of being better acquainted with *them* was expressed towards the two eldest. By Jane this attention was received with the greatest pleasure; but Elizabeth still saw superciliousness in their treatment of everybody, hardly excepting even her sister, and could not like them; though their kindness to Jane, such as it was, had a value, as arising, in all probability, from the influence of their brother's admiration. It was generally evident, whenever they met, that he *did* admire her; and to *her* it was equally evident that Jane was yielding to the preference which she had begun to entertain for him from the first, and was in a way to be very much in love; but she considered with pleasure that it was not likely to be discovered by the world in general, since Jane united with great strength of feeling, a composure of temper and a uniform cheerfulness of manner which would guard her from the suspicions of the impertinent. She mentioned this to her friend Miss Lucas.

'It may, perhaps, be pleasant,' replied Charlotte, 'to be able to impose on the public in such a case; but it is sometimes a disadvantage to be so very guarded. If a woman conceals her affection with the same skill from the object of it, she may lose the opportunity of fixing him; and it will then be but poor consolation to believe the world equally in the dark. There is so much of gratitude or vanity in almost every attachment, that it is not safe to leave any to itself. We can all *begin* freely—a slight preference is natural enough; but there are very few of us who have heart enough to be really in love without encouragement.

In nine cases out of ten, a woman had better show *more* affection than she feels. Bingley likes your sister undoubtedly; but he may never do more than like her, if she does not help him on.'

'But she does help him on, as much as her nature will allow. If *I* can perceive her regard for him, he must be a simpleton indeed not to discover it too.'

'Remember, Eliza, that he does not know Jane's disposition as you do.'

'But if a woman is partial to a man, and does not endeavour to conceal it, he must find it out.'

'Perhaps he must, if he sees enough of her. But though Bingley and Jane meet tolerably often, it is never for many hours together; and as they always see each other in large mixed parties, it is impossible that every moment should be employed in conversing together. Jane should therefore make the most of every half-hour in which she can command his attention. When she is secure of him, there will be leisure for falling in love as much as she chooses.'

'Your plan is a good one,' replied Elizabeth, 'where nothing is in question but the desire of being well married; and if I were determined to get a rich husband, or any husband, I daresay I should adopt it. But these are not Jane's feelings; she is not acting by design. As yet she cannot even be certain of the degree of her own regard, nor of its reasonableness. She has known him only a fortnight. She danced four dances with him at Meryton; she saw him one morning at his own house, and has since dined in company with him four times. This is not quite enough to make her understand his character.'

'Not as you represent it. Had she merely *dined* with him, she might only have discovered whether he had a good appetite; but you must remember that four evenings have been also spent together—and four evenings may do a great deal.'

'Yes: these four evenings have enabled them to ascertain that they both like Vingt-un better than Commerce, but with respect to any other leading characteristic, I do not imagine that much has been unfolded.'

7—C

'Well,' said Charlotte, 'I wish Jane success with all my heart; and if she were married to him to-morrow, I should think she had as good a chance of happiness as if she were to be studying his character for a twelvemonth. Happiness in marriage is entirely a matter of chance. If the dispositions of the parties are ever so well known to each other, or ever so similar beforehand, it does not advance their felicity in the least. They always continue to grow sufficiently unlike afterwards to have their share of vexation; and it is better to know as little as possible of the defects of the person with whom you are to pass your life.'

'You make me laugh, Charlotte; but it is not sound. You know it is not sound, and that you would never act in this way yourself.'

Occupied in observing Mr. Bingley's attentions to her sister, Elizabeth was far from suspecting that she was herself becoming an object of some interest in the eyes of his friend. Mr. Darcy had at first scarcely allowed her to be pretty: he had looked at her without admiration at the ball; and when they next met, he looked at her only to criticise. But no sooner had he made it clear to himself and his friends that she had hardly a good feature in her face, than he began to find it was rendered uncommonly intelligent by the beautiful expression of her dark eyes. To this discovery succeeded some others equally mortifying. Though he had detected with a critical eye more than one failure of perfect symmetry in her form, he was forced to acknowledge her figure to be light and pleasing; and in spite of his asserting that her manners were not those of the fashionable world, he was caught by their easy playfulness. Of this she was perfectly unaware: to her he was only the man who made himself agreeable nowhere, and who had not thought her handsome enough to dance with.

He began to wish to know more of her; and, as a step towards conversing with her himself, attended to her conversation with others. His doing so drew her notice. It was at Sir William Lucas's, where a large party were assembled.

'What does Mr. Darcy mean,' said she to Charlotte, 'by listening to my conversation with Colonel Forster?'

'That is a question which Mr. Darcy only can answer.'

'But if he does it any more, I shall certainly let him know that I see what he is about. He has a very satirical eye, and if I do not begin by being impertinent myself, I shall soon grow afraid of him.'

On his approaching them soon afterwards, though without seeming to have any intention of speaking, Miss Lucas defied her friend to mention such a subject to him, which immediately provoking Elizabeth to do it, she turned to him and said,—

'Did not you think, Mr. Darcy, that I expressed myself uncommonly well just now, when I was teasing Colonel Forster to give us a ball at Meryton?'

'With great energy; but it is a subject which always makes a lady energetic.'

'You are severe on us.'

'It will be *her* turn soon to be teased,' said Miss Lucas. 'I am going to open the instrument, Eliza, and you know what follows.'

'You are a very strange creature by way of a friend!— always wanting me to play and sing before anybody and everybody! If my vanity had taken a musical turn, you would have been invaluable; but as it is, I would really rather not sit down before those who must be in the habit of hearing the very best performers.' On Miss Lucas's persevering, however, she added, 'Very well; if it must be so, it must.' And gravely glancing at Mr. Darcy, 'There is a very fine old saying, which everybody here is of course familiar with—"Keep your breath to cool your porridge,"— and I shall keep mine to swell my song.'

Her performance was pleasing, though by no means capital. After a song or two, and before she could reply to the entreaties of several that she would sing again, she was eagerly succeeded at the instrument by her sister Mary, who having, in consequence of being the only plain one in the family, worked hard for knowledge and accomplishments, was always impatient for display.

Mary had neither genius nor taste; and though vanity had given her application, it had given her likewise a pedantic air and conceited manner, which would have injured a higher degree of excellence than she had reached. Elizabeth, easy and unaffected, had been listened to with much more pleasure, though not playing half so well; and Mary, at the end of a long concerto, was glad to purchase praise and gratitude by Scotch and Irish airs, at the request of her younger sisters, who with some of the Lucases, and two or three officers, joined eagerly in dancing at one end of the room.

Mr. Darcy stood near them in silent indignation at such a mode of passing the evening, to the exclusion of all conversation, and was too much engrossed by his own thoughts to perceive that Sir William Lucas was his neighbour, till Sir William thus began:—

'What a charming amusement for young people this is, Mr. Darcy! There is nothing like dancing, after all. I consider it as one of the first refinements of polished societies.'

'Certainly, sir; and it has the advantage also of being in vogue amongst the less polished societies of the world; every savage can dance.'

Sir William only smiled. 'Your friend performs delightfully,' he continued, after a pause, on seeing Bingley join the group; 'and I doubt not that you are an adept in the science yourself, Mr. Darcy.'

'You saw me dance at Meryton, I believe, sir.'

'Yes, indeed, and received no inconsiderable pleasure from the sight. Do you often dance at St. James's?'

'Never, sir.'

'Do you not think it would be a proper compliment to the place?'

'It is a compliment which I never pay to any place if I can avoid it.'

'You have a house in town, I conclude.'

Mr. Darcy bowed.

'I had once some thoughts of fixing in town myself, for I am fond of superior society; but I did not feel quite certain that the air of London would agree with Lady Lucas.'

He paused in hopes of an answer; but his companion was not disposed to make any; and Elizabeth at that instant moving towards them, he was struck with the notion of doing a very gallant thing, and called out to her,—

'My dear Miss Eliza, why are not you dancing? Mr. Darcy, you must allow me to present this young lady to you as a very desirable partner. You cannot refuse to dance, I am sure, when so much beauty is before you.' And, taking her hand, he would have given it to Mr. Darcy, who, though extremely surprised, was not unwilling to receive it, when she instantly drew back, and said with some discomposure to Sir William,—

'Indeed, sir, I have not the least intention of dancing. I entreat you not to suppose that I moved this way in order to beg for a partner.'

Mr. Darcy, with grave propriety, requested to be allowed the honour of her hand, but in vain. Elizabeth was determined; nor did Sir William at all shake her purpose by his attempt at persuasion.

'You excel so much in the dance, Miss Eliza, that it is cruel to deny me the happiness of seeing you; and though this gentleman dislikes the amusement in general, he can have no objection, I am sure, to oblige us for one half-hour.'

'Mr. Darcy is all politeness,' said Elizabeth, smiling.

'He is, indeed: but considering the inducement, my dear Miss Eliza, we cannot wonder at his complaisance; for who would object to such a partner?'

Elizabeth looked archly, and turned away. Her resistance had not injured her with the gentleman, and he was thinking of her with some complacency, when thus accosted by Miss Bingley,—

'I can guess the subject of your reverie.'

'I should imagine not.'

'You are considering how insupportable it would be to pass many evenings in this manner,—in such society; and, indeed, I am quite of your opinion. I was never more annoyed! The insipidity, and yet the noise—the nothingness, and yet the self-importance, of all these people! What would I give to hear your strictures on them!'

'Your conjecture is totally wrong, I assure you. My mind was more agreeably engaged. I have been meditating on the very great pleasure which a pair of fine eyes in the face of a pretty woman can bestow.'

Miss Bingley immediately fixed her eyes on his face, and desired he would tell her what lady had the credit of inspiring such reflections. Mr. Darcy replied, with great intrepidity,—

'Miss Elizabeth Bennet.'

'Miss Elizabeth Bennet!' repeated Miss Bingley. 'I am all astonishment. How long has she been such a favourite? and pray when am I to wish you joy?'

'That is exactly the question which I expected you to ask. A lady's imagination is very rapid; it jumps from admiration to love, from love to matrimony, in a moment. I knew you would be wishing me joy.'

'Nay, if you are so serious about it, I shall consider the matter as absolutely settled. You will have a charming mother-in-law, indeed, and of course she will be always at Pemberley with you.'

He listened to her with perfect indifference, while she chose to entertain herself in this manner; and as his composure convinced her that all was safe, her wit flowed along.

CHAPTER VII

MR. BENNET'S property consisted almost entirely in an estate of two thousand a year, which, unfortunately for his daughters, was entailed, in default of heirs-male, on a distant relation; and their mother's fortune, though ample for her situation in life, could but ill supply the deficiency of his. Her father had been an attorney in Meryton, and had left her four thousand pounds.

She had a sister married to a Mr. Philips, who had been a clerk to their father, and succeeded him in the business, and a brother settled in London, in a respectable line of trade.

The village of Longbourn was only one mile from Meryton; a most convenient distance for the young ladies, who were usually tempted thither three or four times a week, to pay their duty to their aunt, and to a milliner's shop just over the way. The two youngest of the family, Catherine and Lydia, were particularly frequent in these attentions: their minds were more vacant than their sisters', and when nothing better offered, a walk to Meryton was necessary to amuse their morning hours and furnish conversation for the evening; and, however bare of news the country in general might be, they always contrived to learn some from their aunt. At present, indeed, they were well supplied both with news and happiness by the recent arrival of a militia regiment in the neighbourhood; it was to remain the whole winter, and Meryton was the headquarters.

Their visits to Mrs. Philips were now productive of the most interesting intelligence. Every day added something to their knowledge of the officers' names and connections. Their lodgings were not long a secret, and at length they began to know the officers themselves. Mr. Philips visited them all, and this opened to his nieces a source of felicity

187

unknown before. They could talk of nothing but officers; and Mr. Bingley's large fortune, the mention of which gave animation to their mother, was worthless in their eyes when opposed to the regimentals of an ensign.

After listening one morning to their effusions on this subject, Mr. Bennet coolly observed,—

'From all that I can collect by your manner of talking, you must be two of the silliest girls in the country. I have suspected it some time, but I am now convinced.'

Catherine was disconcerted, and made no answer; but Lydia, with perfect indifference, continued to express her admiration of Captain Carter, and her hope of seeing him in the course of the day, as he was going the next morning to London.

'I am astonished, my dear,' said Mrs. Bennet, 'that you should be so ready to think your own children silly. If I wished to think slightingly of anybody's children, it should not be of my own, however.'

'If my children are silly, I must hope to be always sensible of it.'

'Yes; but as it happens, they are all of them very clever.'

'This is the only point, I flatter myself, on which we do not agree. I had hoped that our sentiments coincided in every particular, but I must so far differ from you as to think our two youngest daughters uncommonly foolish.'

'My dear Mr. Bennet, you must not expect such girls to have the sense of their father and mother. When they get to our age, I daresay they will not think about officers any more than we do. I remember the time when I liked a red coat myself very well—and, indeed, so I do still at my heart; and if a smart young colonel, with five or six thousand a year, should want one of my girls, I shall not say nay to him; and I thought Colonel Forster looked very becoming the other night at Sir William's in his regimentals.'

'Mamma,' cried Lydia, 'my aunt says that Colonel Forster and Captain Carter do not go so often to Miss Watson's as they did when they first came; she sees them now very often standing in Clarke's library.'

Mrs. Bennet was prevented replying by the entrance of the footman with a note for Miss Bennet; it came from Netherfield, and the servant waited for an answer. Mrs. Bennet's eyes sparkled with pleasure, and she was eagerly calling out, while her daughter read,—

'Well, Jane, who is it from? What is it about? What does he say? Well, Jane, make haste and tell us; make haste, my love.'

'It is from Miss Bingley,' said Jane, and then read it aloud.

'My Dear Friend—If you are not so compassionate as to dine to-day with Louisa and me, we shall be in danger of hating each other for the rest of our lives; for a whole day's *tête-à-tête* between two women can never end without a quarrel. Come as soon as you can on the receipt of this. My brother and the gentlemen are to dine with the officers.   Yours ever,
                                'Caroline Bingley.'

'With the officers!' cried Lydia: 'I wonder my aunt did not tell us of *that*.'

'Dining out,' said Mrs. Bennet; 'that is very unlucky.'

'Can I have the carriage?' said Jane.

'No, my dear, you had better go on horseback, because it seems likely to rain; and then you must stay all night.'

'That would be a good scheme,' said Elizabeth, 'if you were sure that they would not offer to send her home.'

'Oh, but the gentlemen will have Mr. Bingley's chaise to go to Meryton; and the Hursts have no horses to theirs.'

'I had much rather go in the coach.'

'But, my dear, your father cannot spare the horses, I am sure. They are wanted in the farm, Mr. Bennet, are not they?'

'They are wanted in the farm much oftener than I can get them.'

'But if you have got them to-day,' said Elizabeth, 'my mother's purpose will be answered.'

She did at last extort from her father an acknowledgment that the horses were engaged; Jane was therefore obliged to go on horseback, and her mother attended her to the door with many cheerful prognostics of a bad day. Her hopes were answered; Jane had not been gone long before it rained hard. Her sisters were uneasy for her, but her mother was delighted. The rain continued the whole even-

ing without intermission; Jane certainly could not come
back.

'This was a lucky idea of mine, indeed!' said Mrs. Bennet,
more than once, as if the credit of making it rain were all
her own. Till the next morning, however, she was not
aware of all the felicity of her contrivance. Breakfast was
scarcely over when a servant from Netherfield brought the
following note for Elizabeth:—

'MY DEAREST LIZZY—I find myself very unwell this morning,
which, I suppose, is to be imputed to my getting wet through yesterday. My kind friends will not hear of my returning home till
I am better. They insist also on my seeing Mr. Jones—therefore do
not be alarmed if you should hear of his having been to me—and,
excepting a sore throat and a headache, there is not much the matter
with me.

'Yours, etc.'

'Well, my dear,' said Mr. Bennet, when Elizabeth had
read the note aloud, 'if your daughter should have a
dangerous fit of illness—if she should die—it would be a
comfort to know that it was all in pursuit of Mr. Bingley,
and under your orders.'

'Oh, I am not at all afraid of her dying. People do not
die of little trifling colds. She will be taken good care of.
As long as she stays there, it is all very well. I would go
and see her if I could have the carriage.'

Elizabeth, feeling really anxious, determined to go to her
though the carriage was not to be had: and as she was no
horsewoman, walking was her only alternative. She declared her resolution.

'How can you be so silly,' cried her mother, 'as to think
of such a thing, in all this dirt! You will not be fit to be
seen when you get there.'

'I shall be very fit to see Jane—which is all I want.'

'Is this a hint to me, Lizzy,' said her father, 'to send for
the horses?'

'No, indeed. I do not wish to avoid the walk. The
distance is nothing, when one has a motive; only three
miles. I shall be back by dinner.'

'I admire the activity of your benevolence,' observed
Mary, 'but every impulse of feeling should be guided by

reason; and, in my opinion, exertion should always be in proportion to what is required.'

'We will go as far as Meryton with you,' said Catherine and Lydia. Elizabeth accepted their company, and the three young ladies set off together.

'If we make haste,' said Lydia, as they walked along, 'perhaps we may see something of Captain Carter, before he goes.'

In Meryton they parted: the two youngest repaired to the lodgings of one of the officers' wives, and Elizabeth continued her walk alone, crossing field after field at a quick pace, jumping over stiles and springing over puddles, with impatient activity, and finding herself at last within view of the house, with weary ankles, dirty stockings, and a face glowing with the warmth of exercise.

She was shown into the breakfast parlour, where all but Jane were assembled, and where her appearance created a great deal of surprise. That she should have walked three miles so early in the day in such dirty weather, and by herself, was almost incredible to Mrs. Hurst and Miss Bingley; and Elizabeth was convinced that they held her in contempt for it. She was received, however, very politely by them; and in their brother's manners there was something better than politeness—there was good-humour and kindness. Mr. Darcy said very little, and Mr. Hurst nothing at all. The former was divided between admiration of the brilliancy which exercise had given to her complexion and doubt as to the occasion's justifying her coming so far alone. The latter was thinking only of his breakfast.

Her inquiries after her sister were not very favourably answered. Miss Bennet had slept ill, and, though up, was very feverish, and not well enough to leave her room. Elizabeth was glad to be taken to her immediately; and Jane, who had only been withheld by the fear of giving alarm or inconvenience, from expressing in her note how much she longed for such a visit, was delighted at her entrance. She was not equal, however, to much conversation; and when Miss Bingley left them together, could attempt little beside expressions of gratitude for the extraordinary kindness she was treated with. Elizabeth silently attended her.

When breakfast was over, they were joined by the sisters; and Elizabeth began to like them herself, when she saw how much affection and solicitude they showed for Jane. The apothecary came; and having examined his patient, said, as might be supposed, that she had caught a violent cold, and that they must endeavour to get the better of it; advised her to return to bed, and promised her some draughts. The advice was followed readily, for the feverish symptoms increased, and her head ached acutely. Elizabeth did not quit her room for a moment, nor were the other ladies often absent; the gentlemen being out, they had in fact nothing to do elsewhere.

When the clock struck three, Elizabeth felt that she must go, and very unwillingly said so. Miss Bingley offered her the carriage, and she only wanted a little pressing to accept it, when Jane testified such concern at parting with her that Miss Bingley was obliged to convert the offer of the chaise into an invitation to remain at Netherfield for the present. Elizabeth most thankfully consented, and a servant was despatched to Longbourn, to acquaint the family with her stay, and bring back a supply of clothes.

CHAPTER VIII

AT five o'clock the two ladies retired to dress, and at half-past six Elizabeth was summoned to dinner. To the civil inquiries which then poured in, and amongst which she had the pleasure of distinguishing the much superior solicitude of Mr. Bingley, she could not make a very favourable answer. Jane was by no means better. The sisters, on hearing this, repeated three or four times how much they were grieved, how shocking it was to have a bad cold, and how excessively they disliked being ill themselves; and then thought no more of the matter: and their indifference towards Jane, when not immediately before them, restored Elizabeth to the enjoyment of all her original dislike.

Their brother, indeed, was the only one of the party whom she could regard with any complacency. His anxiety for Jane was evident, and his attentions to herself most pleasing; and they prevented her feeling herself so much an intruder as she believed she was considered by the others. She had very little notice from any but him. Miss Bingley was engrossed by Mr. Darcy, her sister scarcely less so; and as for Mr. Hurst, by whom Elizabeth sat, he was an indolent man, who lived only to eat, drink, and play at cards, who, when he found her prefer a plain dish to a ragout, had nothing to say to her.

When dinner was over, she returned directly to Jane, and Miss Bingley began abusing her as soon as she was out of the room. Her manners were pronounced to be very bad indeed,—a mixture of pride and impertinence: she had no conversation, no style, no taste, no beauty. Mrs. Hurst thought the same, and added,—

'She has nothing, in short, to recommend her, but being an excellent walker. I shall never forget her appearance this morning. She really looked almost wild.'

'She did, indeed, Louisa. I could hardly keep my countenance. Very nonsensical to come at all! Why must *she* be

193

scampering about the country, because her sister had a cold?
Her hair so untidy, so blowsy!'

'Yes, and her petticoat; I hope you saw her petticoat, six
inches deep in mud, I am absolutely certain, and the gown
which had been let down to hide it not doing its office.'

'Your picture may be very exact, Louisa,' said Bingley;
'but this was all lost upon me. I thought Miss Elizabeth
Bennet looked remarkably well when she came into the room
this morning. Her dirty petticoat quite escaped my notice.'

'*You* observed it, Mr. Darcy, I am sure,' said Miss
Bingley; 'and I am inclined to think that you would not
wish to see *your sister* make such an exhibition.'

'Certainly not.'

'To walk three miles, or four miles, or five miles, or whatever it is, above her ankles in dirt, and alone, quite alone!
what could she mean by it? It seems to me to show an
abominable sort of conceited independence, a most country-
town indifference to decorum.'

'It shows an affection for her sister that is very pleasing,'
said Bingley.

'I am afraid, Mr. Darcy,' observed Miss Bingley, in a
half whisper, 'that this adventure has rather affected your
admiration of her fine eyes.'

'Not at all,' he replied: 'they were brightened by the
exercise.' A short pause followed this speech, and Mrs.
Hurst began again,—

'I have an excessive regard for Jane Bennet,—she is
really a very sweet girl,—and I wish with all my heart she
were well settled. But with such a father and mother, and
such low connections, I am afraid there is no chance of it.'

'I think I have heard you say that their uncle is an attorney in Meryton?'

'Yes; and they have another, who lives somewhere near
Cheapside.'

'That is capital,' added her sister; and they both laughed
heartily.

'If they had uncles enough to fill *all* Cheapside,' cried
Bingley, 'it would not make them one jot less agreeable.'

'But it must very materially lessen their chance of marrying men of any consideration in the world,' replied Darcy.

To this speech Bingley made no answer; but his sisters gave it their hearty assent, and indulged their mirth for some time at the expense of their dear friend's vulgar relations.

With a renewal of tenderness, however, they repaired to her room on leaving the dining-parlour, and sat with her till summoned to coffee. She was still very poorly, and Elizabeth would not quit her at all, till late in the evening, when she had the comfort of seeing her asleep, and when it appeared to her rather right than pleasant that she should go downstairs herself. On entering the drawing-room, she found the whole party at loo, and was immediately invited to join them; but suspecting them to be playing high, she declined it, and making her sister the excuse, said she would amuse herself, for the short time she could stay below, with a book. Mr. Hurst looked at her with astonishment.

'Do you prefer reading to cards?' said he; 'that is rather singular.'

'Miss Eliza Bennet,' said Miss Bingley, 'despises cards. She is a great reader, and has no pleasure in anything else.'

'I deserve neither such praise nor such censure,' cried Elizabeth; 'I am *not* a great reader, and I have pleasure in many things.'

'In nursing your sister I am sure you have pleasure,' said Bingley; 'and I hope it will soon be increased by seeing her quite well.'

Elizabeth thanked him from her heart, and then walked towards a table where a few books were lying. He immediately offered to fetch her others; all that his library afforded.

'And I wish my collection were larger for your benefit and my own credit; but I am an idle fellow; and though I have not many, I have more than I ever looked into.'

Elizabeth assured him that she could suit herself perfectly with those in the room.

'I am astonished,' said Miss Bingley, 'that my father should have left so small a collection of books. What a delightful library you have at Pemberley, Mr. Darcy!'

'It ought to be good,' he replied: 'it has been the work of many generations.'

'And then you have added so much to it yourself—you are always buying books.'

'I cannot comprehend the neglect of a family library in such days as these.'

'Neglect! I am sure you neglect nothing that can add to the beauties of that noble place. Charles, when you build *your* house, I wish it may be half as delightful as Pemberley.'

'I wish it may.'

'But I would really advise you to make your purchase in that neighbourhood, and take Pemberley for a kind of model. There is not a finer county in England than Derbyshire.'

'With all my heart: I will buy Pemberley itself, if Darcy will sell it.'

'I am talking of possibilities, Charles.'

'Upon my word, Caroline, I should think it more possible to get Pemberley by purchase than by imitation.'

Elizabeth was so much caught by what passed as to leave her very little attention for her book; and soon laying it wholly aside, she drew near the card-table, and stationed herself between Mr. Bingley and his eldest sister, to observe the game.

'Is Miss Darcy much grown since the spring?' said Miss Bingley: 'will she be as tall as I am?'

'I think she will. She is now about Miss Elizabeth Bennet's height, or rather taller.'

'How I long to see her again! I never met with anybody who delighted me so much. Such a countenance, such manners, and so extremely accomplished for her age. Her performance on the pianoforte is exquisite.'

'It is amazing to me,' said Bingley, 'how young ladies can have patience to be so very accomplished as they all are.'

'All young ladies accomplished! My dear Charles, what do you mean?'

'Yes, all of them, I think. They all paint tables, cover screens, and net purses. I scarcely know any one who cannot do all this; and I am sure I never heard a young lady spoken of for the first time, without being informed that she was very accomplished.'

'Your list of the common extent of accomplishments,' said Darcy, 'has too much truth. The word is applied to many a woman who deserves it no otherwise than by netting a purse or covering a screen; but I am very far from agreeing with you in your estimation of ladies in general. I cannot boast of knowing more than half a dozen in the whole range of my acquaintance that are really accomplished.'

'Nor I, I am sure,' said Miss Bingley.

'Then,' observed Elizabeth, 'you must comprehend a great deal in your idea of an accomplished woman.'

'Yes; I do comprehend a great deal in it.'

'Oh, certainly,' cried his faithful assistant, 'no one can be really esteemed accomplished who does not greatly surpass what is usually met with. A woman must have a thorough knowledge of music, singing, drawing, dancing, and the modern languages, to deserve the word; and, besides all this, she must possess a certain something in her air and manner of walking, the tone of her voice, her address and expressions, or the word will be but half deserved.'

'All this she must possess,' added Darcy; 'and to all she must yet add something more substantial in the improvement of her mind by extensive reading.'

'I am no longer surprised at your knowing *only* six accomplished women. I rather wonder now at your knowing *any.*'

'Are you so severe upon your own sex as to doubt the possibility of all this?'

'*I* never saw such a woman. *I* never saw such capacity, and taste, and application, and elegance, as you describe, united.'

Mrs. Hurst and Miss Bingley both cried out against the injustice of her implied doubt, and were both protesting that they knew many women who answered this description, when Mr. Hurst called them to order, with bitter complaints of their inattention to what was going forward. As all conversation was thereby at an end, Elizabeth soon afterwards left the room.

'Eliza Bennet,' said Miss Bingley, when the door was closed on her, 'is one of those young ladies who seek to recommend themselves to the other sex by undervaluing their own; and with many men, I daresay, it succeeds; but, in my opinion, it is a paltry device, a very mean art.'

'Undoubtedly,' replied Darcy, to whom this remark was chiefly addressed, 'there is meanness in *all* the arts which ladies sometimes condescend to employ for captivation. Whatever bears affinity to cunning is despicable.'

Miss Bingley was not so entirely satisfied with this reply as to continue the subject.

Elizabeth joined them again only to say that her sister was worse, and that she could not leave her. Bingley urged Mr. Jones's being sent for immediately; while his sisters, convinced that no country advice could be of any service, recommended an express to town for one of the most eminent physicians. This she would not hear of; but she was not so unwilling to comply with their brother's proposal; and it was settled that Mr. Jones should be sent for early in the morning, if Miss Bennet were not decidedly better. Bingley was quite uncomfortable; his sisters declared that they were miserable. They solaced their wretchedness, however, by duets after supper, while he could find no better relief to his feelings than by giving his housekeeper directions that every possible attention might be paid to the sick lady and her sister.

CHAPTER IX

ELIZABETH passed the chief of the night in her sister's room, and in the morning had the pleasure of being able to send a tolerable answer to the inquiries which she very early received from Mr. Bingley by a housemaid, and some time afterwards from the two elegant ladies who waited on his sisters. In spite of this amendment, however, she requested to have a note sent to Longbourn, desiring her mother to visit Jane, and form her own judgment of her situation. The note was immediately despatched, and its contents as quickly complied with. Mrs. Bennet, accompanied by her two youngest girls, reached Netherfield soon after the family breakfast.

Had she found Jane in any apparent danger, Mrs. Bennet would have been very miserable; but being satisfied on seeing her that her illness was not alarming, she had no wish of her recovering immediately, as her restoration to health would probably remove her from Netherfield. She would not listen, therefore, to her daughter's proposal of being carried home; neither did the apothecary, who arrived about the same time, think it at all advisable. After sitting a little while with Jane, on Miss Bingley's appearance and invitation, the mother and three daughters all attended her into the breakfast parlour. Bingley met them with hopes that Mrs. Bennet had not found Miss Bennet worse than she expected.

'Indeed I have, sir,' was her answer. 'She is a great deal too ill to be moved. Mr. Jones says we must not think of moving her. We must trespass a little longer on your kindness.'

'Removed!' cried Bingley. 'It must not be thought of. My sister, I am sure, will not hear of her removal.'

'You may depend upon it, madam,' said Miss Bingley, with cold civility, 'that Miss Bennet shall receive every possible attention while she remains with us.'

Mrs. Bennet was profuse in her acknowledgments.

'I am sure,' she added, 'if it was not for such good friends, I do not know what would become of her, for she is very ill indeed, and suffers a vast deal, though with the greatest patience in the world, which is always the way with her, for she has, without exception, the sweetest temper I ever met with. I often tell my other girls they are nothing to *her*. You have a sweet room here, Mr. Bingley, and a charming prospect over that gravel walk. I do not know a place in the country that is equal to Netherfield. You will not think of quitting it in a hurry, I hope, though you have but a short lease.'

'Whatever I do is done in a hurry,' replied he; 'and therefore if I should resolve to quit Netherfield, I should probably be off in five minutes. At present, however, I consider myself as quite fixed here.'

'That is exactly what I should have supposed of you,' said Elizabeth.

'You begin to comprehend me, do you?' cried he, turning towards her.

'Oh yes—I understand you perfectly.'

'I wish I might take this for a compliment; but to be so easily seen through, I am afraid, is pitiful.'

'That is as it happens. It does not necessarily follow that a deep, intricate character is more or less estimable than such a one as yours.'

'Lizzy,' cried her mother, 'remember where you are, and do not run on in the wild manner that you are suffered to do at home.'

'I did not know before,' continued Bingley, immediately, 'that you were a studier of character. It must be an amusing study.'

'Yes; but intricate characters are the *most* amusing. They have at least that advantage.'

'The country,' said Darcy, 'can in general supply but few subjects for such a study. In a country neighbourhood you move in a very confined and unvarying society.'

'But people themselves alter so much, that there is something new to be observed in them for ever.'

'Yes, indeed,' cried Mrs. Bennet, offended by his manner of mentioning a country neighbourhood. 'I assure you there is quite as much of *that* going on in the country as in town.'

Everybody was surprised; and Darcy, after looking at her for a moment, turned silently away. Mrs. Bennet, who fancied she had gained a complete victory over him, continued her triumph,—

'I cannot see that London has any great advantage over the country, for my part, except the shops and public places. The country is a vast deal pleasanter, is not it, Mr. Bingley?'

'When I am in the country,' he replied, 'I never wish to leave it; and when I am in town, it is pretty much the same. They have each their advantages, and I can be equally happy in either.'

'Ay, that is because you have the right disposition. But that gentleman,' looking at Darcy, 'seemed to think the country was nothing at all.'

'Indeed, mamma, you are mistaken,' said Elizabeth, blushing for her mother. 'You quite mistook Mr. Darcy. He only meant that there was not such a variety of people to be met with in the country as in town, which you must acknowledge to be true.'

'Certainly, my dear, nobody said there were; but as to not meeting with many people in this neighbourhood, I believe there are few neighbourhoods larger. I know we dine with four-and-twenty families.'

Nothing but concern for Elizabeth could enable Bingley to keep his countenance. His sister was less delicate, and directed her eye towards Mr. Darcy with a very expressive smile. Elizabeth, for the sake of saying something that might turn her mother's thoughts, now asked her if Charlotte Lucas had been at Longbourn since *her* coming away.

'Yes, she called yesterday with her father. What an agreeable man Sir William is, Mr. Bingley—is not he? so much the man of fashion! so genteel and so easy! He has always something to say to everybody. *That* is my idea of good-breeding; and those persons who fancy themselves very important and never open their mouths quite mistake the matter.'

'Did Charlotte dine with you?'

'No, she would go home. I fancy she was wanted about the mince-pies. For my part, Mr. Bingley, I always keep servants that can do their own work; my daughters are brought up differently. But everybody is to judge for themselves, and the Lucases are a very good sort of girls, I assure you. It is a pity they are not handsome! Not that I think Charlotte so very plain; but then she is our particular friend.'

'She seems a very pleasant young woman,' said Bingley.

'Oh dear, yes; but you must own she is very plain. Lady Lucas herself has often said so, and envied me Jane's beauty. I do not like to boast of my own child, but to be sure, Jane— one does not often see anybody better looking. It is what everybody says. I do not trust my own partiality. When she was only fifteen there was a gentleman at my brother Gardiner's in town so much in love with her, that my sister-in-law was sure he would make her an offer before we came away. But, however, he did not. Perhaps he thought her too young. However, he wrote some verses on her, and very pretty they were.'

'And so ended his affection,' said Elizabeth, impatiently. 'There has been many a one, I fancy, overcome in the same way. I wonder who first discovered the efficacy of poetry in driving away love!'

'I have been used to consider poetry as the *food* of love,' said Darcy.

'Of a fine, stout, healthy love it may. Everything nourishes what is strong already. But if it be only a slight, thin sort of inclination, I am convinced that one good sonnet will starve it entirely away.'

Darcy only smiled; and the general pause which ensued made Elizabeth tremble lest her mother should be exposing herself again. She longed to speak, but could think of nothing to say; and after a short silence Mrs. Bennet began repeating her thanks to Mr. Bingley for his kindness to Jane, with an apology for troubling him also with Lizzy. Mr. Bingley was unaffectedly civil in his answer, and forced his younger sister to be civil also, and say what the occasion required. She performed her part, indeed, without much graciousness, but Mrs. Bennet was satisfied, and soon afterwards ordered her carriage. Upon this signal, the youngest of her daughters put herself forward. The two girls had been whispering to each other during the whole visit; and the result of it was, that the youngest should tax Mr. Bingley with having promised on his first coming into the country to give a ball at Netherfield.

Lydia was a stout, well-grown girl of fifteen, with a fine complexion and good-humoured countenance; a favourite with her mother, whose affection had brought her into public at an early age. She had high animal spirits, and a sort of natural self-consequence, which the attentions of the officers, to whom her uncle's good dinners and her own easy manners recommended her, had increased into assurance. She was very equal, therefore, to address Mr. Bingley on the subject of the ball, and abruptly reminded him of his promise; adding, that it would be the most shameful thing in the world if he did not keep it. His answer to this sudden attack was delightful to her mother's ear.

'I am perfectly ready, I assure you, to keep my engagement; and, when your sister is recovered, you shall, if you please, name the very day of the ball. But you would not wish to be dancing while she is ill?'

Lydia declared herself satisfied. 'Oh yes—it would be much better to wait till Jane was well; and by that time, most likely, Captain Carter would be at Meryton again. And when you have given *your* ball,' she added, 'I shall insist on their giving one also. I shall tell Colonel Forster it will be quite a shame if he does not.'

Mrs. Bennet and her daughters then departed, and Elizabeth returned instantly to Jane, leaving her own and her relations' behaviour to the remarks of the two ladies and Mr. Darcy; the latter of whom, however, could not be prevailed on to join in their censure of *her,* in spite of all Miss Bingley's witticisms on *fine eyes.*

CHAPTER X

THE day passed much as the day before had done. Mrs. Hurst and Miss Bingley had spent some hours of the morning with the invalid, who continued, though slowly, to mend; and, in the evening, Elizabeth joined their party in the drawing-room. The loo table, however, did not appear. Mr. Darcy was writing, and Miss Bingley, seated near him, was watching the progress of his letter, and repeatedly calling off his attention by messages to his sister. Mr. Hurst and Mr. Bingley were at piquet, and Mrs. Hurst was observing their game.

Elizabeth took up some needlework, and was sufficiently amused in attending to what passed between Darcy and his companion. The perpetual commendations of the lady either on his handwriting, or on the evenness of his lines, or on the length of his letter, with the perfect unconcern with which her praises were received, formed a curious dialogue, and were exactly in unison with her opinion of each.

'How delighted Miss Darcy will be to receive such a letter!'

He made no answer.

'You write uncommonly fast.'

'You are mistaken. I write rather slowly.'

'How many letters you must have occasion to write in the course of a year! Letters of business, too! How odious I should think them!'

'It is fortunate, then, that they fall to my lot instead of to yours.'

'Pray tell your sister that I long to see her.'

'I have already told her so once, by your desire.'

'I am afraid you do not like your pen. Let me mend it for you. I mend pens remarkably well.'

'Thank you—but I always mend my own.'

'How can you contrive to write so even?'

He was silent.

'Tell your sister I am delighted to hear of her improvement on the harp, and pray let her know that I am quite in raptures with her beautiful little design for a table, and I think it infinitely superior to Miss Grantley's.'

'Will you give me leave to defer your raptures till I write again? At present I have not room to do them justice.'

'Oh, it is of no consequence. I shall see her in January. But do you always write such charming long letters to her, Mr. Darcy?'

'They are generally long; but whether always charming, it is not for me to determine.'

'It is a rule with me, that a person who can write a long letter with ease cannot write ill.'

'That will not do for a compliment to Darcy, Caroline,' cried her brother, 'because he does *not* write with ease. He studies too much for words of four syllables. Do not you, Darcy?'

'My style of writing is very different from yours.'

'Oh,' cried Miss Bingley, 'Charles writes in the most careless way imaginable. He leaves out half his words, and blots the rest.'

'My ideas flow so rapidly that I have not time to express them; by which means my letters sometimes convey no ideas at all to my correspondents.'

'Your humility, Mr. Bingley,' said Elizabeth, 'must disarm reproof.'

'Nothing is more deceitful,' said Darcy, 'than the appearance of humility. It is often only carelessness of opinion, and sometimes an indirect boast.'

'And which of the two do you call *my* little recent piece of modesty?'

'The indirect boast; for you are really proud of your defects in writing, because you consider them as proceeding from a rapidity of thought and carelessness of execution, which, if not estimable, you think at least highly interesting. The power of doing anything with quickness is always much prized by the possessor, and often without any attention to the imperfection of the performance. When you told Mrs. Bennet this morning, that if you ever resolved on quitting Netherfield you should be gone in five minutes, you meant it to be a sort of panegyric, of compliment to yourself; and yet what is there so very laudable in a precipitance which must leave very necessary business undone, and can be of no real advantage to yourself or any one else?'

'Nay,' cried Bingley, 'this is too much, to remember at night all the foolish things that were said in the morning. And yet, upon my honour, I believed what I said of myself to be true, and I believe it at this moment. At least, therefore, I did not assume the character of needless precipitance merely to show off before the ladies.'

'I daresay you believed it; but I am by no means convinced that you would be gone with such celerity. Your conduct would be quite as dependent on chance as that of any man I know; and if, as you were mounting your horse, a friend were to say, "Bingley, you had better stay till next week," you would probably do it—you would probably not go —and, at another word, might stay a month.'

'You have only proved by this,' cried Elizabeth, 'that Mr. Bingley did not do justice to his own disposition. You have shown him off now much more than he did himself.'

'I am exceedingly gratified,' said Bingley, 'by your converting what my friend says into a compliment on the sweetness of my temper. But I am afraid you are giving it a turn which that gentleman did by no means intend; for he would certainly think the better of me if, under such a circumstance, I were to give a flat denial, and ride off as fast as I could.'

'Would Mr. Darcy then consider the rashness of your original intention as atoned for by your obstinacy in adhering to it?'

'Upon my word, I cannot exactly explain the matter— Darcy must speak for himself.'

'You expect me to account for opinions which you choose to call mine, but which I have never acknowledged. Allowing the case, however, to stand according to your representation, you must remember, Miss Bennet, that the friend who is supposed to desire his return to the house, and the delay of his plan, has merely desired it, asked it without offering one argument in favour of its propriety.'

'To yield readily—easily—to the *persuasion* of a friend is no merit with you.'

'To yield without conviction is no compliment to the understanding of either.'

'You appear to me, Mr. Darcy, to allow nothing for the influence of friendship and affection. A regard for the requester would often make one readily yield to a request, without waiting for arguments to reason one into it. I am not particularly speaking of such a case as you have supposed about Mr. Bingley. We may as well wait, perhaps, till the circumstance occurs, before we discuss the discretion of his behaviour thereupon. But in general and ordinary cases, between friend and friend, where one of them is desired by the other to change a resolution of no very great moment, should you think ill of that person for complying with the desire, without waiting to be argued into it?'

'Will it not be advisable, before we proceed on this subject, to arrange with rather more precision the degree of importance which is to appertain to this request, as well as the degree of intimacy subsisting between the parties?'

'By all means,' cried Bingley; 'let us hear all the particulars, not forgetting their comparative height and size, for that will have more weight in the argument, Miss Bennet, than you may be aware of. I assure you that if Darcy were not such a great tall fellow, in comparison with myself, I should not pay him half so much deference. I declare I do not know a more awful object than Darcy on particular occasions, and in particular places; at his own house especially, and of a Sunday evening, when he has nothing to do.'

Mr. Darcy smiled; but Elizabeth thought she could perceive that he was rather offended, and therefore checked her laugh. Miss Bingley warmly resented the indignity he had received, in an expostulation with her brother for talking such nonsense.

'I see your design, Bingley,' said his friend. 'You dislike an argument, and want to silence this.'

'Perhaps I do. Arguments are too much like disputes. If you and Miss Bennet will defer yours till I am out of the room, I shall be very thankful; and then you may say whatever you like of me.'

'What you ask,' said Elizabeth, 'is no sacrifice on my side; and Mr. Darcy had much better finish his letter.'

Mr. Darcy took her advice, and did finish his letter.

When that business was over, he applied to Miss Bingley and Elizabeth for the indulgence of some music. Miss Bingley moved with alacrity to the pianoforte, and after a polite request that Elizabeth would lead the way, which the other as politely and more earnestly negatived, she seated herself.

Mrs. Hurst sang with her sister; and while they were thus employed, Elizabeth could not help observing, as she turned over some music-books that lay on the instrument, how frequently Mr. Darcy's eyes were fixed on her. She hardly knew how to suppose that she could be an object of admiration to so great a man, and yet that he should look at her because he disliked her was still more strange. She could only imagine, however, at last, that she drew his notice because there was a something about her more wrong and reprehensible, according to his ideas of right, than in any other person present. The supposition did not pain her. She liked him too little to care for his approbation.

After playing some Italian songs, Miss Bingley varied the charm by a lively Scotch air; and soon afterwards Mr. Darcy, drawing near Elizabeth, said to her,—

'Do not you feel a great inclination, Miss Bennet, to seize such an opportunity of dancing a reel?'

She smiled, but made no answer. He repeated the question, with some surprise at her silence.

'Oh,' said she, 'I heard you before; but I could not immediately determine what to say in reply. You wanted me, I know, to say "Yes," that you might have the pleasure of despising my taste; but I always delight in overthrowing those kind of schemes, and cheating a person of their premeditated contempt. I have, therefore, made up my mind to tell you that I do not want to dance a reel at all; and now despise me if you dare.'

'Indeed I do not dare.'

Elizabeth, having rather expected to affront him, was amazed at his gallantry; but there was a mixture of sweetness and archness in her manner which made it difficult for her to affront anybody, and Darcy had never been so bewitched by any woman as he was by her. He really believed that, were it not for the inferiority of her connections, he should be in some danger.

Miss Bingley saw, or suspected, enough to be jealous; and her great anxiety for the recovery of her dear friend Jane received some assistance from her desire of getting rid of Elizabeth.

She often tried to provoke Darcy into disliking her guest, by talking of their supposed marriage, and planning his happiness in such an alliance.

'I hope,' said she, as they were walking together in the shrubbery the next day, 'you will give your mother-in-law a few hints, when this desirable event takes place, as to the advantage of holding her tongue; and if you can compass it, to cure the younger girls of running after the officers. And, if I may mention so delicate a subject, endeavour to check that little something, bordering on conceit and impertinence, which your lady possesses.'

'Have you anything else to propose for my domestic felicity?'

'Oh yes. Do let the portraits of your uncle and aunt Philips be placed in the gallery at Pemberley. Put them next to your great uncle the judge. They are in the same profession, you know, only in different lines. As for your Elizabeth's picture, you must not attempt to have it taken, for what painter could do justice to those beautiful eyes?'

'It would not be easy, indeed, to catch their expression; but their colour and shape, and the eyelashes, so remarkably fine, might be copied.'

At that moment they were met from another walk by Mrs. Hurst and Elizabeth herself.

'I did not know that you intended to walk,' said Miss Bingley, in some confusion lest they had been overheard.

'You used us abominably ill,' answered Mrs. Hurst 'running away without telling us that you were coming out.'

Then taking the disengaged arm of Mr. Darcy, she left Elizabeth to walk by herself. The path just admitted three. Mr. Darcy felt their rudeness, and immediately said,—

'This walk is not wide enough for our party. We had better go into the avenue.'

But Elizabeth, who had not the least inclination to remain with them, laughingly answered,—

'No, no; stay where you are. You are charmingly grouped, and appear to uncommon advantage. The picturesque would be spoilt by admitting a fourth. Good-bye.'

She then ran gaily off, rejoicing, as she rambled about, in the hope of being at home again in a day or two. Jane was already so much recovered as to intend leaving her room for a couple of hours that evening.

CHAPTER XI

WHEN the ladies removed after dinner Elizabeth ran up to her sister, and seeing her well guarded from cold, attended her into the drawing-room, where she was welcomed by her two friends with many professions of pleasure; and Elizabeth had never seen them so agreeable as they were during the hour which passed before the gentlemen appeared. Their powers of conversation were considerable. They could describe an entertainment with accuracy, relate an anecdote with humour, and laugh at their acquaintance with spirit.

But when the gentlemen entered, Jane was no longer the first object; Miss Bingley's eyes were instantly turned towards Darcy, and she had something to say to him before he had advanced many steps. He addressed himself directly to Miss Bennet with a polite congratulation; Mr. Hurst also made her a slight bow, and said he was 'very glad'; but diffuseness and warmth remained for Bingley's salutation. He was full of joy and attention. The first half-hour was spent in piling up the fire, lest she should suffer from the change of room; and she removed, at his desire, to the other side of the fireplace, that she might be farther from the door. He then sat down by her, and talked scarcely to any one else. Elizabeth, at work in the opposite corner, saw it all with great delight.

When tea was over Mr. Hurst reminded his sister-in-law of the card-table—but in vain. She had obtained private intelligence that Mr. Darcy did not wish for cards, and Mr. Hurst soon found even his open petition rejected. She assured him that no one intended to play, and the silence of the whole party on the subject seemed to justify her. Mr. Hurst had, therefore, nothing to do but to stretch himself on one of the sofas and go to sleep. Darcy took up a book. Miss Bingley did the same; and Mrs. Hurst, principally occupied in playing with her bracelets and rings, joined now and then in her brother's conversation with Miss Bennet.

Miss Bingley's attention was quite as much engaged in watching Mr. Darcy's progress through *his* book, as in reading her own; and she was perpetually either making some inquiry, or looking at his page. She could not win him, however, to any conversation; he merely answered her question and read on. At length, quite exhausted by the attempt to be amused with her own book, which she had only chosen because it was the second volume of his, she gave a great yawn and said, 'How pleasant it is to spend an evening in this way! I declare, after all, there is no enjoyment like reading! How much sooner one tires of anything than of a book! When I have a house of my own, I shall be miserable if I have not an excellent library!'

No one made any reply. She then yawned again, threw aside her book, and cast her eyes round the room in quest of some amusement; when, hearing her brother mentioning a ball to Miss Bennet, she turned suddenly towards him and said,—

'By the bye, Charles, are you really serious in meditating a dance at Netherfield? I would advise you, before you determine on it, to consult the wishes of the present party; I am much mistaken if there are not some among us to whom a ball would be rather a punishment than a pleasure.'

'If you mean Darcy,' cried her brother, 'he may go to bed, if he chooses, before it begins; but as for the ball, it is quite a settled thing, and as soon as Nicholls has made white soup enough I shall send round my cards.'

'I should like balls infinitely better,' she replied, 'if they were carried on in a different manner; but there is something insufferably tedious in the usual process of such a meeting. It would surely be much more rational if conversation instead of dancing made the order of the day.'

'Much more rational, my dear Caroline, I daresay; but it would not be near so much like a ball.'

Miss Bingley made no answer, and soon afterwards got up and walked about the room. Her figure was elegant, and she walked well; but Darcy, at whom it was all aimed, was still inflexibly studious. In the desperation of her feelings she resolved on one effort more; and, turning to Elizabeth, said,—

'Miss Eliza Bennet, let me persuade you to follow my example, and take a turn about the room. I assure you it is very refreshing after sitting so long in one attitude.'

Elizabeth was surprised, but agreed to it immediately. Miss Bingley succeeded no less in the real object of her civility: Mr. Darcy looked up. He was as much awake to the novelty of attention in that quarter as Elizabeth herself could be, and unconsciously closed his book. He was directly invited to join their party, but he declined it, observing that he could imagine but two motives for their choosing to walk up and down the room together, with either of which motives his joining them would interfere. What could he mean? She was dying to know what could be his meaning —and asked Elizabeth whether she could at all understand him.

'Not at all,' was her answer; 'but, depend upon it, he means to be severe on us, and our surest way of disappointing him will be to ask nothing about it.'

Miss Bingley, however, was incapable of disappointing Mr. Darcy in anything, and persevered, therefore, in requiring an explanation of his two motives.

'I have not the smallest objection to explaining them,' said he, as soon as she allowed him to speak. 'You either choose this method of passing the evening because you are in each other's confidence, and have secret affairs to discuss, or because you are conscious that your figures appear to the greatest advantage in walking: if the first, I should be completely in your way; and if the second, I can admire you much better as I sit by the fire.'

'Oh, shocking!' cried Miss Bingley. 'I never heard anything so abominable. How shall we punish him for such a speech?'

'Nothing so easy, if you have but the inclination,' said Elizabeth. 'We can all plague and punish one another. Tease him—laugh at him. Intimate as you are, you must know how it is to be done.'

'But upon my honour I do *not*. I do assure you that my intimacy has not yet taught me *that*. Tease calmness of temper and presence of mind! No, no; I feel he may defy us there. And as to laughter, we will not expose ourselves, if you please, by attempting to laugh without a subject. Mr. Darcy may hug himself.'

'Mr. Darcy is not to be laughed at!' cried Elizabeth. 'That is an uncommon advantage, and uncommon I hope it will continue, for it would be a great loss to *me* to have many such acquaintance. I dearly love a laugh.'

'Miss Bingley,' said he, 'has given me credit for more than can be. The wisest and best of men,—nay, the wisest and best of their actions,—may be rendered ridiculous by a person whose first object in life is a joke.'

'Certainly,' replied Elizabeth, 'there are such people, but I hope I am not one of *them*. I hope I never ridicule what is wise or good. Follies and nonsense, whims and inconsistencies, *do* divert me, I own, and I laugh at them whenever I can. But these, I suppose, are precisely what you are without.'

'Perhaps that is not possible for any one. But it has been the study of my life to avoid those weaknesses which often expose a strong understanding to ridicule.'

'Such as vanity and pride.'

'Yes, vanity is a weakness indeed. But pride—where there is a real superiority of mind—pride will be always under good regulation.'

Elizabeth turned away to hide a smile.

'Your examination of Mr. Darcy is over, I presume,' said Miss Bingley; 'and pray what is the result?'

'I am perfectly convinced by it that Mr. Darcy has no defect. He owns it himself without disguise.'

'No,' said Darcy, 'I have made no such pretension. I have faults enough, but they are not, I hope, of understanding. My temper I dare not vouch for. It is, I believe, too little yielding; certainly too little for the convenience of the world. I cannot forget the follies and vices of others so soon as I ought, nor their offences against myself. My feelings are not puffed about with every attempt to move them. My temper would perhaps be called resentful. My good opinion once lost is lost for ever.'

'*That* is a failing, indeed!' cried Elizabeth. 'Implacable resentment *is* a shade in a character. But you have chosen your fault well. I really cannot *laugh* at it. You are safe from me.'

'There is, I believe, in every disposition a tendency to some particular evil, a natural defect, which not even the best education can overcome.'

'And *your* defect is a propensity to hate everybody.'

'And yours,' he replied, with a smile, 'is wilfully to misunderstand them.'

'Do let us have a little music,' cried Miss Bingley, tired of a conversation in which she had no share. 'Louisa, you will not mind my waking Mr. Hurst.'

Her sister made not the smallest objection, and the pianoforte was opened; and Darcy, after a few moments' recollection, was not sorry for it. He began to feel the danger of paying Elizabeth too much attention.

CHAPTER XII

IN consequence of an agreement between the sisters, Elizabeth wrote the next morning to her mother, to beg that the carriage might be sent for them in the course of the day. But Mrs. Bennet, who had calculated on her daughters remaining at Netherfield till the following Tuesday, which would exactly finish Jane's week, could not bring herself to receive them with pleasure before. Her answer, therefore, was not propitious, at least not to Elizabeth's wishes, for she was impatient to get home. Mrs. Bennet sent them word that they could not possibly have the carriage before Tuesday; and in her postscript it was added, that if Mr. Bingley and his sister pressed them to stay longer, she could spare them very well. Against staying longer, however, Elizabeth was positively resolved—nor did she much expect it would be asked; and fearful, on the contrary, of being considered as intruding themselves needlessly long, she urged Jane to borrow Mr. Bingley's carriage immediately, and at length it was settled that their original design of leaving Netherfield that morning should be mentioned, and the request made.

The communication excited many professions of concern; and enough was said of wishing them to stay at least till the following day to work on Jane; and till the morrow their going was deferred. Miss Bingley was then sorry that she had proposed the delay; for her jealousy and dislike of one sister much exceeded her affection for the other.

The master of the house heard with real sorrow that they were to go so soon, and repeatedly tried to persuade Miss Bennet that it would not be safe for her—that she was not enough recovered; but Jane was firm where she felt herself to be right.

To Mr. Darcy it was welcome intelligence: Elizabeth had been at Netherfield long enough. She attracted him more than he liked; and Miss Bingley was uncivil to *her,* and more teasing than usual to himself. He wisely resolved to be particularly careful that no sign of admiration should *now* escape him—nothing that could elevate her with the hope of influencing his felicity; sensible that, if such an idea had been suggested, his behaviour during the last day must have material weight in confirming or crushing it. Steady to his purpose, he scarcely spoke ten words to her through the whole of Saturday; and though they were at one time left by themselves for half an hour, he adhered most conscientiously to his book and would not even look at her.

On Sunday, after morning service, the separation, so agreeable to almost all, took place. Miss Bingley's civility to Elizabeth increased at last very rapidly, as well as her affection for Jane; and when they parted, after assuring the latter of the pleasure it would always give her to see her either at Longbourn or Netherfield, and embracing her most tenderly, she even shook hands with the former. Elizabeth took leave of the whole party in the liveliest spirits.

They were not welcomed home very cordially by their mother. Mrs. Bennet wondered at their coming, and thought them very wrong to give so much trouble, and was sure Jane would have caught cold again. But their father, though very laconic in his expressions of pleasure, was really glad to see them; he had felt their importance in the family circle. The evening conversation, when they were all assembled, had lost much of its animation, and almost all its sense, by the absence of Jane and Elizabeth.

They found Mary, as usual, deep in the study of thorough bass and human nature; and had some new extracts to admire, and some new observations of threadbare morality to listen to. Catherine and Lydia had information for them of a different sort. Much had been done, and much had been said in the regiment since the preceding Wednesday; several of the officers had dined lately with their uncle; a private had been flogged, and it had actually been hinted that Colonel Forster was going to be married.

CHAPTER XIII

'I HOPE, my dear,' said Mr. Bennet to his wife, as they were at breakfast the next morning, 'that you have ordered a good dinner to-day, because I have reason to expect an addition to our family party.'

'Who do you mean, my dear? I know of nobody that is coming, I am sure, unless Charlotte Lucas should happen to call in; and I hope *my* dinners are good enough for her. I do not believe she often sees such at home.'

'The person of whom I speak is a gentleman and a stranger.' Mrs. Bennet's eyes sparkled. 'A gentleman and a stranger! It is Mr. Bingley, I am sure. Why, Jane—you never dropped a word of this—you sly thing! Well, I am sure I shall be extremely glad to see Mr. Bingley. But—good Lord! how unlucky! there is not a bit of fish to be got to-day. Lydia, my love, ring the bell. I must speak to Hill this moment.'

'It is *not* Mr. Bingley,' said her husband; 'it is a person whom I never saw in the whole course of my life.'

This roused a general astonishment; and he had the pleasure of being eagerly questioned by his wife and five daughters at once.

After amusing himself some time with their curiosity, he thus explained:—'About a month ago I received this letter, and about a fortnight ago I answered it; for I thought it a case of some delicacy, and requiring early attention. It is from my cousin, Mr. Collins, who, when I am dead, may turn you all out of this house as soon as he pleases.'

'Oh, my dear,' cried his wife, 'I cannot bear to hear that mentioned. Pray do not talk of that odious man. I do think it is the hardest thing in the world that your estate should be entailed away from your own children; and I am sure, if I had been you, I should have tried long ago to do something or other about it.'

Jane and Elizabeth attempted to explain to her the nature of an entail. They had often attempted it before: but it was a subject on which Mrs. Bennet was beyond the reach of reason; and she continued to rail bitterly against the cruelty of settling an estate away from a family of five daughters, in favour of a man whom nobody cared anything about.

'It certainly is a most iniquitous affair,' said Mr. Bennet; 'and nothing can clear Mr. Collins from the guilt of inheriting Longbourn. But if you will listen to his letter, you may, perhaps, be a little softened by his manner of expressing himself.'

'No, that I am sure I shall not; and I think it was very impertinent of him to write to you at all, and very hypocritical. I hate such false friends. Why could not he keep on quarrelling with you, as his father did before him?'

'Why, indeed, he does seem to have had some filial scruples on that head, as you will hear:—

'Hunsford, near Westerham, Kent, 15th October.

'DEAR SIR—The disagreement subsisting between yourself and my late honoured father always gave me much uneasiness; and, since I have had the misfortune to lose him, I have frequently wished to heal the breach: but, for some time, I was kept back by my own doubts, fearing lest it might seem disrespectful to his memory for me to be on good terms with any one with whom it had always pleased him to be at variance.'—"There, Mrs. Bennet."—'My mind, however, is now made up on the subject; for, having received ordination at Easter, I have been so fortunate as to be distinguished by the patronage of the Right Honourable Lady Catherine De Bourgh, widow of Sir Lewis De Bourgh, whose bounty and beneficence has preferred me to the valuable rectory of this parish, where it shall be my earnest endeavour to demean myself with grateful respect towards her Ladyship, and be ever ready to perform those rites and ceremonies which are instituted by the Church of England. As a clergyman, moreover, I feel it my duty to promote and establish the blessing of peace in all families within the reach of my influence; and on these grounds I flatter myself that my present overtures of goodwill are highly commendable, and that the circumstance of my being next in the entail of Longbourn estate will be kindly overlooked on your side, and not lead you to reject the offered olive branch. I cannot be otherwise than concerned at being the means of injuring your amiable daughters, and beg leave to apologise for it, as well as to assure you of my readiness to make them every possible amends; but of this hereafter. If you should have no objection to receive me into your house, I propose myself the satisfaction of waiting on you and your family, Monday, November 18th, by four o'clock, and shall probably trespass on your hospitality till the Saturday se'nnight following, which I can do without any inconvenience, as Lady Catherine is far from objecting to my occasional absence on a Sunday, provided that some other clergyman is engaged to do the duty of the day. I remain, dear sir, with respectful compliments to your lady and daughters, your well-wisher and friend,

'WILLIAM COLLINS.'

'At four o'clock, therefore, we may expect this peacemaking gentleman,' said Mr. Bennet, as he folded up the letter. 'He seems to be a most conscientious and polite young man, upon my word; and, I doubt not, will prove a valuable acquaintance, especially if Lady Catherine should be so indulgent as to let him come to us again.'

'There is some sense in what he says about the girls, however; and, if he is disposed to make them any amends, I shall not be the person to discourage him.'

'Though it is difficult,' said Jane, 'to guess in what way he can mean to make us the atonement he thinks our due, the wish is certainly to his credit.'

Elizabeth was chiefly struck with his extraordinary deference for Lady Catherine, and his kind intention of christening, marrying, and burying his parishioners whenever it were required.

'He must be an oddity, I think,' said she. 'I cannot make him out. There is something very pompous in his style. And what can he mean by apologising for being next in the entail? We cannot suppose he would help it, if he could. Can he be a sensible man, sir?'

'No, my dear; I think not. I have great hopes of finding him quite the reverse. There is a mixture of servility and self-importance in his letter which promises well. I am impatient to see him.'

'In point of composition,' said Mary, 'his letter does not seem defective. The idea of the olive branch perhaps is not wholly new, yet I think it is well expressed.'

To Catherine and Lydia neither the letter nor its writer was in any degree interesting. It was next to impossible that their cousin should come in a scarlet coat, and it was now some weeks since they had received pleasure from the society of a man in any other colour. As for their mother, Mr. Collins's letter had done away much of her ill-will, and she was preparing to see him with a degree of composure which astonished her husband and daughters.

Mr. Collins was punctual to his time, and was received with great politeness by the whole family. Mr. Bennet indeed said little; but the ladies were ready enough to talk, and Mr. Collins seemed neither in need of encouragement, nor inclined to be silent himself. He was a tall, heavy-looking young man of five-and-twenty. His air was grave and stately, and his manners were very formal. He had not been long seated before he complimented Mrs. Bennet on having so fine a family of daughters, said he had heard much of their beauty, but that, in this instance, fame had fallen short of the truth; and added, that he did not doubt her seeing them all in due time well disposed of in marriage. This gallantry was not much to the taste of some of his hearers; but Mrs. Bennet, who quarrelled with no compliments, answered most readily,—

'You are very kind, sir, I am sure; and I wish with all my heart it may prove so; for else they will be destitute enough. Things are settled so oddly.'

'You allude, perhaps, to the entail of this estate.'

'Ah, sir, I do indeed. It is a grievous affair to my poor girls, you must confess. Not that I mean to find fault with *you*, for such things I know are all chance in this world. There is no knowing how estates will go when once they come to be entailed.'

'I am very sensible, madam, of the hardship to my fair cousins, and could say much on the subject, but that I am cautious of appearing forward and precipitate. But I can assure the young ladies that I come prepared to admire them. At present I will not say more, but, perhaps, when we are better acquainted——'

He was interrupted by a summons to dinner; and the girls smiled on each other. They were not the only objects of Mr. Collins's admiration. The hall, the dining-room, and all its furniture, were examined and praised; and his commendation of everything would have touched Mrs. Bennet's heart, but for the mortifying supposition of his viewing it all as his own future property. The dinner, too, in its turn, was highly admired; and he begged to know to which of his fair cousins the excellence of its cookery was owing. But here he was set right by Mrs. Bennet, who assured him, with some asperity, that they were very well able to keep a good cook, and that her daughters had nothing to do in the kitchen. He begged pardon for having displeased her. In a softened tone she declared herself not at all offended; but he continued to apologise for about a quarter of an hour.

CHAPTER XIV

DURING dinner, Mr. Bennet scarcely spoke at all; but when the servants were withdrawn, he thought it time to have some conversation with his guest, and therefore started a subject in which he expected him to shine, by observing that he seemed very fortunate in his patroness. Lady Catherine De Bourgh's attention to his wishes, and consideration for his comfort, appeared very remarkable. Mr. Bennet could not have chosen better. Mr. Collins was eloquent in her praise. The subject elevated him to more than usual solemnity of manner; and with a most important aspect he protested that 'he had never in his life witnessed such behaviour in a person of rank—such affability and condescension, as he had himself experienced from Lady Catherine. She had been graciously pleased to approve of both the discourses which he had already had the honour of preaching before her. She had also asked him twice to dine at Rosings, and had sent for him only the Saturday before, to make up her pool of quadrille in the evening. Lady Catherine was reckoned proud by many people, he knew, but *he* had never seen anything but affability in her. She had always spoken to him as she would to any other gentleman; she made not the smallest objection to his joining in the society of the neighbourhood, nor to his leaving his parish occasionally for a week or two to visit his relations. She had even condescended to advise him to marry as soon as he could, provided he chose with discretion; and had once paid him a visit in his humble parsonage, where she had perfectly approved all the alterations he had been making, and had even vouchsafed to suggest some herself,—some shelves in the closets upstairs.'

'That is all very proper and civil, I am sure,' said Mrs. Bennet, 'and I daresay she is a very agreeable woman. It is a pity that great ladies in general are not more like her. Does she live near you, sir?'

'The garden in which stands my humble abode is separated only by a lane from Rosings Park, her Ladyship's residence.'

'I think you said she was a widow, sir? has she any family?'

'She has one only daughter, the heiress of Rosings, and of very extensive property.'

'Ah,' cried Mrs. Bennet, shaking her head, 'then she is better off than many girls. And what sort of young lady is she? Is she handsome?'

'She is a most charming young lady, indeed. Lady Catherine herself says that, in point of true beauty, Miss De Bourgh is far superior to the handsomest of her sex; because there is that in her features which marks the young woman of distinguished birth. She is unfortunately of a sickly constitution, which has prevented her making that progress in many accomplishments which she could not otherwise have failed of, as I am informed by the lady who superintended her education, and who still resides with them. But she is perfectly amiable, and often condescends to drive by my humble abode in her little phaeton and ponies.'

'Has she been presented? I do not remember her name among the ladies at court.'

'Her indifferent state of health unhappily prevents her being in town; and by that means, as I told Lady Catherine myself one day, has deprived the British Court of its brightest ornament. Her Ladyship seemed pleased with the idea; and you may imagine that I am happy on every occasion to offer those little delicate compliments which are always acceptable to ladies. I have more than once observed to Lady Catherine, that her charming daughter seemed born to be a duchess; and that the most elevated rank, instead of giving her consequence, would be adorned by her. These are the kind of little things which please her Ladyship, and it is a sort of attention which I conceive myself peculiarly bound to pay.'

'You judge very properly,' said Mr. Bennet; 'and it is happy for you that you possess the talent of flattering with delicacy. May I ask whether these pleasing attentions proceed from the impulse of the moment, or are the result of previous study?'

'They arise chiefly from what is passing at the time; and though I sometimes amuse myself with suggestions and arranging such little elegant compliments as may be adapted to ordinary occasions, I always wish to give them as unstudied an air as possible.'

Mr. Bennet's expectations were fully answered. His cousin was as absurd as he had hoped; and he listened to him with the keenest enjoyment, maintaining at the same time the most resolute composure of countenance, and, except in an occasional glance at Elizabeth, requiring no partner in his pleasure.

By tea-time, however, the dose had been enough, and Mr. Bennet was glad to take his guest into the drawing-room again, and when tea was over, glad to invite him to read aloud to the ladies. Mr. Collins readily assented, and a book was produced; but on beholding it (for everything announced it to be from a circulating library) he started back, and, begging pardon, protested that he never read novels. Kitty stared at him, and Lydia exclaimed. Other books were produced, and after some deliberation he chose Fordyce's Sermons. Lydia gaped as he opened the volume; and before he had, with very monotonous solemnity, read three pages, she interrupted him with,—

'Do you know, mamma, that my uncle Philips talks of turning away Richard? and if he does, Colonel Forster will hire him. My aunt told me so herself on Saturday. I shall walk to Meryton to-morrow to hear more about it, and to ask when Mr. Denny comes back from town.'

Lydia was bid by her two eldest sisters to hold her tongue; but Mr. Collins, much offended, laid aside his book, and said,—

'I have often observed how little young ladies are interested by books of a serious stamp, though written solely for their benefit. It amazes me, I confess; for certainly there can be nothing so advantageous to them as instruction. But I will no longer importune my young cousin.'

Then turning to Mr. Bennet, he offered himself as his antagonist at backgammon. Mr. Bennet accepted the challenge, observing that he acted very wisely in leaving the girls to their own trifling amusements. Mrs. Bennet and her daughters apologised most civilly for Lydia's interruption, and promised that it should not occur again, if he would resume his book; but Mr. Collins, after assuring them that he bore his young cousin no ill-will, and should never resent her behaviour as any affront, seated himself at another table with Mr. Bennet, and prepared for backgammon.

CHAPTER XV

MR. COLLINS was not a sensible man, and the deficiency of nature had been but little assisted by education or society; the greatest part of his life having been spent under the guidance of an illiterate and miserly father; and though he belonged to one of the universities, he had merely kept the necessary terms without forming at it any useful acquaintance. The subjection in which his father had brought him up had given him originally great humility of manner; but it was now a good deal counteracted by the self-conceit of a weak head, living in retirement, and the consequential feelings of early and unexpected prosperity. A fortunate chance had recommended him to Lady Catherine De Bourgh when the living of Hunsford was vacant; and the respect which he felt for her high rank, and his veneration for her as his patroness, mingling with a very good opinion of himself, of his authority as a clergyman, and his right as a rector, made him altogether a mixture of pride and obsequiousness, self-importance and humility.

Having now a good house and a very sufficient income, he intended to marry; and in seeking a reconciliation with the Longbourn family he had a wife in view, as he meant to choose one of the daughters, if he found them as handsome and amiable as they were represented by common report. This was his plan of amends—of atonement—for inheriting their father's estate; and he thought it an excellent one, full of eligibility and suitableness, and excessively generous and disinterested on his own part.

His plan did not vary on seeing them. Miss Bennet's lovely face confirmed his views, and established all his strictest notions of what was due to seniority; and for the first evening *she* was his settled choice. The next morning, however, made an alteration; for in a quarter of an hour's *tête-à-tête* with Mrs. Bennet before breakfast, a conversation beginning with his parsonage-house, and leading naturally to the avowal

of his hopes that a mistress for it might be found at Longbourn, produced from her, amid very complaisant smiles and
general encouragement, a caution against the very Jane he
had fixed on. 'As to her *younger* daughters, she could not
take upon her to say—she could not positively answer—but
she did not *know* of any prepossession;—her *eldest* daughter
she must just mention—she felt it incumbent on her to hint,
was likely to be very soon engaged.'

Mr. Collins had only to change from Jane to Elizabeth—
and it was soon done—done while Mrs. Bennet was stirring
the fire. Elizabeth, equally next to Jane in birth and beauty,
succeeded her of course.

Mrs. Bennet treasured up the hint, and trusted that she
might soon have two daughters married; and the man whom
she could not bear to speak of the day before was now high
in her good graces.

Lydia's intention of walking to Meryton was not forgotten: every sister except Mary agreed to go with her; and
Mr. Collins was to attend them, at the request of Mr. Bennet,
who was most anxious to get rid of him, and have his library
to himself; for thither Mr. Collins had followed him after
breakfast, and there he would continue, nominally engaged
with one of the largest folios in the collection, but really talking to Mr. Bennet, with little cessation, of his house and
garden at Hunsford. Such doings discomposed Mr. Bennet
exceedingly. In his library he had been always sure of leisure
and tranquillity; and though prepared, as he told Elizabeth,
to meet with folly and conceit in every other room in the
house, he was used to be free from them there: his civility,
therefore, was most prompt in inviting Mr. Collins to join his
daughters in their walk; and Mr. Collins, being in fact much
better fitted for a walker than a reader, was extremely well
pleased to close his large book, and go.

In pompous nothings on his side, and civil assents on that
of his cousins, their time passed till they entered Meryton.
The attention of the younger ones was then no longer to be
gained by *him*. Their eyes were immediately wandering up
the street in quest of the officers, and nothing less than a very
smart bonnet indeed, or a really new muslin in a shop window
could recall them.

But the attention of every lady was soon caught by a young man, whom they had never seen before, of most gentlemanlike appearance, walking with an officer on the other side of the way. The officer was the very Mr. Denny concerning whose return from London Lydia came to inquire, and he bowed as they passed. All were struck with the stranger's air, all wondered who he could be; and Kitty and Lydia, determined if possible to find out, led the way across the street, under pretence of wanting something in an opposite shop, and fortunately had just gained the pavement, when the two gentlemen, turning back, had reached the same spot. Mr. Denny addressed them directly, and entreated permission to introduce his friend, Mr. Wickham, who had returned with him the day before from town, and, he was happy to say, had accepted a commission in their corps. This was exactly as it should be; for the young man wanted only regimentals to make him completely charming. His appearance was greatly in his favour; he had all the best parts of beauty, a fine countenance, a good figure, and very pleasing address. The introduction was followed up on his side by a happy readiness of conversation—a readiness at the same time perfectly correct and unassuming; and the whole party were still standing and talking together very agreeably, when the sound of horses drew their notice, and Darcy and Bingley were seen riding down the street. On distinguishing the ladies of the group the two gentlemen came directly towards them, and began the usual civilities. Bingley was the principal spokesman, and Miss Bennet the principal object. He was then, he said, on his way to Longbourn on purpose to inquire after her. Mr. Darcy corroborated it with a bow, and was beginning to determine not to fix his eyes on Elizabeth, when they were suddenly arrested by the sight of the stranger, and Elizabeth happening to see the countenance of both as they looked at each other, was all astonishment at the effect of the meeting. Both changed colour, one looked white, the other red. Mr. Wickham, after a few moments, touched his hat—a salutation which Mr. Darcy just deigned to return. What could be the meaning of it? It was impossible to imagine; it was impossible not to long to know.

In another minute Mr. Bingley, but without seeming to have noticed what passed, took leave and rode on with his friend.

Mr. Denny and Mr. Wickham walked with the young ladies to the door of Mr. Philips's house, and then made their bows, in spite of Miss Lydia's pressing entreaties that they would come in, and even in spite of Mrs. Philips's throwing up the parlour window, and loudly seconding the invitation.

Mrs. Philips was always glad to see her nieces; and the two eldest, from their recent absence, were particularly welcome; and she was eagerly expressing her surprise at their sudden return home, which, as their own carriage had not fetched them, she should have known nothing about if she had not happened to see Mr. Jones's shop-boy in the street, who had told her that they were not to send any more draughts to Netherfield, because the Miss Bennets were come away, when her civility was claimed towards Mr. Collins by Jane's introduction of him. She received him with her very best politeness, which he returned with as much more, apologising for his intrusion without any previous acquaintance with her, which he could not help flattering himself however might be justified by his relationship to the young ladies who introduced him to her notice. Mrs. Philips was quite awed by such an excess of good breeding; but her contemplation of one stranger was soon put to an end to by exclamations and inquiries about the other, of whom, however, she could only tell her nieces what they already knew, that Mr. Denny had brought him from London, and that he was to have a lieutenant's commission in the ——shire. She had been watching him the last hour, she said, as he walked up and down the street, and had Mr. Wickham appeared, Kitty and Lydia would certainly have continued the occupation; but unluckily no one passed the windows now except a few of the officers, who, in comparison with the stranger, were become 'stupid, disagreeable fellows.' Some of them were to dine with the Philipses the next day, and their aunt promised to make her husband call on Mr. Wickham, and give him an invitation also, if the family from Longbourn would come in the evening. This was agreed to; and Mrs. Philips protested that they would have a nice comfortable noisy game of lottery tickets, and a little bit of hot supper afterwards. The prospect of such delights was very cheering, and they parted in mutual good spirits. Mr. Collins repeated his apologies in quitting the room, and was assured, with unwearying civility, that they were perfectly needless.

As they walked home, Elizabeth related to Jane what she had seen pass between the two gentlemen; but though Jane would have defended either or both, had they appeared to be wrong, she could no more explain such behaviour than her sister.

Mr. Collins on his return highly gratified Mrs. Bennet by admiring Mrs. Philips's manners and politeness. He protested that, except Lady Catherine and her daughter, he had never seen a more elegant woman; for she had not only received him with the utmost civility, but had even pointedly included him in her invitation for the next evening, although utterly unknown to her before. Something, he supposed, might be attributed to his connection with them, but yet he had never met with so much attention in the whole course of his life.

CHAPTER XVI

AS no objection was made the young people's engagement with their aunt, and all Mr. Collins's scruples of leaving Mr. and Mrs. Bennet for a single evening during his visit were most steadily resisted, the coach conveyed him and his five cousins at a suitable hour to Meryton; and the girls had the pleasure of hearing, as they entered the drawing-room, that Mr. Wickham had accepted their uncle's invitation, and was then in the house.

When this information was given, and they had all taken their seats, Mr. Collins was at leisure to look around him and admire, and he was so much struck with the size and furniture of the apartment, that he declared he might almost have supposed himself in the small summer breakfast parlour at Rosings; a comparison that did not at first convey much gratification; but when Mrs. Philips understood from him what Rosings was, and who was its proprietor, when she had listened to the description of only one of Lady Catherine's drawing-rooms, and found that the chimney-piece alone had cost eight hundred pounds, she felt all the force of the compliment, and would hardly have resented a comparison with the housekeeper's room.

In describing to her all the grandeur of Lady Catherine and her mansion, with occasional digressions in praise of his own humble abode, and the improvements it was receiving, he was happily employed until the gentlemen joined them; and he found in Mrs. Philips a very attentive listener. whose opinion of his consequence increased with what she heard, and who was resolving to retail it all among her neighbours as soon as she could. To the girls, who could not listen to their cousin, and who had nothing to do but to wish for an instrument, and examine their own indifferent imitations of china on the mantelpiece, the interval of waiting appeared very long. It was over at last, however. The gentlemen did approach: and when Mr. Wickham walked into the room, Elizabeth felt that she had neither been seeing him before, nor thinking of him since, with the smallest degree of unreasonable admiration. The officers of the ——shire were in general a very creditable, gentlemanlike set, and the best of them were of the present party; but Mr. Wickham was as far beyond them all in person, countenance, air, and walk, as *they* were superior to the broad-faced stuffy uncle Philips, breathing port wine, who followed them into the room.

Mr. Wickham was the happy man towards whom almost every female eye was turned, and Elizabeth was the happy woman by whom he finally seated himself; and the agreeable manner in which he immediately fell into conversation, though it was only on its being a wet night, and on the probability of a rainy season, made her feel that the commonest, dullest, most threadbare topic might be rendered interesting by the skill of the speaker.

With such rivals for the notice of the fair as Mr. Wickham and the officers, Mr. Collins seemed to sink into insignificance; to the young ladies he certainly was nothing; but he had still at intervals a kind listener in Mrs. Philips, and was, by her watchfulness, most abundantly supplied with coffee and muffin.

When the card tables were placed, he had an opportunity of obliging her, in return, by sitting down to whist.

'I know little of the game at present,' said he, 'but I shall be glad to improve myself; for in my situation of life ——' Mrs. Philips was very thankful for his compliance, but could not wait for his reason.

Mr. Wickham did not play at whist, and with ready delight was he received at the other table between Elizabeth and Lydia. At first there seemed danger of Lydia's engrossing him entirely, for she was a most determined talker; but being likewise extremely fond of lottery tickets, she soon grew too much interested in the game, too eager in making bets and exclaiming after prizes, to have attention for any one in particular. Allowing for the common demands of the game, Mr. Wickham was therefore at leisure to talk to Elizabeth, and she was very willing to hear him, though what she chiefly wished to hear she could not hope to be told, the history of his acquaintance with Mr. Darcy.

She dared not even mention that gentleman. Her curiosity, however, was unexpectedly relieved. Mr. Wickham began the subject himself. He inquired how far Netherfield was from Meryton; and, after receiving her answer, asked in a hesitating manner how long Mr. Darcy had been staying there.

'About a month,' said Elizabeth; and then, unwilling to let the subject drop, added, 'he is a man of very large property in Derbyshire, I understand.'

'Yes,' replied Wickham; 'his estate there is a noble one. A clear ten thousand per annum. You could not have met with a person more capable of giving you certain information on that head than myself—for I have been connected with his family, in a particular manner, from my infancy.'

Elizabeth could not but look surprised.

'You may well be surprised, Miss Bennet, at such an assertion, after seeing, as you probably might, the very cold manner of our meeting yesterday. Are you much acquainted with Mr. Darcy?'

'As much as I ever wish to be,' cried Elizabeth, warmly. 'I have spent four days in the same house with him, and I think him very disagreeable.'

'I have no right to give *my* opinion,' said Wickham, 'as to his being agreeable or otherwise. I am not qualified to form one. I have known him too long and too well to be a fair judge. It is impossible for *me* to be impartial. But I believe your opinion of him would in general astonish—and, perhaps, you would not express it quite so strongly anywhere else. Here you are in your own family.'

'Upon my word I say no more *here* than I might say in any house in the neighbourhood, except Netherfield. He is not at all liked in Hertfordshire. Everybody is disgusted with his pride. You will not find him more favourably spoken of by any one.'

'I cannot pretend to be sorry,' said Wickham, after a short interruption, 'that he or that any man should not be estimated beyond their deserts; but with *him* I believe it does not often happen. The world is blinded by his fortune and consequence, or frightened by his high and imposing manners, and sees him only as he chooses to be seen.'

'I should take him, even on *my* slight acquaintance, to be an ill-tempered man.' Wickham only shook his head.

'I wonder,' said he, at the next opportunity of speaking, 'whether he is likely to be in this country much longer.'

'I do not at all know; but I *heard* nothing of his going away when I was at Netherfield. I hope your plans in favour of the ——shire will not be affected by his being in the neighbourhood.'

'Oh no—it is not for *me* to be driven away by Mr. Darcy. If *he* wishes to avoid seeing *me*, he must go. We are not on friendly terms, and it always gives me pain to meet him, but I have no reason for avoiding *him* but what I might proclaim to all the world—a sense of very great ill usage, and most painful regrets at his being what he is. His father, Miss Bennet, the late Mr. Darcy, was one of the best men that ever breathed, and the truest friend I ever had; and I can never be in company with this Mr. Darcy without being grieved to the soul by a thousand tender recollections. His behaviour to myself has been scandalous; but I verily believe I could forgive him anything and everything, rather than his disappointing the hopes and disgracing the memory of his father.'

Elizabeth found the interest of the subject increase, and listened with all her heart; but the delicacy of it prevented further inquiry.

Mr. Wickham began to speak on more general topics, Meryton, the neighbourhood, the society, appearing highly pleased with all that he had yet seen, and speaking of the latter, especially, with gentle but very intelligible gallantry.

'It was the prospect of constant society, and good society,' he added, 'which was my chief inducement to enter the ——shire. I know it to be a most respectable, agreeable corps; and my friend Denny tempted me further by his account of their present quarters, and the very great attentions and excellent acquaintance Meryton had procured them. Society, I own, is necessary to me. I have been a disappointed man, and my spirits will not bear solitude. I *must* have employment and society. A military life is not what I was intended for, but circumstances have now made it eligible. The church *ought* to have been my profession—

I was brought up for the church; and I should at this time
have been in possession of a most valuable living, had it
pleased the gentleman we were speaking of just now.'

'Indeed!'

'Yes—the late Mr. Darcy bequeathed me the next presentation of the best living in his gift. He was my godfather,
and excessively attached to me. I cannot do justice to his
kindness. He meant to provide for me amply, and thought
he had done it; but when the living fell, it was given elsewhere.'

'Good heavens!' cried Elizabeth; 'but how could *that* be?
How could his will be disregarded? Why did not you seek
legal redress?'

'There was just such an informality in the terms of the
bequest as to give me no hope from law. A man of honour
could not have doubted the intention, but Mr. Darcy chose
to doubt it—or to treat it as a merely conditional recommendation, and to assert that I had forfeited all claim to it
by extravagance, imprudence, in short, anything or nothing.
Certain it is that the living became vacant two years ago,
exactly as I was of an age to hold it, and that it was given
to another man; and no less certain is it, that I cannot accuse
myself of having really done anything to deserve to lose it.
I have a warm unguarded temper, and I may perhaps have
sometimes spoken my opinion *of* him, and *to* him, too freely.
I can recall nothing worse. But the fact is, that we are
very different sort of men, and that he hates me.'

'This is quite shocking! He deserves to be publicly dis-
graced.'

'Some time or other he *will* be—but it shall not be by *me*.
Till I can forget his father, I can never defy or expose
him.'

Elizabeth honoured him for such feelings, and thought him
handsomer than ever as he expressed them.

'But what,' said she, after a pause, 'can have been his
motive? what can have induced him to behave so cruelly?'

'A thorough, determined dislike of me—a dislike which I
cannot but attribute in some measure to jealousy. Had the
late Mr. Darcy liked me less, his son might have borne
with me better; but his father's uncommon attachment to

me irritated him, I believe, very early in life. He had not a temper to bear the sort of competition in which we stood—the sort of preference which was often given me.'

'I had not thought Mr. Darcy so bad as this—though I have never liked him, I had not thought so very ill of him—I had supposed him to be despising his fellow-creatures in general, but did not suspect him of descending to such malicious revenge, such injustice, such inhumanity as this!'

After a few minutes' reflection, however, she continued,—'I *do* remember his boasting one day, at Netherfield, of the implacability of his resentments; of his having an unforgiving temper. His disposition must be dreadful.'

'I will not trust myself on the subject,' replied Wickham: '*I* can hardly be just to him.'

Elizabeth was again deep in thought, and after a time exclaimed, 'To treat in such a manner the godson, the friend, the favourite of his father!' She could have added, 'A young man, too, like *you*, whose very countenance may vouch for your being amiable.' But she contented herself with—'And one, too, who had probably been his own companion from childhood, connected together, as I think you said, in the closest manner.'

'We were born in the same parish, within the same park; the greatest part of our youth was passed together: inmates of the same house, sharing the same amusements, objects of the same parental care. *My* father began life in the profession which your uncle, Mr. Philips, appears to do so much credit to: but he gave up everything to be of use to the late Mr. Darcy, and devoted all his time to the care of the Pemberley property. He was most highly esteemed by Mr. Darcy, a most intimate, confidential friend. Mr. Darcy often acknowledged himself to be under the greatest obligations to my father's active superintendence; and when, immediately before my father's death, Mr. Darcy gave him a voluntary promise of providing for me, I am convinced that he felt it to be as much a debt of gratitude to *him* as of affection to myself.'

'How strange!' cried Elizabeth. 'How abominable! I wonder that the very pride of this Mr. Darcy has not made him just to you. If from no better motive, that he

should not have been too proud to be dishonest,—for dis-
honesty I must call it.'

'It *is* wonderful,' replied Wickham; 'for almost all his
actions may be traced to pride; and pride has often been
his best friend. It has connected him nearer with virtue
than any other feeling. But we are none of us consistent;
and in his behaviour to me there were stronger impulses
even than pride.'

'Can such abominable pride as his have ever done him
good?'

'Yes; it has often led him to be liberal and generous;
to give his money freely, to display hospitality, to assist
his tenants, and relieve the poor. Family pride, and *filial*
pride, for he is very proud of what his father was, have
done this. Not to appear to disgrace his family, to degen-
erate from the popular qualities, or lose the influence of
the Pemberley House, is a powerful motive. He has also
brotherly pride, which, with *some* brotherly affection, makes
him a very kind and careful guardian of his sister; and
you will hear him generally cried up as the most attentive and best of brothers.'

'What sort of a girl is Miss Darcy?'

He shook his head. 'I wish I could call her amiable.
It gives me pain to speak ill of a Darcy; but she is too
much like her brother,—very, very proud. As a child, she
was affectionate and pleasing, and extremely fond of me;
and I have devoted hours and hours to her amusement. But
she is nothing to me now. She is a handsome girl, about
fifteen or sixteen, and, I understand, highly accomplished.
Since her father's death her home has been London, where
a lady lives with her, and superintends her education.'

After many pauses and many trials of other subjects,
Elizabeth could not help reverting once more to the first,
and saying,—

'I am astonished at his intimacy with Mr. Bingley. How
can Mr. Bingley, who seems good-humour itself, and is, I
really believe, truly amiable, be in friendship with such a
man? How can they suit each other? Do you know Mr.
Bingley?'

'Not at all.'

'He is a sweet-tempered, amiable, charming man. He cannot know what Mr. Darcy is.'

'Probably not; but Mr. Darcy can please where he chooses. He does not want abilities. He can be a conversible companion if he thinks it worth his while. Among those who are at all his equals in consequence, he is a very different man from what he is to the less prosperous. His pride never deserts him; but with the rich he is liberal-minded, just, sincere, rational, honourable, and, perhaps, agreeable,—allowing something for fortune and figure.'

The whist party soon afterwards breaking up, the players gathered round the other table, and Mr. Collins took his station between his cousin Elizabeth and Mrs. Philips. The usual inquiries as to his success were made by the latter. It had not been very great; he had lost every point; but when Mrs. Philips began to express her concern thereupon, he assured her, with much earnest gravity, that it was not of the least importance; that he considered the money as a mere trifle, and begged she would not make herself uneasy.

'I know very well, madam,' said he, 'that when persons sit down to a card table they must take their chance of these things,—and happily I am not in such circumstances as to make five shillings any object. There are, undoubtedly, many who could not say the same; but, thanks to Lady Catherine de Bourgh, I am removed far beyond the necessity of regarding little matters.'

Mr. Wickham's attention was caught; and after observing Mr. Collins for a few moments, he asked Elizabeth in a low voice whether her relations were very intimately acquainted with the family of De Bourgh.

'Lady Catherine de Bourgh,' she replied, 'has very lately given him a living. I hardly know how Mr. Collins was first introduced to her notice, but he certainly has not known her long.'

'You know of course that Lady Catherine de Bourgh and Lady Anne Darcy were sisters; consequently that she is aunt to the present Mr. Darcy.'

'No, indeed, I did not. I knew nothing at all of Lady Catherine's connections. I never heard of her existence till the day before yesterday.'

'Her daughter, Miss de Bourgh, will have a very large fortune, and it is believed that she and her cousin will unite the two estates.'

This information made Elizabeth smile, as she thought of poor Miss Bingley. Vain indeed must be all her attentions, vain and useless her affection for his sister and her praise of himself, if he were already self-destined to another.

'Mr. Collins,' said she, 'speaks highly both of Lady Catherine and her daughter; but, from some particulars that he has related of her Ladyship, I suspect his gratitude misleads him; and that, in spite of her being his patroness, she is an arrogant, conceited woman.'

'I believe her to be both in a great degree,' replied Wickham: 'I have not seen her for many years; but I very well remember that I never liked her, and that her manners were dictatorial and insolent. She has the reputation of being remarkably sensible and clever; but I rather believe she derives part of her abilities from her rank and fortune, part from her authoritative manner, and the rest from the pride of her nephew, who chooses that every one connected with him should have an understanding of the first class.'

Elizabeth allowed that he had given a very rational account of it, and they continued talking together with mutual satisfaction till supper put an end to cards, and gave the rest of the ladies their share of Mr. Wickham's attentions. There could be no conversation in the noise of Mrs. Philips's supper party, but his manners recommended him to everybody. Whatever he said, was said well; and whatever he did, done gracefully. Elizabeth went away with her head full of him. She could think of nothing but of Mr. Wickham, and of what he had told her, all the way home; but there was not time for her even to mention his name as they went, for neither Lydia nor Mr. Collins was once silent. Lydia talked incessantly of lottery tickets, of the fish she had lost and the fish she had won; and Mr. Collins, in describing the civility of Mr. and Mrs. Philips, protesting that he did not in the least regard his losses at whist, enumerating all the dishes at supper, and repeatedly fearing that he crowded his cousins, had more to say than he could well manage before the carriage stopped at Longbourn House.

CHAPTER XVII

ELIZABETH related to Jane, the next day, what had passed between Mr. Wickham and herself. Jane listened with astonishment and concern: she knew not how to believe that Mr. Darcy could be so unworthy of Mr. Bingley's regard; and yet it was not in her nature to question the veracity of a young man of such amiable appearance as Wickham. The possibility of his having really endured such unkindness was enough to interest all her tender feelings; and nothing therefore remained to be done but to think well of them both, to defend the conduct of each, and throw into the account of accident or mistake whatever could not be otherwise explained.

'They have both,' said she, 'been deceived, I daresay, in some way or other, of which we can form no idea. Interested people have perhaps misrepresented each to the other. It is, in short, impossible for us to conjecture the causes or circumstances which may have alienated them, without actual blame on either side.'

'Very true, indeed; and now, my dear Jane, what have you got to say in behalf of the interested people who have probably been concerned in the business? Do clear *them*, too, or we shall be obliged to think ill of somebody.'

'Laugh as much as you choose, but you will not laugh me out of my opinion. My dearest Lizzy, do but consider in what a disgraceful light it places Mr. Darcy, to be treating his father's favourite in such a manner,—one whom his father had promised to provide for. It is impossible. No man of common humanity, no man who had any value for his character, could be capable of it. Can his most intimate friends be so excessively deceived in him? Oh no.'

'I can much more easily believe Mr. Bingley's being imposed on than that Mr. Wickham should invent such a history of himself as he gave me last night; names, facts, everything mentioned without ceremony. If it be not so, let Mr. Darcy contradict it. Besides, there was truth in his looks.'

'It is difficult, indeed—it is distressing. One does not know what to think.'

'I beg your pardon;—one knows exactly what to think.'

But Jane could think with certainty on only one point,— that Mr. Bingley, if he *had been* imposed on, would have much to suffer when the affair became public.

The two young ladies were summoned from the shrubbery, where this conversation passed, by the arrival of some of the very persons of whom they had been speaking; Mr. Bingley and his sisters came to give their personal invitation for the long-expected ball at Netherfield, which was fixed for the following Tuesday. The two ladies were delighted to see their dear friend again, called it an age since they had met, and repeatedly asked what she had been doing with herself since their separation. To the rest of the family they paid little attention; avoiding Mrs. Bennet as much as possible, saying not much to Elizabeth, and nothing at all to the others. They were soon gone again, rising from their seats with an activity which took their brother by surprise, and hurrying off as if eager to escape from Mrs. Bennet's civilities.

The prospect of the Netherfield ball was extremely agreeable to every female of the family. Mrs. Bennet chose to consider it as given in compliment to her eldest daughter, and was particularly flattered by receiving the invitation from Mr. Bingley himself, instead of a ceremonious card. Jane pictured to herself a happy evening in the society of her two friends, and the attentions of their brother; and Elizabeth thought with pleasure of dancing a great deal with Mr. Wickham, and of seeing a confirmation of everything in Mr. Darcy's look and behaviour. The happiness anticipated by Catherine and Lydia depended less on any single event, or any particular person; for though they each, like Elizabeth, meant to dance half the evening with Mr. Wickham, he was by no means the only partner who could satisfy them, and a ball was, at any rate, a ball. And even Mary could assure her family that she had no disinclination for it.

'While I can have my mornings to myself,' said she, 'it is enough. I think it is no sacrifice to join occasionally in evening engagements. Society has claims on us all; and I profess myself one of those who consider intervals of recreation and amusement as desirable for everybody.'

Elizabeth's spirits were so high on the occasion, that though she did not often speak unnecessarily to Mr. Collins, she could not help asking him whether he intended to accept Mr. Bingley's invitation, and if he did, whether he would think it proper to join in the evening's amusement; and she was rather surprised to find that he entertained no scruple whatever on that head, and was very far from dreading a rebuke, either from the Archbishop or Lady Catherine de Bourgh, by venturing to dance.

'I am by no means of opinion, I assure you,' said he, 'that a ball of this kind, given by a young man of character, to respectable people, can have any evil tendency; and I am so far from objecting to dancing myself, that I shall hope to be honoured with the hands of all my fair cousins in the course of the evening; and I take this opportunity of soliciting yours, Miss Elizabeth, for the two first dances especially; a preference which I trust my cousin Jane will attribute to the right cause, and not to any disrespect for her.'

Elizabeth felt herself completely taken in. She had fully proposed being engaged by Wickham for those very dances; and to have Mr. Collins instead!—her liveliness had been never worse timed. There was no help for it, however. Mr. Wickham's happiness and her own was perforce delayed a little longer, and Mr. Collins's proposal accepted with as good a grace as she could. She was not the better pleased with his gallantry, from the idea it suggested of something more. It now first struck her that *she* was selected from among her sisters as worthy of being the mistress of Hunsford Parsonage, and of assisting to form a quadrille table at Rosings, in the absence of more eligible visitors. The idea soon reached to conviction, as she observed his increasing civilities towards herself, and heard his frequent attempt at a compliment on her wit and vivacity; and though more astonished than gratified herself by this effect of her charms, it was not long before her mother gave her to understand that the probability of their marriage was exceedingly agreeable to *her*. Elizabeth, however, did not choose to take the hint, being well aware that a serious dispute must be the consequence of any reply. Mr. Collins might never make the offer, and, till he did, it was useless to quarrel about him.

If there had not been a Netherfield ball to prepare for and talk of, the younger Miss Bennets would have been in a pitiable state at this time; for from the day of the invitation to the day of the ball there was such a succession of rain as prevented their walking to Meryton once. No aunt, no officers, no news could be sought after; the very shoe-roses for Netherfield were got by proxy. Even Elizabeth might have found some trial of her patience in weather which totally suspended the improvement of her acquaintance with Mr. Wickham; and nothing less than a dance on Tuesday could have made such a Friday, Saturday, Sunday, and Monday endurable to Kitty and Lydia.

CHAPTER XVIII

TILL Elizabeth entered the drawing-room at Netherfield, and looked in vain for Mr. Wickham among the
cluster of red coats there assembled, a doubt of his
being present had never occurred to her. The certainty of
meeting him had not been checked by any of those recollections that might not unreasonably have alarmed her. She
had dressed with more than usual care, and prepared in the
highest spirits for the conquest of all that remained unsub-
dued of his heart, trusting that it was not more than might
be won in the course of the evening. But in an instant arose
the dreadful suspicion of his being purposely omitted, for
Mr. Darcy's pleasure, in the Bingley's invitation to the officers; and though this was not exactly the case, the absolute
fact of his absence was pronounced by his friend Mr. Denny,
to whom Lydia eagerly applied, and who told them that
Wickham had been obliged to go to town on business the
day before, and was not yet returned; adding, with a significant smile,—

'I do not imagine his business would have called him away
just now, if he had not wished to avoid a certain gentleman
here.'

This part of his intelligence, though unheard by Lydia,
was caught by Elizabeth; and, as it assured her that Darcy
was not less answerable for Wickham's absence than if her
first surmise had been just, every feeling of displeasure
against the former was so sharpened by immediate disappointment, that she could hardly reply with tolerable civility
to the polite inquiries which he directly afterwards approached to make. Attention, forbearance, patience with
Darcy, was injury to Wickham. She was resolved against
any sort of conversation with him, and turned away with
a degree of ill-humour which she could not wholly surmount
even in speaking to Mr. Bingley, whose blind partiality provoked her.

But Elizabeth was not formed for ill-humour; and though every prospect of her own was destroyed for the evening, it could not dwell long on her spirits; and, having told all her griefs to Charlotte Lucas, whom she had not seen for a week, she was soon able to make a voluntary transition to the oddities of her cousin, and to point him out to her particular notice. The two first dances, however, brought a return of distress: they were dances of mortification. Mr. Collins, awkward and solemn, apologising instead of attending, and often moving wrong without being aware of it, gave her all the shame and misery which a disagreeable partner for a couple of dances can give. The moment of her release from him was ecstasy.

She danced next with an officer, and had the refreshment of talking of Wickham, and of hearing that he was universally liked. When those dances were over, she returned to Charlotte Lucas, and was in conversation with her, when she found herself suddenly addressed by Mr. Darcy, who took her so much by surprise in his application for her hand, that, without knowing what she did, she accepted him. He walked away again immediately, and she was left to fret over her own want of presence of mind: Charlotte tried to console her.

'I daresay you will find him very agreeable.'

'Heaven forbid! *That* would be the greatest misfortune of all! To find a man agreeable whom one is determined to hate! Do not wish me such an evil.'

When the dancing recommenced, however, and Darcy approached to claim her hand, Charlotte could not help cautioning her, in a whisper, not to be a simpleton, and allow her fancy for Wickham to make her appear unpleasant in the eyes of a man of ten times his consequence. Elizabeth made no answer, and took her place in the set, amazed at the dignity to which she was arrived in being allowed to stand opposite to Mr. Darcy, and reading in her neighbours' looks their equal amazement in beholding it. They stood for some time without speaking a word; and she began to imagine that their silence was to last through the two dances, and, at first, was resolved not to break it; till suddenly fancying that it would be the greater punishment to her partner to oblige him to talk, she made some slight observation on the dance. He replied, and was again silent. After a pause of some minutes, she addressed him a second time, with—

'It is *your* turn to say something now, Mr. Darcy. *I* talked about the dance, and *you* ought to make some kind of remark on the size of the room, or the number of couples.'

He smiled, and assured her that whatever she wished him to say should be said.

'Very well; that will do for the present. Perhaps, by and by, I may observe that private balls are much pleasanter than public ones; but *now* we may be silent.'

'Do you talk by rule, then, while you are dancing?'

'Sometimes. One must speak a little, you know. It would look odd to be entirely silent for half an hour together; and yet, for the advantage of *some,* conversation ought to be so arranged as that they may have the trouble of saying as little as possible.'

'Are you consulting your own feelings in the present case, or do you imagine that you are gratifying mine?'

'Both,' replied Elizabeth archly; 'for I have always seen a great similarity in the turn of our minds. We are each of an unsocial, taciturn disposition, unwilling to speak, unless we expect to say something that will amaze the whole room, and be handed down to posterity with all the *éclat* of a proverb.'

'This is no very striking resemblance of your own character, I am sure,' said he. 'How near it may be to *mine,* I cannot pretend to say. *You* think it a faithful portrait, undoubtedly.'

'I must not decide on my own performance.'

He made no answer, and they were again silent till they had gone down the dance, when he asked her if she and her sisters did not very often walk to Meryton. She answered in the affirmative; and, unable to resist the temptation, added, 'When you met us there the other day, we had just been forming a new acquaintance.'

The effect was immediate. A deeper shade of *hauteur* overspread his features, but he said not a word; and Elizabeth, though blaming herself for her own weakness, could not go on. At length Darcy spoke, and in a constrained manner said,—

'Mr. Wickham is blessed with such happy manners as may insure his *making* friends; whether he may be equally capable of *retaining* them, is less certain.'

'He has been so unlucky as to lose *your* friendship,' replied Elizabeth, with emphasis, 'and in a manner which he is likely to suffer from all his life.'

Darcy made no answer, and seemed desirous of changing the subject.

At that moment Sir William Lucas appeared close to them, meaning to pass through the set to the other side of the room; but, on perceiving Mr. Darcy, he stopped, with a bow of superior courtesy, to compliment him on his dancing and his partner.

'I have been most highly gratified, indeed, my dear sir; such very superior dancing is not often seen. It is evident that you belong to the first circles. Allow me to say, however, that your fair partner does not disgrace you; and that I must hope to have this pleasure often repeated, especially when a certain desirable event, my dear Miss Eliza (glancing at her sister and Bingley), shall take place. What congratulations will then flow in! I appeal to Mr. Darcy;—but let me not interrupt you, sir. You will not thank me for detaining you from the bewitching converse of that young lady, whose bright eyes are also upbraiding me.'

The latter part of this address was scarcely heard by Darcy; but Sir William's allusion to his friend seemed to strike him forcibly, and his eyes were directed, with a very serious expression, towards Bingley and Jane, who were dancing together. Recovering himself, however, shortly, he turned to his partner, and said,—

'Sir William's interruption has made me forget what we were talking of.'

'I do not think we were speaking at all. Sir William could not have interrupted any two people in the room who had less to say for themselves. We have tried two or three subjects already without success, and what we are to talk of next I cannot imagine.'

'What think you of books?' said he, smiling.

'Books—oh no!—I am sure we never read the same, or not with the same feelings.'

'I am sorry you think so; but if that be the case, there can at least be no want of subject. We may compare our different opinions.'

'No—I cannot talk of books in a ball-room; my head is always full of something else.'

'The *present* always occupies you in such scenes—does it?' said he, with a look of doubt.

'Yes, always,' she replied, without knowing what she said; for her thoughts had wandered far from the subject, as soon afterwards appeared by her suddenly exclaiming, 'I remember hearing you once say, Mr. Darcy, that you hardly ever forgave;—that your resentment, once created, was unappeasable. You are very cautious, I suppose, as to its *being created?*'

'I am,' said he, with a firm voice.

'And never allow yourself to be blinded by prejudice?'

'I hope not.'

'It is particularly incumbent on those who never change their opinion, to be secure of judging properly at first.'

'May I ask to what these questions tend?'

'Merely to the illustration of *your* character,' said she, endeavouring to shake off her gravity. 'I'm trying to make it out.'

'And what is your success?'

She shook her head. 'I do not get on at all. I hear such different accounts of you as puzzle me exceedingly.'

'I can readily believe,' answered he, gravely, 'that reports may vary greatly with respect to me; and I could wish, Miss Bennet, that you were not to sketch my character at the present moment, as there is reason to fear that the performance would reflect no credit on either.'

'But if I do not take your likeness now, I may never have another opportunity.'

'I would by no means suspend any pleasure of yours,' he coldly replied. She said no more, and they went down the other dance and parted in silence; on each side dissatisfied, though not to an equal degree; for in Darcy's breast there was a tolerably powerful feeling towards her, which soon procured her pardon, and directed all his anger against another.

They had not long separated when Miss Bingley came towards her, and, with an expression of civil disdain, thus accosted her,—

'So, Miss Eliza, I hear you are quite delighted with George Wickham? Your sister has been talking to me about him, and asking me a thousand questions; and I find that the young man forgot to tell you, among his other communications, that he was the son of old Wickham, the late Mr. Darcy's steward. Let me recommend you, however, as a friend, not to give implicit confidence to all his assertions; for, as to Mr. Darcy's using him ill, it is perfectly false: for, on the contrary, he has been always remarkably kind to him, though George Wickham has treated Mr. Darcy in a most infamous manner. I do not know the particulars, but I know very well that Mr. Darcy is not in the least to blame; that he cannot bear to hear George Wickham mentioned; and that though my brother thought he could not well avoid including him in his invitation to the officers, he was excessively glad to find that he had taken himself out of the way. His coming into the country at all is a most insolent thing, indeed, and I wonder how he could presume to do it. I pity you, Miss Eliza, for this discovery of your favourite's guilt; but really, considering his descent, one could not expect much better.'

'His guilt and his descent appear, by your account, to be the same,' said Elizabeth, angrily; 'for I have heard you accuse him of nothing worse than of being the son of Mr. Darcy's steward, and of *that*, I can assure you, he informed me himself.'

'I beg your pardon,' replied Miss Bingley, turning away with a sneer. 'Excuse my interference; it was kindly meant.'

'Insolent girl!' said Elizabeth to herself. 'You are much mistaken if you expect to influence me by such a paltry attack as this. I see nothing in it but your own wilful ignorance and the malice of Mr. Darcy.' She then sought her eldest sister, who had undertaken to make inquiries on the same subject of Bingley. Jane met her with a smile of such sweet complacency, a glow of such happy expression, as sufficiently marked how well she was satisfied with the occurrences of the evening. Elizabeth instantly read her feelings; and, at that moment. solicitude for Wickham, resentment against his enemies, and everything else, gave way before the hope of Jane's being in the fairest way for happiness.

'I want to know,' said she, with a countenance no less smiling than her sister's, 'what you have learnt about Mr. Wickham. But perhaps you have been too pleasantly engaged to think of any third person, in which case you may be sure of my pardon.'

'No,' replied Jane, 'I have not forgotten him; but I have nothing satisfactory to tell you. Mr. Bingley does not know the whole of his history, and is quite ignorant of the circumstances which have principally offended Mr. Darcy; but he will vouch for the good conduct, the probity and honour, of his friend, and is perfectly convinced that Mr. Wickham has deserved much less attention from Mr. Darcy than he has received; and I am sorry to say that by his account, as well as his sister's, Mr. Wickham is by no means a respectable young man. I am afraid he has been very imprudent, and has deserved to lose Mr. Darcy's regard.'

'Mr. Bingley does not know Mr. Wickham himself.'

'No; he never saw him till the other morning at Meryton.'

'This account then is what he has received from Mr. Darcy. I am perfectly satisfied. But what does he say of the living?'

'He does not exactly recollect the circumstances, though he has heard them from Mr. Darcy more than once, but he believes that it was left to him *conditionally* only.'

'I have not a doubt of Mr. Bingley's sincerity,' said Elizabeth warmly, 'but you must excuse my not being convinced by assurances only. Mr. Bingley's defence of his friend was a very able one, I daresay; but since he is unacquainted with several parts of the story, and has learnt the rest from that friend himself, I shall venture still to think of both gentlemen as I did before.'

She then changed the discourse to one more gratifying to each, and on which there could be no difference of sentiment. Elizabeth listened with delight to the happy though modest hopes which Jane entertained of Bingley's regard, and said all in her power to heighten her confidence in it. On their being joined by Mr. Bingley himself, Elizabeth withdrew to Miss Lucas; to whose inquiry after the pleasantness of her last partner she had scarcely replied before Mr. Collins came up to them, and told her with great exultation that he had just been so fortunate as to make a most important discovery.

'I have found out,' said he, 'by a singular accident, that there is now in the room a near relation to my patroness. I happened to overhear the gentleman himself mentioning to the young lady who does the honours of this house the names of his cousin Miss De Bourgh, and of her mother Lady Catherine. How wonderfully this sort of things occur! Who would have thought of my meeting with—perhaps—a nephew of Lady Catherine de Bourgh in this assembly! I am most thankful that the discovery is made in time for me to pay my respects to him, which I am now going to do, and trust he will excuse my not having done it before. My total ignorance of the connection must plead my apology.'

'You are not going to introduce yourself to Mr. Darcy?'

'Indeed I am. I shall entreat his pardon for not having done it earlier. I believe him to be Lady Catherine's *nephew*. It will be in my power to assure him that her Ladyship was quite well yesterday se'nnight.'

Elizabeth tried hard to dissuade him from such a scheme; assuring him that Mr. Darcy would consider his addressing him without introduction as an impertinent freedom, rather than a compliment to his aunt; that it was not in the least necessary there should be any notice on either side, and that if it were, it must belong to Mr. Darcy, the superior in consequence, to begin the acquaintance. Mr. Collins listened to her with the determined air of following his own inclination, and when she ceased speaking, replied thus,—

'My dear Miss Elizabeth, I have the highest opinion in the world of your excellent judgment in all matters within the scope of your understanding, but permit me to say that there must be a wide difference between the established forms of ceremony amongst the laity and those which regulate the clergy; for, give me leave to observe that I consider the clerical office as equal in point of dignity with the highest rank in the kingdom—provided that a proper humility of behaviour is at the same time maintained. You must, therefore, allow me to follow the dictates of my conscience on this occasion, which leads me to perform what I look on as a point of duty. Pardon me for neglecting to profit by your advice, which on every other subject shall be my constant guide, though in the case before us I consider myself more fitted by education and habitual study to decide on what is right than a young lady like yourself'; and with a low bow he left her to attack Mr. Darcy, whose reception of his advances she eagerly watched, and whose astonishment at being so addressed was very evident. Her cousin prefaced his speech with a solemn bow, and though she could not hear a word of it, she felt as if hearing it all, and saw in the motion of his lips the words 'apology,' 'Hunsford,' and 'Lady Catherine de Bourgh.' It vexed her to see him expose himself to such a man. Mr. Darcy was eyeing him with unrestrained wonder; and when at last Mr. Collins allowed him to speak, replied with an air of distant civility. Mr. Collins, however, was not discouraged from speaking again, and Mr. Darcy's contempt seemed abundantly increasing with the length of his second speech; and at the end of it he only made him a slight bow, and moved another way: Mr. Collins then returned to Elizabeth.

'I have no reason, I assure you,' said he, 'to be dissatisfied with my reception. Mr. Darcy seemed much pleased with the attention. He answered me with the utmost civility, and even paid me the compliment of saying that he was so well convinced of Lady Catherine's discernment as to be certain she could never bestow a favour unworthily. It was really a very handsome thought. Upon the whole, I am much pleased with him.'

As Elizabeth had no longer any interest of her own to pursue, she turned her attention almost entirely on her sister and Mr. Bingley; and the train of agreeable reflections which her observations gave birth to made her perhaps almost as happy as Jane. She saw her in idea settled in that very house, in all the felicity which a marriage of true affection could bestow; and she felt capable, under such circumstances, of endeavouring even to like Bingley's two sisters. Her mother's thoughts she plainly saw were bent the same way, and she determined not to venture near her, lest she might hear too much. When they sat down to supper, therefore, she considered it a most unlucky perverseness which placed them within one of each other; and deeply was she vexed to find that her mother was talking to that one person (Lady Lucas) freely, openly, and of nothing else but of her expectation that Jane would be soon married to Mr. Bingley. It was an animating subject, and Mrs. Bennet seemed incapable of fatigue while enumerating the advantages of the match. His being such a charming young man, and so rich, and living but three miles from them, were the first points of self-gratulation; and then it was such a comfort to think how fond the two sisters were of Jane, and to be certain that they must desire the connection as much as she could do. It was, moreover, such a promising thing for her younger daughters, as Jane's marrying so greatly must throw them in the way of other rich men; and, lastly, it was so pleasant at her time of life to be able to consign her single daughters to the care of their sister, that she might not be obliged to go into company more than she liked. It was necessary to make this circumstance a matter of pleasure, because on such occasions it is the etiquette; but no one was less likely than Mrs. Bennet to find comfort in staying at home at any period of her life. She concluded with many good wishes that Lady Lucas might soon be equally fortunate, though evidently and triumphantly believing there was no chance of it.

In vain did Elizabeth endeavour to check the rapidity of her mother's words, or persuade her to describe her felicity in a less audible whisper; for to her inexpressible vexation she could perceive that the chief of it was overheard by Mr. Darcy, who sat opposite to them. Her mother only scolded her for being nonsensical.

'What is Mr. Darcy to me, pray, that I should be afraid of him? I am sure we owe him no such particular civility as to be obliged to say nothing *he* may not like to hear.'

'For heaven's sake, madam, speak lower. What advantage can it be to you to offend Mr. Darcy? You will never recommend yourself to his friend by so doing.'

Nothing that she could say, however, had any influence. Her mother would talk of her views in the same intelligible tone. Elizabeth blushed and blushed again with shame and vexation. She could not help frequently glancing her eye at Mr. Darcy, though every glance convinced her of what she dreaded; for though he was not always looking at her mother, she was convinced that his attention was invariably fixed by her. The expression of his face changed gradually from indignant contempt to a composed and steady gravity.

At length, however, Mrs. Bennet had no more to say; and Lady Lucas, who had been long yawning at the repetition of delights which she saw no likelihood of sharing, was left to the comforts of cold ham and chicken. Elizabeth now began to revive. But not long was the interval of tranquillity; for when supper was over, singing was talked of, and she had the mortification of seeing Mary, after very little entreaty, preparing to oblige the company. By many significant looks and silent entreaties did she endeavour to prevent such a proof of complaisance,—but in vain; Mary would not understand them; such an opportunity of exhibiting was delightful to her, and she began her song. Elizabeth's eyes were fixed on her, with most painful sensations; and she watched her progress through the several stanzas with an impatience which was very ill rewarded at their close; for Mary, on receiving amongst the thanks of the table the hint of a hope that she might be prevailed on to favour them again, after the pause of half a minute, began another. Mary's powers were by no means fitted for such a display; her voice was weak, and her manner affected. Elizabeth was in agonies. She looked at Jane to see how she bore it; but Jane was very composedly talking to Bingley. She looked at his two sisters, and saw them making signs of derision at each other, and at Darcy, who continued, however, impenetrably grave. She looked at her father to entreat his interference, lest Mary should be singing all night. He took the hint, and, when Mary had finished her second song, said aloud,—

'That will do extremely well, child. You have delighted us long enough. Let the other young ladies have time to exhibit.'

Mary, though pretending not to hear, was somewhat disconcerted; and Elizabeth, sorry for her, and sorry for her father's speech, was afraid her anxiety had done no good. Others of the party were now applied to.

'If I,' said Mr. Collins, 'were so fortunate as to be able to sing, I should have great pleasure, I am sure, in obliging the company with an air; for I consider music as a very innocent diversion, and perfectly compatible with the profession of a clergyman. I do not mean, however, to assert that we can be justified in devoting too much of our time to music, for there are certainly other things to be attended to. The rector of a parish has much to do. In the first place, he must make such an agreement for tithes as may be beneficial to himself and not offensive to his patron. He must write his own sermons; and the time that remains will not be too much for his parish duties, and the care and improvement of his dwelling, which he cannot be excused from making as comfortable as possible. And I do not think it of light importance that he should have attentive and conciliatory manners towards everybody, especially towards those to whom he owes his preferment. I cannot acquit him of that duty; nor could I think well of the man who should omit an occasion of testifying his respect towards anybody connected with the family.' And with a bow to Mr. Darcy, he concluded his speech, which had been spoken so loud as to be heard by half the room. Many stared—many smiled; but no one looked more amused than Mr. Bennet himself, while his wife seriously commended Mr. Collins for having spoken so sensibly, and observed, in a half-whisper to Lady Lucas, that he was a remarkably clever, good kind of young man.

To Elizabeth it appeared, that had her family made an agreement to expose themselves as much as they could during the evening, it would have been impossible for them to play their parts with more spirit, or finer success; and happy did she think it for Bingley and her sister that some of the exhibition had escaped his notice, and that his feelings were not of a sort to be much distressed by the folly which he must have witnessed. That his two sisters and Mr. Darcy, however, should have such an opportunity of ridiculing her relations was bad enough; and she could not determine whether the silent contempt of the gentleman, or the insolent smiles of the ladies, were more intolerable.

The rest of the evening brought her little amusement. She was teased by Mr. Collins, who continued most perseveringly by her side; and though he could not prevail with her to dance with him again, put it out of her power to dance with

others. In vain did she entreat him to stand up with somebody else, and offered to introduce him to any young lady in
the room. He assured her that, as to dancing, he was
perfectly indifferent to it; that his chief object was, by delicate attentions, to recommend himself to her; and that he
should therefore make a point of remaining close to her the
whole evening. There was no arguing upon such a project.
She owed her greatest relief to her friend Miss Lucas, who
often joined them, and good-naturedly engaged Mr. Collins's
conversation to herself.

She was at least free from the offence of Mr. Darcy's
further notice: though often standing within a very short
distance of her, quite disengaged, he never came near enough
to speak. She felt it to be the probable consequence of her
allusions to Mr. Wickham, and rejoiced in it.

The Longbourn party were the last of all the company to
depart; and by a manœuvre of Mrs. Bennet had to wait for
their carriage a quarter of an hour after everybody else was
gone, which gave them time to see how heartily they were
wished away by some of the family. Mrs. Hurst and her
sister scarcely opened their mouths except to complain of
fatigue, and were evidently impatient to have the house to
themselves. They repulsed every attempt of Mrs. Bennet at
conversation, and, by so doing, threw a languor over the
whole party, which was very little relieved by the long
speeches of Mr. Collins, who was complimenting Mr. Bingley
and his sisters on the elegance of their entertainment, and the
hospitality and politeness which had marked their behaviour
to their guests. Darcy said nothing at all. Mr. Bennet, in
equal silence, was enjoying the scene. Mr. Bingley and Jane
were standing together a little detached from the rest, and
talked only to each other. Elizabeth preserved as steady a
silence as either Mrs. Hurst or Miss Bingley; and even Lydia
was too much fatigued to utter more than the occasional exclamation of 'Lord, how tired I am!' accompanied by a
violent yawn.

When at length they arose to take leave, Mrs. Bennet was
most pressingly civil in her hope of seeing the whole family
soon at Longbourn; and addressed herself particularly to Mr.
Bingley, to assure him how happy he would make them by

eating a family dinner with them at any time, without the ceremony of a formal invitation. Bingley was all grateful pleasure; and he readily engaged for taking the earliest opportunity of waiting on her, after his return from London, whither he was obliged to go the next day for a short time.

Mrs. Bennet was perfectly satisfied; and quitted the house under the delightful persuasion that, allowing for the necessary preparations of settlements, new carriages, and wedding clothes, she should undoubtedly see her daughter settled at Netherfield in the course of three or four months. Of having another daughter married to Mr. Collins she thought with equal certainty, and with considerable, though not equal, pleasure. Elizabeth was the least dear to her of all her children; and though the man and the match were quite good enough for *her*, the worth of each was eclipsed by Mr. Bingley and Netherfield.

CHAPTER XIX

THE next day opened a new scene at Longbourn. Mr. Collins made his declaration in form. Having resolved to do it without loss of time, as his leave of absence extended only to the following Saturday, and having no feelings of diffidence to make it distressing to himself even at the moment, he set about it in a very orderly manner, with all the observances which he supposed a regular part of the business. On finding Mrs. Bennet, Elizabeth, and one of the younger girls together, soon after breakfast, he addressed the mother in these words,—

'May I hope, madam, for your interest with your fair daughter Elizabeth, when I solicit for the honour of a private audience with her in the course of this morning?'

Before Elizabeth had time for anything but a blush of surprise, Mrs. Bennet instantly answered,—

'Oh dear! Yes, certainly. I am sure Lizzy will be very happy—I am sure she can have no objection. Come, Kitty, I want you upstairs.' And gathering her work together, she was hastening away, when Elizabeth called out,—

'Dear ma'am, do not go. I beg you will not go. Mr. Collins must excuse me. He can have nothing to say to me that anybody need not hear. I am going away myself.'

'No, no, nonsense, Lizzy. I desire you will stay where you are.' And upon Elizabeth's seeming really, with vexed and embarrassed looks, about to escape, she added, 'Lizzy, I *insist* upon your staying and hearing Mr. Collins.'

Elizabeth would not oppose such an injunction; and a moment's consideration making her also sensible that it would be wisest to get it over as soon and as quietly as possible, she sat down again, and tried to conceal, by incessant employment, the feelings which were divided between distress and diversion. Mrs. Bennet and Kitty walked off, and as soon as they were gone, Mr. Collins began,—

'Believe me, my dear Miss Elizabeth, that your modesty,

so far from doing you any dis-service, rather adds to your other perfections. You would have been less amiable in my eyes had there *not* been this little unwillingness; but allow me to assure you that I have your respected mother's permission for this address. You can hardly doubt the purport of my discourse, however your natural delicacy may lead you to dissemble; my attentions have been too marked to be mistaken. Almost as soon as I entered the house I singled you out as the companion of my future life. But before I am run away with by my feelings on this subject, perhaps it will be advisable for me to state my reasons for marrying—and, moreover, for coming into Hertfordshire with the design of selecting a wife, as I certainly did.'

The idea of Mr. Collins, with all his solemn composure, being run away with by his feelings, made Elizabeth so near laughing that she could not use the short pause he allowed in any attempt to stop him farther, and he continued,—

'My reasons for marrying are, first, that I think it a right thing for every clergyman in easy circumstances (like myself) to set the example of matrimony in his parish; secondly, that I am convinced it will add very greatly to my happiness; and, thirdly, which perhaps I ought to have mentioned earlier, that it is the particular advice and recommendation of the very noble lady whom I have the honour of calling patroness. Twice has she condescended to give me her opinion (unasked too!) on this subject; and it was but the very Saturday night before I left Hunsford,—between our pools at quadrille, while Mrs. Jenkinson was arranging Miss De Bourgh's footstool,—that she said, "Mr. Collins, you must marry. A clergyman like you must marry. Choose properly, choose a gentlewoman for *my* sake, and for your *own;* let her be an active, useful sort of person, not brought up high, but able to make a small income go a good way. This is my advice. Find such a woman as soon as you can, bring her to Hunsford, and I will visit her." Allow me, by the way, to observe, my fair cousin, that I do not reckon the notice and kindness of Lady Catherine de Bourgh as among the least of the advantages in my power to offer. You will find her manners beyond anything I can describe; and your wit and vivacity, I think, must be acceptable to her, especially when tempered with the silence and respect which her rank will inevitably excite. Thus much for my general intention in favour of matrimony; it remains to be told why my views were directed to Longbourn instead of my own neighbourhood, where I assure you there are many amiable young women. But the fact is, that being, as I am, to inherit this estate after the death of your honoured father (who, however, may live many years longer), I could not satisfy myself without resolving to choose a wife from among his daughters, that the loss to them might be as little as possible when the melancholy event takes place which, however, as I have already said, may not be for several years. This has been my motive, my fair cousin, and I flatter myself it will not sink me in your esteem. And now nothing remains for me but to assure you in the most animated language of the violence of my affection. To fortune I am perfectly indifferent, and shall make no demand of that nature on your father, since I am well aware that it could not be complied with; and that one thousand pounds in the four per cents, which will not be yours till after your mother's decease, is all that you may ever be entitled to. On that head, therefore, I shall be uniformly silent: and you may assure yourself that no ungenerous reproach shall ever pass my lips when we are married.'

It was absolutely necessary to interrupt him now.

'You are too hasty, sir,' she cried. 'You forget that I have made no answer. Let me do it without further loss of time. Accept my thanks for the compliment you are paying me. I am very sensible of the honour of your proposals, but it is impossible for me to do otherwise than decline them.'

'I am not now to learn,' replied Mr. Collins, with a formal wave of the hand, 'that it is usual with young ladies to reject the addresses of the man whom they secretly mean to accept, when he first applies for their favour; and that sometimes the refusal is repeated a second or even a third time. I am, therefore, by no means discouraged by what you have just said, and shall hope to lead you to the altar ere long.'

'Upon my word, sir,' cried Elizabeth, 'your hope is rather an extraordinary one after my declaration. I do assure you that I am not one of those young ladies (if such young ladies there are) who are so daring as to risk their happiness on the chance of being asked a second time. I am perfectly serious in my refusal. You could not make *me* happy, and I am convinced that I am the last woman in the world who would make *you* so. Nay, were your friend Lady Catherine to know me, I am persuaded she would find me in every respect ill qualified for the situation.'

'Were it certain that Lady Catherine would think so,' said Mr. Collins, very gravely—'but I cannot imagine that her Ladyship would at all disapprove of you. And you may be certain that when I have the honour of seeing her again I shall speak in the highest terms of your modesty, economy, and other amiable qualifications.'

'Indeed, Mr. Collins, all praise of me will be unnecessary. You must give me leave to judge for myself, and pay me the compliment of believing what I say. I wish you very happy and very rich, and by refusing your hand, do all in my power to prevent your being otherwise. In making me the offer, you must have satisfied the delicacy of your feelings with regard to my family, and may take possession of Longbourn estate whenever it falls, without any self-reproach. This matter may be considered, therefore, as finally settled.' And rising as she thus spoke, she would have quitted the room, had not Mr. Collins thus addressed her, —

'When I do myself the honour of speaking to you next on the subject, I shall hope to receive a more favourable answer than you have now given me; though I am far from accusing you of cruelty at present, because I know it to be the established custom of your sex to reject a man on the first application, and, perhaps, you have even now said as much to encourage my suit as would be consistent with the true delicacy of the female character.'

'Really, Mr. Collins,' cried Elizabeth, with some warmth, 'you puzzle me exceedingly. If what I have hitherto said can appear to you in the form of encouragement, I know not how to express my refusal in such a way as may convince you of its being one.'

'You must give me leave to flatter myself, my dear cousin, that your refusal of my addresses are merely words of course.

My reasons for believing it are briefly these:—It does not appear to me that my hand is unworthy your acceptance, or that the establishment I can offer would be any other than highly desirable. My situation in life, my connections with the family of De Bourgh, and my relationship to your own, are circumstances highly in my favour; and you should take it into further consideration that, in spite of your manifold attractions, it is by no means certain that another offer of marriage may ever be made you. Your portion is unhappily so small, that it will in all likelihood undo the effects of your loveliness and amiable qualifications. As I must, therefore, conclude that you are not serious in your rejection of me, I shall choose to attribute it to your wish of increasing my love by suspense, according to the usual practice of elegant females.'

'I do assure you, sir, that I have no pretensions whatever to that kind of elegance which consists in tormenting a respectable man. I would rather be paid the compliment of being believed sincere. I thank you again and again for the honour you have done me in your proposals, but to accept them is absolutely impossible. My feelings in every respect forbid it. Can I speak plainer? Do not consider me now as an elegant female intending to plague you, but as a rational creature speaking the truth from her heart.'

'You are uniformly charming!' cried he, with an air of awkward gallantry; 'and I am persuaded that, when sanctioned by the express authority of both your excellent parents, my proposals will not fail of being acceptable.'

To such perseverance in wilful self-deception Elizabeth would make no reply, and immediately and in silence withdrew; determined, that if he persisted in considering her repeated refusals as flattering encouragement, to apply to her father, whose negative might be uttered in such a manner as must be decisive, and whose behaviour at least could not be mistaken for the affectation and coquetry of an elegant female.

CHAPTER XX

M R. COLLINS was not left long to the silent contemplation of his successful love; for Mrs. Bennet, having dawdled about in the vestibule to watch for the end of the conference, no sooner saw Elizabeth open the door and with quick step pass her towards the staircase, than she entered the breakfast-room, and congratulated both him and herself in warm terms on the happy prospect of their nearer connection. Mr. Collins received and returned these felicitations with equal pleasure, and then proceeded to relate the particulars of their interview, with the result of which he trusted he had every reason to be satisfied, since the refusal which his cousin had steadfastly given him would naturally flow from her bashful modesty and the genuine delicacy of her character.

This information, however, startled Mrs. Bennet; she would have been glad to be equally satisfied that her daughter had meant to encourage him by protesting against his proposals, but she dared not to believe it, and could not help saying so.

'But depend upon it, Mr. Collins,' she added, 'that Lizzy shall be brought to reason. I will speak to her about it myself directly. She is a very headstrong, foolish girl, and does not know her own interest; but I will *make* her know it.'

'Pardon me for interrupting you, madam,' cried Mr. Collins; 'but if she is really headstrong and foolish, I know not whether she would altogether be a very desirable wife to a man in my situation, who naturally looks for happiness in the marriage state. If, therefore, she actually persists in rejecting my suit, perhaps it were better not to force her into accepting me, because, if liable to such defects of temper, she could not contribute much to my felicity.'

'Sir, you quite misunderstand me,' said Mrs. Bennet, alarmed. 'Lizzy is only headstrong in such matters as these. In everything else she is as good-natured a girl as ever lived.

I will go directly to Mr. Bennet, and we shall very soon settle it with her, I am sure.'

She would not give him time to reply, but hurrying instantly to her husband, called out, as she entered the library,—

'Oh, Mr. Bennet, you are wanted immediately; we are all in an uproar. You must come and make Lizzy marry Mr. Collins, for she vows she will not have him; and if you do not make haste he will change his mind and not have *her*.'

Mr. Bennet raised his eyes from his book as she entered, and fixed them on her face with a calm unconcern, which was not in the least altered by her communication.

'I have not the pleasure of understanding you,' said he, when she had finished her speech. 'Of what are you talking?'

'Of Mr. Collins and Lizzy. Lizzy declares she will not have Mr. Collins, and Mr. Collins begins to say that he will not have Lizzy.'

'And what am I to do on the occasion? It seems a hopeless business.'

'Speak to Lizzy about it yourself. Tell her that you insist upon her marrying him.'

'Let her be called down. She shall hear my opinion.'

Mrs. Bennet rang the bell, and Miss Elizabeth was summoned to the library.

'Come here, child,' cried her father as she appeared. 'I have sent for you on an affair of importance. I understand that Mr. Collins has made yon an offer of marriage. Is it true?' Elizabeth replied that it was. 'Very well— and this offer of marriage you have refused?'

'I have, sir.'

'Very well. We now come to the point. Your mother insists upon your accepting it. Is it not so, Mrs. Bennet?'

'Yes, or I will never see her again.'

'An unhappy alternative is before you, Elizabeth. From this day you must be a stranger to one of your parents. Your mother will never see you again if you do *not* marry Mr. Collins, and I will never see you again if you *do*.'

Elizabeth could not but smile at such a conclusion of such a beginning; but Mrs. Bennet, who had persuaded herself

that her husband regarded the affair as she wished, was excessively disappointed.

'What do you mean, Mr. Bennet, by talking in this way?
You promised me to *insist* upon her marrying him.'

'My dear,' replied her husband, 'I have two small favours
to request. First, that you will allow me the free use of my
understanding on the present occasion; and, secondly, of my
room. I shall be glad to have the library to myself as soon
as may be.'

Not yet, however, in spite of her disappointment in her
husband, did Mrs. Bennet give up the point. She talked to
Elizabeth again and again; coaxed and threatened her by
turns. She endeavoured to secure Jane in her interest, but
Jane, with all possible mildness, declined interfering; and
Elizabeth, sometimes with real earnestness and sometimes
with playful gaiety, replied to her attacks. Though her
manner varied, however, her determination never did.

Mr. Collins, meanwhile, was meditating in solitude on
what had passed. He thought too well of himself to comprehend on what motive his cousin could refuse him; and though
his pride was hurt, he suffered in no other way. His regard
for her was quite imaginary; and the possibility of her
deserving her mother's reproach prevented his feeling any
regret.

While the family were in this confusion, Charlotte Lucas
came to spend the day with them. She was met in the
vestibule by Lydia, who, flying to her, cried in a half-whisper,
'I am glad you are come, for there is such fun here! What
do you think has happened this morning? Mr. Collins has
made an offer to Lizzy, and she will not have him.'

Charlotte had hardly time to answer before they were
joined by Kitty, who came to tell the same news; and no
sooner had they entered the breakfast-room, where Mrs.
Bennet was alone, than she likewise began on the subject,
calling on Miss Lucas for her compassion, and entreating
her to persuade her friend Lizzy to comply with the wishes
of all her family. 'Pray do, my dear Miss Lucas,' she
added, in a melancholy tone; 'for nobody is on my side,
nobody takes part with me; I am cruelly used, nobody feels
for my poor nerves.'

Charlotte's reply was spared by the entrance of Jane and Elizabeth.

'Ay, there she comes,' continued Mrs. Bennet, 'looking as unconcerned as may be, and caring no more for us than if we were at York, provided she can have her own way. But I tell you what, Miss Lizzy, if you take it into your head to go on refusing every offer of marriage in this way, you will never get a husband at all—and I am sure I do not know who is to maintain you when your father is dead. *I* shall not be able to keep you—and so I warn you. I have done with you from this very day. I told you in the library, you know, that I should never speak to you again, and you will find me as good as my word. I have no pleasure in talking to undutiful children. Not that I have much pleasure, indeed, in talking to anybody. People who suffer as I do from nervous complaints can have no great inclination for talking. Nobody can tell what I suffer! But it is always so. Those who do not complain are never pitied.'

Her daughters listened in silence to this effusion, sensible that any attempt to reason with or soothe her would only increase the irritation. She talked on, therefore, without interruption from any of them till they were joined by Mr. Collins, who entered with an air more stately than usual, and on perceiving whom, she said to the girls,—

'Now, I do insist upon it, that you, all of you, hold your tongues, and let Mr. Collins and me have a little conversation together.'

Elizabeth passed quietly out of the room, Jane and Kitty followed, but Lydia stood her ground, determined to hear all she could; and Charlotte, detained first by the civility of Mr. Collins, whose inquiries after herself and all her family were very minute, and then by a little curiosity, satisfied herself with walking to the window and pretending not to hear. In a doleful voice Mrs. Bennet thus began the projected conversation:—'Oh, Mr. Collins.'

'My dear madam,' replied he, 'let us be for ever silent on this point. Far be it from me,' he presently continued, in a voice that marked his displeasure, 'to resent the behaviour of your daughter. Resignation to inevitable evils is the duty of us all: the peculiar duty of a young man who has been so fortunate as I have been, in early preferment; and, I trust, I am resigned. Perhaps not the less so from feeling a doubt of my positive happiness had my fair cousin honoured me with her hand; for I have often observed that resignation is never so perfect as when the blessing denied begins to lose somewhat of its value in our estimation. You will not, I hope, consider me as showing any disrespect to your family, my dear madam, by thus withdrawing my pretensions to your daughter's favour, without having paid yourself and Mr. Bennet the compliment of requesting you to interpose your authority in my behalf. My conduct may, I fear, be objectionable in having accepted my dismission from your daughter's lips instead of your own; but we are all liable to error. I have certainly meant well through the whole affair. My object has been to secure an amiable companion for myself, with due consideration for the advantage of all your family; and if my *manner* has been at all reprehensible, I here beg leave to apologise.'

CHAPTER XXI

THE discussion of Mr. Collins's offer was now nearly at an end, and Elizabeth had only to suffer from the uncomfortable feelings necessarily attending it, and occasionally from some peevish allusion of her mother. As for the gentleman himself, *his* feelings were chiefly expressed, not by embarrassment or dejection, or by trying to avoid her, but by stiffness of manner and resentful silence. He scarcely ever spoke to her; and the assiduous attentions which he had been so sensible of himself were transferred for the rest of the day to Miss Lucas, whose civility in listening to him was a seasonable relief to them all, and especially to her friend.

The morrow produced no abatement of Mrs. Bennet's ill-humour or ill-health. Mr. Collins was also in the same state of angry pride. Elizabeth had hoped that his resentment might shorten his visit, but his plan did not appear in the least affected by it. He was always to have gone on Saturday, and to Saturday he still meant to stay.

After breakfast the girls walked to Meryton, to inquire if Mr. Wickham were returned, and to lament over his absence from the Netherfield ball. He joined them on their entering the town, and attended them to their aunt's, where his regret and vexation and the concern of everybody were well talked over. To Elizabeth, however, he voluntarily acknowledged that the necessity of his absence *had* been self-imposed.

'I found,' said he, 'as the time drew near, that I had better not meet Mr. Darcy;—that to be in the same room, the same party with him for so many hours together, might be more than I could bear, and that scenes might arise unpleasant to more than myself.'

She highly approved his forbearance; and they had leisure for a full discussion of it, and for all the commendations which they civilly bestowed on each other, as Wickham and another officer walked back with them to Longbourn, and during the walk he particularly attended to her. His accompanying them was a double advantage: she felt all the compliment it offered to herself; and it was most acceptable as an occasion of introducing him to her father and mother.

Soon after their return a letter was delivered to Miss Bennet; it came from Netherfield, and was opened immediately. The envelope contained a sheet of elegant, little, hot-pressed paper, well covered with a lady's fair, flowing hand; and Elizabeth saw her sister's countenance change as she read it, and saw her dwelling intently on some particular passages. Jane recollected herself soon; and putting the letter away, tried to join, with her usual cheerfulness, in the general conversation: but Elizabeth felt an anxiety on the subject which drew off her attention even from Wickham; and no sooner had he and his companion taken leave than a glance from Jane invited her to follow her upstairs. When they had gained their own room, Jane, taking out her letter, said, 'This is from Caroline Bingley: what it contains has surprised me a good deal. The whole party have left Netherfield by this time, and are on their way to town, and without any intention of coming back again. You shall hear what she says.'

She then read the first sentence aloud, which comprised the information of their having just resolved to follow their brother to town directly, and of their meaning to dine that day in Grosvenor Street, where Mr. Hurst had a house. The next was in these words:—'I do not pretend to regret anything I shall leave in Hertfordshire except your society, my dearest friend; but we will hope, at some future period, to enjoy many returns of that delightful intercourse we have known, and in the meanwhile may lessen the pain of separation by a very frequent and most unreserved correspondence. I depend on you for that.' To these high-flown expressions Elizabeth listened with all the insensibility of distrust; and though the suddenness of their removal surprised her, she saw nothing in it really to lament: it was not to be supposed that their absence from Netherfield would prevent Mr. Bingley's being there; and as to the loss of their society, she was persuaded that Jane must soon cease to regard it in the enjoyment of his.

'It is unlucky,' said she, after a short pause, 'that you should not be able to see your friends before they leave the country. But may we not hope that the period of future happiness, to which Miss Bingley looks forward, may arrive earlier than she is aware, and that the delightful intercourse you have known as friends will be renewed with yet greater satisfaction as sisters? Mr. Bingley will not be detained in London by them.'

'Caroline decidedly says that none of the party will return into Hertfordshire this winter. I will read it to you.'

' "When my brother left us yesterday, he imagined that the business which took him to London might be concluded in three or four days; but as we are certain it cannot be so, and at the same time convinced that when Charles gets to town he will be in no hurry to leave it again, we have determined on following him thither, that he may not be obliged to spend his vacant hours in a comfortless hotel. Many of my acquaintance are already there for the winter: I wish I could hear that you, my dearest friend, had any intention of making one in the crowd, but of that I despair. I sincerely hope your Christmas in Hertfordshire may abound in the gaieties which that season generally brings, and that your beaux will be so numerous as to prevent your feeling the loss of the three of whom we shall deprive you." '

'It is evident by this,' added Jane, 'that he comes back no more this winter.'

'It is only evident that Miss Bingley does not mean he *should.*'

'Why will you think so? It must be his own doing; he is his own master. But you do not know *all.* I *will* read you the passage which particularly hurts me. I will have no reserves from *you.* "Mr. Darcy is impatient to see his sister; and to confess the truth, *we* are scarcely less eager to meet her again. I really do not think Georgiana Darcy has her equal for beauty, elegance, and accomplishments; and the affection she inspires in Louisa and myself is heightened into something still more interesting from the hope we dare to entertain of her being hereafter our sister. I do not know whether I ever before mentioned to you my feelings on this subject, but I will not leave the country without confiding them, and I trust you will not esteem them unreasonable. My brother admires her greatly already; he will have frequent opportunity now of seeing her on the most intimate footing; her relations all wish the connection as much as his own; and a sister's partiality is not misleading me, I think, when I call Charles most capable of engaging any woman's heart. With all these circumstances to favour an attachment, and nothing to prevent it, am I wrong, my dearest Jane, in indulging the hope of an event which will secure the happiness of so many?" What think you of *this* sentence, my dear Lizzy?' said Jane, as she finished it. 'Is it not clear enough? Does it not expressly declare that Caroline neither expects nor wishes me to be her sister; that she is perfectly convinced of her brother's indifference; and that, if she suspects the nature of my feelings for him, she means (most kindly!) to put me on my guard. Can there be any other opinion on the subject?'

'Yes, there can; for mine is totally different. Will you hear it?'

'Most willingly.'

'You shall have it in a few words. Miss Bingley sees that her brother is in love with you, and wants him to marry Miss Darcy. She follows him to town in the hope of keeping him there, and tries to persuade you that he does not care about you.'

Jane shook her head.

'Indeed, Jane, you ought to believe me. No one who has ever seen you together can doubt his affection; Miss Bingley, I am sure, cannot: she is not such a simpleton. Could she have seen half as much love in Mr. Darcy for herself, she would have ordered her wedding clothes. But the case is this:—we are not rich enough or grand enough for them; and she is the more anxious to get Miss Darcy for her brother, from the notion that when there has been *one* intermarriage, she may have less trouble in achieving a second; in which there is certainly some ingenuity, and I daresay it would succeed if Miss De Bourgh were out of the way. But, my dearest Jane, you cannot seriously imagine that, because Miss Bingley tells you her brother greatly admires Miss Darcy, he is in the smallest degree less sensible of *your* merit than when he took leave of you on Tuesday; or that it will be in her power to persuade him that, instead of being in love with you, he is very much in love with her friend.'

'If we thought alike of Miss Bingley,' replied Jane, 'your representation of all this might make me quite easy. But I know the foundation is unjust. Caroline is incapable of wilfully deceiving any one; and all that I can hope in this case is, that she is deceived herself.'

'That is right. You could not have started a more happy idea, since you will not take comfort in mine: believe her to be deceived, by all means. You have now done your duty by her, and must fret no longer.'

'But, my dear sister, can I be happy, even supposing the best, in accepting a man whose sisters and friends are all wishing him to marry elsewhere?'

'You must decide for yourself,' said Elizabeth; 'and if, upon mature deliberation, you find that the misery of dis-obliging his two sisters is more than equivalent to the hap-piness of being his wife, I advise you, by all means, to refuse him.'

'How can you talk so?' said Jane, faintly smiling; 'you must know that, though I should be exceedingly grieved at their disapprobation, I could not hesitate.'

'I do not think you would; and that being the case, I can-not consider your situation with much compassion.'

'But if he returns no more this winter, my choice will never be required. A thousand things may arise in six months.'

The idea of his returning no more Elizabeth treated with the utmost contempt. It appeared to her merely the sug-gestion of Caroline's interested wishes; and she could not for a moment suppose that those wishes, however openly or art-fully spoken, could influence a young man so totally inde-pendent of every one.

She represented to her sister, as forcibly as possible, what she felt on the subject, and had soon the pleasure of seeing its happy effect. Jane's temper was not desponding; and she was gradually led to hope, though the diffidence of affec-tion sometimes overcame the hope, that Bingley would return to Netherfield, and answer every wish of her heart.

They agreed that Mrs. Bennet should only hear of the departure of the family, without being alarmed on the score of the gentleman's conduct; but even this partial communication gave her a great deal of concern, and she bewailed it as exceedingly unlucky that the ladies should happen to go away just as they were all getting so intimate together. After lamenting it, however, at some length, she had the consolation of thinking that Mr. Bingley would be soon down again, and soon dining at Longbourn; and the conclusion of all was the comfortable declaration, that, though he had been invited only to a family dinner, she would take care to have two full courses.

CHAPTER XXII

THE Bennets were engaged to dine with the Lucases; and again, during the chief of the day, was Miss Lucas so kind as to listen to Mr. Collins. Elizabeth took an opportunity of thanking her. 'It keeps him in good humour,' said she, 'and I am more obliged to you than I can express.' Charlotte assured her friend of her satisfaction in being useful, and that it amply repaid her for the little sacrifice of her time. This was very amiable; but Charlotte's kindness extended farther than Elizabeth had any conception of:— its object was nothing less than to secure her from any return of Mr. Collins's addresses, by engaging them towards herself. Such was Miss Lucas's scheme; and appearances were so favourable, that when they parted at night, she would have felt almost sure of success if he had not been to leave Hertfordshire so very soon. But here she did injustice to the fire and independence of his character; for it led him to escape out of Longbourn House the next morning with admirable slyness, and hasten to Lucas Lodge to throw himself at her feet. He was anxious to avoid the notice of his cousins, from a conviction that, if they saw him depart, they could not fail to conjecture his design, and he was not willing to have the attempt known till its success could be known likewise; for, though feeling almost secure, and with reason, for Charlotte had been tolerably encouraging, he was comparatively diffident since the adventure of Wednesday. His reception, however, was of the most flattering kind. Miss Lucas perceived him from an upper window as he walked towards the house, and instantly set out to meet him accidentally in the lane. But little had she dared to hope that so much love and eloquence awaited her there.

In as short a time as Mr. Collins's long speeches would allow, everything was settled between them to the satisfaction of both; and as they entered the house, he earnestly entreated her to name the day that was to make him the happiest of men; and though such a solicitation must be waived for the present, the lady felt no inclination to trifle with his happiness. The stupidity with which he was favoured by nature must guard his courtship from any charm that could make a woman wish for its continuance; and Miss Lucas, who accepted him solely from the pure and disinterested desire of an establishment, cared not how soon that establishment were gained.

Sir William and Lady Lucas were speedily applied to for their consent; and it was bestowed with a most joyful alacrity. Mr. Collins's present circumstances made it a most eligible match for their daughter, to whom they could give little fortune; and his prospects of future wealth were exceedingly fair. Lady Lucas began directly to calculate, with more interest than the matter had ever excited before, how many years longer Mr. Bennet was likely to live; and Sir William gave it as his decided opinion, that whenever Mr. Collins should be in possession of the Longbourn estate, it would be highly expedient that both he and his wife should make their appearance at St. James's. The whole family in short were properly overjoyed on the occasion. The younger girls formed hopes of *coming out* a year or two sooner than they might otherwise have done; and the boys were relieved from their apprehension of Charlotte's dying an old maid. Charlotte herself was tolerably composed. She had gained her point, and had time to consider of it. Her reflections were in general satisfactory. Mr. Collins, to be sure, was neither sensible nor agreeable; his society was irksome, and his attachment to her must be imaginary. But still he would be her husband. Without thinking highly either of men or of matrimony, marriage had always been her object: it was the only honourable provision for well-educated young women of small fortune, and, however uncertain of giving happiness, must be their pleasantest preservative from want. This preservative she had now obtained; and at the age of twenty-seven, without having ever been handsome, she felt all the good luck of it. The least agreeable circumstance in the business was the surprise it must occasion to Elizabeth Bennet, whose friendship she valued beyond that of any other person. Elizabeth would wonder, and probably would blame her; and though her resolution was not to be shaken, her feelings must be hurt by such a disapprobation. She resolved to give her the information herself; and therefore charged Mr. Collins, when he returned to Longbourn to dinner, to drop no hint of what had passed before any of the family. A promise of secrecy was of course very dutifully given, but it could not be kept without difficulty; for the curiosity excited by his long absence burst forth in such very direct questions on his return, as required some ingenuity to evade, and he was at the same time exercising great self-denial, for he was longing to publish his prosperous love.

As he was to begin his journey too early on the morrow to see any of the family, the ceremony of leave-taking was performed when the ladies moved for the night; and Mrs. Bennet, with great politeness and cordiality, said how happy they should be to see him at Longbourn again, whenever his other engagements might allow him to visit them.

'My dear madam,' he replied, 'this invitation is particularly gratifying, because it is what I have been hoping to receive; and you may be very certain that I shall avail myself of it as soon as possible.'

They were all astonished; and Mr. Bennet, who could by no means wish for so speedy a return, immediately said.—

'But is there not danger of Lady Catherine's disapprobation here, my good sir? You had better neglect your relations than run the risk of offending your patroness.'

'My dear sir,' replied Mr. Collins, 'I am particularly obliged to you for this friendly caution, and you may depend upon my not taking so material a step without her Ladyship's concurrence.'

'You cannot be too much on your guard. Risk anything rather than her displeasure; and if you find it likely to be raised by your coming to us again, which I should think exceedingly probable, stay quietly at home, and be satisfied that *we* shall take no offence.'

'Believe me, my dear sir, my gratitude is warmly excited by such affectionate attention; and, depend upon it, you will speedily receive from me a letter of thanks for this as well as for every other mark of your regard during my stay in Hertfordshire. As for my fair cousins, though my absence may not be long enough to render it necessary, I shall now take the liberty of wishing them health and happiness, not excepting my cousin Elizabeth.'

With proper civilities, the ladies then withdrew; all of them equally surprised to find that he meditated a quick return. Mrs. Bennet wished to understand by it that he thought of paying his addresses to one of her younger girls, and Mary might have been prevailed on to accept him. She rated his abilities much higher than any of the others: there was a solidity in his reflections which often struck her; and though by no means so clever as herself, she thought that, if encouraged to read and improve himself by such an example as hers, he might become a very agreeable companion. But on the following morning every hope of this kind was done away.

Miss Lucas called soon after breakfast, and in a private conference with Elizabeth related the event of the day before.

The possibility of Mr. Collins's fancying himself in love with her friend had once occurred to Elizabeth within the last day or two: but that Charlotte could encourage him seemed almost as far from possibility as that she could encourage him herself; and her astonishment was consequently so great as to overcome at first the bounds of decorum, and she could not help crying out,—

'Engaged to Mr. Collins! my dear Charlotte, impossible!'

The steady countenance which Miss Lucas had commanded in telling her story gave way to a momentary confusion here on receiving so direct a reproach; though, as it was no more than she expected, she soon regained her composure, and calmly replied,—

'Why should you be surprised, my dear Eliza? Do you think it incredible that Mr. Collins should be able to procure any woman's good opinion, because he was not so happy as to succeed with you?'

But Elizabeth had now recollected herself; and, making a strong effort for it, was able to assure her, with tolerable firmness, that the prospect of their relationship was highly grateful to her, and that she wished her all imaginable happiness.

'I see what you are feeling,' replied Charlotte: 'you must be surprised, very much surprised, so lately as Mr. Collins was wishing to marry you. But when you have had time to think it all over, I hope you will be satisfied with what I have done. I am not romantic, you know. I never was. I ask only a comfortable home; and, considering Mr. Collins's character, connections, and situation in life, I am convinced that my chance of happiness with him is as fair as most people can boast on entering the marriage state.'

Elizabeth quietly answered 'undoubtedly'; and, after an awkward pause, they returned to the rest of the family. Charlotte did not stay much longer; and Elizabeth was then left to reflect on what she had heard. It was a long time before she became at all reconciled to the idea of so unsuitable a match. The strangeness of Mr. Collins's making two offers of marriage within three days was nothing in comparison of his being now accepted. She had always felt that Charlotte's opinion of matrimony was not exactly like her own; but she could not have supposed it possible that, when called into action, she would have sacrificed every better feeling to worldly advantage. Charlotte, the wife of Mr. Collins, was a most humiliating picture! And to the pang of a friend disgracing herself, and sunk in her esteem, was added the distressing conviction that it was impossible for that friend to be tolerably happy in the lot she had chosen.

CHAPTER XXIII

ELIZABETH was sitting with her mother and sisters, reflecting on what she had heard, and doubting whether she was authorised to mention it, when Sir William Lucas himself appeared, sent by his daughter to announce her engagement to the family. With many compliments to them, and much self-gratulation on the prospect of a connection between the houses, he unfolded the matter, —to an audience not merely wondering, but incredulous; for Mrs. Bennet, with more perseverance than politeness, protested he must be entirely mistaken; and Lydia, always unguarded and often uncivil, boisterously exclaimed,—

'Good Lord! Sir William, how can you tell such a story? Do you not know that Mr. Collins wants to marry Lizzy?'

Nothing less than the complaisance of a courtier could have borne without anger such treatment: but Sir William's good-breeding carried him through it all; and though he begged leave to be positive as to the truth of his information, he listened to all their impertinence with the most forbearing courtesy.

Elizabeth, feeling it incumbent on her to relieve him from so unpleasant a situation, now put herself forward to confirm his account, by mentioning her prior knowledge of it from Charlotte herself; and endeavoured to put a stop to the exclamations of her mother and sisters, by the earnestness of her congratulations to Sir William, in which she was readily joined by Jane, and by making a variety of remarks on the happiness that might be expected from the match, the excellent character of Mr. Collins, and the convenient distance of Hunsford from London.

Mrs. Bennet was, in fact, too much overpowered to say a great deal while Sir William remained; but no sooner had he left them than her feelings found a rapid vent. In the first place, she persisted in disbelieving the whole of the matter; secondly, she was very sure that Mr. Collins had been taken in; thirdly, she trusted that they would never be happy together; and, fourthly, that the match might be broken off. Two inferences, however, were plainly deduced from the whole: one, that Elizabeth was the real cause of all the mischief; and the other, that she herself had been barbarously used by them all; and on these two points she principally dwelt during the rest of the day. Nothing could console and nothing appease her. Nor did that day wear out her resentment. A week elapsed before she could see Elizabeth without scolding her: a month passed away before she could speak to Sir William or Lady Lucas without being rude; and many months were gone before she could at all forgive their daughter.

Mr. Bennet's emotions were much more tranquil on the occasion, and such as he did experience he pronounced to be of a most agreeable sort; for it gratified him, he said, to dis-cover that Charlotte Lucas, whom he had been used to think tolerably sensible, was as foolish as his wife, and more foolish than his daughter!

Jane confessed herself a little surprised at the match: but she said less of her astonishment than of her earnest desire for their happiness; nor could Elizabeth persuade her to con-sider it as improbable. Kitty and Lydia were far from envy-ing Miss Lucas, for Mr. Collins was only a clergyman; and it affected them in no other way than as a piece of news to spread at Meryton.

Lady Lucas could not be insensible of triumph on being able to retort on Mrs. Bennet the comfort of having a daugh-ter well married; and she called at Longbourn rather oftener than usual to say how happy she was, though Mrs. Bennet's sour looks and ill-natured remarks might have been enough to drive happiness away.

Between Elizabeth and Charlotte there was a restraint which kept them mutually silent on the subject; and Elizabeth felt persuaded that no real confidence could ever subsist between them again. Her disappointment in Charlotte made her turn with fonder regard to her sister, of whose rectitude and delicacy she was sure her opinion could never be shaken, and for whose happiness she grew daily more anxious, as Bingley had now been gone a week, and nothing was heard of his return.

Jane had sent Caroline an early answer to her letter, and was counting the days till she might reasonably hope to hear again. The promised letter of thanks from Mr. Collins arrived on Tuesday, addressed to their father, and written with all the solemnity of gratitude which a twelvemonth's abode in the family might have prompted. After discharging his conscience on that head, he proceeded to inform them, with many rapturous expressions, of his happiness in having obtained the affection of their amiable neighbour, Miss Lucas, and then explained that it was merely with the view of enjoying her society that he had been so ready to close with their kind wish of seeing him again at Longbourn, whither he hoped to be able to return on Monday fortnight; for Lady Catherine, he added, so heartily approved his marriage, that she wished it to take place as soon as possible, which he trusted would be an unanswerable argument with his amiable Charlotte to name an early day for making him the happiest of men.

Mr. Collins's return into Hertfordshire was no longer a matter of pleasure to Mrs. Bennet. On the contrary, she was as much disposed to complain of it as her husband. It was very strange that he should come to Longbourn instead of to Lucas Lodge; it was also very inconvenient and exceedingly troublesome. She hated having visitors in the house while her health was so indifferent, and lovers were of all people the most disagreeable. Such were the gentle murmurs of Mrs. Bennet, and they gave way only to the greater distress of Mr. Bingley's continued absence.

Neither Jane nor Elizabeth was comfortable on this subject. Day after day passed away without bringing any other tidings of him than the report which shortly prevailed in Meryton of his coming no more to Netherfield the whole winter; a report which highly incensed Mrs. Bennet, and which she never failed to contradict as a most scandalous falsehood.

Even Elizabeth began to fear—not that Bingley was indifferent—but that his sisters would be successful in keeping him away. Unwilling as she was to admit an idea so destructive of Jane's happiness, and so dishonourable to the stability of her lover, she could not prevent its frequently recurring. The united efforts of his two unfeeling sisters, and of his overpowering friend, assisted by the attractions of Miss Darcy and the amusements of London, might be too much, she feared, for the strength of his attachment.

As for Jane, *her* anxiety under this suspense was, of course, more painful than Elizabeth's: but whatever she felt she was desirous of concealing; and between herself and Elizabeth, therefore, the subject was never alluded to. But as no such delicacy restrained her mother, an hour seldom passed in which she did not talk of Bingley, express her impatience for his arrival, or even require Jane to confess that if he did not come back she should think herself very ill used. It needed all Jane's steady mildness to bear these attacks with tolerable tranquillity.

Mr. Collins returned most punctually on the Monday fortnight, but his reception at Longbourn was not quite so gracious as it had been on his first introduction. He was too happy, however, to need much attention; and, luckily for the others, the business of love-making relieved them from a great deal of his company. The chief of every day was spent by him at Lucas Lodge, and he sometimes returned to Longbourn only in time to make an apology for his absence before the family went to bed.

Mrs. Bennet was really in a most pitiable state. The very mention of anything concerning the match threw her into an agony of ill-humour, and wherever she went she was sure of hearing it talked of. The sight of Miss Lucas was odious to her. As her successor in that house, she regarded her with jealous abhorrence.

Whenever Charlotte came to see them, she concluded her to be anticipating the hour of possession; and whenever she spoke in a low voice to Mr. Collins, was convinced that they were talking of the Longbourn estate, and resolving to turn herself and her daughters out of the house as soon as Mr. Bennet was dead. She complained bitterly of all this to her husband.

'Indeed, Mr. Bennet,' said she, 'it is very hard to think that Charlotte Lucas should ever be mistress of this house, that *I* should be forced to make way for *her,* and live to see her take my place in it!'

'My dear, do not give way to such gloomy thoughts. Let us hope for better things. Let us flatter ourselves that *I* may be the survivor.'

This was not very consoling to Mrs. Bennet; and, therefore, instead of making any answer, she went on as before.

'I cannot bear to think that they should have all this estate. If it was not for the entail, I should not mind it.'

'What should not you mind?'

'I should not mind anything at all.'

'Let us be thankful that you are preserved from a state of such insensibility.'

'I never can be thankful, Mr. Bennet, for anything about the entail. How any one could have the conscience to entail away an estate from one's own daughters I cannot understand; and all for the sake of Mr. Collins, too! Why should *he* have it more than anybody else?'

'I leave it to yourself to determine,' said Mr. Bennet.

CHAPTER XXIV

MISS BINGLEY'S letter arrived, and put an end to
doubt. The very first sentence conveyed the assurance of their being all settled in London for
the winter, and concluded with her brother's regret at not
having had time to pay his respects to his friends in Hertfordshire before he left the country.

Hope was over, entirely over; and when Jane could attend
to the rest of the letter, she found little, except the professed affection of the writer, that could give her any comfort. Miss Darcy's praise occupied the chief of it. Her
many attractions were again dwelt on; and Caroline boasted
joyfully of their increasing intimacy, and ventured to pre-
dict the accomplishment of the wishes which had been unfolded in her former letter. She wrote also with great
pleasure of her brother's being an intimate of Mr. Darcy's
house, and mentioned with raptures some plans of the latter with regard to new furniture.

Elizabeth, to whom Jane very soon communicated the chief
of all this, heard it in silent indignation. Her heart was
divided between concern for her sister and resentment against
all others. To Caroline's assertion of her brother's being
partial to Miss Darcy she paid no credit. That he was really
fond of Jane she doubted no more than she had ever done;
and much as she had always been disposed to like him, she
could not think without anger, hardly without contempt, on
the easiness of temper, that want of proper resolution, which
now made him the slave of his designing friends, and led him
to sacrifice his own happiness to the caprice of their inclinations. Had his own happiness, however, been the only sacrifice, he might have been allowed to sport with it in whatever
manner he thought best; but her sister's was involved in it,
as she thought he must be sensible himself. It was a subject,
in short, on which reflection would be long indulged, and
must be unavailing. She could think of nothing else; and

yet, whether Bingley's regard had really died away, or were suppressed by his friends' interference; whether he had been aware of Jane's attachment, or whether it had escaped his observation; whatever were the case, though her opinion of him must be materially affected by the difference, her sister's situation remained the same, her peace equally wounded.

A day or two passed before Jane had courage to speak of her feeling to Elizabeth; but at last, on Mrs. Bennet's leaving them together, after a longer irritation than usual about Netherfield and its master, she could not help saying,—

'Oh that my dear mother had more command over herself; she can have no idea of the pain she gives me by her continual reflections on him. But I will not repine. It cannot last long. He will be forgot, and we shall all be as we were before.'

Elizabeth looked at her sister with incredulous solicitude, but said nothing.

'You doubt me,' cried Jane, slightly colouring; 'indeed you have no reason. He may live in my memory as the most amiable man of my acquaintance, but that is all. I have nothing either to hope or fear, and nothing to reproach him with. Thank God I have not *that* pain. A little time, therefore—I shall certainly try to get the better——'

With a stronger voice she soon added, 'I have this comfort immediately, that it has not been more than an error of fancy on my side, and that it has done no harm to any one but myself.'

'My dear Jane,' exclaimed Elizabeth, 'you are too good. Your sweetness and disinterestedness are really angelic; I do not know what to say to you. I feel as if I had never done you justice, or loved you as you deserve.'

Miss Bennet eagerly disclaimed all extraordinary merit, and threw back the praise on her sister's warm affection.

'Nay,' said Elizabeth, 'this is not fair. *You* wish to think all the world respectable, and are hurt if I speak ill of anybody. *I* only want to think *you* perfect, and you set yourself against it. Do not be afraid of my running into any excess, of my encroaching on your privilege of universal goodwill. You need not. There are few people whom I really love, and still fewer of whom I think well. The more I see of the world, the more am I dissatisfied with it; and every day confirms my belief of the inconsistency of all human characters, and of the little dependence that can be placed on the appearance of either merit or sense. I have met with two instances lately: one I will not mention, the other is Charlotte's marriage. It is unaccountable! in every view it is unaccountable!'

'My dear Lizzy, do not give way to such feelings as these. They will ruin your happiness. You do not make allowance enough for difference of situation and temper. Consider Mr. Collins's respectability, and Charlotte's prudent, steady character. Remember that she is one of a large family; that as to fortune it is a most eligible match; and be ready to believe, for everybody's sake, that she may feel something like regard and esteem for our cousin.'

'To oblige you, I would try to believe almost anything, but no one else could be benefited by such a belief as this; for were I persuaded that Charlotte had any regard for him, I should only think worse of her understanding than I now do of her heart. My dear Jane, Mr. Collins is a conceited, pompous, narrow-minded, silly man: you know he is, as well as I do; and you must feel, as well as I do, that the woman who marries him cannot have a proper way of thinking. You shall not defend her, though it is Charlotte Lucas. You shall not, for the sake of one individual, change the meaning of principle and integrity, nor endeavour to persuade yourself or me that selfishness is prudence, and insensibility of danger security for happiness.'

'I must think your language too strong in speaking of both,' replied Jane; 'and I hope you will be convinced of it, by seeing them happy together. But enough of this. You alluded to something else. You mentioned *two* instances. I cannot misunderstand you, but I entreat you, dear Lizzy, not to pain me by thinking *that person* to blame, and saying your opinion of him is sunk. We must not be so ready to fancy ourselves intentionally injured. We must not expect a lively young man to be always so guarded and circumspect. It is very often nothing but our own vanity that deceives us. Women fancy admiration means more than it does.'

'And men take care that they should.'

'If it is designedly done, they cannot be justified; but I have no idea of there being so much design in the world as some persons imagine.'

'I am far from attributing any part of Mr. Bingley's conduct to design,' said Elizabeth; 'but, without scheming to do wrong, or to make others unhappy, there may be error and there may be misery. Thoughtlessness, want of attention to other people's feelings, and want of resolution, will do the business.'

'And do you impute it to either of those?'

'Yes; to the last. But if I go on I shall displease you by saying what I think of persons you esteem. Stop me whilst you can.'

'You persist, then, in supposing his sisters influence him.'

'Yes, in conjunction with his friend.'

'I cannot believe it. Why should they try to influence him? They can only wish his happiness; and if he is attached to me no other woman can secure it.'

'Your first position is false. They may wish many things besides his happiness: they may wish his increase of wealth and consequence; they may wish him to marry a girl who has all the importance of money, great connections, and pride."

'Beyond a doubt they do wish him to choose Miss Darcy,' replied Jane; 'but this may be from better feelings than you are supposing. They have known her much longer than they have known me; no wonder if they love her better. But, whatever may be their own wishes, it is very unlikely they should have opposed their brother's. What sister would think herself at liberty to do it, unless there were something very objectionable? If they believed him attached to me they would not try to part us; if he were so they could not succeed. By supposing such an affection, you make everybody acting unnaturally and wrong, and me most unhappy. Do not distress me by the idea. I am not ashamed of having been mistaken—or, at least it is slight, it is nothing in comparison of what I should feel in thinking ill of him or his sisters. Let me take it in the best light, in the light in which it may be understood.'

Elizabeth could not oppose such a wish; and from this time Mr. Bingley's name was scarcely ever mentioned between them.

Mrs. Bennet still continued to wonder and repine at his returning no more; and though a day seldom passed in which Elizabeth did not account for it clearly, there seemed little chance of her ever considering it with less perplexity. Her daughter endeavoured to convince her of what she did not believe herself, that his attentions to Jane had been merely the effect of a common and transient liking, which ceased when he saw her no more; but though the probability of the statement was admitted at the time, she had the same story to repeat every day. Mrs. Bennet's best comfort was, that Mr. Bingley must be down again in the summer.

Mr. Bennet treated the matter differently. 'So Lizzy,' said he, one day, 'your sister is crossed in love, I find. I congratulate her. Next to being married, a girl likes to be crossed in love a little now and then. It is something to think of, and gives her a sort of distinction among her companions. When is your turn to come? You will hardly bear to be long outdone by Jane. Now is your time. Here are officers enough at Meryton to disappoint all the young ladies in the country. Let Wickham be your man. He is a pleasant fellow, and would jilt you creditably.'

'Thank you, sir, but a less agreeable man would satisfy me. We must not all expect Jane's good fortune.'

'True,' said Mr. Bennet; 'but it is a comfort to think that, whatever of that kind may befall you, you have an affectionate mother who will always make the most of it.'

Mr. Wickham's society was of material service in dispelling the gloom which the late perverse occurrences had thrown on many of the Longbourn family. They saw him often, and to his other recommendations was now added that of general unreserve. The whole of what Elizabeth had already heard, his claims on Mr. Darcy, and all that he had suffered from him, was now openly acknowledged and publicly canvassed; and everybody was pleased to think how much they had always disliked Mr. Darcy before they had known anything of the matter.

Miss Bennet was the only creature who could suppose there might be any extenuating circumstances in the case unknown to the society of Hertfordshire: her mild and steady candour always pleaded for allowances, and urged the possibility of mistakes; but by everybody else Mr. Darcy was condemned as the worst of men.

CHAPTER XXV

AFTER a week spent in professions of love and schemes of felicity, Mr. Collins was called from his amiable Charlotte by the arrival of Saturday. The pain of separation, however, might be alleviated on his side by preparations for the reception of his bride, as he had reason to hope that, shortly after his next return into Hertfordshire, the day would be fixed that was to make him the happiest of men. He took leave of his relations at Longbourn with as much solemnity as before; wished his fair cousins health and happiness again, and promised their father another letter of thanks.

On the following Monday, Mrs. Bennet had the pleasure of receiving her brother and his wife, who came, as usual, to spend the Christmas at Longbourn. Mr. Gardiner was a sensible, gentlemanlike man, greatly superior to his sister, as well by nature as education. The Netherfield ladies would have had difficulty in believing that a man who lived by trade, and within view of his own warehouse, could have been so well bred and agreeable. Mrs. Gardiner, who was several years younger than Mrs. Bennet and Mrs. Philips, was an amiable, intelligent, elegant woman, and a great favourite with her Longbourn nieces. Between the two eldest and herself especially there subsisted a very particular regard. They had frequently been staying with her in town.

The first part of Mrs. Gardiner's business, on her arrival, was to distribute her presents and describe the newest fashions. When this was done, she had a less active part to play. It became her turn to listen. Mrs. Bennet had many grievances to relate, and much to complain of. They had all been very ill used since she last saw her sister. Two of her girls had been on the point of marriage, and after all there was nothing in it.

'I do not blame Jane,' she continued, 'for Jane would have got Mr. Bingley if she could. But, Lizzy! Oh, sister!

it is very hard to think that she might have been Mr. Collins's wife by this time, had not it been for her own perverseness. He made her an offer in this very room, and she refused him. The consequence of it is, that Lady Lucas will have a daughter married before I have, and that Longbourn estate is just as much entailed as ever. The Lucases are very artful people, indeed, sister. They are all for what they can get. I am sorry to say it of them, but it is. It makes me very nervous and poorly, to be thwarted so in my own family, and to have neighbours who think of themselves before anybody else. However, your coming just at this time is the greatest of comforts, and I am very glad to hear what you tell us of long sleeves.'

Mrs. Gardiner, to whom the chief of this news had been given before, in the course of Jane and Elizabeth's correspondence with her, made her sister a slight answer, and, in compassion to her nieces, turned the conversation.

When alone with Elizabeth afterwards, she spoke more on the subject. 'It seems likely to have been a desirable match for Jane,' said she. 'I am sorry it went off. But these things happen so often! A young man, such as you describe Mr. Bingley, so easily falls in love with a pretty girl for a few weeks, and, when accident separates them, so easily forgets her, that these sort of inconstancies are very frequent.'

'An excellent consolation in its way,' said Elizabeth; 'but it will not do for *us*. We do not suffer by accident. It does not often happen that the interference of friends will persuade a young man of independent fortune to think no more of a girl whom he was violently in love with only a few days before.'

'But that expression of "violently in love" is so hackneyed, so doubtful, so indefinite, that it gives me very little idea. It is as often applied to feelings which arise only from a half-hour's acquaintance, as to a real, strong attachment. Pray, how *violent was* Mr. Bingley's love?'

'I never saw a more promising inclination; he was growing quite inattentive to other people, and wholly engrossed by her. Every time they met, it was more decided and remarkable. At his own ball he offended two or three young ladies by not asking them to dance; and I spoke to him twice myself

without receiving an answer. Could there be finer symptoms?
Is not general incivility the very essence of love?'

'Oh yes! of that kind of love which I suppose him to have
felt. Poor Jane! I am sorry for her, because, with her disposition, she may not get over it immediately. It had better
have happened to *you*, Lizzy; you would have laughed yourself out of it sooner. But do you think she would be prevailed on to go back with us? Change of scene might be of
service—and perhaps a little relief from home may be as
useful as anything.'

Elizabeth was exceedingly pleased with this proposal, and
felt persuaded of her sister's ready acquiescence.

'I hope,' added Mrs. Gardiner, 'that no consideration with regard to this young man will influence her. We live in so different a part of town, all our connections are so different, and,
as you well know, we go out so little, that it is very improbable they should meet at all, unless he really comes to see her.'

'And *that* is quite impossible; for he is now in the custody
of his friend, and Mr. Darcy would no more suffer him to call
on Jane in such a part of London! My dear aunt, how could
you think of it? Mr. Darcy may, perhaps, have *heard* of
such a place as Gracechurch Street, but he would hardly think
a month's ablution enough to cleanse him from its impurities,
were he once to enter it; and depend upon it, Mr. Bingley
never stirs without him.'

'So much the better. I hope they will not meet at all. But
does not Jane correspond with his sister? *She* will not be
able to help calling.'

'She will drop the acquaintance entirely.'

But, in spite of the certainty in which Elizabeth affected
to place this point, as well as the still more interesting one
of Bingley's being withheld from seeing Jane, she felt a
solicitude on the subject which convinced her, on examination, that she did not consider it entirely hopeless. It was
possible, and sometimes she thought it probable, that his affection might be reanimated, and the influence of his friends
successfully combated by the more natural influence of
Jane's attractions.

Miss Bennet accepted her aunt's invitation with pleasure;
and the Bingleys were no otherwise in her thoughts at the

same time than as she hoped, by Caroline's not living in the
same house with her brother, she might occasionally spend
a morning with her, without any danger of seeing him.

The Gardiners stayed a week at Longbourn; and what
with the Philipses, the Lucases, and the officers, there was
not a day without its engagement. Mrs. Bennet had so
carefully provided for the entertainment of her brother and
sister, that they did not once sit down to a family dinner.
When the engagement was for home, some of the officers
always made part of it, of which officers Mr. Wickham was
sure to be one; and on these occasions Mrs. Gardiner, rendered suspicious by Elizabeth's warm commendation of him,
narrowly observed them both. Without supposing them,
from what she saw, to be very seriously in love, their preference of each other was plain enough to make her a little uneasy; and she resolved to speak to Elizabeth on the subject
before she left Hertfordshire, and represent to her the imprudence of encouraging such an attachment.

To Mrs. Gardiner Wickham had one means of affording
pleasure, unconnected with his general powers. About ten
or a dozen years ago, before her marriage, she had spent a
considerable time in that very part of Derbyshire to which
he belonged. They had, therefore, many acquaintance in
common; and, though Wickham had been little there since
the death of Darcy's father, five years before, it was yet in
his power to give her fresher intelligence of her former
friends than she had been in the way of procuring.

Mrs. Gardiner had seen Pemberley, and known the late
Mr. Darcy by character perfectly well. Here, consequently,
was an inexhaustible subject of discourse. In comparing her
recollection of Pemberley with the minute description which
Wickham could give, and in bestowing her tribute of praise
on the character of its late possessor, she was delighting
both him and herself. On being made acquainted with the
present Mr. Darcy's treatment of him, she tried to remember
something of that gentleman's reputed disposition, when
quite a lad, which might agree with it; and was confident,
at last, that she recollected having heard Mr. Fitzwilliam
Darcy formerly spoken of as a very proud, ill-natured boy.

CHAPTER XXVI

MRS. GARDINER'S caution to Elizabeth was punctually and kindly given on the first favourable opportunity of speaking to her alone: after honestly telling her what she thought, she thus went on:—

'You are too sensible a girl, Lizzy, to fall in love merely because you are warned against it; and, therefore, I am not afraid of speaking openly. Seriously, I would have you be on your guard. Do not involve yourself, or endeavour to involve him, in an affection which the want of fortune would make so very imprudent. I have nothing to say against *him*: he is a most interesting young man; and if he had the fortune he ought to have, I should think you could not do better. But as it is—you must not let your fancy run away with you. You have sense, and we all expect you to use it. Your father would depend on *your* resolution and good conduct, I am sure. You must not disappoint your father.'

'My dear aunt, this is being serious indeed.'

'Yes, and I hope to engage you to be serious likewise.'

'Well, then, you need not be under any alarm. I will take care of myself, and of Mr. Wickham too. He shall not be in love with me, if I can prevent it.'

'Elizabeth, you are not serious now.'

'I beg your pardon. I will try again. At present I am not in love with Mr. Wickham; no, I certainly am not. But he is, beyond all comparison, the most agreeable man I ever saw—and if he becomes really attached to me—I believe it will be better that he should not. I see the imprudence of it. Oh, *that* abominable Mr. Darcy! My father's opinion of me does me the greatest honour; and I should be miserable to forfeit it. My father, however, is partial to Mr. Wickham. In short, my dear aunt, I should be very sorry to be the means of making any of you unhappy; but since we see, every day, that where there is affection young people are seldom withheld, by immediate want of fortune, from entering into engagements with each other, how can I promise to be wiser than so many of my fellow-creatures, if I am tempted, or how am I even to know that it would be wisdom to resist? All that I can promise you, therefore, is not to be in a hurry. I will not be in a hurry to believe myself his first object. When I am in company with him, I will not be wishing. In short, I will do my best.'

'Perhaps it will be as well if you discourage his coming here so very often. At least you should not *remind* your mother of inviting him.'

'As I did the other day,' said Elizabeth, with a conscious smile; 'very true it will be wise in me to refrain from *that*. But do not imagine that he is always here so often. It is on your account that he has been so frequently invited this week. You know my mother's ideas as to the necessity of constant company for her friends. But really, and upon my honour, I will try to do what I think to be wisest; and now I hope you are satisfied.'

Her aunt assured her that she was; and Elizabeth, having thanked her for the kindness of her hints, they parted,—a wonderful instance of advice being given on such a point without being resented.

Mr. Collins returned into Hertfordshire soon after it had been quitted by the Gardiners and Jane; but, as he took up his abode with the Lucases, his arrival was no great inconvenience to Mrs. Bennet. His marriage was now fast approaching; and she was at length so far resigned as to think it inevitable, and even repeatedly to say, in an ill-natured tone, that she *wished* they might be happy.' Thursday was to be the wedding day, and on Wednesday Miss Lucas paid her farewell visit; and when she rose to take leave, Elizabeth, ashamed of her mother's ungracious and reluctant good wishes, and sincerely affected herself, accompanied her out of the room. As they went downstairs together, Charlotte said,—

'I shall depend on hearing from you very often, Eliza.'

'*That* you certainly shall.'

'And I have another favour to ask. Will you come and see me?'

'We shall often meet, I hope, in Hertfordshire.'

'I am not likely to leave Kent for some time. Promise me, therefore, to come to Hunsford.'

Elizabeth could not refuse, though she foresaw little pleasure in the visit.

'My father and Maria are to come to me in March,' added Charlotte, 'and I hope you will consent to be of the party. Indeed, Eliza, you will be as welcome to me as either of them.'

The wedding took place: the bride and bridegroom set off for Kent from the church door, and everybody had as much to say or to hear on the subject as usual. Elizabeth soon heard from her friend, and their correspondence was as regular and frequent as it ever had been: that it should be equally unreserved was impossible. Elizabeth could never address her without feeling that all the comfort of intimacy was over; and, though determined not to slacken as a correspondent, it was for the sake of what had been rather than what was. Charlotte's first letters were received with a good deal of eagerness: there could not but be curiosity to know how she would speak of her new home, how she would like Lady Catherine, and how happy she would dare pronounce herself to be; though, when the letters were read, Elizabeth felt that Charlotte expressed herself on every point exactly as she might have foreseen. She wrote cheerfully, seemed surrounded with comforts, and mentioned nothing which she could not praise. The house, furniture, neighbourhood, and roads, were all to her taste, and Lady Catherine's behaviour was most friendly and obliging. It was Mr. Collins's picture of Hunsford and Rosings rationally softened; and Elizabeth perceived that she must wait for her own visit there to know the rest.

Jane had already written a few lines to her sister, to announce their safe arrival in London; and when she wrote again, Elizabeth hoped it would be in her power to say something of the Bingleys.

Her impatience for this second letter was as well rewarded as impatience generally is. Jane had been a week in town, without either seeing or hearing from Caroline. She accounted for it, however, by supposing that her last letter to her friend from Longbourn had by some accident been lost.

'My aunt,' she continued, 'is going to-morrow into that part of the town, and I shall take the opportunity of calling in Grosvenor Street.'

She wrote again when the visit was paid, and she had seen Miss Bingley. 'I did not think Caroline in spirits,' were her words, 'but she was very glad to see me, and reproached me for giving her no notice of my coming to London. I was right, therefore; my last letter had never reached her. I inquired after their brother, of course. He was well, but so much engaged with Mr. Darcy, that they scarcely ever saw him. I found that Miss Darcy was expected to dinner: I wish I could see her. My visit was not long, as Caroline and Mrs. Hurst were going out. I daresay I shall soon see them here.'

Elizabeth shook her head over this letter. It convinced her that accident only could discover to Mr. Bingley her sister's being in town.

Four weeks passed away, and Jane saw nothing of him. She endeavoured to persuade herself that she did not regret it; but she could no longer be blind to Miss Bingley's inattention. After waiting at home every morning for a fortnight, and inventing every evening a fresh excuse for her, the visitor did at last appear; but the shortness of her stay, and, yet more, the alteration of her manner, would allow Jane to deceive herself no longer. The letter which she wrote on this occasion to her sister will prove what she felt:—

'My dearest Lizzy will, I am sure, be incapable of triumphing in her better judgment, at my expense, when I confess myself to have been entirely deceived in Miss Bingley's regard for me. But, my dear sister, though the event has proved you right, do not think me obstinate if I still assert that, considering what her behaviour was, my confidence was as natural as your suspicion. I do not at all comprehend her reason for wishing to be intimate with me; but, if the same circumstances were to happen again, I am sure I should be deceived again. Caroline did not return my visit till yesterday; and not a note, not a line, did I receive in the meantime. When she did come, it was very evident that she had no pleasure in it; she made a slight, formal apology for not calling before, said not a word of wishing to see me again, and was, in every respect, so altered a creature, that when she went away I was perfectly resolved to continue the acquaintance no longer. I pity, though I cannot help blaming, her. She was very wrong in singling me out as she did; I can safely say that every advance to intimacy began on her side. But I pity her, because she must feel that she has been acting wrong, and because I am very sure that anxiety for her brother is the cause of it. I need not explain myself farther; and though *we* know this anxiety to be quite needless, yet if she feels it, it will easily account for her behaviour to me; and so deservedly dear as he is to his sister, whatever anxiety she may feel on his behalf is natural and amiable. I cannot but wonder, however, at her having any such fears now, because if he had at all cared about me, we must have met long, long ago. He knows of my being in town, I am certain, from something she said herself; and yet it would seem, by her manner of talking, as if she wanted to persuade herself that he is really partial to Miss Darcy. I cannot understand it. If I were not afraid of judging harshly, I should be almost tempted to say that there is a strong appearance of duplicity in all this. But I will endeavour to banish every painful thought, and think only of what will make me happy, your affection, and the invariable kindness of my dear uncle and aunt. Let me hear from you very soon. Miss Bingley said something of his never returning to Netherfield again, of giving up the house, but not with any certainty. We had better not mention it. I am extremely glad that you have such pleasant accounts from our friends at Hunsford. Pray go to see them, with Sir William and Maria. I am sure you will be very comfortable there. Yours,' etc.

This letter gave Elizabeth some pain; but her spirits returned, as she considered that Jane would no longer be duped, by the sister at least. All expectation from the brother was now absolutely over. She would not even wish for any renewal of his attentions. His character sank on every review of it; and, as a punishment for him, as well as a possible advantage to Jane, she seriously hoped he might really soon marry Mr. Darcy's sister, as, by Wickham's account, she would make him abundantly regret what he had thrown away.

Mrs. Gardiner about this time reminded Elizabeth of her promise concerning that gentleman, and required information; and Elizabeth had such to send as might rather give contentment to her aunt than to herself. His apparent partiality had subsided, his attentions were over, he was the admirer of some one else. Elizabeth was watchful enough to see it all, but she could see it and write of it without material pain. Her heart had been but slightly touched, and her vanity was satisfied with believing that *she* would have been his only choice, had fortune permitted it.

The sudden acquisition of ten thousand pounds was the most remarkable charm of the young lady to whom he was now rendering himself agreeable; but Elizabeth, less clear-sighted perhaps in this case than in Charlotte's, did not quarrel with him for his wish of independence. Nothing, on the contrary, could be more natural; and, while able to suppose that it cost him a few struggles to relinquish her, she was ready to allow it a wise and desirable measure for both, and could very sincerely wish him happy.

All this was acknowledged to Mrs. Gardiner; and, after relating the circumstances, she thus went on:—'I am now convinced, my dear aunt, that I have never been much in love; for had I really experienced that pure and elevating passion, I should at present detest his very name, and wish him all manner of evil. But my feelings are not only cordial towards *him*, they are even impartial towards Miss King. I cannot find out that I hate her at all, or that I am in the least unwilling to think her a very good sort of girl. There can be no love in all this. My watchfulness has been effectual; and though I should certainly be a more interesting object to all my acquaintance, were I distractedly in love with him, I cannot say that I regret my comparative insignificance. Importance may sometimes be purchased too dearly. Kitty and Lydia take his defection much more to heart than I do. They are young in the ways of the world, and not yet open to the mortifying conviction that handsome young men must have something to live on, as well as the plain.'

CHAPTER XXVII

WITH no greater events than these in the Longbourn family, and otherwise diversified by little beyond the walks to Meryton, sometimes dirty and sometimes cold, did January and February pass away. March was to take Elizabeth to Hunsford. She had not at first thought very seriously of going thither; but Charlotte, she soon found, was depending on the plan, and she gradually learned to consider it herself with greater pleasure as well as greater certainty. Absence had increased her desire of seeing Charlotte again, and weakened her disgust of Mr. Collins. There was novelty in the scheme; and as, with such a mother and such uncompanionable sisters, home could not be faultless, a little change was not unwelcome for its own sake. The journey would, moreover, give her a peep at Jane; and, in short, as the time drew near, she would have been very sorry for any delay. Everything, however, went on smoothly, and was finally settled according to Charlotte's first sketch. She was to accompany Sir William and his second daughter. The improvement of spending a night in London was added in time, and the plan became perfect as plan could be.

The only pain was in leaving her father, who would certainly miss her, and who, when it came to the point, so little liked her going, that he told her to write to him, and almost promised to answer her letter.

The farewell between herself and Mr. Wickham was perfectly friendly; on his side even more. His present pursuit could not make him forget that Elizabeth had been the first to excite and to deserve his attention, the first to listen and to pity, the first to be admired; and in his manner of bidding her adieu, wishing her every enjoyment, reminding her of what she was to expect in Lady Catherine de Bourgh, and trusting their opinion of her—their opinion of everybody—would always coincide, there was a solicitude, an interest, which she felt must ever attach her to him with a most sincere regard; and she parted from him convinced that, whether married or single, he must always be her model of the amiable and pleasing.

Her fellow-travellers the next day were not of a kind to make her think him less agreeable. Sir William Lucas, and his daughter Maria, a good-humoured girl, but as empty-headed as himself, had nothing to say that could be worth hearing, and were listened to with about as much delight as the rattle of the chaise. Elizabeth loved absurdities, but she had known Sir William's too long. He could tell her nothing new of the wonders of his presentation and knighthood; and his civilities were worn out like his information.

It was a journey of only twenty-four miles, and they began it so early as to be in Gracechurch Street by noon. As they drove to Mr. Gardiner's door, Jane was at a drawing-room window watching their arrival: when they entered the passage, she was there to welcome them, and Elizabeth, looking earnestly in her face, was pleased to see it healthful and lovely as ever. On the stairs were a troop of little boys and girls, whose eagerness for their cousin's appearance would not allow them to wait in the drawing-room, and whose shyness, as they had not seen her for a twelvemonth, prevented their coming lower. All was joy and kindness. The day passed most pleasantly away; the morning in bustle and shopping, and the evening at one of the theatres.

Elizabeth then contrived to sit by her aunt. Their first subject was her sister; and she was more grieved than astonished to hear, in reply to her minute inquiries, that though Jane always struggled to support her spirits, there were periods of dejection. It was reasonable, however, to hope that they would not continue long. Mrs. Gardiner gave her the particulars also of Miss Bingley's visit in Gracechurch Street, and repeated conversations occurring at different times between Jane and herself, which proved that the former had, from her heart, given up the acquaintance.

Mrs. Gardiner then rallied her niece on Wickham's desertion, and complimented her on bearing it so well.

'But, my dear Elizabeth,' she added, 'what sort of girl is Miss King? I should be sorry to think our friend mercenary.'

'Pray, my dear aunt, what is the difference in matrimonial affairs between the mercenary and the prudent motive? Where does discretion end, and avarice begin? Last Christmas you were afraid of his marrying me, because it would be imprudent; and now, because he is trying to get a girl with only ten thousand pounds, you want to find out that he is mercenary.'

'If you will only tell me what sort of girl Miss King is, I shall know what to think.'

'She is a very good kind of girl, I believe. I know no harm of her.'

'But he paid her not the smallest attention till her grandfather's death made her mistress of this fortune?'

'No—why should he? If it were not allowable for him to gain *my* affections, because I had no money, what occasion could there be for making love to a girl whom he did not care about, and who was equally poor?'

'But there seems indelicacy in directing his attentions towards her so soon after this event.'

'A man in distressed circumstances has not time for all those elegant decorums with other people may observe. If *she* does not object to it, why should *we?*'

'*Her* not objecting does not justify *him*. It only shows her being deficient in something herself—sense or feeling.'

'Well,' cried Elizabeth, 'have it as you choose. *He* shall be mercenary, and *she* shall be foolish.'

'No, Lizzy, that is what I do *not* choose. I should be sorry, you know, to think ill of a young man who has lived so long in Derbyshire.'

'Oh, if that is all, I have a very poor opinion of young men who live in Derbyshire; and their intimate friends who live in Hertfordshire are not much better. I am sick of them all. Thank Heaven! I am going to-morrow where I shall find a man who has not one agreeable quality, who has neither manner nor sense to recommend him. Stupid men are the only ones worth knowing after all.'

'Take care, Lizzy; that speech savours strongly of disappointment.'

Before they were separated by the conclusion of the play, she had the unexpected happiness of an invitation to accompany her uncle and aunt in a tour of pleasure which they proposed taking in the summer.

'We have not quite determined how far it shall carry us,' said Mrs. Gardiner; 'but perhaps, to the Lakes.'

No scheme could have been more agreeable to Elizabeth, and her acceptance of the invitation was most ready and grateful. 'My dear, dear aunt,' she rapturously cried, 'what delight! what felicity! You give me fresh life and vigour. Adieu to disappointment and spleen. What are men to rocks and mountains? Oh, what hours of transport we shall spend! And when we *do* return, it shall not be like other travellers, without being able to give an accurate idea of anything. We *will* know where we have gone—we *will* recollect what we have seen. Lakes, mountains, and rivers, shall not be jumbled together in our imaginations; nor, when we attempt to describe any particular scene, will we begin quarrelling about its relative situation. Let *our* first effusions be less insupportable than those of the generality of travellers.'

CHAPTER XXVIII

EVERY object in the next day's journey was new and interesting to Elizabeth; and her spirits were in a state of enjoyment; for she had seen her sister looking so well as to banish all fear for her health, and the prospect of her northern tour was a constant source of delight.

When they left the highroad for the lane to Hunsford, every eye was in search of the Parsonage, and every turning expected to bring it in view. The paling of Rosings Park was their boundary on one side. Elizabeth smiled at the recollection of all that she had heard of its inhabitants.

At length the Parsonage was discernible. The garden sloping to the road, the house standing in it, the green pales and the laurel hedge, everything declared they were arriving. Mr. Collins and Charlotte appeared at the door, and the carriage stopped at the small gate, which led by a short gravel walk to the house, amidst the nods and smiles of the whole party. In a moment they were all out of the chaise, rejoicing at the sight of each other. Mrs. Collins welcomed her friend with the liveliest pleasure, and Elizabeth was more and more satisfied with coming, when she found herself so affectionately received. She saw instantly that her cousin's manners were not altered by his marriage: his formal civility was just what it had been; and he detained her some minutes at the gate to hear and satisfy his inquiries after all her family. They were then, with no other delay than his pointing out the neatness of the entrance, taken into the house; and as soon as they were in the parlour, he welcomed them a second time, with ostentatious formality, to his humble abode, and punctually repeated all his wife's offers of refreshment.

Elizabeth was prepared to see him in his glory; and she could not help fancying that in displaying the good proportion of the room, its aspect, and its furniture, he addressed himself particularly to her, as if wishing to make her feel what she had lost in refusing him. But though everything

seemed neat and comfortable, she was not able to gratify
him by any sigh of repentance; and rather looked with wonder at her friend, that she could have so cheerful an air
with such a companion. When Mr. Collins said anything of
which his wife might reasonably be ashamed, which certainly
was not seldom, she involuntarily turned her eye on Charlotte. Once or twice she could discern a faint blush; but in
general Charlotte wisely did not hear. After sitting long
enough to admire every article of furniture in the room, from
the sideboard to the fender, to give an account of their
journey, and of all that had happened in London, Mr. Collins
invited them to take a stroll in the garden, which was large
and well laid out, and to the cultivation of which he attended
himself. To work in his garden was one of his most respectable pleasures; and Elizabeth admired the command of
countenance with which Charlotte talked of the healthful-
ness of the exercise, and owned she encouraged it as much
as possible. Here, leading the way through every walk and
cross walk, and scarcely allowing them an interval to utter
the praises he asked for, every view was pointed out with
a minuteness which left beauty entirely behind. He could
number the fields in every direction, and could tell how many
trees there were in the most distant clump. But of all the
views which his garden, or which the country or the kingdom could boast, none were to be compared with the prospect of Rosings, afforded by an opening in the trees that
bordered the park nearly opposite the front of his house. It
was a handsome modern building, well situated on rising
ground.

From his garden, Mr. Collins would have led them round
his two meadows; but the ladies, not having shoes to encounter the remains of a white frost, turned back; and while
Sir William accompanied him, Charlotte took her sister and
friend over the house, extremely well pleased, probably, to
have the opportunity of showing it without her husband's
help. It was rather small, but well built and convenient; and
everything was fitted up and arranged with a neatness and
consistency of which Elizabeth gave Charlotte all the credit.
When Mr. Collins could be forgotten, there was really a
great air of comfort throughout, and by Charlotte's evident

enjoyment of it, Elizabeth supposed he must be often forgotten.

She had already learnt that Lady Catherine was still in the country. It was spoken of again while they were at dinner, when Mr. Collins joining in, observed,—

'Yes, Miss Elizabeth, you will have the honour of seeing Lady Catherine de Bourgh on the ensuing Sunday at church, and I need not say you will be delighted with her. She is all affability and condescension, and I doubt not but you will be honoured with some portion of her notice when service is over. I have scarcely any hesitation in saying that she will include you and my sister Maria in every invitation with which she honours us during your stay here. Her behaviour to my dear Charlotte is charming. We dine at Rosings twice every week, and are never allowed to walk home. Her Ladyship's carriage is regularly ordered for us. I *should* say, one of her Ladyship's carriages, for she has several.'

'Lady Catherine is a very respectable, sensible woman, indeed,' added Charlotte, 'and a most attentive neighbour.'

'Very true, my dear, that is exactly what I say. She is the sort of woman whom one cannot regard with too much deference.'

The evening was spent chiefly in talking over Hertfordshire news, and telling again what had been already written; and when it closed, Elizabeth, in the solitude of her chamber, had to meditate upon Charlotte's degree of contentment, to understand her address in guiding, and composure in bearing with, her husband, and to acknowledge that it was all done very well. She had also to anticipate how her visit would pass, the quiet tenor of their usual employments, the vexatious interruptions of Mr. Collins, and the gaieties of their intercourse with Rosings. A lively imagination soon settled it all.

About the middle of the next day, as she was in her room getting ready for a walk, a sudden noise below seemed to speak the whole house in confusion; and, after listening a moment, she heard somebody running upstairs in a violent hurry, and calling loudly after her. She opened the door and met Maria in the landing-place, who, breathless with agitation, cried out,—

'Oh, my dear Eliza! pray make haste and come into the dining-room, for there is such a sight to be seen! I will not tell you what it is. Make haste, and come down this moment.'

Elizabeth asked questions in vain; Maria would tell her nothing more; and down they ran into the dining-room which fronted the lane, in quest of this wonder; it was two ladies, stopping in a low phaeton at the garden gate.

'And is this all?' cried Elizabeth. 'I expected at least that the pigs were got into the garden, and here is nothing but Lady Catherine and her daughter!'

'La! my dear,' said Maria, quite shocked at the mistake, 'it is not Lady Catherine. The old lady is Mrs. Jenkinson, who lives with them. The other is Miss De Bourgh. Only look at her. She is quite a little creature. Who would have thought she could be so thin and small!'

'She is abominably rude to keep Charlotte out of doors in all this wind. Why does she not come in?'

'Oh, Charlotte says she hardly ever does. It is the greatest of favours when Miss De Bourgh comes in.'

'I like her appearance,' said Elizabeth, struck with other ideas. 'She looks sickly and cross. Yes, she will do for him very well. She will make him a very proper wife.'

Mr. Collins and Charlotte were both standing at the gate in conversation with the ladies; and Sir William, to Elizabeth's high diversion, was stationed in the doorway, in earnest contemplation of the greatness before him, and constantly bowing whenever Miss De Bourgh looked that way.

At length there was nothing more to be said; the ladies drove on, and the others returned into the house. Mr. Collins no sooner saw the two girls than he began to congratulate them on their good fortune, which Charlotte explained by letting them know that the whole party was asked to dine at Rosings the next day.

CHAPTER XXIX

MR. COLLINS'S triumph, in consequence of this invitation, was complete. The power of displaying the grandeur of his patroness to his wondering visitors, and of letting them see her civility towards himself and his wife, was exactly what he had wished for; and that an opportunity of doing it should be given so soon was such an instance of Lady Catherine's condescension as he knew not how to admire enough.

'I confess,' said he, 'that I should not have been at all surprised by her Ladyship's asking us on Sunday to drink tea and spend the evening at Rosings. I rather expected, from my knowledge of her affability, that it would happen. But who could have foreseen such an attention as this? Who could have imagined that we should receive an invitation to dine there (an invitation, moreover, including the whole party) so immediately after your arrival?' —'I am the less surprised at what has happened,' replied Sir William, 'from that knowledge of what the manners of the great really are, which my situation in life has allowed me to acquire. About the court, such instances of elegant breeding are not uncommon.'

Scarcely anything was talked of the whole day or next morning but their visit to Rosings. Mr. Collins was carefully instructing them in what they were to expect, that the sight of such rooms, so many servants, and so splendid a dinner, might not wholly overpower them.

When the ladies were separating for the toilette, he said to Elizabeth,—

'Do not make yourself uneasy, my dear cousin, about your apparel. Lady Catherine is far from requiring that elegance of dress in us which becomes herself and daughter. I would advise you merely to put on whatever of your clothes is superior to the rest, there is no occasion for anything more. Lady Catherine will not think the worse of

309

you for being simply dressed. She likes to have the distinction of rank preserved.'

While they were dressing, he came two or three times to their different doors, to recommend their being quick, as Lady Catherine very much objected to be kept waiting for her dinner. Such formidable accounts of her Ladyship, and her manner of living, quite frightened Maria Lucas, who had been little used to company; and she looked forward to her introduction at Rosings with as much apprehension as her father had done to his presentation at St. James's.

As the weather was fine, they had a pleasant walk of about half a mile across the park. Every park has its beauty and its prospects; and Elizabeth saw much to be pleased with, though she could not be in such raptures as Mr. Collins expected the scene to inspire, and was but slightly affected by his enumeration of the windows in front of the house, and his relation of what the glazing altogether had originally cost Sir Lewis de Bourgh.

When they ascended the steps to the hall, Maria's alarm was every moment increasing, and even Sir William did not look perfectly calm. Elizabeth's courage did not fail her. She had heard nothing of Lady Catherine that spoke her awful from any extraordinary talents or miraculous virtue, and the mere stateliness of money and rank she thought she could witness without trepidation.

From the entrance hall, of which Mr. Collins pointed out, with a rapturous air, the fine proportion and finished ornaments, they followed the servants through an antechamber to the room where Lady Catherine, her daughter, and Mrs. Jenkinson were sitting. Her Ladyship, with great condescension, arose to receive them; and as Mrs. Collins had settled it with her husband that the office of introduction should be hers, it was performed in a proper manner, without any of those apologies and thanks which he would have thought necessary.

In spite of having been at St. James's, Sir William was so completely awed by the grandeur surrounding him, that he had but just courage enough to make a very low bow, and take his seat without saying a word; and his daughter, frightened almost out of her senses, sat on the edge of her chair, not knowing which way to look. Elizabeth found herself quite equal to the scene, and could observe the three ladies before her composedly. Lady Catherine was a tall, large woman, with strongly-marked features, which might once have been handsome. Her air was not conciliating, nor was her manner of receiving them such as to make her visitors forget their inferior rank. She was not rendered formidable by silence: but whatever she said was spoken in so authoritative a tone as marked her self-importance, and brought Mr. Wickham immediately to Elizabeth's mind; and, from the observation of the day altogether, she believed Lady Catherine to be exactly what he had represented.

When, after examining the mother, in whose countenance and deportment she soon found some resemblance of Mr. Darcy, she turned her eyes on the daughter, she could almost have joined in Maria's astonishment at her being so thin and so small. There was neither in figure nor face any likeness between the ladies. Miss De Bourgh was pale and sickly: her features, though not plain, were insignificant; and she spoke very little, except in a low voice, to Mrs. Jenkinson, in whose appearance there was nothing remarkable, and who was entirely engaged in listening to what she said, and placing a screen in the proper direction before her eyes.

After sitting a few minutes, they were all sent to one of the windows to admire the view, Mr. Collins attending them to point out its beauties, and Lady Catherine kindly informing them that it was much better worth looking at in the summer.

The dinner was exceedingly handsome, and there were all the servants, and all the articles of plate which Mr. Collins had promised; and, as he had likewise foretold, he took his seat at the bottom of the table, by her Ladyship's desire, and looked as if he felt that life could furnish nothing greater. He carved and ate and praised with delighted alacrity; and every dish was commended first by him, and then by Sir William, who was now enough recovered to echo whatever his son-in-law said, in a manner which Elizabeth wondered Lady Catherine could bear. But Lady Catherine seemed gratified by their excessive admiration, and gave most gracious smiles, especially when any dish on the table proved a novelty to them. The party did not supply much conversation. Elizabeth was ready to speak whenever there was an opening, but she was seated between Charlotte and Miss De Bourgh—the former of whom was engaged in listening to Lady Catherine, and the latter said not a word to her all dinnertime. Mrs. Jenkinson was chiefly employed in watching how little Miss De Bourgh ate, pressing her to try some other dish and fearing she was indisposed. Maria thought speaking out of the question, and the gentlemen did nothing but eat and admire.

When the ladies returned to the drawing-room, there was little to be done but to hear Lady Catherine talk, which she did without any intermission till coffee came in, delivering her opinion on every subject in so decisive a manner as proved that she was not used to have her judgment controverted. She inquired into Charlotte's domestic concerns familiarly and minutely, and gave her a great deal of advice as to the management of them all; told her how everything ought to be regulated in so small a family as hers, and instructed her as to the care of her cows and her poultry. Elizabeth found that nothing was beneath this great lady's attention which could furnish her with an occasion for dictating to others. In the intervals of her discourse with Mrs. Collins, she addressed a variety of questions to Maria and Elizabeth, but especially to the latter, of whose connections she knew the least, and who, she observed to Mrs. Collins, was a very genteel, pretty kind of girl. She asked her at different times how many sisters she had, whether they were older or younger than herself, whether any of them were likely to be married, whether they were handsome, where they had been educated, what carriage her father kept, and what had been her mother's maiden name? Elizabeth felt all the impertinence of her questions, but answered them very composedly. Lady Catherine then observed,—

'Your father's estate is entailed on Mr. Collins, I think? For your sake,' turning to Charlotte, 'I am glad of it; but otherwise I see no occasion for entailing estates from the female line. It was not thought necessary in Sir Lewis de Bourgh's family. Do you play and sing, Miss Bennet?'

'A little.'

'Oh then—some time or other we shall be happy to hear you. Our instrument is a capital one, probably superior to— you shall try it some day. Do your sisters play and sing?'

'One of them does.'

'Why did not you all learn? You ought all to have learned. The Miss Webbs all play, and their father has not so good an income as yours. Do you draw?'

'No, not at all.'

'What, none of you?'

'Not one.'

'That is very strange. But I suppose you had no opportunity. Your mother should have taken you to town every spring for the benefit of masters.'

'My mother would have no objection, but my father hates London.'

'Has your governess left you?'

'We never had any governess.'

'No governess! How was that possible? Five daughters brought up at home without a governess! I never heard of such a thing. Your mother must have been quite a slave to your education.'

Elizabeth could hardly help smiling, as she assured her that had not been the case.

'Then who taught you? who attended to you? without a governess, you must have been neglected.'

'Compared with some families, I believe we were; but such of us as wished to learn never wanted the means. We were always encouraged to read, and had all the masters that were necessary. Those who chose to be idle certainly might.'

'Ay, no doubt: but that is what a governess will prevent; and if I had known your mother, I should have advised her most strenuously to engage one. I always say that nothing is to be done in education without steady and regular instruction, and nobody but a governess can give it. It is wonderful how many families I have been the means of supplying in

that way. I am always glad to get a young person well placed
out. Four nieces of Mrs. Jenkinson are most delightfully
situated through my means; and it was but the other day that
I recommended another young person, who was merely accidentally mentioned to me, and the family are quite delighted
with her. Mrs. Collins, did I tell you of Lady Metcalfe's
calling yesterday to thank me? She finds Miss Pope a treasure. "Lady Catherine," said she, "you have given me a treasure." Are any of your younger sisters out, Miss Bennet?'

'Yes, ma'am, all.'

'All! What, all five out at once? Very odd! And you only
the second. The younger ones out before the elder are married! Your younger sisters must be very young?'

'Yes, my youngest is not sixteen. Perhaps *she* is full
young to be much in company. But, really, ma'am, I think it
would be very hard upon younger sisters that they should
not have their share of society and amusement, because the
elder may not have the means or inclination to marry early.
The last born has as good a right to the pleasures of youth as
the first. And to be kept back on *such* a motive! I think it
would not be very likely to promote sisterly affection or delicacy of mind.'

'Upon my word,' said her Ladyship, 'you give your opinion
very decidedly for so young a person. Pray, what is your
age?'

'With three younger sisters grown up,' replied Elizabeth,
smiling, 'your Ladyship can hardly expect me to own it.'

Lady Catherine seemed quite astonished at not receiving a
direct answer; and Elizabeth suspected herself to be the
first creature who had ever dared to trifle with so much
dignified impertinence.

'You cannot be more than twenty, I am sure,—therefore
you need not conceal your age.'

'I am not one-and-twenty.'

When the gentlemen had joined them, and tea was over,
the card-tables were placed. Lady Catherine, Sir William,
and Mr. and Mrs. Collins sat down to quadrille; and as Miss
De Bourgh chose to play at cassino, the two girls had the
honour of assisting Mrs. Jenkinson to make up her party.
Their table was superlatively stupid. Scarcely a syllable was

uttered that did not relate to the game, except when Mrs.
Jenkinson expressed her fears of Miss De Bourgh's being too
hot or too cold, or having too much or too little light. A
great deal more passed at the other table. Lady Catherine
was generally speaking—stating the mistakes of the three
others, or relating some anecdote of herself. Mr. Collins was
employed in agreeing to everything her Ladyship said, thanking her for every fish he won, and apologising if he thought
he won too many. Sir William did not say much. He was
storing his memory with anecdotes and noble names.

When Lady Catherine and her daughter had played as
long as they chose, the tables were broken up, the carriage
was offered to Mrs. Collins, gratefully accepted, and immediately ordered. The party then gathered round the fire to hear
Lady Catherine determine what weather they were to have on
the morrow. From these instructions they were summoned
by the arrival of the coach; and with many speeches of
thankfulness on Mr. Collins's side, and as many bows on Sir
William's, they departed. As soon as they had driven from
the door, Elizabeth was called on by her cousin to give her
opinion of all that she had seen at Rosings, which, for
Charlotte's sake, she made more favourable than it really
was. But her commendation, though costing her some trouble, could by no means satisfy Mr. Collins, and he was very
soon obliged to take her Ladyship's praise into his own hands.

CHAPTER XXX

SIR WILLIAM stayed only a week at Hunsford; but his visit was long enough to convince him of his daughter's being most comfortably settled, and of her possessing such a husband and such a neighbour as were not often met with. While Sir William was with them, Mr. Collins devoted his mornings to driving him out in his gig, and showing him the country: but when he went away, the whole family returned to their usual employments, and Elizabeth was thankful to find that they did not see more of her cousin by the alteration; for the chief of the time between breakfast and dinner was now passed by him either at work in the garden, or in reading and writing, and looking out of window in his own book room, which fronted the road. The room in which the ladies sat was backwards. Elizabeth at first had rather wondered that Charlotte should not prefer the dining parlour for common use; it was a better sized room, and had a pleasanter aspect: but she soon saw that her friend had an excellent reason for what she did, for Mr. Collins would undoubtedly have been much less in his own apartment had they sat in one equally lively; and she gave Charlotte credit for the arrangement.

From the drawing-room they could distinguish nothing in the lane, and were indebted to Mr. Collins for the knowledge of what carriages went along, and how often especially Miss De Bourgh drove by in her phaeton, which he never failed coming to inform them of, though it happened almost every day. She not infrequently stopped at the parsonage, and had a few minutes' conversation with Charlotte, but was scarcely ever prevailed on to get out.

Very few days passed in which Mr. Collins did not walk to Rosings, and not many in which his wife did not think it necessary to go likewise; and till Elizabeth recollected that there might be other family livings to be disposed of, she could not understand the sacrifice of so many hours. Now and then they were honoured with a call from her Ladyship, and nothing escaped her observation that was passing in the room during these visits. She examined into their employments, looked at their work, and advised them to do it differently; found fault with the arrangement of the furniture, or detected the housemaid in negligence; and if she accepted any refreshment, seemed to do it only for the sake of finding out that Mrs. Collins's joints of meat were too large for her family.

Elizabeth soon perceived that though this great lady was not in the commission of the peace for the county, she was a most active magistrate in her own parish, the minutest concerns of which were carried to her by Mr. Collins; and whenever any of the cottagers were disposed to be quarrelsome, discontented, or too poor, she sallied forth into the village to settle their differences, silence their complaints, and scold them into harmony and plenty.

The entertainment of dining at Rosings was repeated about twice a week; and, allowing for the loss of Sir William, and there being only one card-table in the evening, every such entertainment was the counterpart of the first. Their other engagements were few; as the style of living of the neighbourhood in general was beyond the Collinses' reach. This, however, was no evil to Elizabeth, and upon the whole she spent her time comfortably enough: there were half-hours of pleasant conversation with Charlotte, and the weather was so fine for the time of year, that she had often great enjoyment out of doors. Her favourite walk, and where she frequently went while the others were calling on Lady Catherine, was along the open grove which edged that side of the park where there was a nice sheltered path, which no one seemed to value but herself, and where she felt beyond the reach of Lady Catherine's curiosity.

In this quiet way the first fortnight of her visit soon passed away. Easter was approaching, and the week preceding it was to bring an addition to the family at Rosings, which in so small a circle must be important. Elizabeth had heard, soon after her arrival, that Mr. Darcy was expected there in the course of a few weeks; and though there were not many of her acquaintance whom she did not prefer, his coming would furnish one comparatively new to look at in their Rosings parties, and she might be amused in seeing how hopeless Miss Bingley's designs on him were, by his behaviour to his cousin, for whom he was evidently destined by Lady Catherine; who talked of his coming with the greatest satisfaction, spoke of him in terms of the highest admiration, and seemed almost angry to find that he had already been frequently seen by Miss Lucas and herself.

His arrival was soon known at the Parsonage; for Mr. Collins was walking the whole morning within view of the lodges opening into Hunsford Lane, in order to have the earliest assurance of it; and, after making his bow as the carriage turned into the park, hurried home with the great intelligence. On the following morning he hastened to Rosings to pay his respects. There were two nephews of Lady Catherine to require them, for Mr. Darcy had brought with him a Colonel Fitzwilliam, the younger son of his uncle Lord ——; and, to the great surprise of all the party, when Mr. Collins returned, the gentleman accompanied him. Charlotte had seen them from her husband's room, crossing the road, and immediately running into the other, told the girls what an honour they might expect, adding,—

'I may thank you, Eliza, for this piece of civility. Mr. Darcy would never have come so soon to wait upon me.'

Elizabeth had scarcely time to disclaim all right to the compliment before their approach was announced by the doorbell, and shortly afterwards the three gentlemen entered the room. Colonel Fitzwilliam, who led the way, was about thirty, not handsome, but in person and address most truly the gentleman. Mr. Darcy looked just as he had been used to look in Hertfordshire, paid his compliments, with his usual reserve, to Mrs. Collins; and, whatever might be his feelings towards her friend, met her with every appearance of composure. Elizabeth merely courtesied to him, without saying a word.

Colonel Fitzwilliam entered into conversation directly, with the readiness and ease of a well-bred man, and talked very pleasantly; but his cousin, after having addressed a slight observation on the house and garden to Mrs. Collins, sat for some time without speaking to anybody. At length, however, his civility was so far awakened as to inquire of Elizabeth after the health of her family. She answered him in the usual way; and, after a moment's pause, added,—

'My eldest sister has been in town these three months. Have you never happened to see her there?'

She was perfectly sensible that he never had: but she wished to see whether he would betray any consciousness of what had passed between the Bingleys and Jane; and she thought he looked a little confused as he answered that he had never been so fortunate as to meet Miss Bennet. The subject was pursued no further, and the gentlemen soon afterwards went away.

CHAPTER XXXI

COLONEL FITZWILLIAM'S manners were very much admired at the Parsonage, and the ladies all felt that he must add considerably to the pleasure of their engagements at Rosings. It was some days, however, before they received any invitation thither, for while there were visitors in the house they could not be necessary; and it was not till Easter-day, almost a week after the gentlemen's arrival, that they were honoured by such an attention, and then they were merely asked on leaving church to come there in the evening. For the last week they had seen very little of either Lady Catherine or her daughter. Colonel Fitzwilliam had called at the Parsonage more than once during the time, but Mr. Darcy they had only seen at church.

The invitation was accepted, of course, and at a proper hour they joined the party in Lady Catherine's drawing-room. Her Ladyship received them civilly, but it was plain that their company was by no means so acceptable as when she could get nobody else; and she was, in fact, almost engrossed by her nephews, speaking to them, especially to Darcy, much more than to any other person in the room.

Colonel Fitzwilliam seemed really glad to see them: anything was a welcome relief to him at Rosings; and Mrs. Collins's pretty friend had, moreover, caught his fancy very much. He now seated himself by her, and talked so agreeably of Kent and Hertfordshire, of travelling and staying at home, of new books and music, that Elizabeth had never been half so well entertained in that room before; and they conversed with so much spirit and flow as to draw the attention of Lady Catherine herself, as well as of Mr. Darcy. *His* eyes had been soon and repeatedly turned towards them with a look of curiosity; and that her Ladyship, after a while, shared the feeling, was more openly acknowledged, for she did not scruple to call out,—

'What is that you are saying, Fitzwilliam? What is it you are talking of? What are you telling Miss Bennet? Let me hear what it is.'

'We are speaking of music, madam,' said he, when no longer able to avoid a reply.

'Of music! Then pray speak aloud. It is of all subjects my delight. I must have my share in the conversation, if you are speaking of music. There are few people in England, I suppose, who have more true enjoyment of music than myself, or a better natural taste. If I had ever learnt, I should have been a great proficient. And so would Anne, if her health had allowed her to apply. I am confident that she would have performed delightfully. How does Georgiana get on, Darcy?'

Mr. Darcy spoke with affectionate praise of his sister's proficiency.

'I am very glad to hear such a good account of her,' said Lady Catherine; 'and pray tell her from me, that she cannot expect to excel if she does not practise a great deal.'

'I assure you, madam, he replied, 'that she does not need such advice. She practises very constantly.'

'So much the better. It cannot be done too much; and when I next write to her, I shall charge her not to neglect it on any account. I often tell young ladies that no excellence in music is to be acquired without constant practice. I have told Miss Bennet several times that she will never play really well unless she practises more; and though Mrs. Collins has no instrument, she is very welcome, as I have often told her, to come to Rosings every day, and play on the pianoforte in Mrs. Jenkinson's room. She would be in nobody's way, you know, in that part of the house.'

Mr. Darcy looked a little ashamed of his aunt's ill-breeding, and made no answer.

When coffee was over, Colonel Fitzwilliam reminded Elizabeth of having promised to play to him; and she sat down directly to the instrument. He drew a chair near her. Lady Catherine listened to half a song, and then talked, as before, to her other nephew; till the latter walked away from her, and, moving with his usual deliberation towards the pianoforte, stationed himself so as to command a full view

of the fair performer's countenance. Elizabeth saw what he
was doing, and at the first convenient pause turned to him
with an arch smile, and said,—

'You mean to frighten me, Mr. Darcy, by coming in all
this state to hear me. But I will not be alarmed though
your sister *does* play so well. There is a stubbornness
about me that never can bear to be frightened at the will
of others. My courage always rises with every attempt to
intimidate me.'

'I shall not say that you are mistaken,' he replied, 'because
you could not really believe me to entertain any design of
alarming you; and I have had the pleasure of your acquaintance long enough to know that you find great enjoyment in
occasionally professing opinions which, in fact, are not your
own.'

Elizabeth laughed heartily at this picture of herself, and
said to Colonel Fitzwilliam, 'Your cousin will give you a very
pretty notion of me, and teach you not to believe a word I say.
I am particularly unlucky in meeting with a person so well
able to expose my real character, in a part of the world where
I had hoped to pass myself off with some degree of credit.
Indeed, Mr. Darcy, it is very ungenerous in you to mention
all that you knew to my disadvantage in Hertfordshire—and,
give me leave to say, very impolitic too—for it is provoking
me to retaliate, and such things may come out as will shock
your relations to hear.'

'I am not afraid of you,' said he, smilingly.

'Pray let me hear what you have to accuse him of,' cried
Colonel Fitzwilliam. 'I should like to know how he behaves
among strangers.'

'You shall hear, then—but prepare for something very
dreadful. The first time of my ever seeing him in Hertfordshire, you must know, was at a ball—and at this ball, what
do you think he did? He danced only four dances! I am
sorry to pain you, but so it was. He danced only four dances,
though gentlemen were scarce; and, to my certain knowledge,
more than one young lady was sitting down in want of a
partner. Mr. Darcy, you cannot deny the fact.'

'I had not at that time the honour of knowing any lady in
the assembly beyond my own party.'

'True; and nobody can ever be introduced in a ballroom. Well, Colonel Fitzwilliam, what do I play next? My fingers wait your orders.'

'Perhaps,' said Darcy, 'I should have judged better had I sought an introduction, but I am ill qualified to recommend myself to strangers.'

'Shall we ask your cousin the reason of this?' said Elizabeth, still addressing Colonel Fitzwilliam. 'Shall we ask him why a man of sense and education, and who has lived in the world, is ill qualified to recommend himself to strangers?'

'I can answer your question,' said Fitzwilliam, 'without applying to him. It is because he will not give himself the trouble.'

'I certainly have not the talent which some people possess,' said Darcy, 'of conversing easily with those I have never seen before. I cannot catch their tone of conversation, or appear interested in their concerns as I often see done.'

'My fingers,' said Elizabeth, 'do not move over this instrument in the masterly manner which I see so many women's do. They have not the same force or rapidity, and do not produce the same expression. But then I have always supposed it to be my own fault—because I would not take the trouble of practising. It is not that I do not believe *my* fingers as capable as any other woman's of superior execution.'

Darcy smiled and said, 'You are perfectly right. You have employed your time much better. No one admitted to the privilege of hearing you can think anything wanting. We neither of us perform to strangers.'

Here they were interrupted by Lady Catherine, who called out to know what they were talking of. Elizabeth immediately began playing again. Lady Catherine approached, and, after listening for a few minutes, said to Darcy,—

'Miss Bennet would not play at all amiss if she practised more, and could have the advantage of a London master. She has a very good notion of fingering, though her taste is not equal to Anne's. Anne would have been a delightful performer, had her health allowed her to learn.'

Elizabeth looked at Darcy to see how cordially he assented to his cousin's praise: but neither at that moment nor at any other could she discern any symptom of love; and from the whole of his behaviour to Miss De Bourgh she derived this comfort for Miss Bingley, that he might have been just as likely to marry *her*, had she been his relation.

Lady Catherine continued her remarks on Elizabeth's performance, mixing with them many instructions on execution and taste. Elizabeth received them with all the forbearance of civility; and at the request of the gentlemen remained at the instrument till her Ladyship's carriage was ready to take them all home.

CHAPTER XXXII

ELIZABETH was sitting by herself the next morning, and writing to Jane, while Mrs. Collins and Maria were gone on business into the village, when she was startled by a ring at the door, the certain signal of a visitor. As she had heard no carriage, she thought it not unlikely to be Lady Catherine; and under that apprehension was putting away her half-finished letter, that she might escape all impertinent questions, when the door opened, and to her very great surprise Mr. Darcy, and Mr. Darcy only, entered the room.

He seemed astonished too on finding her alone, and apologised for his intrusion, by letting her know that he had understood all the ladies to be within.

They then sat down, and when her inquiries after Rosings were made, seemed in danger of sinking into total silence. It was absolutely necessary, therefore, to think of something; and in this emergency recollecting *when* she had seen him last in Hertfordshire, and feeling curious to know what he would say on the subject of their hasty departure, she observed,—

'How very suddenly you all quitted Netherfield last November, Mr. Darcy! It must have been a most agreeable surprise to Mr. Bingley to see you all after him so soon; for, if I recollect right, he went but the day before. He and his sisters were well, I hope, when you left London?'

'Perfectly so, I thank you.'

She found that she was to receive no other answer; and, after a short pause, added,—

'I think I have understood that Mr. Bingley has not much idea of ever returning to Netherfield again?'

'I have never heard him say so; but it is probable that he may spend very little of his time there in future. He has many friends, and he is at a time of life when friends and engagements are continually increasing.'

'If he means to be but little at Netherfield, it would be better for the neighbourhood that he should give up the place entirely, for then we might possibly get a settled family there. But, perhaps, Mr. Bingley did not take the house so much for the convenience of the neighbourhood as for his own, and we must expect him to keep or quit it on the same principle.'

'I should not be surprised,' said Darcy, 'if he were to give it up as soon as any eligible purchase offers.'

Elizabeth made no answer. She was afraid of talking longer of his friend; and, having nothing else to say, was now determined to leave the trouble of finding a subject to him.

He took the hint and soon began with, 'This seems a very comfortable house. Lady Catherine, I believe, did a great deal to it when Mr. Collins first came to Hunsford.'

'I believe she did—and I am sure she could not have bestowed her kindness on a more grateful object.'

'Mr. Collins appears very fortunate in his choice of a wife."

'Yes, indeed; his friends may well rejoice in his having met with one of the very few sensible women who would have accepted him, or have made him happy if they had. My friend has an excellent understanding—though I am not certain that I consider her marrying Mr. Collins as the wisest thing she ever did. She seems perfectly happy, however; and, in a prudential light, it is certainly a very good match for her.'

'It must be very agreeable to her to be settled within so easy a distance of her own family and friends.'

'An easy distance do you call it? It is nearly fifty miles.'

'And what is fifty miles of good road? Little more than half a day's journey. Yes, I call it a very easy distance.'

'I should never have considered the distance as one of the *advantages* of the match,' cried Elizabeth. 'I should never have said Mrs. Collins was settled *near* her family.'

'It is a proof of your own attachment to Hertfordshire. Anything beyond the very neighbourhood of Longbourn, I suppose, would appear far.'

As he spoke there was a sort of smile, which Elizabeth fancied she understood; he must be supposing her to be thinking of Jane and Netherfield, and she blushed as she answered,—

'I do not mean to say that a woman may not be settled too near her family. The far and the near must be relative, and depend on many varying circumstances. Where there is fortune to make the expense of travelling unimportant, distance becomes no evil. But that is not the case *here*. Mr. and Mrs. Collins have a comfortable income, but not such a one as will allow of frequent journeys—and I am persuaded my friend would not call herself *near* her family under less than *half* the present distance.'

Mr. Darcy drew his chair a little towards her, and said, '*You* cannot have a right to such very strong local attachment. *You* cannot have been always at Longbourn.'

Elizabeth looked surprised. The gentleman experienced some change of feeling; he drew back his chair, took a newspaper from the table, and, glancing over it, said, in a colder voice,—

'Are you pleased with Kent?'

A short dialogue on the subject of the country ensued, on either side calm and concise—and soon put an end to by the entrance of Charlotte and her sister, just returned from their walk. The *tête-à-tête* surprised them. Mr. Darcy related the mistake which had occasioned his intruding on Miss Bennet, and, after sitting a few minutes longer, without saying much to anybody, went away.

'What can be the meaning of this?' said Charlotte, as soon as he was gone. 'My dear Eliza, he must be in love with you, or he would never have called on us in this familiar way.'

But when Elizabeth told of his silence, it did not seem very likely, even to Charlotte's wishes, to be the case; and, after various conjectures, they could at last only suppose his visit to proceed from the difficulty of finding anything to do, which was the more probable from the time of year. All field sports were over. Within doors there was Lady Catherine, books, and a billiard table, but gentlemen cannot be always within doors; and in the nearness of the Parsonage, or the pleasantness of the walk to it, or of the people who lived in it, the two cousins found a temptation from this period of walking thither almost every day. They called at various times of the morning, sometimes separately, sometimes together, and now and then accompanied by their aunt. It was plain to them all that Colonel Fitzwilliam came because he had pleasure in their society, a persuasion which of course recommended him still more; and Elizabeth was reminded by her own satisfaction in being with him, as well as by his evident admiration of her former favourite, George Wickham; and though, in comparing them, she saw there was less captivating softness in Colonel Fitzwilliam's manners, she believed he might have the best informed mind.

But why Mr. Darcy came so often to the Parsonage it was more difficult to understand. It could not be for society, as he frequently sat there ten minutes together without opening his lips; and when he did speak, it seemed the effect of necessity rather than of choice—a sacrifice to propriety, not a pleasure to himself. He seldom appeared really animated. Mrs. Collins knew not what to make of him. Colonel Fitzwilliam's occasionally laughing at his stupidity proved that he was generally different, which her own knowledge of him could not have told her; and as she would have liked to believe this change the effect of love, and the object of that love her friend Eliza, she set herself seriously to work to find it out; she watched him whenever they were at Rosings, and whenever he came to Hunsford; but without much success. He certainly looked at her friend a great deal, but the expression of that look was disputable. It was an earnest, steadfast gaze, but she often doubted whether there were much admiration in it, and sometimes it seemed nothing but absence of mind.

She had once or twice suggested to Elizabeth the possibility of his being partial to her, but Elizabeth always laughed at the idea; and Mrs. Collins did not think it right to press the subject, from the danger of raising expectations which might only end in disappointment; for in her opinion it admitted not of a doubt, that all her friend's dislike would vanish, if she could suppose him to be in her power.

In her kind schemes for Elizabeth, she sometimes planned her marrying Colonel Fitzwilliam. He was, beyond comparison, the pleasantest man: he certainly admired her, and his situation in life was most eligible; but, to counterbalance these advantages, Mr. Darcy had considerable patronage in the church, and his cousin could have none at all.

CHAPTER XXXIII

MORE than once did Elizabeth, in her ramble within the park, unexpectedly meet Mr. Darcy. She felt all the perverseness of the mischance that should bring him where no one else was brought; and, to prevent its ever happening again, took care to inform him, at first, that it was a favourite haunt of hers. How it could occur a second time, therefore, was very odd! Yet it did, and even the third. It seemed like wilful ill-nature, or a voluntary penance; for on these occasions is was not merely a few formal inquiries and an awkward pause and then away, but he actually thought it necessary to turn back and walk with her. He never said a great deal, nor did she give herself the trouble of talking or of listening much; but it struck her in the course of their third rencounter that he was asking some odd unconnected questions—about her pleasure in being at Hunsford, her love of solitary walks, and her opinion of Mr. and Mrs. Collins's happiness; and that in speaking of Rosings, and her not perfectly understanding the house, he seemed to expect that whenever she came into Kent again she would be staying *there* too. His words seemed to imply it. Could he have Colonel Fitzwilliam in his thoughts? She supposed, if he meant anything, he must mean an allusion to what might arise in that quarter. It distressed her a little, and she was quite glad to find herself at the gate in the pales opposite the Parsonage.

She was engaged one day, as she walked, in reperusing Jane's last letter, and dwelling on some passages which proved that Jane had not written in spirits, when, instead of being again surprised by Mr. Darcy, she saw, on looking up, that Colonel Fitzwilliam was meeting her. Putting away the letter immediately, and forcing a smile, she said,—

'I did not know before that you ever walked this way.'

'I have been making the tour of the park,' he replied, 'as I generally do every year, and intended to close it with a call at the Parsonage. Are you going much farther?'

'No, I should have turned in a moment.'

And accordingly she did turn, and they walked towards the Parsonage together.

'Do you certainly leave Kent on Saturday?' said she.

'Yes—if Darcy does not put it off again. But I am at his disposal. He arranges the business just as he pleases.'

'And if not able to please himself in the arrangement, he has at least great pleasure in the power of choice. I do not know anybody who seems more to enjoy the power of doing what he likes than Mr. Darcy.'

'He likes to have his own way very well,' replied Colonel Fitzwilliam. 'But so we all do. It is only that he has better means of having it than many others, because he is rich, and many others are poor. I speak feelingly. A younger son, you know, must be inured to self-denial and dependence.'

'In my opinion, the younger son of an earl can know very little of either. Now, seriously, what have you ever known of self-denial and dependence? When have you been prevented by want of money from going wherever you chose or procuring anything you had a fancy for?'

'These are home questions—and perhaps I cannot say that I have experienced many hardships of that nature. But in matters of greater weight I may suffer from the want of money. Younger sons cannot marry where they like.'

'Unless where they like women of fortune, which I think they very often do.'

'Our habits of expense make us too dependent, and there are not many in my rank of life who can afford to marry without some attention to money.'

'Is this,' thought Elizabeth, 'meant for me?' and she coloured at the idea; but, recovering herself, said in a lively tone, 'And pray, what is the usual price of an earl's younger son? Unless the elder brother is very sickly, I suppose you would not ask above fifty thousand pounds.'

He answered her in the same style, and the subject dropped. To interrupt a silence which might make him fancy her affected with what had passed, she soon afterwards said,—

'I imagine your cousin brought you down with him chiefly for the sake of having somebody at his disposal. I wonder he does not marry, to secure a lasting convenience of that kind. But, perhaps, his sister does as well for the present; and, as she is under his sole care, he may do what he likes with her.'

'No,' said Colonel Fitzwilliam, 'that is an advantage which he must divide with me. I am joined with him in the guardianship of Miss Darcy.'

'Are you indeed? And pray what sort of a guardian do you make? Does your charge give you much trouble? Young ladies of her age are sometimes a little difficult to manage; and if she has the true Darcy spirit, she may like to have her own way.'

As she spoke, she observed him looking at her earnestly; and the manner in which he immediately asked her why she supposed Miss Darcy likely to give them any uneasiness, convinced her that she had somehow or other got pretty near the truth. She directly replied,—

'You need not be frightened. I never heard any harm of her; and I daresay she is one of the most tractable creatures in the world. She is a very great favourite with some ladies of my acquaintance, Mrs. Hurst and Miss Bingley. I think I have heard you say that you know them.'

'I know them a little. Their brother is a pleasant, gentlemanlike man—he is a great friend of Darcy's.'

'Oh yes,' said Elizabeth drily—'Mr. Darcy is uncommonly kind to Mr. Bingley, and takes a prodigious deal of care of him.'

'Care of him! Yes, I really believe Darcy *does* take care of him in those points where he most wants care. From something that he told me in our journey hither, I have reason to think Bingley very much indebted to him. But I ought to beg his pardon, for I have no right to suppose that Bingley was the person meant. It was all conjecture.'

'What is it you mean?'

'It is a circumstance which Darcy of course could not wish to be generally known, because if it were to get round to the lady's family it would be an unpleasant thing.'

'You may depend upon my not mentioning it.'

'And remember that I have not much reason for supposing it to be Bingley. What he told me was merely this: that he congratulated himself on having lately saved a friend from the inconveniences of a most imprudent marriage, but without mentioning names or any other particulars; and I only suspected it to be Bingley from believing him the kind of young man to get into a scrape of that sort, and from knowing them to have been together the whole of last summer.'

'Did Mr. Darcy give you his reasons for this interference?'

'I understood that there were some very strong objections against the lady.'

'And what arts did he use to separate them?'

'He did not talk to me of his own arts,' said Fitzwilliam, smiling. 'He only told me what I have now told you.'

Elizabeth made no answer, and walked on, her heart swelling with indignation. After watching her a little, Fitzwilliam asked her why she was so thoughtful.

'I am thinking of what you have been telling me,' said she. 'Your cousin's conduct does not suit my feelings. Why was he to be the judge?'

'You are rather disposed to call his interference officious?'

'I do not see what right Mr. Darcy had to decide on the propriety of his friend's inclination; or why, upon his own judgment alone, he was to determine and direct in what manner that friend was to be happy. But,' she continued, recollecting herself, 'as we know none of the particulars, it is not fair to condemn him. It is not to be supposed that there was much affection in the case.'

'That is not an unnatural surmise,' said Fitzwilliam; 'but it is lessening the honour of my cousin's triumph very sadly.'

This was spoken jestingly, but it appeared to her so just a picture of Mr. Darcy, that she would not trust herself with an answer; and, therefore, abruptly changing the conversation, talked on indifferent matters till they reached the Parsonage. There, shut into her own room, as soon as their visitor left them, she could think without interruption of all that she had heard. It was not to be supposed that any other people could be meant than those with whom she was connected. There could not exist in the world *two* men over whom Mr. Darcy could have such boundless influence. That he had been concerned in the measures taken to separate Mr. Bingley and Jane, she had never doubted; but she had always attributed to Miss Bingley the principal design and arrangement of them. If his own vanity, however, did not mislead him, *he* was the cause—his pride and caprice were the cause—of all that Jane had suffered, and still continued to suffer. He had ruined for a while every hope of happiness for the most affectionate, generous heart in the world; and no one could say how lasting an evil he might have inflicted.

'There were some very strong objections against the lady,' were Colonel Fitzwilliam's words; and these strong objections probably were, her having one uncle who was a country attorney, and another who was in business in London.

'To Jane herself,' she exclaimed, 'there could be no possibility of objection,—all loveliness and goodness as she is! Her understanding excellent, her mind improved, and her manners captivating. Neither could anything be urged against my father, who, though with some peculiarities, has abilities which Mr. Darcy himself need not disdain, and respectability which he will probably never reach.' When she thought of her mother, indeed, her confidence gave way a little; but she would not allow that any objections *there* had material weight with Mr. Darcy, whose pride, she was convinced, would receive a deeper wound from the want of importance in his friend's connections than from their want of sense; and she was quite decided, as last, that he had been partly governed by this worst kind of pride, and partly by the wish of retaining Mr. Bingley for his sister.

The agitation and tears which the subject occasioned brought on a headache; and it grew so much worse towards the evening that, added to her unwillingness to see Mr. Darcy, it determined her not to attend her cousins to Rosings, where they were engaged to drink tea. Mrs. Collins, seeing that she was really unwell, did not press her to go, and as much as possible prevented her husband from pressing her; but Mr. Collins could not conceal his apprehension of Lady Catherine's being rather displeased by her staying at home.

CHAPTER XXXIV

WHEN they were gone, Elizabeth, as if intending to exasperate herself as much as possible against Mr. Darcy, chose for her employment the examination of all the letters which Jane had written to her since her being in Kent. They contained no actual complaint, nor was there any revival of past occurrences, or any communication of present suffering. But in all, and in almost every line of each, there was a want of that cheerfulness which had been used to characterise her style, and which, proceeding from the serenity of a mind at ease with itself, and kindly disposed towards every one, had been scarcely ever clouded. Elizabeth noticed every sentence conveying the idea of uneasiness, with an attention which it had hardly received on the first perusal. Mr. Darcy's shameful boast of what misery he had been able to inflict gave her a keener sense of her sister's sufferings. It was some consolation to think that his visit to Rosings was to end on the day after the next, and a still greater that in less than a fortnight she should herself be with Jane again, and enabled to contribute to the recovery of her spirits, by all that affection could do.

She could not think of Darcy's leaving Kent without remembering that his cousin was to go with him; but Colonel Fitzwilliam had made it clear that he had no intentions at all, and, agreeable as he was, she did not mean to be unhappy about him.

While settling this point, she was suddenly roused by the sound of the door bell; and her spirits were a little fluttered by the idea of its being Colonel Fitzwilliam himself, who had once before called late in the evening, and might now come to inquire particularly after her. But this idea was soon banished, and her spirits were very differently affected, when, to her utter amazement, she saw Mr. Darcy walk into the room. In a hurried manner he immediately began an inquiry after her health, imputing his visit to a wish of hearing that she were better. She answered him with cold civility. He sat down for a few moments, and then getting up, walked about the room. Elizabeth was surprised, but said not a word. After a silence of several minutes, he came towards her in an agitated manner, and thus began:—

'In vain have I struggled. It will not do. My feelings will not be repressed. You must allow me to tell you how ardently I admire and love you.'

Elizabeth's astonishment was beyond expression. She stared, coloured, doubted, and was silent. This he considered sufficient encouragement, and the avowal of all that he felt and had long felt for her immediately followed. He spoke well, but there were feelings besides those of the heart to be detailed, and he was not more eloquent on the subject of tenderness than of pride. His sense of her inferiority, of its being a degradation, of the family obstacles which judgment had always opposed to inclination, were dwelt on with a warmth which seemed due to the consequence he was wounding, but was very unlikely to recommend his suit.

In spite of her deeply-rooted dislike, she could not be insensible to the compliment of such a man's affection, and though her intentions did not vary for an instant, she was at first sorry for the pain he was to receive; till, roused to resentment by his subsequent language, she lost all compassion in anger. She tried, however, to compose herself to answer him with patience, when he should have done. He concluded with representing to her the strength of that attachment which, in spite of all his endeavours, he had found impossible to conquer; and with expressing his hope that it would now be rewarded by her acceptance of his hand. As he said this she could easily see that he had no doubt of a favourable answer. He *spoke* of apprehension and anxiety, but his countenance expressed real security. Such a circumstance could only exasperate farther; and when he ceased the colour rose into her cheeks and she said,—

'In such cases as this, it is, I believe, the established mode to express a sense of obligation for the sentiments avowed, however unequally they may be returned. It is natural that obligation should be felt, and if I could *feel* gratitude, I would now thank you. But I cannot—I have never desired your good opinion, and you have certainly bestowed it most unwillingly. I am sorry to have occasioned pain to any one. It has been most unconsciously done, however, and I hope will be of short duration. The feelings which you tell me have long prevented the acknowledgment of your regard can have little difficulty in overcoming it after this explanation.'

Mr. Darcy, who was leaning against the mantelpiece with his eyes fixed on her face, seemed to catch her words with no less resentment than surprise. His complexion became pale with anger, and the disturbance of his mind was visible in every feature. He was struggling for the appearance of composure, and would not open his lips till he believed himself to have attained it. The pause was to Elizabeth's feelings dreadful. At length, in a voice of forced calmness, he said,—

'And this is all the reply which I am to have the honour of expecting! I might, perhaps, wish to be informed why, with so little *endeavour* at civility, I am thus rejected. But it is of small importance.'

'I might as well inquire,' replied she, 'why, with so evident a design of offending and insulting me, you chose to tell me that you liked me against your will, against your reason, and even against your character? Was not this some excuse for incivility, if I *was* uncivil? But I have other provocations. You know I have. Had not my own feelings decided against you, had they been indifferent, or had they even been favourable, do you think that any consideration would tempt me to accept the man who has been the means of ruining, perhaps for ever, the happiness of a most beloved sister?'

As she pronounced these words, Mr. Darcy changed colour; but the emotion was short, and he listened without attempting to interrupt her while she continued,—

'I have every reason in the world to think ill of you. No motive can excuse the unjust and ungenerous part you acted *there*. You dare not, you cannot, deny that you have been the principal, if not the only means of dividing them from each other, of exposing one to the censure of the world for caprice and instability, the other to its derision for disappointed hopes, and involving them both in misery of the acutest kind.'

She paused, and saw with no slight indignation that he was listening with an air which proved him wholly unmoved by any feeling of remorse. He even looked at her with a smile of affected incredulity.

'Can you deny that you have done it?' she repeated.

With assumed tranquillity he then replied, 'I have no wish of denying that I did everything in my power to separate my friend from your sister, or that I rejoice in my success. Towards *him* I have been kinder than towards myself.'

Elizabeth disdained the appearance of noticing this civil reflection, but its meaning did not escape, nor was it likely to conciliate her.

'But it is not merely this affair,' she continued, 'on which my dislike is founded. Long before it had taken place, my opinion of you was decided. Your character was unfolded in the recital which I received many months ago from Mr. Wickham. On this subject, what can you have to say? In what imaginary act of friendship can you here defend yourself? or under what misrepresentation can you here impose upon others?'

'You take an eager interest in that gentleman's concerns,' said Darcy, in a less tranquil tone, and with a heightened colour.

'Who that knows what his misfortunes have been can help feeling an interest in him?'

'His misfortunes!' repeated Darcy, contemptuously,—'yes, his misfortunes have been great indeed.'

'And of your infliction,' cried Elizabeth, with energy. 'You have reduced him to his present state of poverty—comparative poverty. You have withheld the advantages which you must know to have been designed for him. You have deprived the best years of his life of that independence which was no less his due than his desert. You have done all this! and yet you can treat the mention of his misfortunes with contempt and ridicule.'

'And this,' cried Darcy, as he walked with quick steps across the room, 'is your opinion of me! This is the estimation in which you hold me! I thank you for explaining it so fully. My faults, according to this calculation, are heavy indeed! But, perhaps,' added he, stopping in his walk, and turning towards her, 'these offences might have been over-looked, had not your pride been hurt by my honest confession of the scruples that had long prevented my forming any serious design. These bitter accusations might have been suppressed, had I, with greater policy, concealed my struggles, and flattered you into the belief of my being impelled by unqualified, unalloyed inclination; by reason, by reflection, by everything. But disguise of every sort is my abhorrence. Nor am I ashamed of the feelings I related. They were natural and just. Could you expect me to rejoice in the inferiority of your connections? To congratulate myself on the hope of relations whose condition in life is so decidedly beneath my own?'

Elizabeth felt herself growing more angry every moment; yet she tried to the utmost to speak with composure when she said,—

'You are mistaken, Mr. Darcy, if you suppose that the mode of your declaration affected me in any other way than as it spared me the concern which I might have felt in refusing you, had you behaved in a more gentlemanlike manner.'

She saw him start at this; but he said nothing, and she continued,—

'You could not have made me the offer of your hand in any possible way that would have tempted me to accept it.'

Again his astonishment was obvious; and he looked at her with an expression of mingled incredulity and mortification. She went on,—

'From the very beginning, from the first moment, I may almost say, of my acquaintance with you, your manners, impressing me with the fullest belief of your arrogance, your conceit, and your selfish disdain of the feelings of others, were such as to form that groundwork of disapprobation on which succeeding events have built so immovable a dislike; and I had not known you a month before I felt that you were the last man in the world whom I could ever be prevailed on to marry.'

'You have said quite enough, madam. I perfectly comprehend your feelings, and have now only to be ashamed of what my own have been. Forgive me for having taken up so much of your time, and accept my best wishes for your health and happiness.'

And with these words he hastily left the room, and Elizabeth heard him the next moment open the front door and quit the house. The tumult of her mind was now painfully great. She knew not how to support herself, and, from actual weakness, sat down and cried for half an hour. Her astonishment, as she reflected on what had passed, was increased by every review of it. That she should receive an offer of marriage from Mr. Darcy! that he should have been in love with her for so many months! so much in love as to wish to marry her in spite of all the objections which had made him prevent his friend's marrying her sister, and which must appear at least with equal force in his own case, was almost incredible! it was gratifying to have inspired unconsciously so strong an affection. But his pride, his abominable pride, his shameless avowal of what he had done with respect to Jane, his unpardonable assurance in acknowledging, though he could not justify it, and the unfeeling manner in which he had mentioned Mr. Wickham, his cruelty towards whom he had not attempted to deny, soon overcame the pity which the consideration of his attachment had for a moment excited.

She continued in very agitating reflections till the sound of Lady Catherine's carriage made her feel how unequal she was to encounter Charlotte's observation, and hurried her away to her room.

CHAPTER XXXV

ELIZABETH awoke the next morning to the same thoughts and meditations which had at length closed her eyes. She could not yet recover from the surprise of what had happened: it was impossible to think of anything else; and, totally indisposed for employment, she resolved soon after breakfast to indulge herself in air and exercise. She was proceeding directly to her favourite walk, when the recollection of Mr. Darcy's sometimes coming there stopped her, and instead of entering the park, she turned up the lane which led her farther from the turnpike road. The park paling was still the boundary on one side, and she soon passed one of the gates into the ground.

After walking two or three times along that part of the lane, she was tempted, by the pleasantness of the morning, to stop at the gates and look into the park. The five weeks which she had now passed in Kent had made a great difference in the country, and every day was adding to the verdure of the early trees. She was on the point of continuing her walk, when she caught a glimpse of a gentleman within the sort of grove which edged the park: he was moving that way; and fearful of its being Mr. Darcy, she was directly retreating. But the person who advanced was now near enough to see her, and stepping forward with eagerness, pronounced her name. She had turned away; but on hearing herself called, though in a voice which proved it to be Mr. Darcy, she moved again towards the gate. He had by that time reached it also; and, holding out a letter, which she instinctively took, said, with a look of haughty composure, 'I have been walking in the grove some time, in the hope of meeting you. Will you do me the honour of reading that letter?' and then, with a slight bow, turned again into the plantation, and was soon out of sight.

With no expectation of pleasure, but with the strongest curiosity, Elizabeth opened the letter, and to her still increasing wonder, perceived an envelope containing two sheets of letter paper, written quite through, in a very close hand. The envelope itself was likewise full. Pursuing her way along the lane, she then began it. It was dated from Rosings, at eight o'clock in the morning, and was as follows:—

'Be not alarmed, madam, on receiving this letter, by the apprehension of its containing any repetition of those sentiments, or renewal of those offers, which were last night so disgusting to you. I write without any intention of paining you, or humbling myself, by dwelling on wishes, which, for the happiness of both, cannot be too soon forgotten; and the effort which the formation and the perusal of this letter must occasion should have been spared, had not my character required it to be written and read. You must, therefore, pardon the freedom with which I demand your attention; your feelings, I know, will bestow it unwillingly, but I demand it of your justice.

'Two offences of a very different nature, and by no means of equal magnitude, you last night laid to my charge. The first mentioned was, that, regardless of the sentiments of either, I had detached Mr. Bingley from your sister,—and the other, that I had, in defiance of various claims, in defiance of honour and humanity, ruined the immediate prosperity and blasted the prospects of Mr. Wickham. Wilfully and wantonly to have thrown off the companion of my youth, the acknowledged favourite of my father, a young man who had scarcely any other dependence than on our patronage, and who had been brought up to expect its exertion, would be a depravity, to which the separation of two young persons whose affection could be the growth of only a few weeks could bear no comparison. But from the severity of that blame which was last night so liberally bestowed, respecting each circumstance, I shall hope to be in future secured, when the following account of my actions and their motives has been read. If, in the explanation of them which is due to myself, I am under the necessity of relating feelings which may be offensive to yours, I can only say that I am sorry. The necessity must be obeyed, and further apology would be absurd. I had not been long in Hertfordshire before I saw, in common with others, that Bingley preferred your elder sister to any other young woman in the country. But it was not till the evening of the dance at Netherfield that I had any apprehension of his feeling a serious attachment. I had often seen him in love before. At that ball, while I had the honour of dancing with you, I was first made acquainted, by Sir William Lucas's accidental information, that Bingley's attentions to your sister had given rise to a general expectation of their marriage. He spoke of it as a certain event, of which the time alone could be undecided. From that moment I observed my friend's behaviour attentively; and I could then perceive that his partiality for Miss Bennet was beyond what I had ever witnessed in him. Your sister I also watched. Her look and manners were open, cheerful, and engaging as ever, but without any symptom of peculiar regard; and I remained convinced, from the evening's scrutiny, that though she received his attentions with pleasure, she did not invite them by any participation of sentiment. If *you* have not been mistaken here, *I* must have been in an error. Your superior knowledge of your sister must make the latter probable. If it be so, if I have been misled by such error to inflict pain on her, your resentment has not been unreasonable. But I shall not scruple to assert that the serenity of your sister's countenance and air was such as might have given the most acute observer a conviction that, however amiable her temper, her heart was not likely to be easily touched. That I was desirous of believing her indifferent is certain; but I will venture to say that my investigations and decisions are not usually influenced by my hopes or fears. I did not believe her to be indifferent because I wished it; I believed it on impartial conviction, as truly as I wished it in reason. My objections to the marriage were not merely those which I last night acknowledged to have required the utmost force of passion to put aside in my own case; the want of connection could not be so great an evil to my friend as to me. But there were other causes of repugnance; causes which, though still existing, and existing to an equal degree in both instances, I had myself endeavoured to forget, because they were not immediately before me. These causes must be stated, though briefly. The situation of your mother's family, though objectionable, was nothing in comparison of that total want of propriety so frequently, so almost uniformly betrayed by herself, by your three younger sisters, and occasionally even by your father:—pardon me,—it pains me to offend you. But amidst your concern for the defects of your nearest relations, and your displeasure at this representation of them, let it give you consolation to consider that to have conducted yourselves so as to avoid any share of the like censure is praise no less generally bestowed on you and your elder sister than it is honourable to the sense and disposition of both. I will only say, farther, that from what passed that evening my opinion of all parties was confirmed, and every inducement heightened, which could have led me before to preserve my friend from what I esteemed a most unhappy connection. He left Netherfield for London on the day following, as you, I am certain, remember, with the design of soon returning. The part which I acted is now to be explained. His sisters' uneasiness had been equally excited with my own: our coincidence of feeling was soon discovered; and, alike sensible that no time was to be lost in detaching their brother, we shortly resolved on joining him directly in London. We accordingly went—and there I readily engaged in the office of pointing out to my friend the certain evils of such a choice. I described and enforced them earnestly. But however this remonstrance might have staggered or delayed his determination, I do not suppose that it would ultimately have prevented the marriage, had it not been seconded by the assurance, which I hesitated not in giving, of your sister's indifference. He had before believed her to return his affection with sincere, if not with equal, regard. But

Bingley has great natural modesty, with a stronger dependence on my judgment than on his own. To convince him, therefore, that he had deceived himself was no very difficult point. To persuade him against returning into Hertfordshire, when that conviction had been given, was scarcely the work of a moment. I cannot blame myself for having done thus much. There is but one part of my conduct, in the whole affair, on which I do not reflect with satisfaction; it is that I condescended to adopt the measures of art so far as to conceal from him your sister's being in town. I knew it myself, as it was known to Miss Bingley; but her brother is even yet ignorant of it. That they might have met without ill consequence is, perhaps, probable; but his regard did not appear to me enough extinguished for him to see her without some danger. Perhaps this concealment, this disguise, was beneath me. It is done, however, and it was done for the best. On this subject I have nothing more to say, no other apology to offer. If I have wounded your sister's feelings, it was unknowingly done; and though the motives which governed me may to you very naturally appear insufficient, I have not yet learnt to condemn them.—With respect to that other, more weighty accusation, of having injured Mr. Wickham, I can only refute it by laying before you the whole of his connection with my family. Of what he has *particularly* accused me I am ignorant; but of the truth of what I shall relate I can summon more than one witness of undoubted veracity. Mr. Wickham is the son of a very respectable man, who had for many years the management of all the Pemberley estates, and whose good conduct in the discharge of his trust naturally inclined my father to be of service to him; and on George Wickham, who was his godson, his kindness was therefore liberally bestowed. My father supported him at school, and afterwards at Cambridge; most important assistance, as his own father, always poor from the extravagance of his wife, would have been unable to give him a gentleman's education. My father was not only fond of this young man's society, whose manners were always engaging, he had also the highest opinion of him, and hoping the church would be his profession, intended to provide for him in it. As for myself, it is many, many years since I first began to think of him in a very different manner. The vicious propensities, the want of principle, which he was careful to guard from the knowledge of his best friend, could not escape the observation of a young man of nearly the same age with himself, and who had opportunities of seeing him in unguarded moments, which Mr. Darcy could not have. Here again I shall give you pain—to what degree you only can tell. But whatever may be the sentiments which Mr. Wickham has created, a suspicion of their nature shall not prevent me from unfolding his real character. It adds even another motive. My excellent father died about five years ago; and his attachment to Mr. Wickham was to the last so steady, that in his will he particularly recommended it to me to promote his advancement in the best manner that his profession might allow, and if he took orders, desired that a valuable family living might be his as soon as it became vacant. There was also a legacy of one thousand pounds. His own father did not long survive mine; and within half a year from these events Mr. Wickham wrote to inform me that, having finally resolved against taking orders, he hoped I should not think it unreasonable for him to expect some more immediate pecuniary advantage, in lieu of the preferment, by which he could not be benefited. He had some intention, he added, of studying the law, and I must be aware that the interest of one thousand pounds would be a very insufficient support therein. I rather wished than believed him to be sincere; but, at any rate, was perfectly ready to accede to his proposal. I knew that Mr. Wickham ought not to be a clergyman. The business was therefore soon settled. He resigned all claim to assistance in the church, were it possible that he could ever be in a situation to receive it, and accepted in return three thousand pounds. All connection between us seemed now dissolved. I thought too ill of him to invite him to Pemberley, or admit his society in town. In town, I believe, he chiefly lived, but his studying the law was a mere pretence; and being now free from all restraint, his life was a life of idleness and dissipation. For about three years I heard little of him; but on the decease of the incumbent of the living which had been designed for him, he applied to me again by letter for the presentation. His circumstances, he assured me, and I had no difficulty in believing it, were exceedingly bad. He had found the law a most unprofitable study, and was now absolutely resolved on being ordained, if I would present him to the living in question—of which he trusted there could be little doubt, as he was well assured that I had no other person to provide for, and I could not have forgotten my revered father's intentions. You will hardly blame me for refusing to comply with this entreaty, or for resisting every repetition of it. His resentment was in proportion to the distress of his circumstances—and he was doubtless as violent in his abuse of me to others as in his reproaches to myself. After this period, every appearance of acquaintance was dropped. How he lived, I know not. But last summer he was again most painfully obtruded on my notice. I must now mention a circumstance which I would wish to forget myself, and which no obligation less than the present should induce me to unfold to any human being. Having said thus much, I feel no doubt of your secrecy. My sister, who is more than ten years my junior, was left to the guardianship of my mother's nephew, Colonel Fitzwilliam, and myself. About a year ago, she was taken from school, and an establishment formed for her in London; and last summer she went with the lady who presided over it to Ramsgate; and thither also went Mr. Wickham, undoubtedly by design; for there proved to have been a prior acquaintance between him and Mrs. Younge, in whose character we were most unhappily deceived; and by her connivance and aid he so far recommended himself to Georgiana, whose affectionate heart retained a strong impression of his kindness to her as a child, that she was persuaded to believe herself in love and to consent to an elopement. She was then but fifteen, which must be her excuse; and after stating her imprudence,

I am happy to add that I owed the knowledge of it to herself. I joined them unexpectedly a day or two before the intended elopement; and then Georgiana, unable to support the idea of grieving and offending a brother whom she almost looked up to as a father, acknowledged the whole to me. You may imagine what I felt and how I acted. Regard for my sister's credit and feelings prevented any public exposure; but I wrote to Mr. Wickham, who left the place immediately, and Mrs. Younge was of course removed from her charge. Mr. Wickham's chief object was unquestionably my sister's fortune, which is thirty thousand pounds; but I cannot help supposing that the hope of revenging himself on me was a strong inducement. His revenge would have been complete indeed. This, madam, is a faithful narrative of every event in which we have been concerned together; and if you do not absolutely reject it as false, you will, I hope, acquit me henceforth of cruelty towards Mr. Wickham. I know not in what manner, under what form of falsehood, he has imposed on you; but his success is not perhaps to be wondered at, ignorant as you previously were of everything concerning either. Detection could not be in your power, and suspicion certainly not in your inclination. You may possibly wonder why all this was not told you last night. But I was not then master enough of myself to know what could or ought to be revealed. For the truth of everything here related, I can appeal more particularly to the testimony of Colonel Fitzwilliam, who, from our near relationship and constant intimacy, and still more as one of the executors of my father's will, has been unavoidably acquainted with every particular of these transactions. If your abhorrence of *me* should make *my* assertions valueless, you cannot be prevented by the same cause from confiding in my cousin; and that there may be the possibility of consulting him, I shall endeavour to find some opportunity of putting this letter in your hands in the course of the morning. I will only add, God bless you.

'FITZWILLIAM DARCY.'

CHAPTER XXXVI

I F Elizabeth, when Mr. Darcy gave her the letter, did not expect it to contain a renewal of his offers, she had formed no expectation at all of its contents. But, such as they were, it may be well supposed how eagerly she went through them, and what a contrariety of emotion they excited. Her feelings as she read were scarcely to be defined. With amazement did she first understand that he believed any apology to be in his power; and steadfastly was she persuaded that he could have no explanation to give, which a just sense of shame would not conceal. With a strong prejudice against everything he might say, she began his account of what had happened at Netherfield. She read with an eagerness which hardly left her power of comprehension; and from impatience of knowing what the next sentence might bring, was incapable of attending to the sense of the one before her eyes. His belief of her sister's insensibility she instantly resolved to be false; and his account of the real, the worst objections to the match, made her too angry to have any wish of doing him justice. He expressed no regret for what he had done which satisfied her; his style was not penitent, but haughty. It was all pride and insolence.

But when this subject was succeeded by his account of Mr. Wickham—when she read, with somewhat clearer attention, a relation of events which, if true, must overthrow every cherished opinion of his worth, and which bore so alarming an affinity to his own history of himself—her feelings were yet more acutely painful and more difficult of definition. Astonishment, apprehension, and even horror, oppressed her. She wished to discredit it entirely, repeatedly exclaiming, 'This must be false! This cannot be! This must be the grossest falsehood!'—and when she had gone through the whole letter, though scarcely knowing anything of the last page or two, put it hastily away, protesting that she would not regard it, that she would never look in it again.

In this perturbed state of mind, with thoughts that could rest on nothing, she walked on; but it would not do: in half a minute the letter was unfolded again; and, collecting herself as well as she could, she again began the mortifying perusal of all that related to Wickham, and commanded herself so far as to examine the meaning of every sentence. The account of his connection with the Pemberley family was exactly what he had related himself; and the kindness of the late Mr. Darcy, though she had not before known its extent, agreed equally well with his own words. So far each recital confirmed the other; but when she came to the will, the difference was great. What Wickham had said of the living was fresh in her memory; and as she recalled his very words, it was impossible not to feel that there was gross duplicity on one side or the other, and, for a few moments, she flattered herself that her wishes did not err. But when she read and re-read with the closest attention, the particulars immediately following, of Wickham's resigning all pretensions to the living, of his receiving in lieu so considerable a sum as three thousand pounds, again was she forced to hesitate.

She put down the letter, weighed every circumstance with what she meant to be impartiality—deliberated on the probability of each statement—but with little success. On both sides it was only assertion. Again she read on. But every line proved more clearly that the affair, which she had believed it impossible that any contrivance could so represent as to render Mr. Darcy's conduct in it less than infamous, was capable of a turn which must make him entirely blameless throughout the whole.

The extravagance and general profligacy which he scrupled not to lay to Mr. Wickham's charge exceedingly shocked her; the more so, as she could bring no proof of its injustice. She had never heard of him before his entrance into the ——shire militia, in which he had engaged at the persuasion of the young man who, on meeting him accidentally in town, had there renewed a slight acquaintance. Of his former way of life nothing had been known in Hertfordshire but what he told himself. As to his real character, had information been in her power, she had never felt a wish of inquiring. His countenance, voice, and manner, had established him at once in the possession of every virtue. She tried to recollect some instance of goodness, some distinguished trait of integrity or benevolence, that might rescue him from the attacks of Mr. Darcy; or at least, by the predominance of virtue, atone for those casual errors, under which she would endeavour to class what Mr. Darcy had described as the idleness and vice of many years' continuance. But no such recollection befriended her. She could see him instantly before her, in every charm of air and address, but she could remember no more substantial good than the general approbation of the neighbourhood, and the regard which his social powers had gained him in the mess. After pausing on this point a considerable while, she once more continued to read. But, alas! the story which followed, of his designs on Miss Darcy, received some confirmation from what had passed between Colonel Fitzwilliam and herself only the morning before; and at last she was referred for the truth of every particular to Colonel Fitzwilliam himself—from whom she had previously received the information of his near concern in all his cousin's affairs, and whose character she had no reason to question. At one time she had almost resolved on applying to him, but the idea was checked by the awkwardness of the application, and at length wholly banished by the conviction that Mr. Darcy would never have hazarded such a proposal, if he had not been well assured of his cousin's corroboration.

She perfectly remembered everything that had passed in conversation between Wickham and herself in their first evening at Mr. Philips's. Many of his expressions were still fresh in her memory. She was *now* struck with the impropriety of such communications to a stranger, and wondered it had escaped her before. She saw the indelicacy of putting himself forward as he had done, and the inconsistency of his professions with his conduct. She remembered that he had boasted of having no fear of seeing Mr. Darcy— that Mr. Darcy might leave the country, but that *he* should stand his ground; yet he had avoided the Netherfield ball the very next week. She remembered, also, that till the Netherfield family had quitted the country, he had told his story to no one but herself; but that after their removal, it had been everywhere discussed; that he had then no reserves, no scruples in sinking Mr. Darcy's character, though he had assured her that respect for the father would always prevent his exposing the son.

How differently did everything now appear in which he was concerned! His attentions to Miss King were now the consequence of views solely and hatefully mercenary; and the mediocrity of her fortune proved no longer the moderation of his wishes, but his eagerness to grasp at anything. His behaviour to herself could now have had no tolerable motive: he had either been deceived with regard to her fortune, or had been gratifying his vanity by encouraging the preference which she believed she had most incautiously shown. Every lingering struggle in his favour grew fainter and fainter; and in further justification of Mr. Darcy, she could not but allow that Mr. Bingley, when questioned by Jane, had long ago asserted his blamelessness in the affair;— that, proud and repulsive as were his manners, she had never, in the whole course of their acquaintance—an acquaintance which had latterly brought them much together, and given her a sort of intimacy with his ways—seen anything that betrayed him to be unprincipled or unjust—anything that spoke him of irreligious or immoral habits;— that among his own connections he was esteemed and valued —that even Wickham had allowed him merit as a brother, and that she had often heard him speak so affectionately of his sister as to prove him capable of some amiable feeling; —that had his actions been what Wickham represented them, so gross a violation of everything right could hardly have been concealed from the world; and that friendship between a person capable of it and such an amiable man as Mr. Bingley was incomprehensible.

She grew absolutely ashamed of herself. Of neither Darcy nor Wickham could she think, without feeling that she had been blind, partial, prejudiced, absurd.

'How despicably have I acted!' she cried. 'I, who have prided myself on my discernment! I, who have valued myself on my abilities! who have often disdained the generous candour of my sister, and gratified my vanity in useless or blameless distrust. How humiliating is this discovery! Yet, how just a humiliation! Had I been in love, I could not have been more wretchedly blind. But vanity, not love, has been my folly. Pleased with the preference of one, and offended by the neglect of the other, on the very beginning of our acquaintance I have courted prepossession and ignorance, and driven reason away where either was concerned. Till this moment, I never knew myself.'

From herself to Jane, from Jane to Bingley, her thoughts were in a line which soon brought to her recollection that Mr. Darcy's explanation *there* had appeared very insufficient; and she read it again. Widely different was the effect of a second perusal. How could she deny that credit to his assertions, in one instance, which she had been obliged to give in the other? He declared himself to have been totally unsuspicious of her sister's attachment; and she could not help remembering what Charlotte's opinion had always been. Neither could she deny the justice of his description of Jane. She felt that Jane's feelings, though fervent, were little displayed, and that there was a constant complacency in her air and manner, not often united with great sensibility.

When she came to that part of the letter in which her family were mentioned, in terms of such mortifying, yet merited, reproach, her sense of shame was severe. The justice of the charge struck her too forcibly for denial; and the circumstances to which he particularly alluded, as having passed at the Netherfield ball, and as confirming all his first disapprobation, could not have made a stronger impression on his mind than on hers.

The compliment to herself and her sister was not unfelt. It soothed, but it could not console her for the contempt which had been thus self-attracted by the rest of her family; and as she considered that Jane's disappointment had, in fact, been the work of her nearest relations, and reflected how materially the credit of both must be hurt by such impropriety of conduct, she felt depressed beyond anything she had ever known before.

After wandering along the lane for two hours, giving way to every variety of thought, reconsidering events, determining probabilities, and reconciling herself, as well as she could, to a change so sudden and so important, fatigue, and a recollection of her long absence, made her at length return home; and she entered the house with the wish of appearing cheerful as usual, and the resolution of repressing such reflections as must make her unfit for conversation.

She was immediately told that the two gentlemen from Rosings had each called during her absence; Mr. Darcy, only for a few minutes, to take leave, but that Colonel Fitzwilliam had been sitting with them at least an hour, hoping for her return, and almost resolving to walk after her till she could be found. Elizabeth could but just *affect* concern in missing him; she really rejoiced at it. Colonel Fitzwilliam was no longer an object. She could think only of her letter.

CHAPTER XXXVII

THE two gentlemen left Rosings the next morning; and Mr. Collins having been in waiting near the lodges, to make them his parting obeisance, was able to bring home the pleasing intelligence of their appearing in very good health, and in as tolerable spirits as could be expected, after the melancholy scene so lately gone through at Rosings. To Rosings he then hastened to console Lady Catherine and her daughter; and on his return brought back, with great satisfaction, a message from her Ladyship, importing that she felt herself so dull as to make her very desirous of having them all to dine with her.

Elizabeth could not see Lady Catherine without recollecting that, had she chosen it, she might by this time have been presented to her as her future niece; nor could she think, without a smile, of what her Ladyship's indignation would have been. 'What would she have said? how would she have behaved?' were questions with which she amused herself.

Their first subject was the diminution of the Rosings party. 'I assure you I feel it exceedingly,' said Lady Catherine; 'I believe nobody feels the loss of friends so much as I do. But I am particularly attached to these young men; and know them to be so much attached to me! They were excessively sorry to go! But so they always are. The dear Colonel rallied his spirits tolerably till just at last; but Darcy seemed to feel it most acutely—more, I think, than last year. His attachment to Rosings certainly increases.'

Mr. Collins had a compliment and an allusion to throw in here, which were kindly smiled on by the mother and daughter.

Lady Catherine observed, after dinner, that Miss Bennet seemed out of spirits; and immediately accounting for it herself, by supposing that she did not like to go home again so soon, she added,—

'But if that is the case, you must write to your mother to

352

beg that you may stay a little longer. Mrs. Collins will be very glad of your company, I am sure.'

'I am much obliged to your Ladyship for your kind invitation,' replied Elizabeth; 'but it is not in my power to accept it. I must be in town next Saturday.'

'Why, at that rate, you will have been here only six weeks. I expected you to stay two months. I told Mrs. Collins so before you came. There can be no occasion for your going so soon. Mrs. Bennet could certainly spare you for another fortnight.'

'But my father cannot. He wrote last week to hurry my return.'

'Oh, your father, of course, may spare you, if your mother can. Daughters are never of so much consequence to a father. And if you will stay another *month* complete, it will be in my power to take one of you as far as London, for I am going there early in June, for a week; and as Dawson does not object to the barouche-box, there will be very good room for one of you—and, indeed, if the weather should happen to be cool, I should not object to taking you both, as you are neither of you large.'

'You are all kindness, madam; but I believe we must abide by our original plan.'

Lady Catherine seemed resigned. 'Mrs. Collins, you must send a servant with them. You know I always speak my mind, and I cannot bear the idea of two young women travelling post by themselves. It is highly improper. You must contrive to send somebody. I have the greatest dislike in the world to that sort of thing. Young women should always be properly guarded and attended, according to their situation in life. When my niece Georgiana went to Ramsgate last summer, I made a point of her having two men-servants go with her. Miss Darcy, the daughter of Mr. Darcy of Pemberley, and Lady Anne, could not have appeared with propriety in a different manner. I am excessively attentive to all those things. You must send John with the young ladies, Mrs. Collins. I am glad it occurred to me to mention it; for it would really be discreditable to *you* to let them go alone.'

'My uncle is to send a servant for us.'

'Oh! Your uncle! He keeps a man-servant, does he? I am very glad you have somebody who thinks of those things. Where shall you change horses? Oh, Bromley, of course. If you mention my name at the Bell, you will be attended to.'

Lady Catherine had many other questions to ask respecting their journey, and as she did not answer them all herself attention was necessary, which Elizabeth believed to be lucky for her; or, with a mind so occupied, she might have forgotten where she was. Reflection must be reserved for solitary hours: whenever she was alone, she gave way to it as the greatest relief; and not a day went by without a solitary walk, in which she might indulge in all the delight of unpleasant recollections.

Mr. Darcy's letter she was in a fair way of soon knowing by heart. She studied every sentence; and her feelings towards its writer were at times widely different. When she remembered the style of his address, she was still full of indignation: but when she considered how unjustly she had condemned and upbraided him, her anger was turned against herself; and his disappointed feelings became the object of compassion. His attachment excited gratitude, his general character respect: but she could not approve him; nor could she for a moment repent her refusal, or feel the slightest inclination ever to see him again. In her own past behaviour there was a constant source of vexation and regret: and in the unhappy defects of her family a subject of yet heavier chagrin. They were hopeless of remedy. Her father, contented with laughing at them, would never exert himself to restrain the wild giddiness of his youngest daughters; and her mother, with manners so far from right herself, was entirely insensible of the evil. Elizabeth had frequently united with Jane in an endeavour to check the imprudence of Catherine and Lydia; but while they were supported by their mother's indulgence, what chance could there be of improvement? Catherine, weak-spirited, irritable, and completely under Lydia's guidance, had been always affronted by their advice; and Lydia, self-willed and careless, would scarcely give them a hearing. They were ignorant, idle, and vain. While there was an officer in Meryton, they would flirt with him; and while Meryton was within a walk of Longbourn, they would be going there for ever.

Anxiety on Jane's behalf was another prevailing concern; and Mr. Darcy's explanation, by restoring Bingley to all her former good opinion, heightened the sense of what Jane had lost. His affection was proved to have been sincere, and his conduct cleared of all blame, unless any could attach to the implicitness of his confidence in his friend. How grievous then was the thought that, of a situation so desirable in every respect, so replete with advantage, so promising for happiness, Jane had been deprived, by the folly and indecorum of her own family!

When to these recollections was added the development of Wickham's character, it may be easily believed that the happy spirits which had seldom been depressed before were now so much affected as to make it almost impossible for her to appear tolerably cheerful.

Their engagements at Rosings were as frequent during the last week of her stay as they had been at first. The very last evening was spent there; and her Ladyship again inquired minutely into the particulars of their journey, gave them directions as to the best method of packing, and was so urgent on the necessity of placing gowns in the only right way, that Maria thought herself obliged, on her return, to undo all the work of the morning, and pack her trunk afresh.

When they parted, Lady Catherine, with great condescension, wished them a good journey, and invited them to come to Hunsford again next year; and Miss De Bourgh exerted herself so far as to courtesy and hold out her hand to both.

CHAPTER XXXVIII

O N Saturday morning Elizabeth and Mr. Collins met for breakfast a few minutes before the others appeared; and he took the opportunity of paying the parting civilities which he deemed indispensably necessary.

'I know not, Miss Elizabeth,' said he, 'whether Mrs. Collins has yet expressed her sense of your kindness in coming to us; but I am very certain you will not leave the house without receiving her thanks for it. The favour of your company has been much felt, I assure you. We know how little there is to tempt any one to our humble abode. Our plain manner of living, our small rooms, and few domestics, and the little we see of the world, must make Hunsford extremely dull to a young lady like yourself; but I hope you will believe us grateful for the condescension, and that we have done everything in our power to prevent your spending your time unpleasantly.'

Elizabeth was eager with her thanks and assurances of happiness. She had spent six weeks with great enjoyment; and the pleasure of being with Charlotte, and the kind attentions she had received, must make *her* feel the obliged. Mr. Collins was gratified; and with a more smiling solemnity replied,—

'It gives me the greatest pleasure to hear that you have passed your time not disagreeably. We have certainly done our best; and most fortunately having it in our power to introduce you to very superior society, and from our connection with Rosings, the frequent means of varying the humble home scene, I think we may flatter ourselves that your Hunsford visit cannot have been entirely irksome. Our situation with regard to Lady Catherine's family is, indeed, the sort of extraordinary advantage and blessing which few can boast. You see on what a footing we are. You see how continually we are engaged there. In truth, I must acknowledge that, with all the disadvantages of this humble parsonage, I should not think any one abiding in it an object of compassion while they are sharers of our intimacy at Rosings.'

Words were insufficient for the elevation of his feelings; and he was obliged to walk about the room, while Elizabeth tried to unite civility and truth in a few short sentences.

'You may, in fact, carry a very favourable report of us into Hertfordshire, my dear cousin. I flatter myself, at least, that you will be able to do so. Lady Catherine's great attentions to Mrs. Collins you have been a daily witness of; and altogether I trust it does not appear that your friend has drawn an unfortunate—but on this point it will be as well to be silent. Only let me assure you, my dear Miss Elizabeth, that I can from my heart most cordially wish you equal felicity in marriage. My dear Charlotte and I have but one mind and one way of thinking. There is in everything a most remarkable resemblance of character and ideas between us. We seem to have been designed for each other.'

Elizabeth could safely say that it was a great happiness where that was the case, and with equal sincerity could add, that she firmly believed and rejoiced in his domestic comforts. She was not sorry, however, to have the recital of them interrupted by the entrance of the lady from whom they sprang. Poor Charlotte! it was melancholy to leave her to such society! But she had chosen it with her eyes open; and though evidently regretting that her visitors were to go, she did not seem to ask for compassion. Her home and her housekeeping, her parish and her poultry, and all their dependent concerns, had not yet lost their charms.

At length the chaise arrived, the trunks were fastened on, the parcels placed within, and it was pronounced to be ready.

After an affectionate parting between the friends, Elizabeth was attended to the carriage by Mr. Collins; and as they walked down the garden, he was commissioning her with his best respects to all her family, not forgetting his thanks for the kindness he had received at Longbourn in the winter, and his compliments to Mr. and Mrs. Gardiner, though unknown. He then handed her in, Maria followed, and the door was on the point of being closed, when he suddenly reminded them, with some consternation, that they had hitherto forgotten to leave any message for the ladies of Rosings.

'But,' he added, 'you will of course wish to have your humble respects delivered to them, with your grateful thanks for their kindness to you while you have been here.'

Elizabeth made no objection: the door was then allowed to be shut, and the carriage drove off.

'Good gracious!' cried Maria, after a few minutes' silence, 'it seems but a day or two since we first came! and yet how many things have happened!'

'A great many, indeed,' said her companion, with a sigh.

'We have dined nine times at Rosings, besides drinking tea there twice! How much I shall have to tell!'

Elizabeth privately added, 'And how much I shall have to conceal.'

Their journey was performed without much conversation, or any alarm; and within four hours of their leaving Hunsford they reached Mr. Gardiner's house, where they were to remain a few days.

Jane looked well, and Elizabeth had little opportunity of studying her spirits, amidst the various engagements which the kindness of her aunt had reserved for them. But Jane was to go home with her, and at Longbourn there would be leisure enough for observation.

It was not without an effort, meanwhile, that she could wait even for Longbourn, before she told her sister of Mr. Darcy's proposals. To know that she had the power of revealing what would so exceedingly astonish Jane, and must, at the same time, so highly gratify whatever of her own vanity she had not yet been able to reason away, was such a temptation to openness as nothing could have conquered, but the state of indecision in which she remained as to the extent of what she should communicate, and her fear, if she once entered on the subject, of being hurried into repeating something of Bingley, which might only grieve her sister further.

CHAPTER XXXIX

IT was the second week in May, in which the three young ladies set out together from Gracechurch Street for the town of ——, in Hertfordshire; and, as they drew near the appointed inn where Mr. Bennet's carriage was to meet them, they quickly perceived, in token of the coachman's punctuality, both Kitty and Lydia looking out of a dining-room upstairs. These two girls had been above an hour in the place, happily employed in visiting an opposite milliner, watching the sentinel on guard, and dressing a salad and cucumber.

After welcoming their sisters, they triumphantly displayed a table set out with such cold meat as an inn larder usually affords, exclaiming, 'Is not this nice? is not this an agreeable surprise?'

'And we mean to treat you all,' added Lydia; 'but you must lend us the money, for we have just spent ours at the shop out there.' Then showing her purchases,—'Look here, I have bought this bonnet. I do not think it is very pretty; but I thought I might as well buy it as not. I shall pull it to pieces as soon as I get home, and see if I can make it up any better.'

And when her sisters abused it as ugly, she added, with perfect unconcern, 'Oh, but there were two or three much uglier in the shop; and when I have bought some prettier-coloured satin to trim it with fresh, I think it will be very tolerable. Besides, it will not much signify what one wears this summer, after the ——shire have left Meryton, and they are going in a fortnight.'

'Are they, indeed?' cried Elizabeth, with the greatest satisfaction.

'They are going to be encamped near Brighton; and I do so want papa to take us all there for the summer! It would be such a delicious scheme, and I daresay would hardly cost anything at all. Mamma would like to go, too, of all things! Only think what a miserable summer else we shall have!'

'Yes,' thought Elizabeth; 'that would be a delightful scheme, indeed, and completely do for us at once. Good Heaven! Brighton and a whole campful of soldiers, to us, who have been overset already by one poor regiment of militia, and the monthly balls of Meryton!'

'Now I have got some news for you,' said Lydia, as they sat down to table. 'What do you think? It is excellent news, capital news, and about a certain person that we all like.'

Jane and Elizabeth looked at each other, and the waiter was told that he need not stay. Lydia laughed, and said,—

'Ay, that is just like your formality and discretion. You thought the waiter must not hear, as if he cared! I daresay he often hears worse things said than I am going to say. But he is an ugly fellow! I am glad he is gone. I never saw such a long chin in my life. Well, but now for my news: it is about dear Wickham; too good for the waiter, is not it? There is no danger of Wickham's marrying Mary King— there's for you! She is gone down to her uncle at Liverpool; gone to stay. Wickham is safe.'

'And Mary King is safe!' added Elizabeth; 'safe from a connection imprudent as to fortune.'

'She is a great fool for going away, if she liked him.'

'But I hope there is no strong attachment on either side,' said Jane.

'I am sure there is not on *his*. I will answer for it, he never cared three straws about her. Who *could* about such a nasty little freckled thing?'

Elizabeth was shocked to think that, however incapable of such coarseness of *expression* herself, the coarseness of the *sentiment* was little other than her own breast had formerly harboured and fancied liberal!

As soon as all had ate, and the elder ones paid, the carriage was ordered; and, after some contrivance, the whole party, with all their boxes, workbags, and parcels, and the unwelcome addition of Kitty's and Lydia's purchases, were seated in it.

'How nicely we are crammed in!' cried Lydia. 'I am glad I brought my bonnet, if it is only for the fun of having another band-box! Well, now let us be quite comfortable and snug, and talk and laugh all the way home. And in the first place, let us hear what has happened to you all since you went away. Have you seen any pleasant men? Have you had any flirting? I was in great hopes that one of you would have got a husband before you came back. Jane will be quite an old maid soon, I declare. She is almost three-and-twenty! Lord! how ashamed I should be of not being married before three-and-twenty! My aunt Philips wants you so to get husbands, you can't think. She says Lizzy had better have taken Mr. Collins; but *I* do not think there would have been any fun in it. Lord! how I should like to be married before any of you! and then I would *chaperon* you about to all the balls. Dear me! we had such a good piece of fun the other day at Colonel Forster's! Kitty and me were to spend the day there, and Mrs. Forster promised to have a little dance in the evening (by the bye, Mrs. Forster and me are *such* friends!); and so she asked the two Harringtons to come; but Harriet was ill, and so Pen was forced to come by herself; and then, what do you think we did? We dressed up Chamberlayne in woman's clothes, on purpose to pass for a lady,—only think what fun! Not a soul knew of it, but Colonel and Mrs. Forster, and Kitty and me, except my aunt, for we were forced to borrow one of her gowns; and you cannot imagine how well he looked! When Denny, and Wickham, and Pratt, and two or three more of the men came in, they did not know him in the least. Lord! how I laughed! and so did Mrs. Forster. I thought I should have died. And *that* made the men suspect something, and then they soon found out what was the matter.'

With such kind of histories of their parties and good jokes did Lydia, assisted by Kitty's hints and additions, endeavour to amuse her companions all the way to Longbourn. Elizabeth listened as little as she could, but there was no escaping the frequent mention of Wickham's name.

Their reception at home was most kind. Mrs. Bennet rejoiced to see Jane in undiminished beauty; and more than once during dinner did Mr. Bennet say voluntarily to Elizabeth,—

'I am glad you are come back, Lizzy.'

Their party in the dining-room was large, for almost all the Lucases came to meet Maria and hear the news; and various were the subjects which occupied them: Lady Lucas was inquiring of Maria, across the table, after the welfare and poultry of her eldest daughter; Mrs. Bennet was doubly engaged, on one hand collecting an account of the present fashions from Jane, who sat some way below her, and on the other, retailing them all to the younger Miss Lucases; and Lydia, in a voice rather louder than any other person's, was enumerating the various pleasures of the morning to anybody who would hear her.

'Oh, Mary,' said she, 'I wish you had gone with us, for we had such fun! as we went along Kitty and me drew up all the blinds, and pretended there was nobody in the coach; and I should have gone so all the way, if Kitty had not been sick; and when we got to the George, I do think we behaved very handsomely, for we treated the other three with the nicest cold luncheon in the world, and if you would have gone, we would have treated you too. And then when we came away it was such fun! I thought we never should have got into the coach. I was ready to die of laughter. And then we were so merry all the way home! we talked and laughed so loud, that anybody might have heard us ten miles off!'

To this Mary very gravely replied, 'Far be it from me, my dear sister, to depreciate such pleasures. They would doubtless be congenial with the generality of female minds. But I confess they would have no charms for *me*. I should infinitely prefer a book.'

But of this answer Lydia heard not a word. She seldom listened to anybody for more than half a minute, and never attended to Mary at all.

In the afternoon Lydia was urgent with the rest of the girls to walk to Meryton, and see how everybody went on; but Elizabeth steadily opposed the scheme. It should not be said that the Miss Bennets could not be at home half a day before they were in pursuit of the officers. There was another reason, too, for her opposition. She dreaded seeing Wickham again, and was resolved to avoid it as long as possible. The comfort to *her*, of the regiment's approaching removal, was indeed beyond expression. In a fortnight they

discovery. Most earnestly did she labour to prove the probability of error, and to seek to clear one, without involving
the other.

'This will not do,' said Elizabeth; 'you never will be able
to make both of them good for anything. Take your choice,
but you must be satisfied with only one. There is but such a
quantity of merit between them; just enough to make one
good sort of man; and of late it has been shifting about
pretty much. For my part, I am inclined to believe it all Mr.
Darcy's, but you shall do as you choose.'

It was some time, however, before a smile could be extorted
from Jane.

'I do not know when I have been more shocked,' said she.
'Wickham so very bad! It is almost past belief. And poor
Mr. Darcy! dear Lizzy, only consider what he must have
suffered. Such a disappointment! and with the knowledge
of your ill opinion too! and having to relate such a thing of
his sister! It is really too distressing, I am sure you must
feel it so.'

'Oh no, my regret and compassion are all done away by
seeing you so full of both. I know you will do him such
ample justice, that I am growing every moment more unconcerned and indifferent. Your profusion makes me saving;
and if you lament over him much longer, my heart will be
as light as a feather.'

'Poor Wickham! there is such an expression of goodness
in his countenance! such an openness and gentleness in his
manner.'

'There certainly was some great mismanagement in the
education of those two young men. One has got all the goodness, and the other all the appearance of it.'

'I never thought Mr. Darcy so deficient in the *appearance*
of it as you used to do.'

'And yet I meant to be uncommonly clever in taking so
decided a dislike to him, without any reason. It is such a
spur to one's genius, such an opening for wit, to have a dislike of that kind. One may be continually abusive without
saying anything just; but one cannot be always laughing
at a man without now and then stumbling on something
witty.'

'Lizzy, when you first read that letter, I am sure you could not treat the matter as you do now.'

'Indeed I could not. I was uncomfortable enough, I was very uncomfortable—I may say unhappy. And with no one to speak to of what I felt, no Jane to comfort me, and say that I had not been so very weak, and vain, and nonsensical, as I knew I had! Oh, how I wanted you!'

'How unfortunate that you should have used such very strong expressions in speaking of Wickham to Mr. Darcy, for now they *do* appear wholly undeserved.'

'Certainly. But the misfortune of speaking with bitterness is a most natural consequence of the prejudices I had been encouraging. There is one point on which I want your advice. I want to be told whether I ought, or ought not, to make our acquaintance in general understand Wickham's character.'

Miss Bennet paused a little, and then replied, 'Surely there can be no occasion for exposing him so dreadfully. What is your own opinion?'

'That it ought not to be attempted. Mr. Darcy has not authorised me to make his communication public. On the contrary, every particular relative to his sister was meant to be kept as much as possible to myself; and if I endeavour to undeceive people as to the rest of his conduct, who will believe me? The general prejudice against Mr. Darcy is so violent, that it would be the death of half the good people in Meryton, to attempt to place him in an amiable light. I am not equal to it. Wickham will soon be gone; and, therefore, it will not signify to anybody here what he really is. Some time hence it will be all found out, and then we may laugh at their stupidity in not knowing it before. At present I will say nothing about it.'

'You are quite right. To have his errors made public might ruin him for ever. He is now, perhaps, sorry for what he has done, and anxious to re-establish a character. We must not make him desperate.'

The tumult of Elizabeth's mind was allayed by this conversation. She had got rid of two of the secrets which had weighed on her for a fortnight, and was certain of a willing listener in Jane, whenever she might wish to talk again of either. But there was still something lurking behind, of which prudence forbade the disclosure. She dared not relate the other half of Mr. Darcy's letter, nor explain to her sister how sincerely she had been valued by his friend. Here was knowledge in which no one could partake; and she was sensible that nothing less than a perfect understanding between the parties could justify her in throwing off this last encumbrance of mystery. 'And then,' said she, 'if that very improbable event should ever take place, I shall merely be able to tell what Bingley may tell in a much more agreeable manner himself. The liberty of communication cannot be mine till it has lost all its value!'

She was now, on being settled at home, at leisure to observe the real state of her sister's spirits. Jane was not happy. She still cherished a very tender affection for Bingley. Having never even fancied herself in love before, her regard had all the warmth of first attachment, and from her age and disposition, greater steadiness than first attachments often boast; and so fervently did she value his remembrance, and prefer him to every other man, that all her good sense, and all her attention to the feelings of her friends, were requisite to check the indulgence of those regrets which must have been injurious to her own health and their tranquillity.

'Well, Lizzy,' said Mrs. Bennet, one day, 'what is your opinion *now* of this sad business of Jane's? For my part, I am determined never to speak of it again to anybody. I told my sister Philips so the other day. But I cannot find out that Jane saw anything of him in London. Well, he is a very undeserving young man—and I do not suppose there is the least chance in the world of her ever getting him now. There is no talk of his coming to Netherfield again in the summer; and I have inquired of everybody, too, who is likely to know.'

'I do not believe that he will ever live at Netherfield any more.'

'Oh, well! it is just as he chooses. Nobody wants him to come; though I shall always say that he used my daughter extremely ill; and, if I was her, I would not have put up with it. Well, my comfort is, I am sure Jane will die of a broken heart, and then he will be sorry for what he has done.'

But as Elizabeth could not receive comfort from any such expectation she made no answer.

'Well, Lizzy,' continued her mother, soon afterwards, 'and so the Collinses live very comfortable, do they? Well, well, I only hope it will last. And what sort of table do they keep? Charlotte is an excellent manager, I daresay. If she is half as sharp as her mother, she is saving enough. There is nothing extravagant in *their* housekeeping, I daresay.'

'No, nothing at all.'

'A great deal of good management, depend upon it. Yes, yes. *They* will take care not to outrun their income. *They* will never be distressed for money. Well, much good may it do them! And so, I suppose, they often talk of having Longbourn when your father is dead. They look upon it quite as their own, I daresay, whenever that happens.'

'It was a subject which they could not mention before me.'

'No; it would have been strange if they had. But I make no doubt they often talk of it between themselves. Well, if they can be easy with an estate that is not lawfully their own, so much the better. *I* should be ashamed of having one that was only entailed on me.'

CHAPTER XLI

THE first week of their return was soon gone. The second began. It was the last of the regiment's stay in Meryton, and all the young ladies in the neighbourhood were drooping apace. The dejection was almost universal. The elder Miss Bennets alone were still able to eat, drink, and sleep, and pursue the usual course of their employments. Very frequently were they reproached for this insensibility by Kitty and Lydia, whose own misery was extreme, and who could not comprehend such hard-heartedness in any of the family.

'Good Heaven! What is to become of us? What are we to do?' would they often exclaim in the bitterness of woe. 'How can you be smiling so, Lizzy?' Their affectionate mother shared all their grief; she remembered what she had herself endured on a similar occasion five-and-twenty years ago.

'I am sure,' said she, 'I cried for two days together when Colonel Millar's regiment went away. I thought I should have broke my heart.'

'I am sure I shall break *mine*,' said Lydia.

'If one could but go to Brighton!' observed Mrs. Bennet.

'Oh yes!—if one could but go to Brighton! But papa is so disagreeable.'

'A little sea-bathing would set me up for ever.'

'And my aunt Philips is sure it would do *me* a great deal of good,' added Kitty.

Such were the kind of lamentations resounding perpetually through Longbourn House. Elizabeth tried to be diverted by them; but all sense of pleasure was lost in shame. She felt anew the justice of Mr. Darcy's objections; and never had she before been so much disposed to pardon his interference in the views of his friend.

But the gloom of Lydia's prospect was shortly cleared away; for she received an invitation from Mrs. Forster, the wife of the colonel of the regiment, to accompany her to Brighton. This invaluable friend was a very young woman, and very lately married. A resemblance in good-humour and good spirits had recommended her and Lydia to each other, and out of their *three* months' acquaintance they had been intimate *two*.

The rapture of Lydia on this occasion, her adoration of Mrs. Forster, the delight of Mrs. Bennet, and the mortification of Kitty, are scarcely to be described. Wholly inattentive to her sister's feelings, Lydia flew about the house in restless ecstasy, calling for every one's congratulations, and laughing and talking with more violence than ever; whilst the luckless Kitty continued in the parlour repining at her fate in terms as unreasonable as her accent was peevish.

'I cannot see why Mrs. Forster should not ask *me* as well as Lydia,' said she, 'though I am *not* her particular friend. I have just as much right to be asked as she has, and more too, for I am two years older.'

In vain did Elizabeth attempt to make her reasonable, and Jane to make her resigned. As for Elizabeth herself, this invitation was so far from exciting in her the same feelings as in her mother and Lydia, that she considered it as the death-warrant of all possibility of common sense for the latter; and, detestable as such a step must make her were it known, she could not help secretly advising her father not to let her go. She represented to him all the improprieties of Lydia's general behaviour, the little advantage she could derive from the friendship of such a woman as Mrs. Forster, and the probability of her being yet more imprudent with such a companion at Brighton, where the temptations must be greater than at home. He heard her attentively, and then said,—

'Lydia will never be easy till she has exposed herself in some public place or other, and we can never expect her to do it with so little expense or inconvenience to her family as under the present circumstances.'

'If you were aware,' said Elizabeth, 'of the very great disadvantage to us all, which must arise from the public notice of Lydia's unguarded and imprudent manner, nay, which has already arisen from it, I am sure you would judge differently in the affair.'

'Already arisen!' repeated Mr. Bennet. 'What! has she frightened away some of your lovers? Poor little Lizzy. But do not be cast down. Such squeamish youths as cannot bear to be connected with a little absurdity are not worth a regret. Come, let me see the list of the pitiful fellows who have been kept aloof by Lydia's folly.'

'Indeed, you are mistaken. I have no such injuries to resent. It is not of peculiar, but of general evils, which I am now complaining. Our importance, our respectability in the world, must be affected by the wild volatility, the assurance and disdain of all restraint which mark Lydia's character. Excuse me,—for I must speak plainly. If you, my dear father, will not take the trouble of checking her exuberant spirits, and of teaching her that her present pursuits are not to be the business of her life, she will soon be beyond the reach of amendment. Her character will be fixed; and she will, at sixteen, be the most determined flirt that ever made herself and her family ridiculous. A flirt, too, in the worst and meanest degree of flirtation; without any attraction beyond youth and a tolerable person; and, from the ignorance and emptiness of her mind, wholly unable to ward off any portion of that universal contempt which her rage for admiration will excite. In this danger Kitty is also comprehended. She will follow wherever Lydia leads. Vain, ignorant, idle, and absolutely uncontrolled! Oh, my dear father, can you suppose it possible that they will not be censured and despised wherever they are known, and that their sisters will not be often involved in the disgrace?'

Mr. Bennet saw that her whole heart was in the subject; and, affectionately taking her hand, said in reply,—

'Do not make yourself uneasy, my love. Wherever you and Jane are known, you must be respected and valued; and you will not appear to less advantage for having a couple of— or I may say, three—very silly sisters. We shall have no peace at Longbourn if Lydia does not go to Brighton. Let her go, then. Colonel Forster is a sensible man, and will keep her out of any real mischief; and she is luckily too poor to be an object of prey to anybody. At Brighton she will be of less importance even as a common flirt than she has been here. The officers will find women better worth their notice. Let us hope, therefore, that her being there may teach her her own insignificance. At any rate, she cannot grow many degrees worse, without authorising us to lock her up for the rest of her life.'

With this answer Elizabeth was forced to be content; but her own opinion continued the same, and she left him disappointed and sorry. It was not in her nature, however, to increase her vexations by dwelling on them. She was confident of having performed her duty; and to fret over unavoidable evils, or augment them by anxiety, was no part of her disposition.

Had Lydia and her mother known the substance of her conference with her father, their indignation would hardly have found expression in their united volubility. In Lydia's imagination, a visit to Brighton comprised every possibility of earthly happiness. She saw, with the creative eye of fancy, the streets of that gay bathing-place covered with officers. She saw herself the object of attention to tens and to scores of them at present unknown. She saw all the glories of the camp: its tents stretched forth in beauteous uniformity of lines, crowded with the young and the gay, and dazzling with scarlet; and, to complete the view, she saw herself seated beneath a tent, tenderly flirting with at least six officers at once.

Had she known that her sister sought to tear her from such prospects and such realities as these, what would have been her sensations? They could have been understood only by her mother, who might have felt nearly the same. Lydia's going to Brighton was all that consoled her for the melancholy conviction of her husband's never intending to go there himself.

But they were entirely ignorant of what had passed; and their raptures continued, with little intermission, to the very day of Lydia's leaving home.

Elizabeth was now to see Mr. Wickham for the last time. Having been frequently in company with him since her return, agitation was pretty well over; the agitations of former partiality entirely so. She had even learnt to detect, in the very gentleness which had first delighted her, an affectation and a sameness to disgust and weary. In his present behaviour to herself, moreover, she had a fresh source of displeasure; for the inclination he soon testified of renewing those attentions which had marked the early part of their acquaintance could only serve, after what had since passed, to provoke her. She lost all concern for him in finding herself thus selected as the object of such idle and frivolous gallantry; and while she steadily repressed it, could not but feel the reproof contained in his believing that, however long and for whatever cause his attentions had been withdrawn, her vanity would be gratified, and her preference secured at any time, by their renewal.

On the very last day of the regiment's remaining in Meryton, he dined, with others of the officers, at Longbourn; and so little was Elizabeth disposed to part from him in good-humour, that, on his making some inquiry as to the manner in which her time had passed at Hunsford, she mentioned Colonel Fitzwilliam's and Mr. Darcy's having both spent three weeks at Rosings, and asked him if he were acquainted with the former.

He looked surprised, displeased, alarmed; but, with a moment's recollection, and a returning smile, replied that he had formerly seen him often; and, after observing that he was a very gentlemanlike man, asked her how she had liked him. Her answer was warmly in his favour. With an air of indifference, he soon afterwards added, 'How long did you say that he was at Rosings?'

'Nearly three weeks.'

'And you saw him frequently?'

'Yes, almost every day.'

'His manners are very different from his cousin's.'

'Yes, very different; but I think Mr. Darcy improves on acquaintance.'

'Indeed!' cried Wickham, with a look which did not escape her. 'And pray may I ask——' but checking himself, he added, in a gayer tone, 'Is it in address that he improves? Has he deigned to add aught of civility to his ordinary style? for I dare not hope,' he continued, in a lower and more serious tone, 'that he is improved in essentials.'

13—C

'Oh no!' said Elizabeth. 'In essentials, I believe, he is very much what he ever was.'

While she spoke, Wickham looked as if scarcely knowing whether to rejoice over her words or to distrust their meaning. There was a something in her countenance which made him listen with an apprehensive and anxious attention, while she added,—

'When I said that he improved on acquaintance, I did not mean that either his mind or manners were in a state of improvement; but that, from knowing him better, his disposition was better understood.'

Wickham's alarm now appeared in a heightened complexion and agitated look; for a few minutes he was silent; till, shaking off his embarrassment, he turned to her again, and said in the gentlest of accents,—

'You, who so well know my feelings towards Mr. Darcy, will readily comprehend how sincerely I must rejoice that he is wise enough to assume even the *appearance* of what is right. His pride, in that direction, may be of service, if not to himself, to many others, for it must deter him from such foul misconduct as I have suffered by. I only fear that the sort of cautiousness to which you, I imagine, have been alluding, is merely adopted on his visits to his aunt, of whose good opinion and judgment he stands much in awe. His fear of her has always operated, I know, when they were together; and a good deal is to be imputed to his wish of forwarding the match with Miss De Bourgh, which I am certain he has very much at heart.'

Elizabeth could not repress a smile at this, but she answered only by a slight inclination of the head. She saw that he wanted to engage her on the old subject of his grievances, and she was in no humour to indulge him. The rest of the evening passed with the *appearance*, on his side, of usual cheerfulness, but with no further attempt to distinguish Elizabeth; and they parted at last with mutual civility, and possibly a mutual desire of never meeting again.

When the party broke up, Lydia returned with Mrs. Forster to Meryton, from whence they were to set out early the next morning. The separation between her and her family was rather noisy than pathetic. Kitty was the only one who shed tears; but she did weep from vexation and envy. Mrs. Bennet was diffuse in her good wishes for the felicity of her daughter, and impressive in her injunctions that she would not miss the opportunity of enjoying herself as much as possible,—advice which there was every reason to believe would be attended to; and, in the clamorous happiness of Lydia herself in bidding farewell, the more gentle adieus of her sisters were uttered without being heard.

CHAPTER XLII

HAD Elizabeth's opinion been all drawn from her own family, she could not have formed a very pleasing picture of conjugal felicity or domestic comfort. Her father, captivated by youth and beauty, and that appearance of good-humour which youth and beauty generally give, had married a woman whose weak understanding and illiberal mind had very early in their marriage put an end to all real affection for her. Respect, esteem, and confidence had vanished for ever; and all his views of domestic happiness were overthrown.

But Mr. Bennet was not of a disposition to seek comfort for the disappointment which his own imprudence had brought on in any of those pleasures which too often console the unfortunate for their folly or their vice. He was fond of the country and of books; and from these tastes had arisen his principal enjoyments. To his wife he was very little otherwise indebted than as her ignorance and folly had contributed to his amusement. This is not the sort of happiness which a man would in general wish to owe to his wife; but where other powers of entertainment are wanting, the true philosopher will derive benefit from such as are given.

Elizabeth, however, had never been blind to the impropriety of her father's behaviour as a husband. She had always seen it with pain; but respecting his abilities, and grateful for his affectionate treatment of herself, she endeavoured to forget what she could not overlook, and to banish from her thoughts that continual breach of conjugal obligation and decorum which, in exposing his wife to the contempt of her own children, was so highly reprehensible. But she had never felt so strongly as now the disadvantages which must attend the children of so unsuitable a marriage, nor ever been so fully aware of the evils arising from so ill-judged a direction of talents—talents which, rightly used, might at least have preserved the respectability of his daughters, even if incapable of enlarging the mind of his wife.

When Elizabeth had rejoiced over Wickham's departure, she found little other cause for satisfaction in the loss of the regiment. Their parties abroad were less varied than before; and at home she had a mother and sister, whose constant repinings at the dulness of everything around them threw a real gloom over their domestic circle; and, though Kitty might in time regain her natural degree of sense, since the disturbers of her brain were removed, her other sister, from whose disposition greater evil might be apprehended, was likely to be hardened in all her folly and assurance by a situation of such double danger as a watering-place and a camp. Upon the whole, therefore, she found, what has been sometimes found before, that an event to which she had looked forward with impatient desire, did not, in taking place, bring all the satisfaction she had promised herself. It was consequently necessary to name some other period for the commencement of actual felicity; to have some other point on which her wishes and hopes might be fixed, and by again enjoying the pleasure of anticipation, console herself for the present, and prepare for another disappointment. Her tour to the Lakes was now the object of her happiest thoughts: it was her best consolation for all the uncomfortable hours which the discontentedness of her mother and Kitty made inevitable; and could she have included Jane in the scheme every part of it would have been perfect.

'But it is fortunate,' thought she, 'that I have something to wish for. Were the whole arrangement complete, my disappointment would be certain. But here, by carrying with me one ceaseless source of regret in my sister's absence, I may reasonably hope to have all my expectations of pleasure realised. A scheme of which every part promises delight can never be successful; and general disappointment is only warded off by the defence of some little peculiar vexation.'

When Lydia went away she promised to write very often and very minutely to her mother and Kitty; but her letters were always long expected, and always very short. Those to 'her mother contained little else than that they were just returned from the library, where such and such officers had

attended them, and where she had seen such beautiful ornaments as made her quite wild; that she had a new gown, or
a new parasol, which she would have described more fully,
but was obliged to leave off in a violent hurry, as Mrs.
Forster called her, and they were going to the camp; and
from her correspondence with her sister there was still less
to be learnt, for her letters to Kitty, though rather longer,
were much too full of lines under the words to be made public.

After the first fortnight or three weeks of her absence,
health, good-humour, and cheerfulness began to reappear at
Longbourn. Everything wore a happier aspect. The families who had been in town for the winter came back again,
and summer finery and summer engagements arose. Mrs.
Bennet was restored to her usual querulous serenity; and
by the middle of June Kitty was so much recovered as to be
able to enter Meryton without tears,—an event of such happy
promise as to make Elizabeth hope that by the following
Christmas she might be so tolerably reasonable as not to mention an officer above once a day, unless, by some cruel and
malicious arrangement at the War Office, another regiment
should be quartered in Meryton.

The time fixed for the beginning of their northern tour
was now fast approaching; and a fortnight only was wanting
of it, when a letter arrived from Mrs. Gardiner, which at
once delayed its commencement and curtailed its extent. Mr.
Gardiner would be prevented by business from setting out
till a fortnight later in July, and must be in London again
within a month; and as that left too short a period for them
to go so far and see so much as they had proposed, or at
least to see it with the leisure and comfort they had built on,
they were obliged to give up the Lakes, and substitute a more
contracted tour; and, according to the present plan, were to
go no farther northward than Derbyshire. In that county
there was enough to be seen to occupy the chief of their
three weeks; and to Mrs. Gardiner it had a peculiarly strong
attraction. The town where she had formerly passed some
years of her life, and where they were now to spend a few
days, was probably as great an object of her curiosity as all
the celebrated beauties of Matlock, Chatsworth, Dovedale, or
the Peak.

Elizabeth was excessively disappointed: she had set her heart on seeing the Lakes; and still thought there might have been time enough. But it was her business to be satisfied—and certainly her temper to be happy; and all was soon right again.

With the mention of Derbyshire there were many ideas connected. It was impossible for her to see the word without thinking of Pemberley and its owner. 'But surely,' said she, 'I may enter his county with impunity, and rob it of a few petrified spars, without his perceiving me.'

The period of expectation was now doubled. Four weeks were to pass away before her uncle and aunt's arrival. But they did pass away, and Mr. and Mrs. Gardiner, with their four children, did at length appear at Longbourn. The children, two girls of six and eight years old, and two younger boys, were to be left under the particular care of their cousin Jane, who was the general favourite, and whose steady sense and sweetness of temper exactly adapted her for attending to them in every way—teaching them, playing with them, and loving them.

The Gardiners stayed only one night at Longbourn, and set off the next morning with Elizabeth in pursuit of novelty and amusement. One enjoyment was certain—that of suitableness as companions—a suitableness which comprehended health and temper to bear inconveniences—cheerfulness to enhance every pleasure—and affection and intelligence, which might supply it among themselves if there were disappointments abroad.

It is not the object of this work to give a description of Derbyshire, nor of any of the remarkable places through which their route thither lay—Oxford, Blenheim, Warwick, Kenilworth, Birmingham, etc., are sufficiently known. A small part of Derbyshire is all the present concern. To the little town of Lambton, the scene of Mrs. Gardiner's former residence, and where she had lately learned that some acquaintance still remained, they bent their steps, after having seen all the principal wonders of the country; and within five miles of Lambton, Elizabeth found, from her aunt, that Pemberley was situated. It was not in their direct road; nor more than a mile or two out of it. In talking over their route the evening before, Mrs. Gardiner expressed an inclination to see the place again. Mr. Gardiner declared his willingness, and Elizabeth was applied to for her approbation.

'My love, should not you like to see a place of which you have heard so much?' said her aunt. 'A place, too, with which so many of your acquaintance are connected. Wickham passed all his youth there, you know.'

Elizabeth was distressed. She felt that she had no business at Pemberley, and was obliged to assume a disinclination for seeing it. 'She must own that she was tired of great houses: after going over so many, she really had no pleasure in fine carpets or satin curtains.'

Mrs. Gardiner abused her stupidity. 'If it were merely a fine house richly furnished,' said she, 'I should not care about it myself; but the grounds are delightful. They have some of the finest woods in the country.'

Elizabeth said no more; but her mind could not acquiesce. The possibility of meeting Mr. Darcy, while viewing the place, instantly occurred. It would be dreadful! She blushed at the very idea; and thought it would be better to speak openly to her aunt, than to run such a risk. But against this there were objections; and she finally resolved that it could be the last resource, if her private inquiries as to the absence of the family were unfavourably answered.

Accordingly, when she retired at night, she asked the chambermaid whether Pemberley were not a very fine place, what was the name of its proprietor, and, with no little alarm, whether the family were down for the summer. A most welcome negative followed the last question; and her alarms being now removed, she was at leisure to feel a great deal of curiosity to see the house herself; and when the subject was revived the next morning, and she was again applied to, could readily answer, and with a proper air of indifference, that she had not really any dislike to the scheme.

To Pemberley, therefore, they were to go.

CHAPTER XLIII

ELIZABETH, as they drove along, watched for the first appearance of Pemberley Woods with some perturbation; and when at length they turned in at the lodge, her spirits were in a high flutter.

The park was very large, and contained great variety of ground. They entered it in one of its lowest points, and drove for some time through a beautiful wood stretching over a wide extent.

Elizabeth's mind was too full for conversation, but she saw and admired every remarkable spot and point of view. They gradually ascended for half a mile, and then found themselves at the top of a considerable eminence, where the wood ceased, and the eye was instantly caught by Pemberley House, situated on the opposite side of the valley, into which the road with some abruptness wound. It was a large, handsome stone building, standing well on rising ground, and backed by a ridge of high woody hills; and in front a stream of some natural importance was swelled into greater, but without any artificial appearance. Its banks were neither formal nor falsely adorned. Elizabeth was delighted. She had never seen a place for which nature had done more, or where natural beauty had been so little counteracted by an awkward taste. They were all of them warm in their admiration; and at that moment she felt that to be mistress of Pemberley might be something!

They descended the hill, crossed the bridge, and drove to the door; and, while examining the nearer aspect of the house, all her apprehension of meeting its owner returned. She dreaded lest the chambermaid had been mistaken. On applying to see the place, they were admitted into the hall; and Elizabeth, as they waited for the housekeeper, had leisure to wonder at her being where she was.

The housekeeper came, a respectable-looking elderly woman, much less fine, and more civil, than she had any notion of finding her. They followed her into the dining-parlour. It was a large, well-proportioned room, handsomely fitted up. Elizabeth, after slightly surveying it, went to a window to enjoy its prospect. The hill, crowned with wood, from which they had descended, receiving increased abruptness from the distance, was a beautiful object. Every disposition of the ground was good; and she looked on the whole scene, the river, the trees scattered on its banks, and the winding of the valley, as far as she could trace it, with delight. As they passed into other rooms, these objects were taking different positions; but from every window there were beauties to be seen. The rooms were lofty and handsome, and their furniture suitable to the fortune of their proprietor; but Elizabeth saw, with admiration of his taste, that it was neither gaudy nor uselessly fine,——with less of splendour, and more real elegance, than the furniture of Rosings.

'And of this place,' thought she, 'I might have been mistress! With these rooms I might have now been familiarly acquainted! Instead of viewing them as a stranger, I might have rejoiced in them as my own, and welcomed to them as visitors my uncle and aunt. But no,' recollecting herself, 'that could never be; my uncle and aunt would have been lost to me; I should not have been allowed to invite them.'

This was a lucky recollection—it saved her from something like regret.

She longed to inquire of the housekeeper whether her master were really absent, but had not courage for it. At length, however, the question was asked by her uncle; and she turned away with alarm, while Mrs. Reynolds replied that he was; adding, 'But we expect him to-morrow, with a large party of friends.' How rejoiced was Elizabeth that their own journey had not by any circumstance been delayed a day.

Her aunt now called her to look at a picture. She approached, and saw the likeness of Mr. Wickham, suspended, amongst several other miniatures, over the mantelpiece. Her aunt asked her, smilingly, how she liked it. The housekeeper came forward, and told them it was the picture of a young gentleman, the son of her late master's steward, who had been brought up by him at his own expense. 'He is now gone into the army,' she added; 'but I am afraid he has turned out very wild.'

Mrs. Gardiner looked at her niece with a smile, but Elizabeth could not return it.

'And that,' said Mrs. Reynolds, pointing to another of the miniatures, 'is my master—and very like him. It was drawn at the same time as the other—about eight years ago.'

'I have heard much of your master's fine person,' said Mrs. Gardiner, looking at the picture; 'it is a handsome face. But, Lizzy, you can tell us whether it is like or not.'

Mrs. Reynolds's respect for Elizabeth seemed to increase on this intimation of her knowing her master.

'Does that young lady know Mr. Darcy?'

Elizabeth coloured and said, 'A little.'

'And do not you think him a very handsome gentleman, ma'am?'

'Yes, very handsome.'

'I am sure *I* know none so handsome; but in the gallery upstairs you will see a finer, larger picture of him than this. This room was my late master's favourite room, and these miniatures are just as they used to be then. He was very fond of them.'

This accounted to Elizabeth for Mr. Wickham's being among them.

Mrs. Reynolds then directed their attention to one of Miss Darcy, drawn when she was only eight years old.

'And is Miss Darcy as handsome as her brother?' said Mr. Gardiner.

'Oh yes—the handsomest young lady that ever was seen; and so accomplished! She plays and sings all day long. In the next room is a new instrument just come down for her—a present from my master; she comes here to-morrow with him.'

Mr. Gardiner, whose manners were easy and pleasant, encouraged her communicativeness by his questions and remarks: Mrs. Reynolds, either from pride or attachment, had evidently great pleasure in talking of her master and his sister.

'Is your master much at Pemberley in the course of the year?'

'Not so much as I could wish, sir: but I daresay he may spend half his time here; and Miss Darcy is always down for the summer months.'

Except, thought Elizabeth, when she goes to Ramsgate.

'If your master would marry, you might see more of him.'

'Yes, sir; but I do not know when *that* will be. I do not know who is good enough for him.'

Mr. and Mrs. Gardiner smiled. Elizabeth could not help saying, 'It is very much to his credit, I am sure, that you should think so.'

'I say no more than the truth, and what everybody will say that knows him,' replied the other. Elizabeth thought this was going pretty far; and she listened with increasing astonishment as the housekeeper added, 'I have never had a cross word from him in my life, and I have known him ever since he was four years old.'

This was praise of all others most extraordinary, most opposite to her ideas. That he was not a good-tempered man had been her firmest opinion. Her keenest attention was awakened: she longed to hear more; and was grateful to her uncle for saying,—

'There are very few people of whom so much can be said. You are lucky in having such a master.'

'Yes, sir, I know I am. If I were to go through the world, I could not meet with a better. But I have always observed that they who are good-natured when children are good-natured when they grow up; and he was always the sweetest-tempered, most generous-hearted boy in the world.'

Elizabeth almost stared at her. 'Can this be Mr. Darcy?' thought she.

'His father was an excellent man,' said Mrs. Gardiner.

'Yes, ma'am, that he was indeed; and his son will be just like him—just as affable to the poor.'

Elizabeth listened, wondered, doubted, and was impatient for more. Mrs. Reynolds could interest her on no other point. She related the subjects of the pictures, the dimensions of the rooms, and the price of the furniture in vain. Mr. Gardiner, highly amused by the kind of family prejudice, to which he attributed her excessive commendation of her master, soon led again to the subject; and she dwelt with energy on his many merits, as they proceeded together up the great staircase.

'He is the best landlord, and the best master,' said she, 'that ever lived. Not like the wild young men nowadays, who think of nothing but themselves. There is not one of his tenants or servants but what will give him a good name. Some people call him proud; but I am sure I never saw anything of it. To my fancy, it is only because he does not rattle away like other young men.'

'In what an amiable light does this place him!' thought Elizabeth.

'This fine account of him,' whispered her aunt as they walked, 'is not quite consistent with his behaviour to our poor friend.'

'Perhaps we might be deceived.'

'That is not very likely; our authority was too good.'

On reaching the spacious lobby above, they were shown into a very pretty sitting-room, lately fitted up with greater elegance and lightness than the apartments below; and were informed that it was but just done to give pleasure to Miss Darcy, who had taken a liking to the room when last at Pemberley.

'He is certainly a good brother,' said Elizabeth, as she walked towards one of the windows.

Mrs. Reynolds anticipated Miss Darcy's delight when she should enter the room. 'And this is always the way with him,' she added. 'Whatever can give his sister any pleasure, is sure to be done in a moment. There is nothing he would not do for her.'

The picture gallery, and two or three of the principal bedrooms, were all that remained to be shown. In the former were many good paintings: but Elizabeth knew nothing of the art; and from such as had been already visible below, she had willingly turned to look at some drawings of Miss Darcy's, in crayons, whose subjects were usually more interesting, and also more intelligible.

In the gallery there were many family portraits, but they could have little to fix the attention of a stranger. Elizabeth walked on in quest of the only face whose features would be known to her. At last it arrested her—and she beheld a striking resemblance of Mr. Darcy, with such a smile over the face as she remembered to have sometimes seen when he looked at her. She stood several minutes before the picture, in earnest contemplation, and returned to it again before they quitted the gallery. Mrs. Reynolds informed them that it had been taken in his father's lifetime.

There was certainly at this moment, in Elizabeth's mind, a more gentle sensation towards the original than she had ever felt in the height of their acquaintance. The commendation bestowed on him by Mrs. Reynolds was of no trifling nature. What praise is more valuable than the praise of an intelligent servant? As a brother, a landlord, a master, she considered how many people's happiness was in his guardianship! How much of pleasure or pain it was in his power to bestow! How much of good or evil must be done by him! Every idea that had been brought forward by the housekeeper was favourable to his character; and as she stood before the canvas on which he was represented, and fixed his eyes upon herself, she thought of his regard with a deeper sentiment of gratitude than it had ever raised before: she remembered its warmth, and softened its impropriety of expression.

When all of the house that was open to general inspection had been seen, they returned downstairs; and, taking leave of the housekeeper, were consigned over to the gardener, who met them at the hall door.

As they walked across the lawn towards the river, Elizabeth turned back to look again; her uncle and aunt stopped also: and while the former was conjecturing as to the date of the building, the owner of it himself suddenly came forward from the road which led behind it to the stables.

They were within twenty yards of each other, and so abrupt was his appearance, that it was impossible to avoid his sight. Their eyes instantly met, and the cheeks of each were overspread with the deepest blush. He absolutely started, and for a moment seemed immovable from surprise; but shortly recovering himself, advanced towards the party, and spoke to Elizabeth, if not in terms of perfect composure, at least of perfect civility.

She had instinctively turned away; but, stopping on his approach, received his compliments with an embarrassment impossible to be overcome. Had his first appearance, or his resemblance to the picture they had just been examining, been insufficient to assure the other two that they now saw Mr. Darcy, the gardener's expression of surprise, on beholding his master, must immediately have told it. They stood a little aloof while he was talking to their niece, who, astonished and confused, scarcely dared lift her eyes to his face, and knew not what answer she returned to his civil inquiries after her family. Amazed at the alteration of his manner since they last parted, every sentence that he uttered was increasing her embarrassment; and every idea of the impropriety of her being found there recurring to her mind, the few minutes in which they continued together were some of the most uncomfortable of her life. Nor did he seem much more at ease; when he spoke, his accent had none of its usual sedateness; and he repeated his inquiries as to the time of her having left Longbourn, and of her stay in Derbyshire, so often, and in so hurried a way, as plainly spoke the distraction of his thoughts.

At length every idea seemed to fail him; and after standing a few moments without saying a word, he suddenly recollected himself, and took leave.

The others then joined her, and expressed their admiration of his figure; but Elizabeth heard not a word, and, wholly engrossed by her own feelings, followed them in silence. She was overpowered by shame and vexation. Her coming there was the most unfortunate, the most ill-judged thing in the world! How strange must it appear to him! In what a disgraceful light might it not strike so vain a man! It might seem as if she had purposely thrown herself in his way again! Oh! why did she come? or, why did he thus come a day before he was expected? Had they been only ten minutes sooner, they should have been beyond the reach of his discrimination; for it was plain that he was that moment arrived, that moment alighted from his horse or his carriage. She blushed again and again over the perverseness of the meeting. And his behaviour, so strikingly altered,—what could it mean? That he should even speak to her was amazing!—but to speak with such civility, to inquire after her family! Never in her life had she seen his manner so little dignified, never had he spoken with such gentleness as on this unexpected meeting. What a contrast did it offer to his last address in Rosings Park, when he put his letter into her hand! She knew not what to think, or how to account for it.

They had now entered a beautiful walk by the side of the water, and every step was bringing forward a nobler fall of ground, or a finer reach of the woods to which they were approaching: but it was some time before Elizabeth was sensible of any of it; and, though she answered mechanically to the repeated appeals of her uncle and aunt, and seemed to direct her eyes to such objects as they pointed out, she distinguished no part of the scene. Her thoughts were all fixed on that one spot of Pemberley House, whichever it might be, where Mr. Darcy then was. She longed to know what at that moment was passing in his mind; in what manner he thought of her, and whether, in defiance of everything, she was still dear to him. Perhaps he had been civil only because he felt himself at ease; yet there had been *that* in his voice, which was not like ease. Whether he had felt more of pain or of pleasure in seeing her she could not tell, but he certainly had not seen her with composure.

At length, however, the remarks of her companions on her absence of mind roused her, and she felt the necessity of appearing more like herself.

They entered the woods, and, bidding adieu to the river for a while, ascended some of the higher ground; whence, in spots where the opening of the trees gave the eye power to wander, were many charming views of the valley, the opposite hills, with the long range of woods overspreading many, and occasionally part of the stream. Mr. Gardiner expressed a wish of going round the whole park, but feared it might be beyond a walk. With a triumphant smile they were told that it was ten miles round. It settled the matter; and they pursued the accustomed circuit; which brought them again, after some time, in a descent among hanging woods, to the edge of the water, and one of its narrowest parts. They crossed it by a simple bridge, in character with the general air of the scene: it was a spot less adorned than any they had yet visited; and the valley, here contracted into a glen, allowed room only for the stream and a narrow walk amidst the rough coppice-wood which bordered it. Elizabeth longed to explore its windings; but when they had crossed the bridge, and perceived their distance from the house, Mrs. Gardiner, who was not a great walker, could go no farther, and thought only of returning to the carriage as quickly as possible. Her niece was, therefore, obliged to submit, and they took their way towards the house on the opposite side of the river, in the nearest direction; but their progress was slow, for Mr. Gardiner, though seldom able to indulge the taste, was very fond of fishing, and was so much engaged in watching the occasional appearance of some trout in the water, and talking to the man about them, that he advanced but little. Whilst wandering on in this slow manner, they were again surprised, and Elizabeth's astonishment was quite equal to what it had been at first, by the sight of Mr. Darcy approaching them, and at no great distance. The walk, being here less sheltered than on the other side, allowed them to see him before they met. Elizabeth, however astonished, was at least more prepared for an interview than before, and resolved to appear and to speak with calmness, if he really intended to meet them. For a few moments, indeed, she felt that he would probably strike into some other path. The idea lasted while a turning in the walk concealed him from their view; the turning passed, he was immediately before them. With a glance she saw that he had lost none of his recent civility; and, to imitate his politeness, she began as they met to admire the beauty of the place; but she had not got beyond the words 'delightful' and 'charming,' when some unlucky recollections obtruded, and she fancied that praise of Pemberley from her might be mischievously construed. Her colour changed, and she said no more.

Mr. Gardiner was standing a little behind; and on her pausing, he asked her if she would do him the honour of introducing him to her friends. This was a stroke of civility for which she was quite unprepared; and she could hardly suppress a smile at his being now seeking the acquaintance of some of those very people, against whom his pride had revolted in his offer to herself. 'What will be his surprise,' thought she, 'when he knows who they are! He takes them now for people of fashion.'

The introduction, however, was immediately made; and as she named their relationship to herself, she stole a sly look at him, to see how he bore it; and was not without the expectation of his decamping as fast as he could from such disgraceful companions. That he was *surprised* by the connection was evident: he sustained it, however, with fortitude: and, so far from going away, turned back with them, and entered into conversation with Mr. Gardiner. Elizabeth could not but be pleased, could not but triumph. It was consoling that he should know she had some relations for whom there was no need to blush. She listened most attentively to all that passed between them, and gloried in every expression, every sentence of her uncle, which marked his intelligence, his taste, or his good manners.

The conversation soon turned upon fishing; and she heard Mr. Darcy invite him, with the greatest civility, to fish there as often as he chose, while he continued in the neighbourhood, offering at the same time to supply him with fishing tackle, and pointing out those parts of the stream where there was usually most sport. Mrs. Gardiner, who was walking arm in arm with Elizabeth, gave her a look expressive of her wonder. Elizabeth said nothing, but it gratified her exceedingly; the compliment must be all for herself. Her astonishment, however, was extreme; and continually was she repeating, 'Why is he so altered? From what can it proceed? It cannot be for *me,* it cannot be for *my* sake that his manners are thus softened. My reproofs at Hunsford could not work such a change as this. It is impossible that he should still love me.'

After walking some time in this way, the two ladies in front, the two gentlemen behind, on resuming their places, after descending to the brink of the river for the better inspection of some curious water-plant, there chanced to be a little alteration. It originated in Mrs. Gardiner, who, fatigued by the exercise of the morning, found Elizabeth's arm inadequate to her support, and consequently preferred her husband's. Mr. Darcy took her place by her niece, and they walked on together. After a short silence the lady first spoke. She wished him to know that she had been assured of his absence before she came to the place, and accordingly began by observing, that his arrival had been very unexpected—'for your housekeeper,' she added, 'informed us that you would certainly not be here till to-morrow; and, indeed, before we left Bakewell, we understood that you were not immediately expected in the country.' He acknowledged the truth of it all; and said that business with his steward had occasioned his coming forward a few hours before the rest of the party with whom he had been travelling. 'They will join me early to-morrow,' he continued, 'and among them are some who will claim an acquaintance with you,—Mr. Bingley and his sisters.'

Elizabeth answered only by a slight bow. Her thoughts were instantly driven back to the time when Mr. Bingley's name had been last mentioned between them; and if she might judge from his complexion, *his* mind was not very differently engaged.

'There is also one other person in the party,' he continued after a pause, 'who more particularly wishes to be known to you. Will you allow me, or do I ask too much to introduce my sister to your acquaintance during your stay at Lambton?'

The surprise of such an application was great indeed; it was too great for her to know in what manner she acceded to it. She immediately felt that whatever desire Miss Darcy might have of being acquainted with her must be the work of her brother, and without looking farther, it was satisfactory; it was gratifying to know that his resentment had not made him think really ill of her.

They now walked on in silence; each of them deep in thought. Elizabeth was not comfortable; that was impossible; but she was flattered and pleased. His wish of introducing his sister to her was a compliment of the highest kind. They soon outstripped the others; and when they had reached the carriage, Mr. and Mrs. Gardiner were half a quarter of a mile behind.

He then asked her to walk into the house—but she declared herself not tired, and they stood together on the lawn. At such a time much might have been said, and silence was very awkward. She wanted to talk, but there seemed an embargo on every subject. At last she recollected that she had been travelling, and they talked of Matlock and Dovedale with great perseverance. Yet time and her aunt moved slowly—and her patience and her ideas were nearly worn out before the *tête-à-tête* was over.

On Mr. and Mrs. Gardiner's coming up they were all pressed to go into the house and take some refreshment; but this was declined, and they parted on each side with the utmost politeness. Mr. Darcy handed the ladies into the carriage, and when it drove off, Elizabeth saw him walking slowly towards the house.

The observations of her uncle and aunt now began; and each of them pronounced him to be infinitely superior to anything they had expected. 'He is perfectly well behaved, polite, and unassuming,' said her uncle.

'There *is* something a little stately in him to be sure,' replied her aunt; 'but it is confined to his air, and is not unbecoming. I can now say with the housekeeper, that though some people may call him proud, *I* have seen nothing of it.'

'I was never more surprised than by his behaviour to us. It was more than civil; it was really attentive; and there was no necessity for such attention. His acquaintance with Elizabeth was very trifling.'

'To be sure, Lizzy,' said her aunt, 'he is not so handsome as Wickham; or rather he has not Wickham's countenance, for his features are perfectly good. But how came you to tell us that he was so disagreeable?'

Elizabeth excused herself as well as she could: said that she had liked him better when they met in Kent than before, and that she had never seen him so pleasant as this morning.

'But perhaps he may be a little whimsical in his civilities,' replied her uncle. 'Your great men often are; and, therefore, I shall not take him at his word about fishing, as he might change his mind another day, and warn me off his grounds.'

Elizabeth felt that they had entirely mistaken his character, but said nothing.

'From what we have seen of him,' continued Mrs. Gardiner, 'I really should not have thought that he could have behaved in so cruel a way by anybody, as he has done by poor Wickham. He has not an ill-natured look. On the contrary, there is something pleasing about his mouth when he speaks. And there is something of dignity in his countenance, that would not give one an unfavorable idea of his heart. But, to be sure, the good lady who showed us the house did give him a most flaming character! I could hardly help laughing aloud sometimes. But he is a liberal master, I suppose, and *that,* in the eye of a servant, comprehends every virtue.'

Elizabeth here felt herself called on to say something in vindication of his behaviour to Wickham; and, therefore, gave them to understand, in as guarded a manner as she could, that by what she had heard from his relations in Kent, his actions were capable of a very different construction; and that his character was by no means so faulty, nor Wickham's so amiable, as they had been considered in Hertfordshire. In confirmation of this, she related the particulars of all the pecuniary transactions in which they had been connected, without actually naming her authority, but stating it to be such as might be relied on.

Mrs. Gardiner was surprised and concerned: but as they were now approaching the scene of her former pleasures, every idea gave way to the charm of recollection; and she was too much engaged in pointing out to her husband all the interesting spots in its environs, to think of anything else. Fatigued as she had been by the morning's walk, they had no sooner dined than she set off again in quest of her former acquaintance, and the evening was spent in the satisfactions of an intercourse renewed after many years' discontinuance.

The occurrences of the day were too full of interest to leave Elizabeth much attention for any of these new friends; and she could do nothing but think, and think with wonder, of Mr. Darcy's civility, and above all, of his wishing her to be acquainted with his sister.

CHAPTER XLIV

ELIZABETH had settled it that Mr. Darcy would bring his sister to visit her the very day after her reaching Pemberley; and was, consequently, resolved not to be out of sight of the inn the whole of that morning. But her conclusion was false; for on the very morning after their own arrival at Lambton these visitors came. They had been walking about the place with some of their new friends, and were just returned to the inn to dress themselves for dining with the same family, when the sound of a carriage drew them to a window, and they saw a gentleman and lady in a curricle driving up the street. Elizabeth, immediately recognising the livery, guessed what it meant, and imparted no small degree of surprise to her relations by acquainting them with the honour which she expected. Her uncle and aunt were all amazement; and the embarrassment of her manner as she spoke, joined to the circumstance itself, and many of the circumstances of the preceding day, opened to them a new idea on the business. Nothing had ever suggested it before, but they now felt that there was no other way of accounting for such attentions from such a quarter than by supposing a partiality for their niece. While these newly-born notions were passing in their heads, the perturbation of Elizabeth's feelings was every moment increasing. She was quite amazed at her own discomposure; but, amongst other causes of disquiet, she dreaded lest the partiality of the brother should have said too much in her favour; and, more than commonly anxious to please, she naturally suspected that every power of pleasing would fail her.

She retreated from the window, fearful of being seen; and as she walked up and down the room, endeavouring to compose herself, saw such looks of inquiring surprise in her uncle and aunt as made everything worse.

Miss Darcy and her brother appeared, and this formidable introduction took place. With astonishment did Elizabeth see that her new acquaintance was at least as much embarrassed as herself. Since her being at Lambton, she had heard that Miss Darcy was exceedingly proud; but the observation of a very few minutes convinced her that she was only exceedingly shy. She found it difficult to obtain even a word from her beyond a monosyllable.

Miss Darcy was tall, and on a larger scale than Elizabeth; and, though little more than sixteen, her figure was formed, and her appearance womanly and graceful. She was less handsome than her brother, but there was sense and good-humour in her face, and her manners were perfectly unassuming and gentle. Elizabeth, who had expected to find in her as acute and unembarrassed an observer as ever Mr. Darcy had been, was much relieved by discerning such different feelings.

They had not been long together before Darcy told her that Bingley was also coming to wait on her; and she had barely time to express her satisfaction, and prepare for such a visitor, when Bingley's quick step was heard on the stairs, and in a moment he entered the room. All Elizabeth's anger against him had been long done away; but had she still felt any, it could hardly have stood its ground against the unaffected cordiality with which he expressed himself on seeing her again. He inquired in a friendly, though general, way, after her family, and looked and spoke with the same good-humoured ease that he had ever done.

To Mr. and Mrs. Gardiner he was scarcely a less interesting personage than to herself. They had long wished to see him. The whole party before them, indeed, excited a lively attention. The suspicions which had just arisen of Mr. Darcy and their niece directed their observation towards each with an earnest, though guarded, inquiry; and they soon drew from those inquiries the full conviction that one of them at least knew what it was to love. Of the lady's sensations they remained a little in doubt; but that the gentleman was overflowing with admiration was evident enough.

Elizabeth, on her side, had much to do. She wanted to ascertain the feelings of each of her visitors, she wanted to compose her own, and to make herself agreeable to all; and

in the latter object, where she feared most to fail, she was
most sure of success, for those to whom she endeavoured to
give pleasure were prepossessed in her favour. Bingley was
ready, Georgiana was eager, and Darcy determined, to be
pleased.

In seeing Bingley, her thoughts naturally flew to her sister;
and oh! how ardently did she long to know whether any
of his were directed in a like manner. Sometimes she could
fancy that he talked less than on former occasions, and once
or twice pleased herself with the notion that as he looked at
her he was trying to trace a resemblance. But, though this
might be imaginary, she could not be deceived as to his
behaviour to Miss Darcy, who had been set up as a rival to
Jane. No look appeared on either side that spoke particular
regard. Nothing occurred between them that could justify
the hopes of his sister. On this point she was soon satisfied;
and two or three little circumstances occurred ere they
parted, which, in her anxious interpretation, denoted a
recollection of Jane, not untinctured by tenderness, and
a wish of saying more that might lead to the mention of her,
had he dared.

He observed to her, at a moment when the others were
talking together, and in a tone which had something of real
regret, that, it 'was a very long time since he had had the
pleasure of seeing her'; and, before she could reply, he added,
'It is above eight months. We have not met since the 26th of
November, when we were all dancing together at Netherfield.'

Elizabeth was pleased to find his memory so exact; and he
afterwards took occasion to ask her, when unattended to by
any of the rest, whether *all* her sisters were at Longbourn.
There was not much in the question, nor in the preceding
remark; but there was a look and a manner which gave them
meaning.

It was not often that she could turn her eyes on Mr.
Darcy himself; but whenever she did catch a glimpse she
saw an expression of general complaisance, and in all that he
said she heard an accent so far removed from *hauteur* or
disdain of his companions, as convinced her that the improvement of manners which she had yesterday witnessed, however

temporary its existence might prove, had at least outlived one day. When she saw him thus seeking the acquaintance and courting the good opinion of people with whom any intercourse a few months ago would have been a disgrace; when she saw him thus civil, not only to herself, but to the very relations whom he had openly disdained, and recollected their last lively scene in Hunsford Parsonage, the difference, the change was so great, and struck so forcibly on her mind, that she could hardly restrain her astonishment from being visible. Never, even in the company of his dear friends at Netherfield, or his dignified relations at Rosings, had she seen him so desirous to please, so free from self-consequence or unbending reserve, as now when no importance could result from the success of his endeavours, and when even the acquaintance of those to whom his attentions were addressed would draw down the ridicule and censure of the ladies both of Netherfield and Rosings.

Their visitors stayed with them above half an hour; and when they arose to depart, Mr. Darcy called on his sister to join him in expressing their wish of seeing Mr. and Mrs. Gardiner, and Miss Bennet, to dinner at Pemberley, before they left the country. Miss Darcy, though with a diffidence which marked her little in the habit of giving invitations, readily obeyed.

Mrs. Gardiner looked at her niece, desirous of knowing how *she*, whom the invitation most concerned, felt disposed as to its acceptance, but Elizabeth had turned away her head. Presuming, however, that this studied avoidance spoke rather a momentary embarrassment than any dislike of the proposal, and seeing in her husband, who was fond of society, a perfect willingness to accept it, she ventured to engage for her attendance, and the day after the next was fixed on.

Bingley expressed great pleasure in the certainty of seeing Elizabeth again, having still a great deal to say to her, and many inquiries to make after all their Hertfordshire friends. Elizabeth, construing all this into a wish of hearing her speak of her sister, was pleased; and on this account, as well as some others, found herself, when their visitors left them, capable of considering the last half-hour with some satisfaction, though while it was passing the enjoyment of it had been little. Eager to be alone, and fearful of inquiries or hints from her uncle and aunt, she stayed with them only long enough to hear their favourable opinion of Bingley, and then hurried away to dress.

But she had no reason to fear Mr. and Mrs. Gardiner's curiosity; it was not their wish to force her communication. It was evident that she was much better acquainted with Mr. Darcy than they had before any idea of; it was evident that he was very much in love with her. They saw much to interest, but nothing to justify inquiry.

Of Mr. Darcy it was now a matter of anxiety to think well; and, as far as their acquaintance reached, there was no fault to find. They could not be untouched by his politeness; and had they drawn his character from their own feelings and his servant's report, without any reference to any other account, the circle in Hertfordshire to which he was known would not have recognised it for Mr. Darcy. There was now an interest, however, in believing the housekeeper; and they soon became sensible that the authority of a servant, who had known him since he was four years old, and whose own manners indicated respectability, was not to be hastily rejected. Neither had anything occurred in the intelligence of their Lambton friends that could materially lessen its weight. They had nothing to accuse him of but pride; pride he probably had, and if not, it would certainly be imputed by the inhabitants of a small market town where the family did not visit. It was acknowledged, however, that he was a liberal man, and did much good among the poor.

With respect to Wickham, the travellers soon found that he was not held there in much estimation; for though the chief of his concerns with the son of his patron were imperfectly understood, it was yet a well-known fact that, on his quitting Derbyshire, he had left many debts behind him, which Mr. Darcy afterwards discharged.

As for Elizabeth, her thoughts were at Pemberley this evening more than the last; and the evening, though as it passed it seemed long, was not long enough to determine her feelings towards *one* in that mansion; and she lay awake two whole hours, endeavouring to make them out. She certainly did not hate him. No; hatred had vanished long ago, and she had almost as long been ashamed of ever feeling a dislike against him that could be so called. The respect created by the conviction of his valuable qualities, though at first unwillingly admitted, had for some time ceased to be repugnant to her feelings; and it was now heightened into somewhat of a friendlier nature by the testimony so highly in his favour, and bringing forward his disposition in so amiable a light, which yesterday had produced. But above all, above respect and esteem, there was a motive within her of goodwill which could not be overlooked. It was gratitude;—gratitude, not merely for having once loved her, but for loving her still well enough to forgive all the petulance and acrimony of her manner in rejecting him, and all the unjust accusations accompanying her rejection. He who, she had been persuaded, would avoid her as his greatest enemy, seemed, on this accidental meeting, most eager to preserve the acquaintance, and without any indelicate display of regard, or any peculiarity of manner, where their two selves only were concerned, was soliciting the good opinion of her friends, and bent on making her known to his sister. Such a change in a man of so much pride excited not only astonishment but gratitude—for to love, ardent love, it must be attributed; and, as such, its impression on her was of a sort to be encouraged, as by no means unpleasing, though it could not be exactly defined. She respected, she esteemed, she was grateful to him, she felt a real interest in his welfare; and she only wanted to know how far she wished that welfare to depend upon herself, and how far it would be for the happiness of both that she should employ the power, which her fancy told her she still possessed, of bringing on the renewal of his addresses.

It had been settled in the evening, between the aunt and niece, that such a striking civility as Miss Darcy's in coming to them on the very day of her arrival at Pemberley, for she had reached it only to a late breakfast, ought to be imitated, though it could not be equalled, by some exertion of politeness on their side; and, consequently, that it would be highly expedient to wait on her at Pemberley the following morning. They were, therefore, to go. Elizabeth was pleased; though when she asked herself the reason, she had very little to say in reply.

Mr. Gardiner left them soon after breakfast. The fishing scheme had been renewed the day before, and a positive engagement made of his meeting some of the gentlemen at Pemberley by noon.

CHAPTER XLV

CONVINCED as Elizabeth now was that Miss Bingley's dislike of her had originated in jealousy, she could not help feeling how very unwelcome her appearance at Pemberley must be to her, and was curious to know with how much civility on that lady's side the acquaintance would now be renewed.

On reaching the house they were shown through the hall into the saloon, whose northern aspect rendered it delightful for summer. Its windows, opening to the ground, admitted a most refreshing view of the high woody hills behind the house, and of the beautiful oaks and Spanish chestnuts which were scattered over the intermediate lawn.

In this room they were received by Miss Darcy, who was sitting there with Mrs. Hurst and Miss Bingley, and the lady with whom she lived in London. Georgiana's reception of them was very civil, but attended with all that embarrassment which, though proceeding from shyness and the fear of doing wrong, would easily give to those who felt themselves inferior the belief of her being proud and reserved. Mrs. Gardiner and her niece, however, did her justice, and pitied her.

By Mrs. Hurst and Miss Bingley they were noticed only by a courtesy; and on their being seated, a pause, awkward as such pauses must always be, succeeded for a few moments. It was first broken by Mrs. Annesley, a genteel, agreeable-looking woman, whose endeavour to introduce some kind of discourse proved her to be more truly well-bred than either of the others; and between her and Mrs. Gardiner, with occasional help from Elizabeth, the conversation was carried on. Miss Darcy looked as if she wished for courage enough to join in it; and sometimes did venture a short sentence, when there was least danger of its being heard.

Elizabeth soon saw that she was herself closely watched by Miss Bingley, and that she could not speak a word, especially to Miss Darcy, without calling her attention. This observation would not have prevented her from trying to talk to the latter, had they not been seated at an inconvenient distance; but she was not sorry to be spared the necessity of saying much: her own thoughts were employing her. She expected every moment that some of the gentlemen would enter the room: she wished, she feared, that the master of the house might be amongst them; and whether she wished or feared it most, she could scarcely determine. After sitting in this manner a quarter of an hour, without hearing Miss Bingley's voice, Elizabeth was aroused by receiving from her a cold inquiry after the health of her family. She answered with equal indifference and brevity, and the other said no more.

The next variation which their visit afforded was produced by the entrance of servants with cold meat, cake, and a variety of all the finest fruits in season; but this did not take place till after many a significant look and smile from Mrs. Annesley to Miss Darcy had been given, to remind her of her post. There was now employment for the whole party; for though they could not all talk, they could all eat; and the beautiful pyramids of grapes, nectarines, and peaches, soon collected them round the table.

While thus engaged, Elizabeth had a fair opportunity of deciding whether she most feared or wished for the appearance of Mr. Darcy, by the feelings which prevailed on his entering the room; and then, though but a moment before she had believed her wishes to predominate, she began to regret that he came.

He had been some time with Mr. Gardiner, who with two or three other gentlemen from the house, was engaged by the river, and had left him only on learning that the ladies of the family intended a visit to Georgiana that morning. No sooner did he appear, than Elizabeth wisely resolved to be perfectly easy and unembarrassed;—a resolution the more necessary to be made, but perhaps not the more easily kept, because she saw that the suspicions of the whole party were awakened against them, and that there was scarcely an eye which did not watch his behaviour when he first came into the room. In no countenance was attentive curiosity so strongly marked as in Miss Bingley's, in spite of the smiles which overspread her face whenever she spoke to one of its objects; for jealousy had not yet made her desperate, and her attentions to Mr. Darcy were by no means over. Miss Darcy, on her brother's entrance, exerted herself much more to talk; and Elizabeth saw that he was anxious for his sister and herself to get acquainted, and forwarded, as much as possible, every attempt at conversation on either side. Miss Bingley saw all this likewise; and, in the imprudence of anger, took the first opportunity of saying, with sneering civility,—

'Pray, Miss Eliza, are not the ——shire militia removed from Meryton? They must be a great loss to *your* family.'

In Darcy's presence she dared not mention Wickham's name; but Elizabeth instantly comprehended that he was uppermost in her thoughts; and the various recollections connected with him gave her a moment's distress; but, exerting herself vigorously to repel the ill-natured attack, she presently answered the question in a tolerably disengaged tone. While she spoke, an involuntary glance showed her Darcy with a heightened complexion, earnestly looking at her, and his sister overcome with confusion, and unable to lift up her eyes. Had Miss Bingley known what pain she was then giving her beloved friend, she undoubtedly would have refrained from the hint; but she had merely intended to discompose Elizabeth, by bringing forward the idea of a man to whom she believed her partial, to make her betray a sensibility which might injure her in Darcy's opinion, and, perhaps, to remind the latter of all the follies and absurdities by which some part of her family were connected with that corps. Not a syllable had ever reached her of Miss Darcy's meditated elopement. To no creature had it been revealed, where secrecy was possible, except to Elizabeth; and from all Bingley's connections her brother was particularly anxious to conceal it, from that very wish which Elizabeth had long ago attributed to him, of their becoming hereafter her own. He had certainly formed such a plan; and without meaning that it should affect his endeavour to separate him from Miss Bennet, it is probable that it might add something to his lively concern for the welfare of his friend.

Elizabeth's collected behaviour, however, soon quieted his emotion; and as Miss Bingley, vexed and disappointed, dared not approach nearer to Wickham, Georgiana also recovered in time, though not enough to be able to speak any more. Her brother, whose eye she feared to meet, scarcely recollected her interest in the affair; and the very circumstance which had been designed to turn his thoughts from Elizabeth seemed to have fixed them on her more and more cheerfully.

Their visit did not continue long after the question and answer above mentioned; and while Mr. Darcy was attending them to their carriage, Miss Bingley was venting her feelings in criticisms on Elizabeth's person, behaviour, and dress. But Georgiana would not join her. Her brother's recommendation was enough to insure her favour: his judgment could not err; and he had spoken in such terms of Elizabeth as to leave Georgiana without the power of finding her otherwise than lovely and amiable. When Darcy returned to the saloon, Miss Bingley could not help repeating to him some part of what she had been saying to his sister.

'How very ill Eliza Bennet looks this morning, Mr. Darcy,' she cried: 'I never in my life saw any one so much altered as she is since the winter. She is grown so brown and coarse. Louisa and I were agreeing that we should not have known her again.'

However little Mr. Darcy might have liked such an address, he contented himself with coolly replying that he perceived no other alteration than her being rather tanned,—no miraculous consequence of travelling in the summer.

'For my own part,' she rejoined, 'I must confess that I never could see any beauty in her. Her face is too thin; her complexion has no brilliancy; and her features are not at all handsome. Her nose wants character; there is nothing marked in its lines. Her teeth are tolerable, but not out of the common way; and as for her eyes, which have sometimes been called so fine, I never could perceive anything extraordinary in them. They have a sharp, shrewish look, which I do not like at all; and in her air altogether there is a self-sufficiency without fashion, which is intolerable.'

Persuaded as Miss Bingley was that Darcy admired Elizabeth, this was not the best method of recommending herself; but angry people are not always wise; and in seeing him at last look somewhat nettled, she had all the success she expected. He was resolutely silent, however; and, from a determination of making him speak, she continued,—

'I remember, when we first knew her in Hertfordshire, how amazed we all were to find that she was a reputed beauty; and I particularly recollect your saying one night, after they had been dining at Netherfield, "*She* a beauty! I should as soon call her mother a wit." But afterwards she seemed to improve on you, and I believe you thought her rather pretty at one time.'

'Yes,' replied Darcy, who could contain himself no longer, 'but *that* was only when I first knew her; for it is many months since I have considered her as one of the handsomest women of my acquaintance.'

He then went away, and Miss Bingley was left to all the satisfaction of having forced him to say what gave no one any pain but herself.

Mrs. Gardiner and Elizabeth talked of all that had occurred during their visit, as they returned, except what had particularly interested them both. The looks and behaviour of everybody they had seen were discussed, except of the person who had mostly engaged their attention. They talked of his sister, his friends, his house, his fruit, of everything but himself; yet Elizabeth was longing to know what Mrs. Gardiner thought of him, and Mrs. Gardiner would have been highly gratified by her niece's beginning the subject.

CHAPTER XLVI

ELIZABETH had been a good deal disappointed in not finding a letter from Jane on their first arrival at Lambton; and this disappointment had been renewed on each of the mornings that had now been spent there; but on the third her repining was over, and her sister justified, by the receipt of two letters from her at once, on one of which was marked that it had been mis-sent elsewhere. Elizabeth was not surprised at it, as Jane had written the direction remarkably ill.

They had just been preparing to walk as the letters came in; and her uncle and aunt, leaving her to enjoy them in quiet, set off by themselves. The one mis-sent must be first attended to; it had been written five days ago. The beginning contained an account of all their little parties and engagements, with such news as the country afforded; but the latter half, which was dated a day later, and written in evident agitation, gave more important intelligence. It was to this effect:—

'Since writing the above, dearest Lizzy, something has occurred of a most unexpected and serious nature; but I am afraid of alarming you—be assured that we are all well. What I have to say relates to poor Lydia. An express came at twelve last night, just as we were all gone to bed, from Colonel Forster, to inform us that she had gone off to Scotland with one of his officers; to own the truth, with Wickham! Imagine our surprise. To Kitty, however, it does not seem so wholly unexpected. I am very, very sorry. So imprudent a match on both sides! But I am willing to hope the best, and that his character has been misunderstood. Thoughtless and indiscreet I can easily believe him, but this step (and let us rejoice over it) marks nothing bad at heart. His choice is disinterested at least, for he must know my father can give her nothing. Our poor mother is sadly grieved. My father bears it better. How thankful am I, that we never let them know what has been said against him; we must forget it ourselves. They were off Saturday night about twelve, as is conjectured, but were not missed till yesterday morning at eight. The express was sent off directly. My dear Lizzy, they must have passed within ten miles of us. Colonel Forster gives us reason to expect him here soon. Lydia left a few lines for his wife, informing her of their intention. I must conclude, for I cannot be long from my poor mother. I am afraid you will not be able to make it out, but I hardly know what I have written.'

Without allowing herself time for consideration and scarcely knowing what she felt, Elizabeth, on finishing this letter, instantly seized the other, and opening it with the utmost impatience, read as follows: it had been written a day later than the conclusion of the first.

'By this time, my dearest sister, you have received my hurried letter; I wish this may be more intelligible, but though not confined for time, my head is so bewildered that I cannot answer for being coherent. Dearest Lizzy, I hardly know what I would write, but I have bad news for you, and it cannot be delayed. Imprudent as a marriage between Mr. Wickham and our poor Lydia would be, we are now anxious to be assured it has taken place, for there is but too much reason to fear they are not gone to Scotland. Colonel Forster came yesterday, having left Brighton the day before, not many hours after the express. Though Lydia's short letter to Mrs. F. gave them to understand that they were going to Gretna Green, something was dropped by Denny expressing his belief that W. never intended to go there, or to marry Lydia at all, which was repeated to Colonel F., who, instantly taking the alarm, set off from B., intending to trace their route. He did trace them easily to Clapham, but no farther; for on entering that place, they removed into a hackney-coach, and dismissed the chaise that brought them from Epsom. All that is known after this is, that they were seen to continue the London road. I know not what to think. After making every possible inquiry on that side London, Colonel F. came on into Hertfordshire, anxiously renewing them at all the turnpikes, and at the inns in Barnet and Hatfield, but without any success,—no such people had been seen to pass through. With the kindest concern he came on to Longbourn, and broke his apprehensions to us in a manner most creditable to his heart. I am sincerely grieved for him and Mrs. F.; but no one can throw any blame on them. Our distress, my dear Lizzy, is very great. My father and mother believe the worst, but I cannot think so ill of him. Many circumstances might make it more eligible for them to be married privately in town than to pursue their first plan; and even if *he* could form such a design against a young woman of Lydia's connections, which is not likely, can I suppose her so lost to everything? Impossible! I grieve to find, however, that Colonel F. is not disposed to depend upon their marriage: he shook his head when I expressed my hopes, and said he feared W. was not a man to be trusted. My poor mother is really ill, and keeps her room. Could she exert herself, it would be better, but this is not to be expected; and as to my father, I never in my life saw him so affected. Poor Kitty has anger for having concealed their attachment; but as it was a matter of confidence, one cannot wonder. I am truly glad, dearest Lizzy, that you have been spared something of these distressing scenes; but now, as the first shock is over, shall I own that I long for your return? I am not so selfish, however, as to press for it, if inconvenient. Adieu! I take up my pen again to do what I have just told you I would not; but circumstances are such, that I cannot help earnestly begging you all to come here as soon as possible. I know my dear uncle and aunt so well, that I am not afraid of requesting it, though I have still something more to ask of the former. My father is going to London with Colonel Forster instantly, to try to discover her. What he means to do, I am sure I know not; but his excessive distress will not allow him to pursue any measure in the best and safest way, and Colonel Forster is obliged to be at Brighton again to-morrow evening. In such an exigence my uncle's advice and assistance would be everything in the world; he will immediately comprehend what I must feel, and I rely upon his goodness.'

'Oh! where, where is my uncle?' cried Elizabeth, darting from her seat as she finished the letter, in eagerness to follow him, without losing a moment of the time so precious; but as she reached the door, it was opened by a servant, and Mr. Darcy appeared. Her pale face and impetuous manner made him start, and before he could recover himself enough to speak, she, in whose mind every idea was superseded by Lydia's situation, hastily exclaimed, 'I beg your pardon, but I must leave you. I must find Mr. Gardiner this moment on business that cannot be delayed; I have not an instant to lose.'

'Good God! what is the matter?' cried he, with more feeling than politeness; then recollecting himself, 'I will not detain you a minute; but let me, or let the servant, go after Mr. and Mrs. Gardiner. You are not well enough; you cannot go yourself.'

Elizabeth hesitated, but her knees trembled under her, and she felt how little would be gained by her attempting to pursue them. Calling back the servant, therefore, she commissioned him, though in so breathless an accent as made her almost unintelligible, to fetch his master and mistress home instantly.

On his quitting the room, she sat down, unable to support herself, and looking so miserably ill, that it was impossible for Darcy to leave her, or to refrain from saying, in a tone of gentleness and commiseration, 'Let me call your maid. Is there nothing you could take to give you present relief? A glass of wine; shall I get you one? You are very ill.'

'No, I thank you,' she replied, endeavouring to recover herself. 'There is nothing the matter with me. I am quite well, I am only distressed by some dreadful news which I have just received from Longbourn.'

She burst into tears as she alluded to it, and for a few minutes could not speak another word. Darcy, in wretched suspense, could only say something indistinctly of his concern, and observe her in compassionate silence. At length she spoke again. 'I have just had a letter from Jane, with such dreadful news. It cannot be concealed from any one. My youngest sister has left all her friends—has eloped; has thrown herself into the power of—of Mr. Wickham. They are gone off together from Brighton. *You* know him too well to doubt the rest. She has no money, no connections, nothing that can tempt him to—she is lost for ever.'

Darcy was fixed in astonishment. 'When I consider,' she added, in a yet more agitated voice, 'that *I* might have prevented it! *I* who knew what he was. Had I but explained some part of it only—some part of what I learnt, to my own family! Had his character been known, this could not have happened. But it is all, all too late now.'

'I am grieved, indeed,' cried Darcy: 'grieved—shocked. But is it certain, absolutely certain?'

'Oh, yes! They left Brighton together on Sunday night, and were traced almost to London, but not beyond: they are certainly not gone to Scotland.'

'And what has been done, what has been attempted, to recover her?'

'My father has gone to London, and Jane has written to beg my uncle's immediate assistance, and we shall be off, I hope, in half an hour. But nothing can be done; I know very well that nothing can be done. How is such a man to be worked on? How are they even to be discovered? I have not the smallest hope. It is every way horrible!'

Darcy shook his head in silent acquiescence.

'When *my* eyes were open to his real character. Oh! had I known what I ought, what I dared to do! But I knew not—I was afraid of doing too much. Wretched, wretched mistake!'

Darcy made no answer. He seemed scarcely to hear her, and was walking up and down the room in earnest meditation; his brow contracted, his air gloomy. Elizabeth soon observed, and instantly understood it. Her power was sinking; everything *must* sink under such a proof of family weakness, such an assurance of the deepest disgrace. She could neither wonder nor condemn, but the belief of his self-conquest brought nothing consolatory to her bosom, afforded no palliation of her distress. It was, on the contrary, exactly calculated to make her understand her own wishes; and never had she so honestly felt that she could have loved him, as now, when all love must be vain.

But self, though it would intrude, could not engross her. Lydia—the humiliation, the misery she was bringing on them all—soon swallowed up every private care; and covering her face with her handkerchief, Elizabeth was soon lost to everything else; and, after a pause of several minutes, was only recalled to a sense of her situation by the voice of her companion, who, in a manner which, though it spoke compassion, spoke likewise restraint, said, 'I am afraid you have been long· desiring my absence, nor have I anything to plead in excuse of my stay, but real, though unavailing concern. Would to Heaven that anything could be either said or done on my part, that might offer consolation to such distress! But I will not torment you with vain wishes, which may seem purposely to ask for your thanks. This unfortunate affair will, I fear, prevent my sister's having the pleasure of seeing you at Pemberley to-day.'

'Oh yes. Be so kind as to apologise for us to Miss Darcy. Say that urgent business calls us home immediately. Conceal the unhappy truth as long as it is possible. I know it cannot be long.'

He readily assured her of his secrecy, again expressed his sorrow for her distress, wished it a happier conclusion than there was at present reason to hope, and, leaving his compliments for her relations, with only one serious parting look went away.

As he quitted the room, Elizabeth felt how improbable it was that they should ever see each other again on such terms of cordiality as had marked their several meetings in Derbyshire; and as she threw a retrospective glance over the whole of their acquaintance, so full of contradictions and varieties, sighed at the perverseness of those feelings which would now have promoted its continuance, and would formerly have rejoiced in its termination.

If gratitude and esteem are good foundations of affection, Elizabeth's change of sentiment will be neither improbable nor faulty. But if otherwise, if the regard springing from such sources is unreasonable or unnatural, in comparison of what is so often described as arising on a first interview with its object, and even before two words have been exchanged, nothing can be said in her defence, except that she had given somewhat of a trial to the latter method, in her partiality for Wickham, and that its ill success might, perhaps, authorize her to seek the other less interesting mode of attachment. Be that as it may, she saw him go with regret; and in this early example of what Lydia's infamy must produce, found additional anguish as she reflected on that wretched business. Never since reading Jane's second letter had she entertained a hope of Wickham's meaning to marry her. No one but Jane, she thought, could flatter herself with such an expectation. Surprise was the least of all her feelings on this development. While the contents of the first letter remained on her mind, she was all surprise, all astonishment, that Wickham should marry a girl, whom it was impossible he could marry for money; and how Lydia could ever have attached him had appeared incomprehensible. But now it was all too natural. For such an attachment as this she might have sufficient charms; and though she did not suppose Lydia to be deliberately engaging in an elopement, without the intention of marriage, she had no difficulty in believing that neither her virtue nor her understanding would preserve her from falling an easy prey.

She had never perceived, while the regiment was in Hertfordshire, that Lydia had any partiality for him; but she was convinced that Lydia had wanted only encouragement to attach herself to anybody. Sometimes one officer, sometimes another, had been her favourite, as their attentions raised them in her opinion. Her affections had been continually fluctuating, but never without an object. The mischief of neglect and mistaken indulgence towards such a girl—oh! how acutely did she now feel it.

She was wild to be at home—to hear, to see, to be upon the spot to share with Jane in the cares that must now fall wholly upon her, in a family so deranged; a father absent, a mother incapable of exertion, and requiring constant attendance; and though almost persuaded that nothing could be done for Lydia, her uncle's interference seemed of the utmost importance, and till he entered the room the misery of her impatience was severe. Mr. and Mrs. Gardiner had hurried back in alarm, supposing, by the servant's account, that their niece was taken suddenly ill; but satisfying them instantly on that head, she eagerly communicated the cause of their summons, reading the two letters aloud, and dwelling on the postscript of the last with trembling energy, though Lydia had never been a favourite with them. Mr. and Mrs. Gardiner could not but be deeply afflicted. Not Lydia only, but all were concerned in it; and after the first exclamations of surprise and horror, Mr. Gardiner readily promised every assistance in his power. Elizabeth, though expecting no less, thanked him with tears of gratitude; and all three being actuated by one spirit, everything relating to their journey was speedily settled. They were to be off as soon as possible. 'But what is to be done about Pemberley?' cried Mrs. Gardiner. 'John told us Mr. Darcy was here when you sent for us;—was it so?'

'Yes; and I told him we should not be able to keep our engagement. *That* is all settled.'

'What is all settled?' repeated the other, as she ran into her room to prepare. 'And are they upon such terms as for her to disclose the real truth! Oh that I knew how it was!'

But wishes were vain; or, at best, could serve only to amuse her in the hurry and confusion of the following hour. Had Elizabeth been at leisure to be idle, she would have remained certain that all employment was impossible to one so wretched as herself; but she had her share of business as well as her aunt, and amongst the rest there were notes to be written to all their friends at Lambton, with false excuses for their sudden departure. An hour, however, saw the whole completed; and Mr. Gardiner, meanwhile, having settled his account at the inn, nothing remained to be done but to go; and Elizabeth, after all the misery of the morning, found herself, in a shorter space of time than she could have supposed, seated in the carriage, and on the road to Longbourn.

CHAPTER XLVII

'I HAVE been thinking it over again, Elizabeth,' said her uncle, as they drove from the town; 'and really, upon serious consideration, I am much more inclined than I was to judge as your eldest sister does of the matter. It appears to me so very unlikely that any young man should form such a design against a girl who is by no means unprotected or friendless, and who was actually staying in his Colonel's family, that I am strongly inclined to hope the best. Could he expect that her friends would not step forward? Could he expect to be noticed again by the regiment, after such an affront to Colonel Forster? His temptation is not adequate to the risk.'

'Do you really think so?' cried Elizabeth, brightening up for a moment.

'Upon my word,' said Mrs. Gardiner, 'I begin to be of your uncle's opinion. It is really too great a violation of decency, honour, and interest, for him to be guilty of it. I cannot think so very ill of Wickham. Can you, yourself, Lizzy, so wholly give him up, as to believe him capable of it?'

'Not perhaps of neglecting his own interest. But of every other neglect I can believe him capable. If, indeed, it should be so! But I dare not hope it. Why should they not go on to Scotland, if that had been the case?'

'In the first place,' replied Mr. Gardiner, 'there is no absolute proof that they are not gone to Scotland.'

'Oh, but their removing from the chaise into a hackney coach is such a presumption! And, besides, no traces of them were to be found on the Barnet road.'

'Well, then,—supposing them to be in London. They may be there, though for the purpose of concealment, for no more exceptionable purpose. It is not likely that money should be very abundant on either side; and it might strike them that they could be more economically, though less expeditiously, married in London than in Scotland.'

'But why all this secrecy? Why any fear of detection? Why must their marriage be private? Oh no, no, this is not likely. His most particular friend, you see by Jane's account, was persuaded of his never intending to marry her. Wickham will never marry a woman without some money. He cannot afford it. And what claims has Lydia, what attractions has she beyond youth, health, and good humour, that could make him for her sake forego every chance of benefiting himself by marrying well? As to what restraint the apprehensions of disgrace in the corps might throw on a dishonourable elopement with her, I am not able to judge; for I know nothing of the effects that such a step might produce. But as to your other objection, I am afraid it will hardly hold good. Lydia has no brothers to step forward; and he might imagine, from my father's behaviour, from his indolence and the little attention he has ever seemed to give to what was going forward in his family, that *he* would do as little and think as little about it, as any father could do, in such a matter.'

'But can you think that Lydia is so lost to everything but love of him, as to consent to live with him on any other terms than marriage?'

'It does seem, and it is most shocking, indeed,' replied Elizabeth, with tears in her eyes, 'that a sister's sense of decency and virtue in such a point should admit of doubt. But, really, I know not what to say. Perhaps I am not doing her justice. But she is very young; she has never been taught to think on serious subjects; and for the last half-year, nay, for a twelvemonth, she has been given up to nothing but amusement and vanity. She has been allowed to dispose of her time in the most idle and frivolous manner, and to adopt any opinions that came in her way. Since the ——shire were first quartered in Meryton, nothing but love flirtation, and officers, has been in her head. She has been doing everything in her power, by thinking and talking on the subject, to give greater—what shall I call it?—susceptibility to her feelings; which are naturally lively enough. And we all know that Wickham has every charm of person and address that can captivate a woman.'

'But you see that Jane,' said her aunt, 'does not think so ill of Wickham as to believe him capable of the attempt.'

'Of whom does Jane ever think ill? And who is there, whatever might be their former conduct, that she would believe capable of such an attempt, till it were proved against them? But Jane knows, as well as I do, what Wickham really is. We both know that he has been profligate in every sense of the word. That he has neither integrity nor honour. That he is as false and deceitful as he is insinuating.'

'And do you really know all this?' cried Mrs. Gardiner, whose curiosity as to the mode of her intelligence was all alive.

'I do, indeed,' replied Elizabeth, colouring. 'I told you the other day of his infamous behaviour to Mr. Darcy; and you, yourself, when last at Longbourn, heard in what manner he spoke of the man who had behaved with such forbearance and liberality towards him. And there are other circumstances which I am not at liberty—which it is not worth while to relate; but his lies about the whole Pemberley family are endless. From what he said of Miss Darcy, I was thoroughly prepared to see a proud, reserved, disagreeable girl. Yet he knew to the contrary himself. He must know that she was as amiable and unpretending as we have found her.'

'But does Lydia know nothing of this; can she be ignorant of what you and Jane seem so well to understand?'

'Oh yes!—that, that is the worst of all. Till I was in Kent, and saw so much both of Mr. Darcy and his relation Colonel Fitzwilliam, I was ignorant of the truth myself. And when I returned home the ——shire was to leave Meryton in a week or fortnight's time. As that was the case, neither Jane, to whom I related the whole, nor I, thought it necessary to make our knowledge public; for of what use could it apparently be to any one, that the good opinion which all the neighbourhood had of him should then be overthrown? And even when it was settled that Lydia should go with Mrs. Forster, the necessity of opening her eyes to his character never occurred to me. That *she* could be in any danger from the deception never entered my head. That such a consequence as *this* should ensue, you may easily believe was far enough from my thoughts.'

'When they all removed to Brighton, therefore, you had no reason, I suppose, to believe them fond of each other?'

'Not the slightest. I can remember no symptom of affection on either side; and had anything of the kind been perceptible, you must be aware that ours is not a family on which it could be thrown away. When first he entered the corps, she was ready enough to admire him; but so we all were. Every girl in or near Meryton was out of her senses about him for the first two months; but he never distinguished *her* by any particular attention; and, consequently, after a moderate period of extravagant and wild admiration, her fancy for him gave way, and others of the regiment, who treated her with more distinction, again became her favourites.'

It may be easily believed that, however little of novelty could be added to their fears, hopes, and conjectures, on this interesting subject, by its repeated discussion, no other could detain them from it long, during the whole of the journey. From Elizabeth's thoughts it was never absent. Fixed there by the keenest of all anguish, self-reproach, she could find no interval of ease or forgetfulness.

They travelled as expeditiously as possible; and, sleeping one night on the road, reached Longbourn by dinner-time the next day. It was a comfort to Elizabeth to consider that Jane could not have been wearied by long expectations.

The little Gardiners, attracted by the sight of a chaise, were standing on the steps of the house, as they entered the paddock; and when the carriage drove up to the door, the joyful surprise that lighted up their faces and displayed itself over their whole bodies, in a variety of capers and frisks, was the first pleasing earnest of their welcome.

Elizabeth jumped out; and after giving each of them a hasty kiss, hurried into the vestibule, where Jane, who came running downstairs from her mother's apartment, immediately met her.

Elizabeth, as she affectionately embraced her, whilst tears filled the eyes of both, lost not a moment in asking whether anything had been heard of the fugitives.

'Not yet,' replied Jane. 'But now that my dear uncle is come, I hope everything will be well.'

'Is my father in town?'

'Yes, he went on Tuesday, as I wrote you word.'

'And have you heard from him often?'

'We have heard only once. He wrote me a few lines on Wednesday, to say that he had arrived in safety, and to give me his directions, which I particularly begged him to do. He merely added, that he should not write again, till he had something of importance to mention.'

'And my mother—how is she? How are you all?'

'My mother is tolerably well, I trust; though her spirits are greatly shaken. She is upstairs, and will have great satisfaction in seeing you all. She does not yet leave her dressing-room. Mary and Kitty, thank Heaven! are quite well.'

'But you—how are you?' cried Elizabeth. 'You look pale. How much you must have gone through!'

Her sister, however, assured her of her being perfectly well; and their conversation, which had been passing while Mr. and Mrs. Gardiner were engaged with their children, was now put an end to by the approach of the whole party. Jane ran to her uncle and aunt, and welcomed and thanked them both, with alternate smiles and tears.

When they were all in the drawing-room, the questions which Elizabeth had already asked were of course repeated by the others, and they soon found that Jane had no intelligence to give. The sanguine hope of good, however, which the benevolence of her heart suggested, had not yet deserted her; she still expected that it would all end well, and that every morning would bring some letter, either from Lydia or her father, to explain their proceedings, and, perhaps, announce the marriage.

Mrs. Bennet, to whose apartment they all repaired, after a few minutes' conversation together, received them exactly as might be expected; with tears and lamentations of regret, invectives against the villainous conduct of Wickham, and complaints of her own sufferings and ill-usage. Blaming everybody but the person to whose ill-judging indulgence the errors of her daughter must be principally owing.

'If I had been able,' said she, 'to carry my point in going to Brighton with all my family, *this* would not have happened: but poor dear Lydia had nobody to take care of her. Why did the Forsters ever let her go out of their sight? I am sure there was some great neglect or other on their side, for she is not the kind of girl to do such a thing, if she had been well looked after. I always thought they were very unfit to have the charge of her; but I was overruled, as I always am. Poor, dear child! And now here's Mr. Bennet gone away, and I know he will fight Wickham, wherever he meets him, and then he will be killed, and what is to become of us all? The Collinses will turn us out, before he is cold in his grave; and if you are not kind to us, brother, I do not know what we shall do.'

They all exclaimed against such terrific ideas; and Mr. Gardiner, after general assurances of his affection for her and all her family, told her that he meant to be in London the very next day, and would assist Mr. Bennet in every endeavour for recovering Lydia.

'Do not give way to useless alarm,' added he: 'though it is right to be prepared for the worst, there is no occasion to look on it as certain. It is not quite a week since they left Brighton. In a few days more we may gain some news of them; and till we know that they are not married, and have no design of marrying, do not let us give the matter over as lost. As soon as I get to town, I shall go to my brother, and make him come home with me to Gracechurch Street, and then we may consult together as to what is to be done.'

'Oh, my dear brother,' replied Mrs. Bennet, 'that is exactly what I could most wish for. And now do, when you get to town, find them out, wherever they may be; and if they are not married already, *make* them marry. And as for wedding clothes, do not let them wait for that, but tell Lydia she shall have as much money as she chooses to buy them, after they are married. And, above all things, keep Mr. Bennet from fighting. Tell him what a dreadful state I am in—that I am frightened out of my wits; and have such tremblings, such flutterings, all over me, such spasms in my side, and pains in my head, and such beatings at heart that I can get no rest by night nor by day. And tell my dear Lydia not to give any directions about her clothes till she has seen me, for she does not know which are the best warehouses. Oh, brother, how kind you are! I know you will contrive it all.'

But Mr. Gardiner, though he assured her again of his earnest endeavours in the cause, could not avoid recommending moderation to her, as well in her hopes as her fears; and after talking with her in this manner till dinner was on table, they left her to vent all her feelings on the housekeeper, who attended in the absence of her daughters.

Though her brother and sister were persuaded that there was no real occasion for such a seclusion from the family, they did not attempt to oppose it, for they knew that she had not prudence enough to hold her tongue before the servants, while they waited at table, and judged it better that *one* only of the household, and the one whom they could most trust, should comprehend all her fears and solicitude on the subject.

In the dining-room they were soon joined by Mary and Kitty, who had been too busily engaged in their separate apartments to make their appearance before. One came from her books, and the other from her toilette. The faces of both, however, were tolerably calm; and no change was visible in either, except that the loss of her favourite sister, or the anger which she had herself incurred in the business, had given something more of fretfulness than usual to the accents of Kitty. As for Mary, she was mistress enough of herself to whisper to Elizabeth, with a countenance of grave reflection, soon after they were seated at table,—

'This is a most unfortunate affair, and will probably be much talked of. But we must stem the tide of malice, and pour into the wounded bosoms of each other the balm of sisterly consolation.'

Then perceiving in Elizabeth no inclination of replying, she added, 'Unhappy as the event must be for Lydia, we may draw from it this useful lesson:—that loss of virtue in a female is irretrievable, that one false step involves her in endless ruin, that her reputation is no less brittle than it is beautiful, and that she cannot be too much guarded in her behaviour towards the undeserving of the other sex.'

Elizabeth lifted up her eyes in amazement, but was too much oppressed to make any reply. Mary, however, continued to console herself with such kind of moral extractions from the evil before them.

In the afternoon, the two elder Miss Bennets were able to be for half an hour by themselves; and Elizabeth instantly availed herself of the opportunity of making any inquiries which Jane was equally eager to satisfy. After joining in general lamentations over the dreadful sequel of this event, which Elizabeth considered as all but certain, and Miss Bennet could not assert to be wholly impossible, the former continued the subject by saying, 'But tell me all and everything about it which I have not already heard. Give me further particulars. What did Colonel Forster say? Had they no apprehension of anything before the elopement took place? They must have seen them together for ever.'

'Colonel Forster did own that he had often suspected some partiality, especially on Lydia's side, but nothing to give him any alarm. I am so grieved for him. His behaviour was attentive and kind to the utmost. He *was* coming to us, in order to assure us of his concern, before he had any idea of their not being gone to Scotland: when that apprehension first got abroad, it hastened his journey.'

'And was Denny convinced that Wickham would not marry? Did he know of their intending to go off? Had Colonel Forster seen Denny himself?'

'Yes; but when questioned by *him* Denny denied knowing anything of their plan, and would not give his real opinion about it. He did not repeat his persuasion of their not marrying, and from *that* I am inclined to hope he might have been misunderstood before.'

'And till Colonel Forster came himself, not one of you entertained a doubt, I suppose, of their being really married?'

'How was it possible that such an idea should enter our brains? I felt a little uneasy—a little fearful of my sister's happiness with him in marriage, because I knew that his conduct had not been always quite right. My father and mother knew nothing of that, they only felt how imprudent a match it must be. Kitty then owned, with a very natural triumph on knowing more than the rest of us, that in Lydia's last letter she had prepared her for such a step. She had known, it seems, of their being in love with each other many weeks.'

'But not before they went to Brighton?'

'No, I believe not.'

'And did Colonel Forster appear to think ill of Wickham himself? Does he know his real character?'

'I must confess that he did not speak so well of Wickham as he formerly did. He believed him to be imprudent and extravagant; and since this sad affair has taken place, it is said that he left Meryton greatly in debt: but I hope this may be false.'

'Oh, Jane, had we been less secret, had we told what we knew of him, this could not have happened!'

'Perhaps it would have been better,' replied her sister.

'But to expose the former faults of any person, without knowing what their present feelings were, seemed unjustifiable.'

'We acted with the best intentions.'

'Could Colonel Forster repeat the particulars of Lydia's note to his wife?'

'He brought it with him for us to see.'

Jane then took it from her pocket-book, and gave it to Elizabeth. These were the contents:—

'MY DEAR HARRIET—You will laugh when you know where I am gone, and I cannot help laughing myself at your surprise to-morrow morning, as soon as I am missed. I am going to Gretna Green, and if you cannot guess with who, I shall think you a simpleton, for there is but one man in the world I love, and he is an angel. I should never be happy without him, so think it no harm to be off. You need not send them word at Longbourn of my going, if you do not like it, for it will make the surprise the greater when I write to them, and sign my name Lydia Wickham. What a good joke it will be! I can hardly write for laughing. Pray make my excuses to Pratt for not keeping my engagement and dancing with him to-night. Tell him I hope he will excuse me when he knows all, and tell him I will dance with him at the next ball we meet with great pleasure. I shall send for my clothes when I get to Longbourn; but I wish you would tell Sally to mend a great slit in my worked muslin gown before they are packed up. Good-bye. Give my love to Colonel Forster. I hope you will drink to our good journey.—Your affectionate friend,   LYDIA BENNET.'

'Oh, thoughtless, thoughtless Lydia!' cried Elizabeth, when she had finished it. 'What a letter is this, to be written at such a moment! But at least it shows that *she* was serious in the object of her journey. Whatever he might afterwards persuade her to, it was not on her side a *scheme* of infamy. My poor father! how he must have felt it!'

'I never saw any one so shocked. He could not speak a word for full ten minutes. My mother was taken ill immediately, and the whole house in such confusion!'

'Oh, Jane,' cried Elizabeth, 'was there a servant belonging to it who did not know the whole story before the end of the day?'

'I do not know: I hope there was. But to be guarded at such a time is very difficult. My mother was in hysterics; and though I endeavoured to give her every assistance in my power, I am afraid I did not do so much as I might have done! but the horror of what might possibly happen almost took from me my faculties.'

'Your attendance upon her has been too much for you. You do not look well. Oh that I had been with you! you have had every care and anxiety upon yourself alone.'

'Mary and Kitty have been very kind, and would have shared in every fatigue, I am sure, but I did not think it right for either of them. Kitty is slight and delicate, and Mary studies so much that her hours of repose should not be broken in on. My aunt Philips came to Longbourn on Tuesday, after my father went away; and was so good as to stay till Thursday with me. She was of great use and comfort to us all, and Lady Lucas has been very kind: she walked here on Wednesday morning to condole with us, and offered her services, or any of her daughters, if they could be of use to us.'

'She had better have stayed at home,' cried Elizabeth: 'perhaps she *meant* well, but, under such a misfortune as this, one cannot see too little of one's neighbours. Assistance is impossible; condolence, insufferable. Let them triumph over us at a distance, and be satisfied.'

She then proceeded to inquire into the measures which her father had intended to pursue, while in town, for the recovery of his daughter.

'He meant, I believe,' replied Jane, 'to go to Epsom, the place where they last changed horses, see the postilions, and try if anything could be made out from them. His principal object must be to discover the number of the hackney coach which took them from Clapham. It had come with a fare from London; and as he thought the circumstance of a gentleman and lady's removing from one carriage into another might be remarked, he meant to make inquiries at Clapham. If he could anyhow discover at what house the coachman had before set down his fare, he determined to make inquiries there, and hoped it might not be impossible to find out the stand and number of the coach. I do not know of any other designs that he had formed; but he was in such a hurry to be gone, and his spirits so greatly discomposed, that I had difficulty in finding out even so much as this.'

CHAPTER XLVIII

THE whole party were in hopes of a letter from Mr. Bennet the next morning, but the post came in without bringing a single line from him. His family knew him to be, on all common occasions, a most negligent and dilatory correspondent; but at such a time they had hoped for exertion. They were forced to conclude that he had no pleasing intelligence to send, but even of *that* they would have been glad to be certain. Mr. Gardiner had waited only for the letters before he set off.

When he was gone, they were certain at least of receiving constant information of what was going on; and their uncle promised, at parting, to prevail on Mr. Bennet to return to Longbourn as soon as he could, to the great consolation of his sister, who considered it as the only security for her husband's not being killed in a duel.

Mrs. Gardiner and the children were to remain in Hertfordshire a few days longer, as the former thought her presence might be serviceable to her nieces. She shared in their attendance on Mrs. Bennet, and was a great comfort to them in their hours of freedom. Their other aunt also visited them frequently, and always, as she said, with the design of cheering and heartening them up, though, as she never came without reporting some fresh instance of Wickham's extravagance or irregularity, she seldom went away without leaving them more dispirited than she found them.

All Meryton seemed striving to blacken the man who, but three months before, had been almost an angel of light. He was declared to be in debt to every tradesman in the place, and his intrigues, all honoured with the title of seduction, had been extended into every tradesman's family. Everybody declared that he was the wickedest young man in the world; and everybody began to find out that they had always distrusted the appearance of his goodness. Elizabeth,

425

though she did not credit above half of what was said, believed enough to make her former assurance of her sister's ruin still more certain; and even Jane, who believed still less of it, became almost hopeless, more especially as the time was now come, when, if they had gone to Scotland, which she had never before entirely despaired of, they must in all probability have gained some news of them.

Mr. Gardiner left Longbourn on Sunday; on Tuesday his wife received a letter from him: it told them that on his arrival he had immediately found out his brother, and persuaded him to come to Gracechurch Street. That Mr. Bennet had been to Epsom and Clapham, before his arrival, but without gaining any satisfactory information; and that he was now determined to inquire at all the principal hotels in town, as Mr. Bennet thought it possible they might have gone to one of them, on their first coming to London, before they procured lodgings. Mr. Gardiner himself did not expect any success from this measure; but as his brother was eager in it, he meant to assist him in pursuing it. He added, that Mr. Bennet seemed wholly disinclined at present to leave London, and promised to write again very soon. There was also a postscript to this effect:—

'I have written to Colonel Forster to desire him to find out, if possible, from some of the young man's intimates in the regiment, whether Wickham has any relations or connections who would be likely to know in what part of the town he has now concealed himself. If there were any one that one could apply to, with a probability of gaining such a clue as that, it might be of essential consequence. At present we have nothing to guide us. Colonel Forster will, I daresay, do everything in his power to satisfy us on this head. But, on second thoughts, perhaps Lizzy could tell us what relations he has now living better than any other person.'

Elizabeth was at no loss to understand from whence this deference for her authority proceeded; but it was not in her power to give any information of so satisfactory a nature as the compliment deserved.

She had never heard of his having had any relations, except a father and mother, both of whom had been dead many years. It was possible, however, that some of his companions in the ——shire might be able to give more information; and though she was not very sanguine in expecting it, the application was a something to look forward to.

Every day at Longbourn was now a day of anxiety; but the most anxious part of each was when the post was expected. The arrival of letters was the first grand object of every morning's impatience. Through letters, whatever of good or bad was to be told would be communicated, and every succeeding day was expected to bring some news of importance.

But before they heard again from Mr. Gardiner, a letter arrived for their father, from a different quarter, from Mr. Collins; which, as Jane had received directions to open all that came for him in his absence, she accordingly read; and Elizabeth, who knew what curiosities his letters always were, looked over her, and read it likewise. It was as follows:—

'MY DEAR SIR—I feel myself called upon, by our relationship, and my situation in life, to condole with you on the grievous affliction you are now suffering under, of which we were yesterday informed by a letter from Hertfordshire. Be assured, my dear sir, that Mrs. Collins and myself sincerely sympathise with you, and all your respectable family, in your present distress, which must be of the bitterest kind, because proceeding from a cause which no time can remove. No arguments shall be wanting on my part, that can alleviate so severe a misfortune; or that may comfort you, under a circumstance that must be, of all others, most afflicting to a parent's mind. The death of your daughter would have been a blessing in comparison of this. And it is the more to be lamented, because there is reason to suppose, as my dear Charlotte informs me, that this licentiousness of behaviour in your daughter has proceeded from a faulty degree of indulgence; though, at the same time, for the consolation of yourself and Mrs. Bennet, I am inclined to think that her own disposition must be naturally bad, or she could not be guilty of such an enormity, at so early an age. Howsoever that may be, you are grievously to be pitied, in which opinion I am not only joined by Mrs. Collins, but likewise by Lady Catherine and her daughter, to whom I have related the affair. They agree with me in apprehending that this false step in one daughter will be injurious to the fortunes of all the others: for who, as Lady Catherine herself condescendingly says, will connect themselves with such a family? And this consideration leads me, moreover, to reflect, with augmented satisfaction, on a certain event of last November; for had it been otherwise, I must have been involved in all your sorrow and disgrace. Let me advise you, then, my dear sir, to console yourself as much as possible, to throw off your unworthy child from your affection for ever, and leave her to reap the fruits of her own heinous offence.—I am, dear sir,' etc. etc.

Mr. Gardiner did not write again till he had received an answer from Colonel Forster; and then he had nothing of a pleasant nature to send. It was not known that Wickham had a single relation with whom he kept up any connection, and it was certain that he had no near one living. His former acquaintance had been numerous; but since he had been in the militia, it did not appear that he was on terms of particular friendship with any of them. There was no one, therefore, who could be pointed out as likely to give any news of him. And in the wretched state of his own finances there was a very powerful motive for secrecy, in addition to his fear of discovery by Lydia's relations; for it had just transpired that he had left gaming debts behind him to a very considerable amount. Colonel Forster believed that more than a thousand pounds would be necessary to clear his expenses at Brighton. He owed a good deal in the town, but his debts of honour were still more formidable. Mr. Gardiner did not attempt to conceal these particulars from the Longbourn family; Jane heard them with horror. 'A gamester!' she cried. 'This is wholly unexpected; I had not an idea of it.'

Mr. Gardiner added, in his letter, that they might expect to see their father at home on the following day, which was Saturday. Rendered spiritless by the ill success of all their endeavours, he had yielded to his brother-in-law's entreaty that he would return to his family and leave it to him to do whatever occasion might suggest to be advisable for continuing their pursuit. When Mrs. Bennet was told of this, she did not express so much satisfaction as her children expected, considering what her anxiety for his life had been before.

'What! is he coming home, and without poor Lydia?' she cried. 'Sure he will not leave London before he has found them. Who is to fight Wickham, and make him marry her, if he comes away?'

As Mrs. Gardiner began to wish to be at home, it was settled that she and her children should go to London at the same time that Mr. Bennet came from it. The coach, therefore, took them the first stage of their journey, and brought its master back to Longbourn.

Mrs. Gardiner went away in all the perplexity about Elizabeth and her Derbyshire friend that had attended her from that part of the world. His name had never been voluntarily mentioned before them by her niece; and the kind of half-expectation which Mrs. Gardiner had formed, of their being followed by a letter from him, had ended in nothing. Elizabeth had received none since her return, that could come from Pemberley.

The present unhappy state of the family rendered any other excuse for the lowness of her spirits unnecessary; nothing, therefore, could be fairly conjectured from *that*, though Elizabeth, who was by this time tolerably well acquainted with her own feelings, was perfectly aware that, had she known nothing of Darcy, she could have borne the dread of Lydia's infamy somewhat better. It would have spared her, she thought, one sleepless night out of two.

When Mr. Bennet arrived, he had all the appearance of his usual philosophic composure. He said as little as he had ever been in the habit of saying; made no mention of the business that had taken him away, and it was some time before his daughters had courage to speak of it.

It was not till the afternoon, when he joined them at tea, that Elizabeth ventured to introduce the subject; and then, on her briefly expressing her sorrow for what he must have endured, he replied, 'Say nothing of that. Who should suffer but myself? It has been my own doing, and I ought to feel it.'

'You must not be too severe upon yourself,' replied Elizabeth.

'You may well warn me against such an evil. Human nature is so prone to fall into it! No, Lizzy, let me once in my life feel how much I have been to blame. I am not afraid of being overpowered by the impression. It will pass away soon enough.'

'Do you suppose them to be in London?'

'Yes; where else can they be so well concealed?'

'And Lydia used to want to go to London,' added Kitty.

'She is happy, then,' said her father, drily; 'and her residence there will probably be of some duration.'

Then, after a short silence, he continued, 'Lizzy, I bear you no ill-will for being justified in your advice to me last May, which, considering the event, shows some greatness of mind.'

They were interrupted by Miss Bennet, who came to fetch her mother's tea.

'This is a parade,' cried he, 'which does one good; it gives such an elegance to misfortune! Another day I will do the same; I will sit in my library, in my night-cap and powdering gown, and give as much trouble as I can,—or perhaps I may defer it till Kitty runs away.'

'I am not going to run away, papa,' said Kitty, fretfully. 'If *I* should ever go to Brighton, I would behave better than Lydia.'

'*You* go to Brighton! I would not trust you so near it as East Bourne, for fifty pounds! No, Kitty, I have at least learnt to be cautious, and you will feel the effects of it. No officer is ever to enter my house again, nor even to pass through the village. Balls will be absolutely prohibited, unless you stand up with one of your sisters. And you are never to stir out of doors, till you can prove that you have spent ten minutes of every day in a rational manner.'

Kitty, who took all these threats in a serious light, began to cry.

'Well, well,' said he, 'do not make yourself unhappy. If you are a good girl for the next ten years, I will take you to a review at the end of them.'

CHAPTER XLIX

TWO days after Mr. Bennet's return, as Jane and Elizabeth were walking together in the shrubbery behind the house, they saw the housekeeper coming towards them, and concluding that she came to call them to their mother, went forward to meet her; but instead of the expected summons, when they approached her, she said to Miss Bennet, 'I beg your pardon, madam, for interrupting you, but I was in hopes you might have got some good news from town, so I took the liberty of coming to ask.'

'What do you mean, Hill? We have heard nothing from town.'

'Dear madam,' cried Mrs. Hill, in great astonishment, 'don't you know there is an express come for master from Mr. Gardiner? He has been here this half-hour, and master has had a letter.'

Away ran the girls, too eager to get in to have time for speech. They ran through the vestibule into the breakfast-room; from thence to the library;—their father was in neither; and they were on the point of seeking him upstairs with their mother, when they were met by the butler, who said,—

'If you are looking for my master, ma'am, he is walking towards the little copse.'

Upon this information, they instantly passed through the hall once more, and ran across the lawn after their father, who was deliberately pursuing his way towards a small wood on one side of the paddock.

Jane, who was not so light, nor so much in the habit of running as Elizabeth, soon lagged behind, while her sister, panting for breath, came up with him, and eagerly cried out,—

'Oh, papa, what news? what news? have you heard from my uncle?'

'Yes, I have had a letter from him by express.'

'Well, and what news does it bring—good or bad?'

'What is there of good to be expected?' said he, taking the letter from his pocket; 'but perhaps you would like to read it.'

Elizabeth impatiently caught it from his hand. Jane now came up.

'Read it aloud,' said their father, 'for I hardly know myself what it is about.'

'Gracechurch Street, Monday, August 2.

'MY DEAR BROTHER—At last I am able to send you some tidings of my niece, and such as, upon the whole, I hope will give you satisfaction. Soon after you left me on Saturday, I was fortunate enough to find out in what part of London they were. The particulars I reserve till we meet. It is enough to know they are discovered; I have seen them both——'

'Then it is as I always hoped,' cried Jane: 'they are married!'

Elizabeth read on:

'I have seen them both. They are not married, nor can I find there was any intention of being so; but if you are willing to perform the engagements which I have ventured to make on your side, I hope it will not be long before they are. All that is required of you is, to assure to your daughter, by settlement, her equal share of the five thousand pounds secured among your children after the decease of yourself and my sister; and, moreover, to enter into an engagement of allowing her, during your life, one hundred pounds per annum. These are conditions which, considering everything, I had no hesitation in complying with, as far as I thought myself privileged, for you. I shall send this by express, that no time may be lost in bringing me your answer. You will easily comprehend, from these particulars, that Mr. Wickham's circumstances are not so hopeless as they are generally believed to be. The world has been deceived in that respect; and I am happy to say there will be some little money, even when all his debts are discharged, to settle on my niece, in addition to her own fortune. If, as I conclude will be the case, you send me full powers to act in your name throughout the whole of this business, I will immediately give directions to Haggerston for preparing a proper settlement. There will not be the smallest occasion for your coming to town again; therefore stay quietly at Longbourn, and depend on my diligence and care. Send back your answer as soon as you can, and be careful to write explicitly. We have judged it best that my niece should be married from this house, of which I hope you will approve. She comes to us to-day. I shall write again as soon as anything more is determined on. Yours, etc.

'EDW. GARDINER.'

'Is it possible?' cried Elizabeth, when she had finished. 'Can it be possible that he will marry her?'

'Wickham is not so undeserving, then, as we have thought him,' said her sister. 'My dear father, I congratulate you.'

'And have you answered the letter?' said Elizabeth.

'No; but it must be done soon.'

Most earnestly did she then entreat him to lose no more time before he wrote.

'Oh, my dear father,' she cried, 'come back and write immediately. Consider how important every moment is in such a case.'

'Let me write for you,' said Jane, 'if you dislike the trouble yourself.'

'I dislike it very much,' he replied; 'but it must be done.'

And so saying, he turned back with them, and walked towards the house.

'And may I ask?' said Elizabeth; 'but the terms, I suppose, must be complied with.'

'Complied with! I am only ashamed of his asking so little.'

'And they *must* marry! Yet he is *such* a man.'

'Yes, yes, they must marry. There is nothing else to be done. But there are two things that I want very much to know:—one is, how much money your uncle has laid down to bring it about; and the other, how I am ever to pay him.'

'Money! my uncle!' cried Jane, 'what do you mean, sir?'

'I mean that no man in his senses would marry Lydia on so slight a temptation as one hundred a year during my life, and fifty after I am gone.'

'That is very true,' said Elizabeth; 'though it had not occurred to me before. His debts to be discharged, and something still to remain! Oh, it must be my uncle's doings! Generous, good man, I am afraid he has distressed himself. A small sum could not do all this.'

'No,' said her father. 'Wickham's a fool if he takes her with a farthing less than ten thousand pounds: I should be sorry to think so ill of him, in the very beginning of our relationship.'

'Ten thousand pounds! Heaven forbid! How is half such a sum to be repaid?'

Mr. Bennet made no answer; and each of them, deep in thought, continued silent till they reached the house. Their

father then went to the library to write, and the girls walked
into the breakfast-room.

'And they are really to be married!' cried Elizabeth,
as soon as they were by themselves. 'How strange this
is! and for *this* we are to be thankful. That they
should marry, small as is their chance of happiness, and
wretched as is his character, we are forced to rejoice!
Oh, Lydia!'

'I comfort myself with thinking,' replied Jane, 'that he
certainly would not marry Lydia if he had not a real regard
for her. Though our kind uncle has done something towards
clearing him, I cannot believe that ten thousand pounds, or
anything like it, has been advanced. He has children of his
own, and may have more. How could he spare half ten
thousand pounds?'

'If we are ever able to learn what Wickham's debts have
been,' said Elizabeth, 'and how much is settled on his side on
our sister, we shall exactly know what Mr. Gardiner has done
for them, because Wickham has not sixpence of his own.
The kindness of my uncle and aunt can never be requited.
Their taking her home, and affording her their personal
protection and countenance, is such a sacrifice to her advantage as years of gratitude cannot enough acknowledge.
By this time she is actually with them! If such goodness
does not make her miserable now, she will never deserve
to be happy! What a meeting for her, when she first sees
my aunt!'

'We must endeavour to forget all that has passed on either
side,' said Jane: 'I hope and trust they will yet be happy.
His consenting to marry her is a proof, I will believe, that he
is come to a right way of thinking. Their mutual affection
will steady them; and I flatter myself they will settle so
quietly, and live in so rational a manner, as may in time
make their past imprudence forgotten.'

'Their conduct has been such,' replied Elizabeth, 'as
neither you, nor I, nor anybody, can ever forget. It is useless to talk of it.'

It now occurred to the girls that their mother was in all
likelihood perfectly ignorant of what had happened. They
went to the library, therefore, and asked their father whether

he would not wish them to make it known to her. He was writing, and, without raising his head, coolly replied,—

'Just as you please.'

'May we take my uncle's letter to read to her?'

'Take whatever you like, and get away.'

Elizabeth took the letter from his writing-table, and they went upstairs together. Mary and Kitty were both with Mrs. Bennet: one communication would, therefore, do for all. After a slight preparation for good news, the letter was read aloud. Mrs. Bennet could hardly contain herself. As soon as Jane had read Mr. Gardiner's hope of Lydia's being soon married, her joy burst forth, and every following sentence added to its exuberance. She was now in an irritation as violent from delight as she had ever been fidgety from alarm and vexation. To know that her daughter would be married was enough. She was disturbed by no fear for her felicity, nor humbled by any remembrance of her misconduct.

'My dear, dear Lydia!' she cried: 'this is delightful indeed! She will be married! I shall see her again! She will be married at sixteen! My good, kind brother! I knew how it would be—I knew he would manage everything. How I long to see her! and to see dear Wickham too! But the clothes, the wedding clothes! I will write to my sister Gardiner about them directly. Lizzy, my dear, run down to your father, and ask him how much he will give her. Stay, stay, I will go myself. Ring the bell, Kitty, for Hill. I will put on my things in a moment. My dear, dear Lydia! How merry we shall be together when we meet!'

Her eldest daughter endeavoured to give some relief to the violence of these transports, by leading her thoughts to the obligations which Mr. Gardiner's behaviour laid them all under.

'For we must attribute this happy conclusion,' she added, 'in a great measure to his kindness. We are persuaded that he has pledged himself to assist Mr. Wickham with money.'

'Well,' cried her mother, 'it is all very right; who should do it but her own uncle? If he had not had a family of his own, I and my children must have had all his money, you know; and it is the first time we have ever had anything from him except a few presents. Well! I am so happy. In a short time I shall have a daughter married. Mrs. Wickham! How well it sounds. And she was only sixteen last June. My dear Jane, I am in such a flutter, that I am sure I can't write; so I will dictate, and you write for me. We will settle with your father about the money afterwards; but the things should be ordered immediately.'

She was then proceeding to all the particulars of calico, muslin, and cambric, and would shortly have dictated some very plentiful orders, had not Jane, though with some difficulty, persuaded her to wait till her father was at leisure to be consulted. One day's delay, she observed, would be of small importance; and her mother was too happy to be quite so obstinate as usual. Other schemes, too, came into her head.

'I will go to Meryton,' said she, 'as soon as I am dressed, and tell the good, good news to my sister Philips. And as I come back, I can call on Lady Lucas and Mrs. Long. Kitty, run down and order the carriage. An airing would do me a great deal of good, I am sure. Girls, can I do anything for you in Meryton? Oh! here comes Hill. My dear Hill, have you heard the good news? Miss Lydia is going to be married; and you shall all have a bowl of punch to make merry at her wedding.'

Mrs. Hill began instantly to express her joy. Elizabeth received her congratulations amongst the rest, and then, sick of this folly, took refuge in her own room, that she might think with freedom. Poor Lydia's situation must, at best, be bad enough; but that it was no worse, she had need to be thankful. She felt it so; and though, in looking forward, neither rational happiness nor worldly prosperity could be justly expected for her sister, in looking back to what they had feared, only two hours ago, she felt all the advantages of what they had gained.

CHAPTER L

MR. BENNET had very often wished, before this period of his life, that, instead of spending his whole income, he had laid by an annual sum, for the better provision of his children, and of his wife, if she survived him. He now wished it more than ever. Had he done his duty in that respect, Lydia need not have been indebted to her uncle for whatever of honour or credit could now be purchased for her. The satisfaction of prevailing on one of the most worthless young men in Great Britain to be her husband might then have rested in its proper place.

He was seriously concerned that a cause of so little advantage to any one should be forwarded at the sole expense of his brother-in-law; and he was determined, if possible, to find out the extent of his assistance, and to discharge the obligation as soon as he could.

When first Mr. Bennet had married, economy was held to be perfectly useless; for, of course, they were to have a son. This son was to join in cutting off the entail, as soon as he should be of age, and the widow and younger children would by that means be provided for. Five daughters successively entered the world, but yet the son was to come; and Mrs. Bennet, for many years after Lydia's birth, had been certain that he would. This event had at last been despaired of, but it was then too late to be saving. Mrs. Bennet had no turn for economy; and her husband's love of independence had alone prevented their exceeding their income.

Five thousand pounds was settled by marriage articles on Mrs. Bennet and the children. But in what proportions it should be divided amongst the latter depended on the will of the parents. This was one point, with regard to Lydia at least, which was now to be settled, and Mr. Bennet could have no hesitation in acceding to the proposal before him. In terms of grateful acknowledgment for the kindness of his brother, though expressed most concisely, he then delivered

437

on paper his perfect approbation of all that was done, and his willingness to fulfil the engagements that had been made for him. He had never before supposed that, could Wickham be prevailed on to marry his daughter, it would be done with so little inconvenience to himself as by the present arrangement. He would scarcely be ten pounds a year the loser, by the hundred that was to be paid them; for, what with her board and pocket allowance, and the continual presents in money which passed to her through her mother's hands, Lydia's expenses had been very little within that sum.

That it would be done with such trifling exertion on his side, too, was another very welcome surprise; for his chief wish at present was to have as little trouble in the business as possible. When the first transports of rage which had produced his activity in seeking her were over, he naturally returned to all his former indolence. His letter was soon despatched; for though dilatory in undertaking business, he was quick in its execution. He begged to know further particulars of what he was indebted to his brother; but was too angry with Lydia to send any message to her.

The good news quickly spread through the house; and with proportionate speed through the neighbourhood. It was borne in the latter with decent philosophy. To be sure, it would have been more for the advantage of conversation, had Miss Lydia Bennet come upon the town; or, as the happiest alternative, been secluded from the world, in some distant farmhouse. But there was much to be talked of, in marrying her; and the good-natured wishes for her well-doing, which had proceeded before from all the spiteful old ladies in Meryton, lost but little of their spirit in this change of circumstances, because with such a husband her misery was considered certain.

It was a fortnight since Mrs. Bennet had been downstairs, but on this happy day she again took her seat at the head of her table, and in spirits oppressively high. No sentiment of shame gave a damp to her triumph. The marriage of a daughter, which had been the first object of her wishes since Jane was sixteen, was now on the point of accomplishment, and her thoughts and her words ran wholly on those attendants of elegant nuptials, fine muslins, new carriages, and servants. She was busily searching through the neighbourhood for a proper situation for her daughter; and, without knowing or considering what their income might be, rejected many as deficient in size and importance.

'Haye Park might do,' said she, 'if the Gouldings would quit it, or the great house at Stoke, if the drawing-room were larger; but Ashworth is too far off. I could not bear to have her ten miles from me; and as for Purvis Lodge, the attics are dreadful.'

Her husband allowed her to talk on without interruption while the servants remained. But when they had withdrawn, he said to her, 'Mrs. Bennet, before you take any, or all of these houses, for your son and daughter, let us come to a right understanding. Into *one* house in this neighbourhood they shall never have admittance. I will not encourage the imprudence of either, by receiving them at Longbourn.'

A long dispute followed this declaration; but Mr. Bennet was firm: it soon led to another; and Mrs. Bennet found, with amazement and horror, that her husband would not advance a guinea to buy clothes for his daughter. He protested that she should receive from him no mark of affection whatever on the occasion. Mrs. Bennet could hardly comprehend it. That his anger could be carried to such a point of inconceivable resentment as to refuse his daughter a privilege, without which her marriage would scarcely seem valid, exceeded all that she could believe possible. She was more alive to the disgrace which her want of new clothes must reflect on her daughter's nuptials, than to any sense of shame at her eloping and living with Wickham a fortnight before they took place.

Elizabeth was now most heartily sorry that she had, from the distress of the moment, been led to make Mr. Darcy acquainted with their fears for her sister; for since her marriage would so shortly give the proper termination to the elopement, they might hope to conceal its unfavourable beginning from all those who were not immediately on the spot.

She had no fear of its spreading farther through his means. There were few people on whose secrecy she would have more confidently depended; but at the same time there was no one whose knowledge of a sister's frailty would have mortified her so much. Not, however, from any fear of disadvantage from it individually to herself; for at any rate there seemed a gulf impassable between them. Had Lydia's marriage been concluded on the most honourable terms, it was not to be supposed that Mr. Darcy would connect himself with a family, where to every other objection would now be added an alliance and relationship of the nearest kind with the man whom he so justly scorned.

From such a connection she could not wonder that he should shrink. The wish of procuring her regard, which she had assured herself of his feeling in Derbyshire, could not in rational expectation survive such a blow as this. She was humbled, she was grieved; she repented, though she hardly knew of what. She became jealous of his esteem, when she could no longer hope to be benefited by it. She wanted to hear of him, when there seemed the least chance of gaining intelligence. She was convinced that she could have been happy with him, when it was no longer likely they should meet.

What a triumph for him, as she often thought, could he know that the proposals which she had proudly spurned only four months ago would now have been gladly and gratefully received! He was as generous, she doubted not, as the most generous of his sex. But while he was mortal, there must be a triumph.

She began now to comprehend that he was exactly the man who, in disposition and talents, would most suit her. His understanding and temper, though unlike her own, would have answered all her wishes. It was an union that must have been to the advantage of both; by her ease and liveliness his mind might have been softened, his manners improved; and from his judgment, information, and knowledge of the world, she must have received benefit of greater importance.

But no such happy marriage could now teach the admiring multitude what connubial felicity really was. An union of a different tendency, and precluding the possibility of the other, was soon to be formed in their family.

How Wickham and Lydia were to be supported in tolerable independence she could not imagine. But how little of permanent happiness could belong to a couple who were only brought together because their passions were stronger than their virtue, she could easily conjecture.

Mr. Gardiner soon wrote again to his brother. To Mr. Bennet's acknowledgments he briefly replied, with assurances of his eagerness to promote the welfare of any of his family; and concluded with entreaties that the subject might never be mentioned to him again. The principal purport of his letter was to inform them that Mr. Wickham had resolved on quitting the militia.

'It was greatly my wish that he should do so,' he added, 'as soon as his marriage was fixed on. And I think you will agree with me in considering a removal from that corps as highly advisable, both on his account and my niece's. It is Mr. Wickham's intention to go into the Regulars; and, among his former friends, there are still some who are able and willing to assist him in the army. He has the promise of an ensigncy in General ——'s regiment, now quartered in the north. It is an advantage to have it so far from this part of the kingdom. He promises fairly; and I hope among different people, where they may each have a character to preserve, they will both be more prudent. I have written to Colonel Forster, to inform him of our present arrangements, and to request that he will satisfy the various creditors of Mr. Wickham in and near Brighton with assurances of speedy payment, for which I have pledged myself. And will you give yourself the trouble of carrying similar assurances to his creditors in Meryton, of whom I shall subjoin a list, according to his information? He has given in all his debts; I hope at least he has not deceived us. Haggerston has our directions, and all will be completed in a week. They will then join his regiment, unless they are first invited to Longbourn; and I understand from Mrs. Gardiner that my niece is very desirous of seeing you all before she leaves the south. She is well, and begs to be dutifully remembered to you and her mother.—Yours, etc.

'E. GARDINER.'

Mr. Bennet and his daughters saw all the advantages of Wickham's removal from the ——shire, as clearly as Mr. Gardiner could do. But Mrs. Bennet was not so well pleased with it. Lydia's being settled in the north, just when she had expected most pleasure and pride in her company, for she had by no means given up her plan of their residing in Hertfordshire, was a severe disappointment; and, besides, it was such a pity that Lydia should be taken from a regiment where she was acquainted with everybody, and had so many favourites.

'She is so fond of Mrs. Forster,' said she, 'It will be quite shocking to send her away! And there are several of the young men, too, that she likes very much. The officers may not be so pleasant in General ——'s regiment.'

His daughter's request, for such it might be considered, of being admitted into her family again, before she set off for the north, received at first an absolute negative. But Jane and Elizabeth, who agreed in wishing, for the sake of their sister's feelings and consequence, that she should be noticed on her marriage by her parents, urged him so earnestly, yet so rationally and so mildly, to receive her and her husband at Longbourn, as soon as they were married, that he was prevailed on to think as they thought and act as they wished. And their mother had the satisfaction of knowing that she should be able to show her married daughter in the neighbourhood, before she was banished to the north. When Mr. Bennet wrote again to his brother, therefore, he sent his permission for them to come; and it was settled that, as soon as the ceremony was over, they should proceed to Longbourn. Elizabeth was surprised, however, that Wickham should consent to such a scheme; and, had she consulted only her own inclination, any meeting with him would have been the last object of her wishes.

CHAPTER LI

THEIR sister's wedding day arrived; and Jane and Elizabeth felt for her probably more than she felt for herself. The carriage was sent to meet them at ——, and they were to return in it by dinner-time. Their arrival was dreaded by the elder Miss Bennets; and Jane more especially, who gave Lydia the feelings which would have attended herself had *she* been the culprit, and was wretched in the thought of what her sister must endure.

They came. The family were assembled in the breakfast-room to receive them. Smiles decked the face of Mrs. Bennet, as the carriage drove up to the door; her husband looked impenetrably grave; her daughters, alarmed, anxious, uneasy.

Lydia's voice was heard in the vestibule; the door was thrown open, and she ran into the room. Her mother stepped forwards, embraced her, and welcomed her with rapture; gave her hand with an affectionate smile to Wickham, who followed his lady, and wished them both joy, with an alacrity which showed no doubt of their happiness.

Their reception from Mr. Bennet, to whom they then turned, was not quite so cordial. His countenance rather gained in austerity; and he scarcely opened his lips. The easy assurance of the young couple, indeed, was enough to provoke him. Elizabeth was disgusted, and even Miss Bennet was shocked. Lydia was Lydia still; untamed, unabashed, wild, noisy, and fearless. She turned from sister to sister, demanding their congratulations; and when at length they all sat down, looked eagerly round the room, took notice of some little alteration in it, and observed, with a laugh, that it was a great while since she had been there.

Wickham was not at all more distressed than herself; but his manners were always so pleasing, that had his character and his marriage been exactly what they ought, his smiles and his easy address, while he claimed their relationship,

443

would have delighted them all. Elizabeth had not before believed him quite equal to such assurance; but she sat down, resolving within herself to draw no limits in future to the impudence of an impudent man. *She* blushed, and Jane blushed; but the cheeks of the two who caused their confusion suffered no variation of colour.

There was no want of discourse. The bride and her mother could neither of them talk fast enough; and Wickham, who happened to sit near Elizabeth, began inquiring after his acquaintance in that neighbourhood, with a good-humoured ease which she felt very unable to equal in her replies. They seemed each of them to have the happiest memories in the world. Nothing of the past was recollected with pain; and Lydia led voluntarily to subjects which her sisters would not have alluded to for the world.

'Only think of its being three months,' she cried, 'since I went away: it seems but a fortnight, I declare; and yet there have been things enough happened in the time. Good gracious! when I went away, I am sure I had no more idea of being married till I came back again! though I thought it would be very good fun if I was.'

Her father lifted up his eyes, Jane was distressed, Elizabeth looked expressively at Lydia; but she, who never heard nor saw anything of which she chose to be insensible, gaily continued, 'Oh, mamma, do the people hereabouts know I am married to-day? I was afraid they might not; and we overtook William Goulding in his curricle, so I was determined he should know it, and so I let down the side glass next to him, and took off my glove and let my hand just rest upon the window frame, so that he might see the ring, and then I bowed and smiled like anything.'

Elizabeth could bear it no longer. She got up and ran out of the room; and returned no more till she heard them passing through the hall to the dining parlour. She then joined them soon enough to see Lydia, with anxious parade, walk up to her mother's right hand, and hear her say to her eldest sister, 'Ah, Jane I take your place now, and you must go lower, because I am a married woman.'

It was not to be supposed that time would give Lydia that embarrassment from which she had been so wholly free at first. Her ease and good spirits increased. She longed to see Mrs. Philips, the Lucases, and all their other neighbours, and to hear herself called 'Mrs. Wickham' by each of them; and in the meantime she went after dinner to show her ring and boast of being married to Mrs. Hill and the two house-maids.

'Well, mamma,' said she, when they were all returned to the breakfast-room, 'and what do you think of my husband? Is not he a charming man? I am sure my sisters must all envy me. I only hope they may have half my good luck. They must all go to Brighton. That is the place to get husbands. What a pity it is, mamma, we did not all go.'

'Very true; and if I had my will we should. But, my dear Lydia, I don't at all like your going such a way off. Must it be so?'

'O Lord! yes; there is nothing in that. I shall like it of all things. You and papa, and my sisters, must come down and see us. We shall be at Newcastle all the winter, and I daresay there will be some balls, and I will take care to get good partners for them all.'

'I should like it beyond anything!' said her mother.

'And then when you go away, you may leave one or two of my sisters behind you; and I daresay I shall get husbands for them before the winter is over.'

'I thank you for my share of the favour,' said Elizabeth; 'but I do not particularly like your way of getting husbands.'

Their visitors were not to remain above ten days with them. Mr. Wickham had received his commission before he left London, and he was to join his regiment at the end of a fortnight.

No one but Mrs. Bennet regretted that their stay would be so short; and she made the most of the time by visiting about with her daughter, and having very frequent parties at home. These parties were acceptable to all; to avoid a family circle was even more desirable to such as did think than such as did not.

Wickham's affection for Lydia was just what Elizabeth had expected to find it; not equal to Lydia's for him. She had scarcely needed her present observation to be satisfied, from the reason of things, that their elopement had been brought on by the strength of her love rather than by his; and she would have wondered why, without violently caring for her, he chose to elope with her at all, had she not felt certain that his flight was rendered necessary by distress of circumstances; and if that were the case, he was not the young man to resist an opportunity of having a companion.

Lydia was exceedingly fond of him. He was her dear Wickham on every occasion; no one was to be put in competition with him. He did everything best in the world; and she was sure he would kill more birds on the first of September than anybody else in the country.

One morning, soon after their arrival, as she was sitting with her two elder sisters, she said to Elizabeth,—

'Lizzy, I never gave *you* an account of my wedding, I believe. You were not by when I told mamma and the others all about it. Are not you curious to hear how it was managed?'

'No, really,' replied Elizabeth; 'I think there cannot be too little said on the subject.'

'La! You are so strange! But I must tell you how it went off. We were married, you know, at St. Clement's, because Wickham's lodgings were in that parish. And it was settled that we should all be there by eleven o'clock. My uncle and aunt and I were to go together; and the others were to meet us at the church. Well, Monday morning came, and I was in such a fuss! I was so afraid, you know, that something would happen to put it off, and then I should have gone quite distracted. And there was my aunt, all the time I was dressing, preaching and talking away just as if she was reading a sermon. However, I did not hear above one word in ten, for I was thinking, you may suppose, of my dear Wickham. I longed to know whether he would be married in his blue coat.

'Well, and so we breakfasted at ten as usual: I thought it would never be over; for, by the bye, you are to understand that my uncle and aunt were horrid unpleasant all the time I was with them. If you'll believe me, I did not once put my foot out of doors, though I was there a fortnight. Not one party, or scheme, or anything. To be sure, London was rather thin, but, however, the Little Theatre was open.

Well, and so just as the carriage came to the door, my uncle was called away upon business to that horrid man Mr. Stone. And then, you know, when once they get together, there is no end of it. Well, I was so frightened I did not know what to do, for my uncle was to give me away; and if we were beyond the hour we could not be married all day. But, luckily, he came back again in ten minutes' time, and then we all set out. However, I recollected afterwards, that if he *had* been prevented going, the wedding need not be put off, for Mr. Darcy might have done as well.'

'Mr. Darcy!' repeated Elizabeth, in utter amazement.

'Oh yes! he was to come there with Wickham, you know. But gracious me! I quite forgot! I ought not to have said a word about it. I promised them so faithfully! What will Wickham say? It was to be such a secret!'

'If it was to be a secret,' said Jane, 'say not another word on the subject. You may depend upon my seeking no further.'

'Oh, certainly,' said Elizabeth, though burning with curiosity; 'we will ask you no questions.'

'Thank you,' said Lydia; 'for if you did, I should certainly tell you all, and then Wickham would be so angry.'

On such encouragement to ask, Elizabeth was forced to put it out of her power by running away.

But to live in ignorance on such a point was impossible; or at least it was impossible not to try for information. Mr. Darcy had been at her sister's wedding. It was exactly a scene, and exactly among people, where he had apparently least to do, and least temptation to go. Conjectures as to the meaning of it, rapid and wild, hurried into her brain, but she was satisfied with none. Those that best pleased her, as placing his conduct in the noblest light, seemed most improbable. She could not bear such suspense; and hastily seizing a sheet of paper, wrote a short letter to her aunt, to request an explanation of what Lydia had dropped, if it were compatible with the secrecy which had been intended.

'You may readily comprehend,' she added, 'what my curiosity must be to know how a person unconnected with any of us, and, comparatively speaking, a stranger to our family, should have been amongst you at such a time. Pray write instantly, and let me understand it—unless it is, for very cogent reasons, to remain in the secrecy which Lydia seems to think necessary; and then I must endeavour to be satisfied with ignorance.'

'Not that I *shall* though,' she added to herself, and she finished the letter; 'and, my dear aunt, if you do not tell me in an honourable manner, I shall certainly be reduced to tricks and stratagems to find it out.'

Jane's delicate sense of honour would not allow her to speak to Elizabeth privately of what Lydia had let fall; Elizabeth was glad of it:—till it appeared whether her inquiries would receive any satisfaction, she had rather be without a confidante.

CHAPTER LII

ELIZABETH had the satisfaction of receiving an answer to her letter as soon as she possibly could. She was no sooner in possession of it, than hurrying into the little copse, where she was least likely to be interrupted, she sat down on one of the benches, and prepared to be happy; for the length of the letter convinced her that it did not contain a denial.

'Gracechurch Street, Sept. 6.

'MY DEAR NIECE—I have just received your letter, and shall devote this whole morning to answering it, as I foresee that a *little* writing will not comprise what I have to tell you. I must confess myself surprised by your application; I did not expect it from *you*. Don't think me angry, however, for I only mean to let you know that I had not imagined such inquiries to be necessary on *your* side. If you do not choose to understand me, forgive my impertinence. Your uncle is as much surprised as I am; and nothing but the belief of your being a party concerned would have allowed him to act as he has done. But if you are really innocent and ignorant, I must be more explicit. On the very day of my coming home from Longbourn, your uncle had a most unexpected visitor. Mr. Darcy called, and was shut up with him several hours. It was all over before I arrived; so my curiosity was not so dreadfully racked as *yours* seems to have been. He came to tell Mr. Gardiner that he had found out where your sister and Mr. Wickham were, and that he had seen and talked with them both—Wickham repeatedly, Lydia once. From what I can collect, he left Derbyshire only one day after ourselves, and came to town with the resolution of hunting for them. The motive professed was his conviction of its being owing to himself that Wickham's worthlessness had not been so well known as to make it impossible for any young woman of character to love or confide in him. He generously imputed the whole to his mistaken pride, and confessed that he had before thought it beneath him to lay his private actions open to the world. His character was to speak for itself. He called it, therefore, his duty to step forward, and endeavour to remedy an evil which had been brought on by himself. If he *had another* motive, I am sure it would never disgrace him. He had been some days in town before he was able to discover them; but he had something to direct his search, which was more than *we* had; and the consciousness of this was another reason for his resolving to follow us. There is a lady, it seems, a Mrs. Younge,

449

who was some time ago governess to Miss Darcy, and was dismissed
from her charge on some cause of disapprobation, though he did
not say what. She then took a large house in Edward Street, and
has since maintained herself by letting lodgings. This Mrs. Younge
was, he knew, intimately acquainted with Wickham; and he went to
her for intelligence of him, as soon as he got to town. But it was
two or three days before he could get from her what he wanted. She
would not betray her trust, I suppose, without bribery and corruption,
for she really did know where her friend was to be found. Wickham, indeed, had gone to her on their first arrival in London, and
had she been able to receive them into her house, they would have
taken up their abode with her. At length, however, our kind friend
procured the wished-for direction. They were in ———— Street. He
saw Wickham, and afterwards insisted on seeing Lydia. His first
object with her, he acknowledged had been to persuade her to quit
her present disgraceful situation, and return to her friends as soon
as they could be prevailed on to receive her, offering his assistance
as far as it would go. But he found Lydia absolutely resolved on
remaining where she was. She cared for none of her friends; she
wanted no help of his; she would not hear of leaving Wickham. She
was sure they should be married some time or other, and it did not
much signify when. Since such were her feelings, it only remained,
he thought, to secure and expedite a marriage, which, in his very
first conversation with Wickham, he easily learnt had never been *his*
design. He confessed himself obliged to leave the regiment on
account of some debts of honour which were very pressing; and
scrupled not to lay all the ill consequences of Lydia's flight on her
own folly alone. He meant to resign his commission immediately;
and as to his future situation, he could conjecture very little about
it. He must go somewhere, but he did not know where, and he
knew he should have nothing to live on. Mr. Darcy asked why he
did not marry your sister at once. Though Mr. Bennet was not
imagined to be very rich, he would have been able to do something
for him, and his situation must have been benefited by marriage.
But he found, in reply to this question, that Wickham still cherished
the hope of more effectually making his fortune by marriage, in some
other country. Under such circumstances, however, he was not likely
to be proof against the temptation of immediate relief. They met
several times, for there was much to be discussed. Wickham, of
course, wanted more than he could get; but at length was reduced
to be reasonable. Everything being settled betwen *them,* Mr.
Darcy's next step was to make your uncle acquainted with it, and
he first called in Gracechurch Street the evening before I came home.
But Mr. Gardiner could not be seen; and Mr. Darcy found, on
further inquiry, that your father was still with him, but would quit
town the next morning. He did not judge your father to be a person
whom he could so properly consult as your uncle, and therefore
readily postponed seeing him till after the departure of the former.
He did not leave his name, and till the next day it was only known
that a gentleman had called on business. On Saturday he came

again. Your father was gone, your uncle at home, and, as I said before, they had a great deal of talk together. They met again on Sunday, and then *I* saw him too. It was not all settled before Monday : as soon as it was, the express was sent off to Longbourn. But our visitor was very obstinate. I fancy, Lizzy, that obstinacy is the real defect of his character, after all. He has been accused of many faults at different times ; but *this* is the true one. Nothing was to be done that he did not do himself; though I am sure (and I do not speak it to be thanked, therefore say nothing about it) your uncle would most readily have settled the whole. They battled it together for a long time, which was more than either the gentleman or lady concerned in it deserved. But at last your uncle was forced to yield, and instead of being allowed to be of use to his niece, was forced to put up with only having the probable credit of it, which went sorely against the grain; and I really believe your letter this morning gave him great pleasure, because it required an explanation that would rob him of his borrowed feathers, and give the praise where it was due. But, Lizzy, this must go no further than yourself, or Jane at most. You know pretty well, I suppose, what has been done for the young people. His debts are to be paid, amounting, I believe, to considerably more than a thousand pounds, another thousand in addition to her own settled upon *her,* and his commission purchased. The reason why all this was to be done by him alone was such as I have given above. It was owing to him, to his reserve and want of proper consideration, that Wickham's character had been so misunderstood, and consequently that he had been received and noticed as he was. Perhaps there was some truth in *this;* though I doubt whether *his* reserve, or *anybody's* reserve, can be answerable for the event. But in spite of all this fine talking, my dear Lizzy, you may rest perfectly assured that your uncle would never have yielded, if we had not given him credit for *another interest* in the affair. When all this was resolved on, he returned again to his friends, who were still staying at Pemberley; but it was agreed that he should be in London once more when the wedding took place, and all money matters were then to receive the last finish. — I believe I have now told you everything. It is a relation which you tell me is to give you great surprise; I hope at least it will not afford you any displeasure. Lydia came to us, and Wickham had constant admission to the house. *He* was exactly what he had been when I knew him in Hertfordshire; but I would not tell you how little I was satisfied with *her* behaviour while she stayed with us, if I had not perceived, by Jane's letter last Wednesday, that her conduct on coming home was exactly of a piece with it, and therefore what I now tell you can give you no fresh pain. I talked to her repeatedly in the most serious manner, representing to her the wickedness of what she had done, and all the unhappiness she had brought on her family. If she heard me, it was by good luck, for I am sure she did not listen. I was sometimes quite provoked ; but then I recollected my dear Elizabeth and Jane, and for their sakes had patience with her. Mr. Darcy was punctual in his return, and, as Lydia informed you, attended the wedding. He dined with us the next day, and was to leave town again on Wednesday or Thursday. Will you be very angry with me, my dear Lizzy, if I take this opportunity of saying (what I was never bold enough to say before) how much I like him? His behaviour to us has, in every respect, been as pleasing as when we were in Derbyshire. His understanding and opinions all please me; he wants nothing but a little more liveliness, and *that*, if he marry *prudently*, his wife may teach him. I thought him very sly; he hardly ever mentioned your name. But slyness seems the fashion. Pray forgive me, if I have been very presuming, or at least do not punish me so far as to exclude me from P. I shall never be quite happy till I have been all round the park. A low phaeton with a nice little pair of ponies would be the very thing. But I must write no more. The children have been wanting me this half-hour.—Yours very sincerely,

'M. GARDINER.'

The contents of this letter threw Elizabeth into a flutter of spirits, in which it was difficult to determine whether pleasure or pain bore the greatest share. The vague and unsettled suspicions which uncertainty had produced of what Mr. Darcy might have been doing to forward her sister's match, which she had feared to encourage, as an exertion of goodness too great to be probable, and at the same time dreaded to be just, from the pain of obligation, were proved beyond their greatest extent to be true! He had followed them purposely to town, he had taken on himself all the trouble and mortification attendant on such a research; in which supplication had been necessary to a woman whom he must abominate and despise, and where he was reduced to meet, frequently meet, reason with, persuade, and finally bribe, the man whom he always most wished to avoid, and whose very name it was punishment to him to pronounce. He had done all this for a girl whom he could neither regard nor esteem. Her heart did whisper that he had done it for her. But it was a hope shortly checked by other considerations; and she soon felt that even her vanity was insufficient, when required to depend on his affection for her, for a woman who had already refused him, as able to overcome a sentiment so natural as abhorrence against relationship with Wickham. Brother-in-law of Wickham! Every kind of pride must revolt from the connection. He had, to be sure, done much. She was ashamed to think how much. But he had given a reason for his interference, which asked no extraordinary stretch of belief. It was reasonable that he should feel he had been wrong; he had liberality, and he had the means of exercising it; and though she would not place herself as his principal inducement, she could perhaps believe that remaining partiality for her might assist his endeavours in a cause where her peace of mind must be materially concerned. It was painful, exceedingly painful, to know that they were under obligations to a person who could never receive a return. They owed the restoration of Lydia, her character, everything, to him. Oh how heartily did she grieve over every ungracious sensation she had ever encouraged, every saucy speech she had ever directed towards him. For herself she was humbled; but she was proud of him,—proud that in a cause of compassion and honour he had been able to get the better of himself. She read over her aunt's commendation of him again and again. It was hardly enough; but it pleased her. She was even sensible of some pleasure, though mixed with regret, on finding how steadfastly both she and her uncle had been persuaded that affection and confidence subsisted between Mr. Darcy and herself.

She was roused from her seat and her reflections by some one's approach; and, before she could strike into another path, she was overtaken by Wickham.

'I am afraid I interrupt your solitary ramble, my dear sister?' said he, as he joined her.

'You certainly do,' she replied with a smile; 'but it does not follow that the interruption must be unwelcome.'

'I should be sorry, indeed, if it were. *We* were always good friends, and now we are better.'

'True. Are the others coming out?'

'I do not know. Mrs. Bennet and Lydia are going in the carriage to Meryton. And so, my dear sister, I find, from our uncle and aunt, that you have actually seen Pemberley.'

She replied in the affirmative.

'I almost envy you the pleasure, and yet I believe it would be too much for me, or else I could take it in my way to Newcastle. And you saw the old housekeeper, I suppose? Poor Reynolds, she was always very fond of me. But of course she did not mention my name to you.'

'Yes, she did.'

'And what did she say?'

'That you were gone into the army, and she was afraid had—not turned out well. At such a distance as *that*, you know, things are strangely misrepresented.'

'Certainly,' he replied, biting his lips. Elizabeth hoped she had silenced him; but he soon afterwards said,—

'I was surprised to see Darcy in town last month. We passed each other several times. I wonder what he can be doing there.'

'Perhaps preparing for his marriage with Miss De Bourgh,' said Elizabeth. 'It must be something particular to take him there at this time of year.'

'Undoubtedly. Did you see him while you were at Lambton? I thought I understood from the Gardiners that you had.'

'Yes; he introduced us to his sister.'

'And do you like her?'

'Very much.'

'I have heard, indeed, that she is uncommonly improved within this year or two. When I last saw her, she was not very promising. I am very glad you liked her. I hope she will turn out well.'

'I daresay she will; she has got over the most trying age.'

'Did you go by the village of Kympton?'

'I do not recollect that we did.'

'I mention it because it is the living which I ought to have had. A must delightful place! Excellent parsonage house! It would have suited me in every respect.'

'How should you have liked making sermons?'

'Exceedingly well. I should have considered it as part of my duty, and the exertion would soon have been nothing. One ought not to repine; but, to be sure, it would have been such a thing for me! The quiet, the retirement of such a life, would have answered all my ideas of happiness! But it was not to be. Did you ever hear Darcy mention the circumstance when you were in Kent?'

'I *have* heard from authority, which I thought *as good,* that it was left you conditionally only, and at the will of the present patron.'

'You have! Yes, there was something in *that;* I told you so from the first, you may remember.'

'I *did* hear, too, that there was a time when sermon-making was not so palatable to you as it seems to be at present; that you actually declared your resolution of never taking orders, and that the business had been compromised accordingly.'

'You did! and it was not wholly without foundation. You may remember what I told you on that point, when first we talked of it.'

They were now almost at the door of the house, for she had walked fast to get rid of him; and unwilling, for her sister's sake, to provoke him, she only said in reply, with a good-humoured smile,—

'Come, Mr. Wickham, we are brother and sister, you know. Do not let us quarrel about the past. In future, I hope we shall be always of one mind.'

She held out her hand: he kissed it with affectionate gallantry, though he hardly knew how to look, and they entered the house.

CHAPTER LIII

MR. WICKHAM was so perfectly satisfied with this conversation, that he never again distressed himself, or provoked his dear sister Elizabeth, by introducing the subject of it; and she was pleased to find that she had said enough to keep him quiet.

The day of his and Lydia's departure soon came, and Mrs. Bennet was forced to submit to a separation, which, as her husband by no means entered into her scheme of their all going to Newcastle, was likely to continue at least a twelvemonth.

'Oh, my dear Lydia,' she cried, 'when shall we meet again?'

'O Lord! I don't know. Not these two or three years, perhaps.'

'Write to me very often, my dear.'

'As often as I can. But you know married women have never much time for writing. My sisters may write to *me*. They will have nothing else to do.'

Mr. Wickham's adieus were much more affectionate than his wife's. He smiled, looked handsome, and said many pretty things.

'He is as fine a fellow,' said Mr. Bennet, as soon as they were out of the house, 'as ever I saw. He simpers, and smirks, and makes love to us all. I am prodigiously proud of him. I defy even Sir Wiliam Lucas himself to produce a more valuable son-in-law.'

The loss of her daughter made Mrs. Bennet very dull for several days.

'I often think,' said she, 'that there is nothing so bad as parting with one's friends. One seems so forlorn without them.'

'This is the consequence, you see, madam, of marrying a daughter,' said Elizabeth. 'It must make you better satisfied that your other four are single.'

'It is no such thing. Lydia does not leave me because she is married; but only because her husband's regiment happens to be so far off. If that had been nearer, she would not have gone so soon.'

But the spiritless condition which this event threw her into was shortly relieved, and her mind opened again to the agitation of hope, by an article of news, which then began to be in circulation. The housekeeper at Netherfield had received orders to prepare for the arrival of her master, who was coming down in a day or two, to shoot there for several weeks. Mrs. Bennet was quite in the fidgets. She looked at Jane, and smiled, and shook her head, by turns.

'Well, well, and so Mr. Bingley is coming down, sister,' (for Mrs. Philips first brought her the news). 'Well, so much the better. Not that I care about it, though. He is nothing to us, you know, and I am sure I never want to see him again. But, however, he is very welcome to come to Netherfield, if he likes it. And who knows what *may* happen? But that is nothing to us. You know, sister, we agreed long ago never to mention a word about it. And so, it is quite certain he is coming?'

'You may depend on it,' replied the other, 'for Mrs. Nichols was in Meryton last night: I saw her passing by, and went out myself on purpose to know the truth of it; and she told me that it was certainly true. He comes down on Thursday, at the latest, very likely on Wednesday. She was going to the butcher's, she told me, on purpose to order in some meat on Wednesday, and she has got three couple of ducks just fit to be killed.'

Miss Bennet had not been able to hear of his coming without changing colour. It was many months since she had mentioned his name to Elizabeth; but now, as soon as they were alone together, she said,—

'I saw you look at me to-day, Lizzy, when my aunt told us of the present report; and I know I appeared distressed; but don't imagine it was from any silly cause. I was only confused for the moment, because I felt that I *should* be looked at. I do assure you that the news does not affect me either with pleasure or pain. I am glad of one thing, that he comes alone; because we shall see the less of him.

Not that I am afraid of *myself*, but I dread other people's remarks.'

Elizabeth did not know what to make of it. Had she not seen him in Derbyshire, she might have supposed him capable of coming there with no other view than what was acknowledged; but she still thought him partial to Jane, and she wavered as to the greater probability of his coming there *with* his friend's permission, or being bold enough to come without it.

'Yet it is hard,' she sometimes thought, 'that this poor man cannot come to a house, which he has legally hired, without raising all this speculation! I *will* leave him to himself.'

In spite of what her sister declared, and really believed to be her feelings, in the expectation of his arrival, Elizabeth could easily perceive that her spirits were affected by it. They were more disturbed, more unequal, than she had often seen them.

The subject which had been so warmly canvassed between their parents, about a twelvemonth ago, was now brought forward again.

'As soon as ever Mr. Bingley comes, my dear,' said Mrs. Bennet, 'you will wait on him of course.'

'No, no. You forced me into visiting him last year, and promised, if I went to see him, he should marry one of my daughters. But it ended in nothing, and I will not be sent on a fool's errand again.'

His wife represented to him how absolutely necessary such an attention would be from all the neighbouring gentlemen, on his returning to Netherfield.

''Tis an *etiquette* I despise,' said he. 'If he wants our society, let him seek it. He knows where we live. I will not spend *my* hours in running after my neighbours every time they go away and come back again.'

'Well, all I know is, that it will be abominably rude if you do not wait on him. But, however, that shan't prevent my asking him to dine here, I am determined. We must have Mrs. Long and the Gouldings soon. That will make thirteen with ourselves, so there will be just room at the table for him.'

Consoled by this resolution, she was the better able to bear her husband's incivility; though it was very mortifying to know that her neighbours might all see Mr. Bingley in consequence of it before *they* did. As the day of his arrival drew near,—

'I begin to be sorry that he comes at all,' said Jane to her sister. 'It would be nothing; I could see him with perfect indifference; but I can hardly bear to hear it thus perpetually talked off. My mother means well; but she does not know, no one can know, how much I suffer from what she says. Happy shall I be when his stay at Netherfield is over!'

'I wish I could say anything to comfort you,' replied Elizabeth; 'but it is wholly out of my power. You must feel it; and the usual satisfaction of preaching patience to a sufferer is denied me, because you have always so much.'

Mr. Bingley arrived. Mrs. Bennet, through the assistance of servants, contrived to have the earliest tidings of it, that the period of anxiety and fretfulness on her side might be as long as it could. She counted the days that must intervene before their invitation could be sent; hopeless of seeing him before. But on the third morning after his arrival in Hertfordshire, she saw him from her dressing-room window enter the paddock, and ride towards the house.

Her daughters were eagerly called to partake of her joy. Jane resolutely kept her place at the table; but Elizabeth, to satisfy her mother, went to the window—she looked—she saw Mr. Darcy with him, and sat down again by her sister.

'There is a gentleman with him, mamma,' said Kitty; 'who can it be?'

'Some acquaintance or other, my dear, I suppose; I am sure I do not know.'

'La!' replied Kitty, 'it looks just like that man that used to be with him before. Mr. what's his name—that tall, proud man.'

'Good gracious! Mr. Darcy!—and so it does, I vow. Well, any friend of Mr. Bingley's will always be welcome here to be sure; but else I must say that I hate the very sight of him.'

Jane looked at Elizabeth with surprise and concern. She knew but little of their meeting in Derbyshire, and therefore felt for the awkwardness which must attend her sister, in seeing him almost for the first time after receiving his explanatory letter. Both sisters were uncomfortable enough. Each felt for the other, and of course for themselves; and their mother talked on of her dislike of Mr. Darcy, and her resolution to be civil to him only as Mr. Bingley's friend, without being heard by either of them. But Elizabeth had sources of uneasiness which could not be suspected by Jane, to whom she had never yet had courage to show Mrs. Gardiner's letter, or to relate her own change of sentiment towards him.

To Jane he could be only a man whose proposals she had refused, and whose merits she had undervalued; but to her own more extensive information he was the person to whom the whole family were indebted for the first of benefits, and whom she regarded herself with an interest, if not quite so tender, at least as reasonable and just, as what Jane felt for Bingley. Her astonishment at his coming—at his coming to Netherfield, to Longbourn, and voluntarily seeking her again, was almost equal to what she had known on first witnessing his altered behaviour in Derbyshire.

The colour which had been driven from her face returned for half a minute with an additional glow, and a smile of delight added lustre to her eyes, as she thought for that space of time that his affection and wishes must still be unshaken; but she would not be secure.

'Let me first see how he behaves,' said she; 'it will then be early enough for expectation.'

She sat intently at work, striving to be composed, and without daring to lift up her eyes, till anxious curiosity carried them to the face of her sister as the servant was approaching the door. Jane looked a little paler than usual, but more sedate than Elizabeth had expected. On the gentlemen's appearing, her colour increased; yet she received them with tolerable ease, and with a propriety of behaviour equally free from any symptom of resentment, or any unnecessary complaisance.

Elizabeth said as little to either as civility would allow, and sat down again to her work, with an eagerness which it did not often command. She had ventured only one glance at Darcy. He looked serious as usual; and she thought, more as he had been used to look in Hertfordshire, than as she had seen him at Pemberley. But, perhaps, he could not in her mother's presence be what he was before her uncle and aunt. It was a painful, but not an improbable, conjecture.

Bingley she had likewise seen for an instant, and in that short period saw him looking both pleased and embarrassed. He was received by Mrs. Bennet with a degree of civility which made her two daughters ashamed, especially when contrasted with the cold and ceremonious politeness of her courtesy and address of his friend.

Elizabeth particularly, who knew that her mother owed to the latter the preservation of her favourite daughter from irremediable infamy, was hurt and distressed to a most painful degree by a distinction so ill applied.

Darcy, after inquiring of her how Mr. and Mrs. Gardiner did, a question which she could not answer without confusion, said scarcely anything. He was not seated by her: perhaps that was the reason of his silence; but it had not been so in Derbyshire. There he had talked to her friends when he could not to herself. But now several minutes elapsed, without bringing the sound of his voice; and when occasionally, unable to resist the impulse of curiosity, she raised her eyes to his face, she as often found him looking at Jane as at herself, and frequently on no object but the ground. More thoughtfulness and less anxiety to please, than when they last met, were plainly expressed. She was disappointed, and angry with herself for being so.

'Could I expect it to be otherwise?' said she. 'Yet why did he come?'

She was in no humour for conversation with any one but himself; and to him she had hardly courage to speak.

She inquired after his sister, but could do no more.

'It is a long time, Mr. Bingley, since you went away,' said Mrs. Bennet.

He readily agreed to it. ·

'I began to be afraid you would never come back again. People *did* say, you meant to quit the place entirely at Michaelmas; but, however, I hope it is not true. A great many changes have happened in the neighbourhood since you went away. Miss Lucas is married and settled: and one of my own daughters. I suppose you have heard of it; indeed, you must have seen it in the papers. In was in the *Times* and the *Courier,* I know; though it was not put in as it ought to be. It was only said, "Lately, George Wickham, Esq., to Miss Lydia Bennet," without there being a syllable said of her father, or the place where she lived, or anything. It was my brother Gardiner's drawing up, too, and I wonder how he came to make such an awkward business of it. Did you see it?'

Bingley replied that he did, and made his congratulations. Elizabeth dared not lift up her eyes. How Mr. Darcy looked, therefore, she could not tell.

'It is a delightful thing, to be sure, to have a daughter well married,' continued her mother; 'but at the same time, Mr. Bingley, it is very hard to have her taken away from me. They are gone down to Newcastle, a place quite northward it seems, and there they are to stay, I do not know how long. His regiment is there; for I suppose you have heard of his leaving the ——shire, and of his being gone into the Regulars. Thank heaven! he has *some* friends, though, perhaps, not so many as he deserves.'

Elizabeth, who knew this to be levelled at Mr. Darcy, was in such misery of shame that she could hardly keep her seat. It drew from her, however, the exertion of speaking, which nothing else had so effectually done before; and she asked Bingley whether he meant to make any stay in the country at present. A few weeks, he believed.

'When you have killed all your own birds, Mr. Bingley,' said her mother, 'I beg you will come here and shoot as many as you please on Mr. Bennet's manor. I am sure he will be vastly happy to oblige you, and will save all the best of the coveys for you.'

Elizabeth's misery increased at such unnecessary, such officious attention! Were the same fair prospect to arise at present, as had flattered them a year ago, everything, she was persuaded, would be hastening to the same vexatious conclusion. At that instant she felt that years of happiness could not make Jane or herself amends for moments of such painful confusion.

'The first wish of my heart,' said she to herself, 'is never more to be in company with either of them. Their society can afford no pleasure that will atone for such wretchedness as this! Let me never see either one or the other again!'

Yet the misery, for which years of happiness were to offer no compensation, received soon afterwards material relief, from observing how much the beauty of her sister rekindled the admiration of her former lover. When first he came in, he had spoken to her but little; but every five minutes seemed to be giving her more of his attention. He found her as handsome as she had been last year; as good-natured, and as unaffected, though not quite so chatty. Jane was anxious that no difference should be perceived in her at all, and was really persuaded that she talked as much as ever; but her mind was so busily engaged, that she did not always know when she was silent.

When the gentlemen rose to go away, Mrs. Bennet was mindful of her intended civility, and they were invited and engaged to dine at Longbourn in a few days' time.

'You are quite a visit in my debt, Mr. Bingley,' she added; 'for when you went to town last winter, you promised to take a family dinner with us as soon as you returned. I have not forgot, you see; and I assure you I was very much disappointed that you did not come back and keep your engagement.'

Bingley looked a little silly at this reflection, and said something of his concern at having been prevented by business. They then went away.

Mrs. Bennet had been strongly inclined to ask them to stay and dine there that day; but, though she always kept a very good table, she did not think anything less than two courses could be good enough for a man on whom she had such anxious designs, or satisfy the appetite and pride of one who had ten thousand a year.

CHAPTER LIV

AS soon as they were gone, Elizabeth walked out to recover her spirits; or, in other words, to dwell without interruption on those subjects that must deaden them more. Mr. Darcy's behaviour astonished and vexed her.

'Why, if he came only to be silent, grave, and indifferent,' said she, 'did he come at all?'

She could settle it in no way at all that gave her pleasure.

'He could be still amiable, still pleasing, to my uncle and aunt, when he was in town; and why not to me? If he fears me, why come hither? If he no longer cares for me, why silent? Teasing, teasing man! I will think no more about him.'

Her resolution was for a short time involuntarily kept by the approach of her sister, who joined her with a cheerful look which showed her better satisfied with their visitors than Elizabeth.

'Now,' said she, 'that this first meeting is over, I feel perfectly easy. I know my own strength, and I shall never be embarrassed again by his coming. I am glad he dines here on Tuesday. It will then be publicly seen that on both sides we meet only as common and indifferent acquaintance.'

'Yes, very indifferent indeed,' said Elizabeth, laughingly. 'Oh, Jane! take care.'

'My dear Lizzy, you cannot think me so weak as to be in danger now.'

'I think you are in very great danger of making him as much in love with you as ever.'

They did not see the gentlemen again till Tuesday; and Mrs. Bennet, in the meanwhile, was giving way to all the happy schemes which the good-humour and common politeness of Bingley, in half an hour's visit, had revived.

On Tuesday there was a large party assembled at Longbourn; and the two who were most anxiously expected, to the credit of their punctuality as sportsmen, were in very good time. When they repaired to the dining-room, Elizabeth eagerly watched to see whether Bingley would take the place which, in all their former parties, had belonged to him, by her sister. Her prudent mother, occupied by the same ideas, forbore to invite him to sit by herself. On entering the room, he seemed to hesitate; but Jane happened to look round, and happened to smile: it was decided. He placed himself by her.

Elizabeth, with a triumphant sensation, looked towards his friend. He bore it with noble indifference; and she would have imagined that Bingley had received his sanction to be happy, had she not seen his eyes likewise turned towards Mr. Darcy, with an expression of half-laughing alarm.

His behaviour to her sister was such during dinner-time as showed an admiration of her, which, though more guarded than formerly, persuaded Elizabeth that, if left wholly to himself, Jane's happiness, and his own, would be speedily secured. Though she dared not depend upon the consequence, she yet received pleasure from observing his behaviour. It gave her all the animation that her spirits could boast; for she was in no cheerful humour. Mr. Darcy was almost as far from her as the table could divide them. He was on one side of her mother. She knew how little such a situation would give pleasure to either, or make either appear to advantage. She was not near enough to hear any of their discourse; but she could see how seldom they spoke to each other, and how formal and cold was their manner whenever they did. Her mother's ungraciousness made the sense of what they owed him more painful to Elizabeth's mind; and she would, at times, have given anything to be privileged to tell him that his kindness was neither unknown nor unfelt by the whole of the family.

She was in hopes that the evening would afford some opportunity of bringing them together; that the whole of the visit would not pass away without enabling them to enter into something more of conversation than the mere ceremonious salutation attending his entrance. Anxious and uneasy, the period which passed in the drawing-room before the gentlemen came was wearisome and dull to a degree that almost made her uncivil. She looked forward to their entrance as the point on which all her chance of pleasure for the evening must depend.

'If he does not come to me, *then,*' said she, 'I shall give him up for ever.'

The gentlemen came; and she thought he looked as if he would have answered her hopes; but, alas! the ladies had crowded round the table, where Miss Bennet was making tea and Elizabeth pouring out the coffee, in so close a confederacy, that there was not a single vacancy near her which would admit of a chair. And on the gentlemen's approaching, one of the girls moved closer to her than ever, and said, in a whisper,—

'The men shan't come and part us, I am determined. We want none of them; do we?'

Darcy had walked away to another part of the room. She followed him with her eyes, envied every one to whom he spoke, had scarcely patience enough to help anybody to coffee, and then was enraged against herself for being so silly!

'A man who has once been refused! How could I ever be foolish enough to expect a renewal of his love? Is there one among the sex who would not protest against such a weakness as a second proposal to the same woman? There is no indignity so abhorrent to their feelings.'

She was a little revived, however, by his bringing back his coffee-cup himself; and she seized the opportunity of saying,—

'Is your sister at Pemberley still?'

'Yes; she will remain there till Christmas.'

'And quite alone? Have all her friends left her?'

'Mrs. Annesley is with her. The others have been gone on to Scarborough these three weeks.'

She could think of nothing more to say; but if he wished to converse with her, he might have better success. He stood by her, however, for some minutes, in silence; and, at last, on the young lady's whispering to Elizabeth again, he walked away.

When the tea things were removed, and the card-tables placed, the ladies all rose, and Elizabeth was then hoping to be soon joined by him, when all her views were overthrown by seeing him fall a victim to her mother's rapacity for whist-players, and in a few moments after seated with the rest of the party. She now lost every expectation of pleasure. They were confined for the evening at different tables, and she had nothing to hope, but that his eyes were so often turned towards her side of the room as to make him play as unsuccessfully as herself.

Mrs. Bennet had designed to keep the two Netherfield gentlemen to supper; but their carriage was, unluckily, ordered before any of the others, and she had no opportunity of detaining them.

'Well, girls,' said she, as soon as they were left to themselves, 'what say you to the day? I think everything has passed off uncommonly well, I assure you. The dinner was as well dressed as any I ever saw. The venison was roasted to a turn—and everybody said they never saw so fat a haunch. The soup was fifty times better than what we had at the Lucases' last week; and even Mr. Darcy acknowledged that the partridges were remarkably well done; and I suppose he has two or three French cooks at least. And, my dear Jane, I never saw you look in greater beauty. Mrs. Long said so too, for I asked her whether you did not. And what do you think she said besides? "Ah! Mrs. Bennet, we shall have her at Netherfield at last!" She did, indeed. I do think Mrs. Long is as good a creature as ever lived—and her nieces are very pretty behaved girls, and not at all handsome: I like them prodigiously.'

Mrs. Bennet, in short, was in very great spirits: she had seen enough of Bingley's behaviour to Jane to be convinced that she would get him at last; and her expectations of advantage to her family, when in a happy humour, were so far beyond reason, that she was quite disappointed at not seeing him there again the next day to make his proposals.

'It has been a very agreeable day,' said Miss Bennet to Elizabeth. 'The party seemed so well selected, so suitable one with the other. I hope we may often meet again.'

Elizabeth smiled.

'Lizzy, you must not do so. You must not suspect me. It mortifies me. I assure you that I have now learnt to enjoy his conversation as an agreeable and sensible young man without having a wish beyond it. 'I am perfectly satisfied, from what his manners now are, that he never had any design of engaging my affection. It is only that he is blessed with greater sweetness of address, and a stronger desire of generally pleasing, than any other man.'

'You are very cruel,' said her sister; 'you will not let me smile, and are provoking me to it every moment.'

'How hard it is in some cases to be believed! And how impossible in others! But why should you wish to persuade me that I feel more than I acknowledge?'

'That is a question which I hardly know how to answer. We all love to instruct, though we can teach only what is not worth knowing. Forgive me; and if you persist in indifference, do not make *me* your confidante.'

'Jane, I congratulate you. You will be a very happy woman.'

Jane went to him instantly, kissed him, and thanked him for his goodness.

'You are a good girl,' he replied, 'and I have great pleasure in thinking you will be so happily settled. I have not a doubt of your doing very well together. Your tempers are by no means unlike. You are each of you so complying, that nothing will ever be resolved on; so easy, that every servant will cheat you; and so generous, that you will always exceed your income.'

'I hope not so. Imprudence or thoughtlessness in money matters would be unpardonable in *me*.'

'Exceed their income! My dear Mr. Bennet,' cried his wife, 'what are you talking of? Why, he has four or five thousand a year, and very likely more.' Then addressing her daughter, 'Oh, my dear, dear Jane, I am so happy! I am sure I shan't get a wink of sleep all night. I knew how it would be. I always said it must be so, at last. I was sure you could not be so beautiful for nothing! I remember, as soon as ever I saw him, when he first came into Hertfordshire last year, I thought how likely it was that you should come together. Oh, he is the handsomest young man that ever was seen!'

Wickham, Lydia, were all forgotten. Jane was beyond competition her favourite child. At that moment she cared for no other. Her younger sisters soon began to make interest with her for objects of happiness which she might in future be able to dispense.

Mary petitioned for the use of the library at Netherfield; and Kitty begged very hard for a few balls there every winter.

Bingley, from this time, was of course a daily visitor at Longbourn; coming frequently before breakfast, and always remaining till after supper; unless when some barbarous neighbour, who could not be enough detested, had given him an invitation to dinner, which he thought himself obliged to accept.

Elizabeth had now but little time for conversation with her sister; for while he was present Jane had no attention to bestow on any one else: but she found herself considerably useful to both of them in those hours of separation that must sometimes occur. In the absence of Jane, he always attached himself to Elizabeth for the pleasure of talking of her; and when Bingley was gone, Jane constantly sought the same means of relief.

'He has made me so happy,' said she, one evening, 'by telling me that he was totally ignorant of my being in town last spring! I had not believed it possible.'

'I suspected as much,' replied Elizabeth. 'But how did he account for it?'

'It must have been his sisters' doing. They were certainly no friends to his acquaintance with me, which I cannot wonder at, since he might have chosen so much more advantageously in many respects. But when they see, as I trust they will, that their brother is happy with me, they will learn to be contented, and we shall be on good terms again: though we can never be what we once were to each other.'

'That is the most unforgiving speech,' said Elizabeth, 'that I ever heard you utter. Good girl! It would vex me, indeed, to see you again the dupe of Miss Bingley's pretended regard.'

'Would you believe it, Lizzy, that when he went to town last November he really loved me, and nothing but a persuasion of *my* being indifferent would have prevented his coming down again?'

'He made a little mistake, to be sure; but it is to the credit of his modesty.'

This naturally introduced a panegyric from Jane on his diffidence, and the little value he put on his own good qualities.

Elizabeth was pleased to find that he had not betrayed the interference of his friend; for, though Jane had the most generous and forgiving heart in the world, she knew it was a circumstance which must prejudice her against him.

'I am certainly the most fortunate creature that ever existed!' cried Jane. 'Oh, Lizzy, why am I thus singled from my family, and blessed above them all? If I could but see you as happy! If there were but such another man for you!'

'If you were to give me forty such men I never could be so happy as you. Till I have your disposition, your goodness,

I never can have your happiness. No, no, let me shift for myself; and, perhaps, if I have very good luck, I may meet with another Mr. Collins in time.'

The situation of affairs in the Longbourn family could not be long a secret. Mrs. Bennet was privileged to whisper it to Mrs. Philips, and she ventured, without any permission, to do the same by all her neighbours in Meryton.

The Bennets were speedily pronounced to be the luckiest family in the world; though only a few weeks before, when Lydia had first run away, they had been generally proved to be marked out for misfortune.

CHAPTER LVI

ONE morning, about a week after Bingley's engagement with Jane had been formed, as he and the females of the family were sitting together in the dining-room, their attention was suddenly drawn to the window by the sound of a carriage; and they perceived a chaise and four driving up the lawn. It was too early in the morning for visitors, and besides, the equipage did not answer to that of any of their neighbours. The horses were post; and neither the carriage, nor the livery of the servant who preceded it, was familiar to them. As it was certain, however, that some-body was coming, Bingley instantly prevailed on Miss Bennet to avoid the confinement of such an intrusion, and walk away with him into the shrubbery. They both set off, and the conjectures of the remaining three continued, though with little satisfaction, till the door was thrown open, and their visitor entered. It was Lady Catherine de Bourgh.

They were of course all intending to be surprised: but their astonishment was beyond their expectation; and on the part of Mrs. Bennet and Kitty, though she was perfectly un-known to them, even inferior to what Elizabeth felt.

She entered the room with an air more than usually un-gracious, made no other reply to Elizabeth's salutation than a slight inclination of the head, and sat down without saying a word. Elizabeth had mentioned her name to her mother on her Ladyship's entrance, though no request of introduc-tion had been made.

Mrs. Bennet, all amazement, though flattered by having a guest of such high importance, received her with the utmost politeness. After sitting for a moment in silence, she said, very stiffly, to Elizabeth,—

'I hope you are well, Miss Bennet. That lady, I suppose, is your mother?'

Elizabeth replied very concisely that she was.

'And *that*, I suppose, is one of your sisters?'

'Yes, madam,' said Mrs. Bennet, delighted to speak to a Lady Catherine. 'She is my youngest girl but one. My youngest of all is lately married, and my eldest is somewhere about the ground, walking with a young man, who, I believe, will soon become a part of the family.'

'You have a very small park here,' returned Lady Catherine, after a short silence.

'It is nothing in comparison of Rosings, my Lady, I daresay; but I assure you it is much larger than Sir William Lucas's.'

'This must be a most inconvenient sitting-room for the evening in summer; the windows are full west.'

Mrs. Bennet assured her that they never sat there after dinner; and then added,—

'May I take the liberty of asking your Ladyship whether you left Mr. and Mrs. Collins well?'

'Yes, very well. I saw them the night before last.'

Elizabeth now expected that she would produce a letter for her from Charlotte, as it seemed the only probable motive for her calling. But no letter appeared, and she was completely puzzled.

Mrs. Bennet, with great civility, begged her Ladyship to take some refreshment: but Lady Catherine very resolutely, and not very politely, declined eating anything; and then, rising up, said to Elizabeth,—

'Miss Bennet, there seemed to be a prettyish kind of a little wilderness on one side of your lawn. I should be glad to take a turn in it, if you will favour me with your company.'

'Go, my dear,' cried her mother, 'and show her Ladyship about the different walks. I think she will be pleased with the hermitage.'

Elizabeth obeyed; and, running into her own room for her parasol, attended her noble guest downstairs. As they passed through the hall, Lady Catherine opened the doors into the dining-parlour and drawing-room, and pronouncing them, after a short survey, to be decent-looking rooms, walked on.

Her carriage remained at the door, and Elizabeth saw that her waiting-woman was in it. They proceeded in silence along the gravel walk that led to the copse: Elizabeth was determined to make no effort for conversation with a woman who was now more than usually insolent and disagreeable.

'How could I ever think her like her nephew?' said she, as she looked in her face.

As soon as they entered the copse, Lady Catherine began in the following manner:—

'You can be at no loss, Miss Bennet, to understand the reason of my journey hither. Your own heart, your own conscience, must tell you why I come.'

Elizabeth looked with unaffected astonishment.

'Indeed, you are mistaken, madam; I have not been at all able to account for the honour of seeing you here.'

'Miss Bennet,' replied her Ladyship, in an angry tone, 'you ought to know that I am not to be trifled with. But however insincere *you* may choose to be, you shall not find *me* so. My character has ever been celebrated for its sincerity and frankness; and in a cause of such moment as this, I shall certainly not depart from it. A report of a most alarming nature reached me two days ago. I was told, that not only your sister was on the point of being most advantageously married, but that *you*, that Miss Elizabeth Bennet would, in all likelihood, be soon afterwards united to my nephew, my own nephew, Mr. Darcy. Though I *know* it must be a scandalous falsehood, though I would not injure him so much as to suppose the truth of it possible, I instantly resolved on setting off for this place, that I might make my sentiments known to you.'

'If you believed it impossible to be true,' said Elizabeth, colouring with astonishment and disdain, 'I wonder you took the trouble of coming so far. What could your Ladyship propose by it?'

'At once to insist upon having such a report universally contradicted.'

'Your coming to Longbourn, to see me and my family,' said Elizabeth coolly, 'will be rather a confirmation of it; if, indeed, such a report is in existence.'

'If! do you then pretend to be ignorant of it? Has it not been industriously circulated by yourselves? Do you not know that such a report is spread abroad?'

'I never heard that it was.'

'And can you likewise declare that there is no *foundation* for it?'

'I do not pretend to possess equal frankness with your Ladyship. *You* may ask questions which *I* shall not choose to answer.'

'This is not to be borne. Miss Bennet, I insist on being satisfied. Has he, has my nephew, made you an offer of marriage?'

'Your Ladyship has declared it to be impossible.'

'It ought to be so; it must be so while he retains the use of his reason. But *your* arts and allurements may, in a moment of infatuation, have made him forget what he owes to himself and to all his famly. You may have drawn him in.'

'If I have, I shall be the last person to confess it.'

'Miss Bennet, do you know who I am? I have not been accustomed to such language as this. I am almost the nearest relation he has in the world, and am entitled to know all his dearest concerns.'

'But you are not entitled to know *mine;* nor will such behaviour as this ever induce me to be explicit.'

'Let me be rightly understood. This match, to which you have the presumption to aspire, can never take place. No, never. Mr. Darcy is engaged to *my daughter*. Now, what have you to say?'

'Only this,—that if he is so, you can have no reason to suppose he will make an offer to me.'

Lady Catherine hesitated for a moment, and then replied,—

'The engagement between them is of a peculiar kind. From their infancy, they have been intended for each other. It was the favourite wish of *his* mother, as well as of hers. While in their cradles we planned the union; and now, at the moment when the wishes of both sisters would be accomplished, in their marriage, to be prevented by a young woman of inferior birth, of no importance in the world, and wholly unallied to the family! Do you pay no regard to the wishes of his friends? To his tacit engagement with Miss De Bourgh? Are you lost to every feeling of propriety and delicacy? Have you not heard me say that from his earliest hours he was destined for his cousin?'

'Yes; and I had heard it before. But what is that to me? If there is no other objection to my marrying your nephew, I shall certainly not be kept from it by knowing that his mother and aunt wished him to marry Miss De Bourgh. You both did as much as you could in planning the marriage. Its completion depended on others. If Mr. Darcy is neither by honour nor inclination confined to his cousin, why is not he to make another choice? And if I am that choice, why may not I accept him?'

'Because honour, decorum, prudence, nay interest, forbid it. Yes, Miss Bennet, interest; for do not expect to be noticed by his family or friends, if you wilfully act against the inclinations of all. You will be censured, slighted, and despised by every one connected with him. Your alliance will be a disgrace; your name will never even be mentioned by any of us.'

'These are heavy misfortunes,' replied Elizabeth. 'But the wife of Mr. Darcy must have such extraordinary sources of happiness necessarily attached to her situation, that she could, upon the whole, have no cause to repine.'

'Obstinate, headstrong girl! I am ashamed of you! Is this your gratitude for my attentions to you last spring? Is nothing due to me on that score? Let us sit down. You are to understand, Miss Bennet, that I came here with the determined resolution of carrying my purpose; nor will I be dissuaded from it. I have not been used to submit to any person's whims. I have not been in the habit of brooking disappointment.'

'*That* will make your Ladyship's situation at present more pitiable; but it will have no effect on *me*.'

'I will not be interrupted! Hear me in silence. My daughter and my nephew are formed for each other. They are descended, on the maternal side, from the same noble line; and, on the father's, from respectable, honourable, and ancient, though untitled, families. Their fortune on both sides is splendid. They are destined for each other by the voice of every member of their respective houses; and what is to divide them?—the upstart pretensions of a young woman without family, connections, or fortune! Is this to be endured? But it must not, shall not be! If you were sensible of your own good, you would not wish to quit the sphere in which you have been brought up.'

'In marrying your nephew, I should not consider myself as quitting that sphere. He is a gentleman; I a gentleman's daughter; so far we are equal.'

'True. You *are* a gentleman's daughter. But what was your mother? Who are your uncles and aunts? Do not imagine me ignorant of their condition.'

'Whatever my connection may be,' said Elizabeth, 'if your nephew does not object to them, they can be nothing to *you.*'

'Tell me, once for all, are you engaged to him?'

Though Elizabeth would not, for the mere purpose of obliging Lady Catherine, have answered this question, she could not but say, after a moment's deliberation,—

'I am not.'

Lady Catherine seemed pleased.

'And will you promise me never to enter into such an engagement?'

'I will make no promise of the kind.'

'Miss Bennet, I am shocked and astonished. I expected to find a more reasonable young woman. But do not deceive yourself into a belief that I will ever recede. I shall not go away till you have given me the assurance I require.'

'And I certainly *never* shall give it. I am not to be intimidated into anything so wholly unreasonable. Your Ladyship wants Mr. Darcy to marry your daughter; but would my giving you the wished-for promise make *their* marriage at all more probable? Supposing him to be attached to me, would *my* refusing to accept his hand make him wish to bestow it on his cousin? Allow me to say, Lady Catherine, that the arguments with which you have supported this extraordinary application have been as frivolous as the application was ill-judged. You have widely mistaken my character, if you think I can be worked on by such persuasions as these. How far your nephew might approve of your interference in his affairs, I cannot tell; but you have certainly no right to concern yourself in mine. I must beg, therefore, to be importuned no further on the subject.'

'Not so hasty, if you please. I have by no means done. To all the objections I have already urged I have still another to add. I am no stranger to the particulars of your youngest sister's infamous elopement. I know it all; that the young man's marrying her was a patched-up business, at the expense of your father and uncle. And is *such* a girl to be my nephew's sister? Is *her* husband, who is the son of his late father's steward, to be his brother? Heaven and earth!—of what are you thinking? Are the shades of Pemberley to be thus polluted?'

'You can *now* have nothing further to say,' she resentfully answered. 'You have insulted me in every possible method. I must beg to return to the house.'

And she rose as she spoke. Lady Catherine rose also, and they turned back. Her Ladyship was highly incensed.

'You have no regard, then, for the honour and credit of my nephew! Unfeeling, selfish girl! Do you not consider that a connection with you must disgrace him in the eyes of everybody?'

'Lady Catherine, I have nothing further to say. You know my sentiments.'

'You are then resolved to have him?'

'I have said no such thing. I am only resolved to act in that manner which will, in my own opinion, constitute my happiness, without reference to *you*, or to any person so wholly unconnected with me.'

'It is well. You refuse, then, to oblige me. You refuse to obey the claims of duty, honour, and gratitude. You are determined to ruin him in the opinion of all his friends, and make him the contempt of the world.'

'Neither duty, nor honour, nor gratitude,' replied Elizabeth, 'has any possible claim on me, in the present instance. No principle of either would be violated by my marriage with Mr. Darcy. And with regard to the resentment of his family, or the indignation of the world, if the former *were* excited by his marrying me, it would not give me one moment's concern —and the world in general would have too much sense to join in the scorn.'

'And this is your real opinion! This is your final resolve! Very well. I shall now know how to act. Do not imagine,

Miss Bennet, that your ambition will ever be gratified. I came to try you. I hoped to find you reasonable; but depend upon it I will carry my point.'

In this manner Lady Catherine talked on till they were at the door of the carriage, when, turning hastily round, she added,—

'I take no leave of you, Miss Bennet. I send no compliments to your mother. You deserve no such attention. I am most seriously displeased.'

Elizabeth made no answer; and without attempting to persuade her Ladyship to return into the house, walked quietly into it herself. She heard the carriage drive away as she proceeded upstairs. Her mother impatiently met her at the door of her dressing-room, to ask why Lady Catherine would not come in again and rest herself.

'She did not choose it,' said her daughter; 'she would go.'

'She is a very fine-looking woman! and her calling here was prodigiously civil! for she only came, I suppose, to tell us the Collinses were well. She is on her road somewhere, I daresay; and so, passing through Meryton, thought she might as well call on you. I suppose she had nothing particular to say to you, Lizzy?'

Elizabeth was forced to give in to a little falsehood here; for to acknowledge the substance of their conversation was impossible.

CHAPTER LVII

THE discomposure of spirits which this extraordinary visit threw Elizabeth into could not be easily overcome; nor could she for many hours learn to think of it less than incessantly. Lady Catherine, it appeared, had actually taken the trouble of this journey from Rosings for the sole purpose of breaking off her supposed engagement with Mr. Darcy. It was a rational scheme to be sure! but from what the report of their engagement could originate, Elizabeth was at a loss to imagine; till she recollected that *his* being the intimate friend of Bingley, and *her* being the sister of Jane, was enough, at a time when the expectation of one wedding made everybody eager for another, to supply the idea. She had not herself forgotten to feel that the marriage of her sister must bring them more frequently together. And her neighbours at Lucas Lodge, therefore (for through their communication with the Collinses, the report, she concluded, had reached Lady Catherine), had only set *that* down as almost certain and immediate which *she* had looked forward to as possible at some future time.

In revolving Lady Catherine's expressions, however, she could not help feeling some uneasiness as to the possible consequence of her persisting in this interference. From what she had said of her resolution to prevent the marriage, it occurred to Elizabeth that she must meditate an application to her nephew; and how he might take a similar representation of the evils attached to a connection with her she dared not pronounce. She knew not the exact degree of his affection for his aunt, or his dependence on her judgment, but it was natural to suppose that he thought much higher of her Ladyship than *she* could do; and it was certain, that in enumerating the miseries of a marriage with *one* whose immediate connections were so unequal to his own, his aunt would address him on his weakest side. With his notions of dignity, he would probably feel that the arguments, which

484

to Elizabeth had appeared weak and ridiculous, contained much good sense and solid reasoning.

If he had been wavering before as to what he should do, which had often seemed likely, the advice and entreaty of so near a relation might settle every doubt, and determine him at once to be as happy as dignity unblemished could make him. In that case he would return no more. Lady Catherine might see him in her way through town; and his engagement to Bingley of coming again to Netherfield must give way.

'If, therefore an excuse for not keeping his promise should come to his friend within a few days,' she added, 'I shall know how to understand it. I shall then give over every expectation, every wish, of his constancy. If he is satisfied with only regretting me, when he might have obtained my affections and hand, I shall soon cease to regret him at all.'

The surprise of the rest of the family, on hearing who their visitor had been, was very great: but they obligingly satisfied it with the same kind of supposition which had appeased Mrs. Bennet's curiosity; and Elizabeth was spared from much teasing on the subject.

The next morning, as she was going downstairs, she was met by her father, who came out of his library with a letter in his hand.

'Lizzy,' said he, 'I was going to look for you: come into my room.'

She followed him thither; and her curiosity to know what he had to tell her was heightened by the supposition of its being in some manner connected with the letter he held. It suddenly struck her that it might be from Lady Catherine, and she anticipated with dismay all the consequent explanations.

She followed her father to the fireplace, and they both sat down. He then said,—

'I have received a letter this morning that has astonished me exceedingly. As it principally concerns yourself, you ought to know its contents. I did not know before that I had *two* daughters on the brink of matrimony. Let me congratulate you on a very important conquest.'

The colour now rushed into Elizabeth's cheeks in the instantaneous conviction of its being a letter from the nephew, instead of the aunt; and she was undetermined whether most to be pleased that he explained himself at all, or offended that his letter was not rather addressed to herself, when her father continued,—

'You look conscious. Young ladies have great penetration in such matters as these; but I think I may defy even *your* sagacity to discover the name of your admirer. This letter is from Mr. Collins.'

'From Mr. Collins! and what can *he* have to say?'

'Something very much to the purpose, of course. He begins with congratulations on the approaching nuptials of my eldest daughter, of which, it seems, he has been told by some of the good-natured, gossiping Lucases. I shall not sport with your impatience by reading what he says on that point. What relates to yourself is as follows:—"Having thus offered you the sincere congratulations of Mrs. Collins and myself on this happy event, let me now add a short hint on the subject of another, of which we have been advertised by the same authority. Your daughter Elizabeth, it is presumed, will not long bear the name of Bennet, after her eldest sister has resigned it; and the chosen partner of her fate may be reasonably looked up to as one of the most illustrious personages in this land."

'Can you possibly guess, Lizzy, who is meant by this?'

'"This young gentleman is blessed, in a peculiar way, with everything the heart of mortal can most desire,—splendid property, noble kindred, and extensive patronage. Yet, in spite of all these temptations, let me warn my cousin Elizabeth, and yourself, of what evils you may incur by a precipitate closure with this gentleman's proposals, which, of course, you will be inclined to take immediate advantage of."

'Have you any idea, Lizzy, who this gentleman is? But now it comes out.'

'"My motive for cautioning you is as follows:—We have reason to imagine that his aunt, Lady Catherine de Bourgh, does not look on the match with a friendly eye."

'*Mr. Darcy*, you see, is the man! Now, Lizzy, I think I *have* surprised you. Could he, or the Lucases, have pitched on any man, within the circle of our acquaintance, whose name would have given the lie more effectually to what they related? Mr. Darcy, who never looks at any woman but to see a blemish, and who probably never looked at *you* in his life! It is admirable!'

Elizabeth tried to join in her father's pleasantry, but could only force one most reluctant smile. Never had his wit been directed in a manner so little agreeable to her.

'Are you not diverted?'

'Oh yes. Pray read on.'

' "After mentioning the likelihood of this marriage to her Ladyship last night, she immediately, with her usual condescension, expressed what she felt on the occasion; when it became apparent that on the score of some family objections on the part of my cousin she would never give her consent to what she termed so disgraceful a match. I thought it my duty to give the speediest intelligence of this to my cousin, that she and her noble admirer may be aware of what they are about, and not run hastily into a marriage which has not been properly sanctioned." Mr. Collins, moreover, adds, "I am truly rejoiced that my cousin Lydia's sad business has been so well hushed up, and am only concerned that their living together before the marriage took place should be so generally known. I must not, however, neglect the duties of my station, or refrain from declaring my amazement, at hearing that you received the young couple into your house as soon as they were married. It was an encouragement of vice; and had I been the rector of Longbourn, I should very strenuously have opposed it. You ought certainly to forgive them as a Christian, but never to admit them in your sight, or allow their names to be mentioned in your hearing." *That* is his notion of Christian forgiveness! The rest of his letter is only about his dear Charlotte's situation, and his expectation of a young olive-branch. But, Lizzy, you look as if you did not enjoy it. You are not going to be *missish*, I hope and pretend to be affronted at an idle report. For what do we live, but to make sport for our neighbours. and laugh at them in our turn?'

'Oh,' cried Elizabeth, 'I am exceedingly diverted. But it is so strange!'

'Yes, *that* is what makes it amusing. Had they fixed on any other man it would have been nothing; but *his* perfect indifference and *your* pointed dislike make it so delightfully absurd! Much as I abominate writing, I would not give up Mr. Collins's correspondence for any consideration. Nay, when I read a letter of his, I cannot help giving him the preference even over Wickham, much as I value the impudence and hypocrisy of my son-in-law. And pray, Lizzy, what said Lady Catherine about this report? Did she call to refuse her consent?'

To this question his daughter replied only with a laugh; and as it had been asked without the least suspicion, she was not distressed by his repeating it. Elizabeth had never been more at a loss to make her feelings appear what they were not. It was necessary to laugh when she would rather have cried. Her father had most cruelly mortified her by what he said of Mr. Darcy's indifference; and she could do nothing but wonder at such a want of penetration, or fear that, perhaps, instead of his seeing too *little,* she might have fancied too *much.*

CHAPTER LVIII

INSTEAD of receiving any such letter of excuse from his friend as Elizabeth half expected Mr. Bingley to do, he was able to bring Darcy with him to Longbourn before many days had passed after Lady Catherine's visit. The gentlemen arrived early; and, before Mrs. Bennet had time to tell him of their having seen his aunt, of which her daughter sat in momentary dread, Bingley, who wanted to be alone with Jane, proposed their all walking out. It was agreed to. Mrs. Bennet was not in the habit of walking, Mary could never spare time, but the remaining five set off together. Bingley and Jane, however, soon allowed the others to outstrip them. They lagged behind, while Elizabeth, Kitty, and Darcy were to entertain each other. Very little was said by either; Kitty was too much afraid of him to talk; Elizabeth was secretly forming a desperate resolution; and, perhaps, he might be doing the same.

They walked toward the Lucases', because Kitty wished to call upon Maria; and as Elizabeth saw no occasion for making it a general concern, when Kitty left them she went boldly on with him alone. Now was the moment for her resolution to be executed; and while her courage was high she immediately said,—

'Mr. Darcy, I am a very selfish creature, and for the sake of giving relief to my own feelings care not how much I may be wounding yours. I can no longer help thanking you for your unexampled kindness to my poor sister. Ever since I have known it I have been most anxious to acknowledge to you how gratefully I feel it. Were it known to the rest of my family I should not have merely my own gratitude to express.'

'I am sorry, exceedingly sorry,' replied Darcy, in a tone of surprise and emotion, 'that you have ever been informed of what may, in a mistaken light, have given you uneasiness. I did not think Mrs. Gardiner was so little to be trusted.'

'You must not blame my aunt. Lydia's thoughtlessness first betrayed to me that you had been concerned in the matter; and, of course, I could not rest till I knew the particulars. Let me thank you again and again, in the name of all my family, for that generous compassion which induced you to take so much trouble, and bear so many mortifications, for the sake of discovering them.'

'If you *will* thank me,' he replied, 'let it be for yourself alone. That the wish of giving happiness to you might add force to the other inducements which led me on I shall not attempt to deny. But your *family* owe me nothing. Much as I respect them, I believe I thought only of *you*.'

Elizabeth was too much embarrassed to say a word. After a short pause, her companion added, 'You are too generous to trifle with me. If your feelings are still what they were last April, tell me so at once. *My* affections and wishes are unchanged; but one word from you will silence me on this subject for ever.'

Elizabeth, feeling all the more than common awkwardness and anxiety for his situation, now forced herself to speak; and immediately, though not very fluently, gave him to understand that her sentiments had undergone so material a change since the period to which he alluded as to make her receive with gratitude and pleasure his present assurances. The happiness which this reply produced was such as he had probably never felt before; and he expressed himself on the occasion as sensibly and as warmly as a man violently in love can be supposed to do. Had Elizabeth been able to encounter his eyes, she might have seen how well the expression of heartfelt delight, diffused over his face, became him; but though she could not look she could listen; and he told her of feelings which, in proving of what importance she was to him, made his affection every moment more valuable.

They walked on without knowing in what direction. There was too much to be thought, and felt, and said, for attention to any other objects. She soon learnt that they were indebted for their present good understanding to the efforts of his aunt, who *did* call on him in her return through London, and there relate her journey to Longbourn, its motive, and the substance of her conversation with Elizabeth; dwelling emphatically on every expression of the latter, which, in her Ladyship's apprehension, peculiarly denoted her perverseness and assurance, in the belief that such a relation must assist her endeavours to obtain that promise from her nephew which *she* had refused to give. But, unluckily for her Ladyship, its effect had been exactly contrariwise.

'It taught me to hope,' said he, 'as I had scarcely ever allowed myself to hope before. I knew enough of your disposition to be certain that had you been absolutely, irrevocably decided against me, you would have acknowledged it to Lady Catherine frankly and openly.'

Elizabeth coloured and laughed as she replied, 'Yes, you know enough of my *frankness* to believe me capable of *that*. After abusing you so abominably to your face, I could have no scruple in abusing you to all your relations.'

'What did you say of me that I did not deserve? For though your accusations were ill founded, formed on mistaken premises, my behaviour to you at the time had merited the severest reproof. It was unpardonable. I cannot think of it without abhorrence.'

'We will not quarrel for the greater share of blame annexed to that evening,' said Elizabeth. 'The conduct of neither, if strictly examined, will be irreproachable; but since then we have both, I hope, improved in civility.'

'I cannot be so easily reconciled to myself. The recollection of what I then said, of my conduct, my manners, my expressions, during the whole of it, is now, and has been many months, inexpressibly painful to me. Your reproof, so well applied, I shall never forget: "Had you behaved in a more gentlemanlike manner." Those were your words. You know not, you can scarcely conceive, how they have tortured me; though it was some time, I confess, before I was reasonable enough to allow their justice.'

'I was certainly very far from expecting them to make so strong an impression. I had not the smallest idea of their being ever felt in such a way.'

'I can easily believe it. You thought me then devoid of every proper feeling, I am sure you did. The turn of your countenance I shall never forget, as you said that I could not have addressed you in any possible way that would induce you to accept me.'

'Oh, do not repeat what I then said. These recollections will not do at all. I assure you that I have long been most heartily ashamed of it.'

Darcy mentioned his letter. 'Did it,' said he,—'did it *soon* make you think better of me? Did you, on reading it, give any credit to its contents?'

She explained what its effects on her had been, and how gradually all her former prejudices had been removed.

'I knew,' said he, 'that what I wrote must give you pain, but it was necessary. I hope you have destroyed the letter. There was one part, especially the opening of it, which I should dread your having the power of reading again. I can remember some expressions which might justly make you hate me.'

'The letter shall certainly be burnt, if you believe it essential to the preservation of my regard; but, though we have both reason to think my opinions not entirely unalterable, they are not, I hope, quite so easily changed as that implies.'

'When I wrote that letter,' replied Darcy, 'I believed myself perfectly calm and cool; but I am since convinced that it was written in a dreadful bitterness of spirit.'

'The letter, perhaps, began in bitterness, but it did not end so. The adieu is charity itself. But think no more of the letter. The feelings of the person who wrote and the person who received it are now so widely different from what they were then, that every unpleasant circumstance attending it ought to be forgotten. You must learn some of my philosophy. Think only of the past as its remembrance gives you pleasure.'

'I cannot give you credit for any philosophy of the kind. *Your* retrospections must be so totally void of reproach, that the contentment arising from them is not of philosophy, but, what is much better, of ignorance. But with *me*, it is not so. Painful recollections will intrude, which cannot, which ought not to be repelled. I have been a selfish being all my life, in practice, though not in principle. As a child

I was taught what was *right,* but I was not taught to correct my temper. I was given good principles, but left to follow them in pride and conceit. Unfortunately an only son (for many years an only *child*), I was spoiled by my parents, who, though good themselves (my father particularly, all that was benevolent and amiable), allowed, encouraged, almost taught me to be selfish and overbearing, to care for none beyond my own family circle, to think meanly of all the rest of the world, to *wish* at least to think meanly of their sense and worth compared with my own. Such I was, from eight to eight-and-twenty; and such I might still have been but for you, dearest, loveliest Elizabeth! What do I owe you! You taught me a lesson hard indeed at first, but most advantageous. By you I was properly humbled. I came to you without a doubt of my reception. You showed me how insufficient were all my pretensions to please a woman worthy of being pleased.'

'Had you then persuaded yourself that I should?'

'Indeed I had. What will you think of my vanity? I believed you to be wishing, expecting my addresses.'

'My manners must have been in fault, but not intentionally, I assure you. I never meant to deceive you, but my spirits might often lead me wrong. How you must have hated me after *that* evening!'

'Hate you! I was angry, perhaps, at first, but my anger soon began to take a proper direction.'

'I am almost afraid of asking what you thought of me when we met at Pemberley. You blamed me for coming?'

'No, indeed, I felt nothing but surprise.'

'Your surprise could not be greater than *mine* in being noticed by you. My conscience told me that I deserved no extraordinary politeness, and I confess that I did not expect to receive *more* than my due.'

'My object *then,*' replied Darcy, 'was to show you, by every civility in my power, that I was not so mean as to resent the past; and I hoped to obtain your forgiveness, to lessen your ill-opinion, by letting you see that your reproofs had been attended to. How soon any other wishes introduced themselves I can hardly tell, but I believe in about half an hour after I had seen you.'

He then told her of Georgiana's delight in her acquaintance, and of her disappointment at its sudden interruption; which naturally leading to the cause of that interruption, she soon learnt that his resolution of following her from Derbyshire in quest of her sister had been formed before he quitted the inn, and that his gravity and thoughtfulness there had arisen from no other struggles than what such a purpose must comprehend.

She expressed her gratitude again, but it was too painful a subject for each to be dwelt on farther.

After walking several miles in a leisurely manner, and too busy to know anything about it, they found at last, on examining their watches, that it was time to be at home.

'What could have become of Mr. Bingley and Jane!' was a wonder which introduced the discussion of *their* affairs. Darcy was delighted with their engagement; his friend had given him the earliest information of it.

'I must ask whether you were surprised?' said Elizabeth.

'Not at all. When I went away, I felt that it would soon happen.'

'That is to say, you had given your permission. I guessed as much.' And though he exclaimed at the term, she found that it had been pretty much the case.

'On the evening before my going to London,' said he, 'I made a confession to him, which I believe I ought to have made long ago. I told him of all that had occurred to make my former interference in his affairs absurd and impertinent. His surprise was great. He had never had the slightest suspicion. I told him, moreover, that I believed myself mistaken in supposing, as I had done, that your sister was indifferent to him; and as I could easily perceive that his attachment to her was unabated, I felt no doubt of their happiness together.'

Elizabeth could not help smiling at his easy manner of directing his friend.

'Did you speak from your own observation,' said she, 'when you told him that my sister loved him, or merely from my information last spring?'

'From the former. I had narrowly observed her, during the two visits which I had lately made her here; and I was convinced of her affection.'

'And your assurance of it, I suppose, carried immediate conviction to him.'

'It did. Bingley is most unaffectedly modest. His diffidence had prevented his depending on his own judgment in so anxious a case, but his reliance on mine made everything easy. I was obliged to confess one thing, which for a time, and not unjustly, offended him. I could not allow myself to conceal that your sister had been in town three months last winter, that I had known it, and purposely kept it from him. He was angry. But his anger, I am persuaded, lasted no longer than he remained in any doubt of your sister's sentiments. He has heartily forgiven me now.'

Elizabeth longed to observe that Mr. Bingley had been a most delightful friend; so easily guided that his worth was invaluable; but she checked herself. She remembered that he had yet to learn to be laughed at, and it was rather too early to begin. In anticipating the happiness of Bingley, which of course was to be inferior only to his own, he continued the conversation till they reached the house. In the hall they parted.

CHAPTER LIX

'MY dear Lizzy, where can you have been walking to?' was a question which Elizabeth received from Jane as soon as she entered the room, and from all the others when they sat down to table. She had only to say in reply, that they had wandered about till she was beyond her own knowledge. She coloured as she spoke; but neither that, nor anything else, awakened a suspicion of the truth.

The evening passed quietly, unmarked by anything extraordinary. The acknowledged lovers talked and laughed; the unacknowledged were silent. Darcy was not of a disposition in which happiness overflows in mirth: and Elizabeth, agitated and confused, rather *knew* that she was happy than *felt* herself to be so; for, besides the immediate embarrassment, there were other evils before her. She anticipated what would be felt in the family when her situation became known: she was aware that no one liked him but Jane; and even feared that with the others it was a *dislike* which not all his fortune and consequence might do away.

At night she opened her heart to Jane. Though suspicion was very far from Miss Bennet's general habits, she was absolutely incredulous here.

'You are joking, Lizzy. This cannot be! Engaged to Mr. Darcy! No, no, you shall not deceive me: I know it to be impossible.'

'This is a wretched beginning, indeed! My sole dependence was on you; and I am sure nobody else will believe me, if you do not. Yet, indeed, I am in earnest. I speak nothing but the truth. He still loves me, and we are engaged.'

Jane looked at her doubtingly. 'Oh, Lizzy, it cannot be. I know how much you dislike him.'

'You know nothing of the matter. *That* is all to be forgot. Perhaps I did not always love him so well as I do now; but in such cases as these a good memory is unpardonable. This is the last time I shall ever remember it myself.'

Miss Bennet still looked all amazement. Elizabeth again, and more seriously, assured her of its truth.

'Good heaven! can it be really so? Yet now I must believe you,' cried Jane. 'My dear, dear Lizzy, I would, I do congratulate you; but are you certain—forgive the question—are you quite certain that you can be happy with him?'

'There can be no doubt of that. It is settled between us already that we are to be the happiest couple in the world. But are you pleased, Jane? Shall you like to have such a brother?'

'Very, very much. Nothing could give either Bingley or myself more delight. But we considered it, we talked of it as impossible. And do you really love him quite well enough? Oh, Lizzy, do anything rather than marry without affection. Are you quite sure that you feel what you ought to do?'

'Oh, yes! You will only think I feel *more* than I ought to do when I tell you all.'

'What do you mean?'

'Why, I must confess that I love him better than I do Bingley. I am afraid you will be angry.'

'My dearest sister, now *be*, be serious. I want to talk very seriously. Let me know everything that I am to know without delay. Will you tell me how long you have loved him?'

'It has been coming on so gradually, that I hardly know when it began; but I believe I must date it from my first seeing his beautiful grounds at Pemberley.'

Another entreaty that she would be serious, however, produced the desired effect; and she soon satisfied Jane by her solemn assurances of attachment. When convinced on that article, Miss Bennet had nothing further to wish.

'Now I am quite happy,' said she, 'for you will be as happy as myself. I always had a value for him. Were it for nothing but his love of you, I must always have esteemed him; but now, as Bingley's friend and your husband, there can be only Bingley and yourself more dear to me. But, Lizzy, you have been very sly, very reserved with me. How little did you tell me of what passed at Pemberley and Lambton! I owe all that I know of it to another, not to you.'

Elizabeth told her the motives of her secrecy. She had been unwilling to mention Bingley; and the unsettled state of her own feelings had made her equally avoid the name of his friend: but now she would no longer conceal from her his share in Lydia's marriage. All was acknowledged, and half the night spent in conversation.

'Good gracious!' cried Mrs. Bennet, as she stood at a window the next morning, 'if that disagreeable Mr. Darcy is not coming here again with our dear Bingley! What can he mean by being so tiresome as to be always coming here? I had no notion but he would go a shooting, or something or other, and not disturb us with his company. What shall we do with him? Lizzy, you must walk out with him again, that he may not be in Bingley's way.'

Elizabeth could hardly help laughing at so convenient a proposal; yet was really vexed that her mother should be always giving him such an epithet.

As soon as they entered, Bingley looked at her so expressively, and shook hands with such warmth, as left no doubt of his good information; and he soon afterwards said aloud, 'Mrs. Bennet, have you no more lanes hereabouts in which Lizzy may lose her way again to-day?'

'I advise Mr. Darcy, and Lizzy, and Kitty,' said Mrs. Bennet, 'to walk to Oakham Mount this morning. It is a nice long walk, and Mr. Darcy has never seen the view.'

'It may do very well for the others,' replied Mr. Bingley; 'but I am sure it will be too much for Kitty. Won't it Kitty?'

Kitty owned that she had rather stay at home. Darcy professed a great curiosity to see the view from the Mount, and Elizabeth silently consented. As she went upstairs to get ready, Mrs. Bennet followed her, saying,—

'I am quite sorry, Lizzy, that you should be forced to have that disagreeable man all to yourself; but I hope you will not mind it. It is all for Jane's sake, you know; and there is no occasion for talking to him except just now and then, so do not put yourself to inconvenience.'

During their walk, it was resolved that Mr. Bennet's consent should be asked in the course of the evening: Elizabeth reserved to herself the application for her mother's. She could not determine how her mother would take it; sometimes doubting whether all his wealth and grandeur would be enough to overcome her abhorrence of the man; but whether she were violently set against the match, or violently delighted with it, it was certain that her manner would be equally ill adapted to do credit to her sense; and she could no more bear that Mr. Darcy should hear the first raptures of her joy, than the first vehemence of her disapprobation.

In the evening, soon after Mr. Bennet withdrew to the library, she saw Mr. Darcy rise also and follow him, and her agitation on seeing it was extreme. She did not fear her father's opposition, but he was going to be made unhappy, and that it should be through her means; that *she,* his favourite child, should be distressing him by her choice, should be filling him with fears and regrets in disposing of her, was a wretched reflection, and she sat in misery till Mr. Darcy appeared again, when, looking at him, she was a little relieved by his smile. In a few minutes he approached the table where she was sitting with Kitty; and, while pretending to admire her work, said in a whisper, 'Go to your father; he wants you in the library.' She was gone directly.

Her father was walking about the room, looking grave and anxious. 'Lizzy,' said he, 'what are you doing? Are you out of your senses to be accepting this man? Have not you always hated him?'

How earnestly did she then wish that her former opinions had been more reasonable, her expressions more moderate! It would have spared her from explanations and professions which it was exceedingly awkward to give; but they were now necessary, and she assured him, with some confusion, of her attachment to Mr. Darcy.

'Or, in other words, you are determined to have him. He is rich, to be sure, and you may have more fine clothes and fine carriages than Jane. But will they make you happy?'

'Have you any other object,' said Elizabeth, 'than your belief of my indifference?'

'None at all. We all know him to be a proud, unpleasant sort of man; but this would be nothing if you really liked him.'

'I do, I do like him,' she replied, with tears in her eyes; 'I love him. Indeed he has no improper pride. He is perfectly amiable. You do not know what he really is; then pray do not pain me by speaking of him in such terms.'

'Lizzy,' said her father, 'I have given him my consent. He is the kind of man, indeed, to whom I should never dare refuse anything which he condescended to ask. I now give it to *you,* if you are resolved on having him. But let me advise you to think better of it. I know your disposition, Lizzy. I know that you could be neither happy nor respectable, unless you truly esteemed your husband; unless you looked up to him as a superior. Your lively talents would place you in the greatest danger in an unequal marriage. You could scarcely escape discredit and misery. My child, let me not have the grief of seeing *you* unable to respect your partner in life. You know not what you are about.'

Elizabeth, still more affected, was earnest and solemn in her reply; and, at length, by repeated assurances that Mr. Darcy was really the object of her choice, by explaining the gradual change which her estimation of him had undergone, relating her absolute certainty that his affection was not the work of a day, but had stood the test of many months' suspense, and enumerating with energy all his good qualities, she did conquer her father's incredulity, and reconcile him to the match.

'Well, my dear,' said he, when she ceased speaking, 'I have no more to say. If this be the case, he deserves you. I could not have parted with you, my Lizzy, to any one less worthy.'

To complete the favourable impression, she then told him what Mr. Darcy had voluntarily done for Lydia. He heard her with astonishment.

'This is an evening of wonders, indeed! And so, Darcy did everything; made up the match, gave the money, paid the fellow's debts, and got him his commission! So much the better. It will save me a world of trouble and economy. Had it been your uncle's doing, I must and *would* have paid him; but these violent young lovers carry everything their own way. I shall offer to pay him to-morrow, he will rant and storm about his love for you, and there will be an end of the matter.'

He then recollected her embarrassment a few days before on his reading Mr. Collins's letter; and after laughing at her some time, allowed her at last to go, saying, as she quitted the room, 'If any young men come for Mary or Kitty, send them in, for I am quite at leisure.'

Elizabeth's mind was now relieved from a very heavy weight; and, after half an hour's quiet reflection in her own room, she was able to join the others with tolerable composure. Everything was too recent for gaiety, but the evening passed tranquilly away; there was no longer anything material to be dreaded, and the comfort of ease and familiarity would come in time.

When her mother went up to her dressing-room at night, she followed her, and made the important communication. Its effect was most extraordinary; for, on first hearing it, Mrs. Bennet sat quite still, and unable to utter a syllable. Nor was it under many, many minutes, that she could comprehend what she heard, though not in general backward to credit what was for the advantage of her family, or that came in the shape of a lover to any of them. She began at length to recover, to fidget about in her chair, get up, sit down again, wonder, and bless herself.

'Good gracious! Lord bless me! only think! dear me! Mr. Darcy! Who would have thought it? And is it really true? Oh, my sweetest Lizzy! how rich and how great you will be! What pin-money, what jewels, what carriages you will have! Jane's is nothing to it—nothing at all. I am so pleased—so happy. Such a charming man! so handsome! so tall! Oh, my dear Lizzy! pray apologise for my having disliked him so much before. I hope he will overlook it. Dear, dear Lizzy. A house in town! Everything that is charming! Three daughters married! Ten thousand a year! Oh, Lord! what will become of me? I shall go distracted.'

This was enough to prove that her approbation need not be doubted; and Elizabeth, rejoicing that such an effusion

17—C

was heard only by herself, soon went away. But before she had been three minutes in her room, her mother followed her.

'My dearest child,' she cried, 'I can think of nothing else. Ten thousand a year, and very likely more! 'Tis as good as a lord! And a special license—you must and shall be married by a special license. But, my dearest love, tell me what dish Mr. Darcy is particularly fond of, that I may have it to-morrow.'

This was a sad omen of what her mother's behaviour to the gentleman himself might be; and Elizabeth found that, though in the certain possession of his warmest affection, and secure of her relations' consent, there was still something to be wished for. But the morrow passed off much better than she expected; for Mrs. Bennet luckily stood in such awe of her intended son-in-law, that she ventured not to speak to him, unless it was in her power to offer him any attention, or mark her deference for his opinion.

Elizabeth had the satisfaction of seeing her father taking pains to get acquainted with him; and Mr. Bennet soon assured her that he was rising every hour in his esteem.

'I admire all my three sons-in-law highly,' said he. 'Wickham, perhaps, is my favourite; but I think I shall like your husband quite as well as Jane's.'

CHAPTER LX

ELIZABETH'S spirits soon rising to playfulness again, she wanted Mr. Darcy to account for his having ever fallen in love with her. 'How could you begin?' said she. 'I can comprehend your going on charmingly, when you had once made a beginning, but what could set you off in the first place?'

'I cannot fix on the hour, or the spot, or the look, or the words, which laid the foundation. It is too long ago. I was in the middle before I knew that I *had* begun.'

'My beauty you had early withstood, and as for my manners—my behaviour to *you* was at least always bordering on the uncivil, and I never spoke to you without rather wishing to give you pain than not. Now, be sincere; did you admire me for my impertinence?'

'For the liveliness of your mind I did.'

'You may as well call it impertinence at once. It was very little less. The fact is, that you were sick of civility, of deference, of officious attention. You were disgusted with the women who were always speaking, and looking, and thinking for *your* approbation alone. I roused and interested you, because I was so unlike *them*. Had you not been really amiable you would have hated me for it: but in spite of the pains you took to disguise yourself, your feelings were always noble and just; and in your heart you thoroughly despised the persons who so assiduously courted you. There —I have saved you the trouble of accounting for it; and really, all things considered, I begin to think it perfectly reasonable. To be sure you know no actual good of me— but nobody thinks of *that* when they fall in love.'

'Was there no good in your affectionate behaviour to Jane, while she was ill at Netherfield?'

'Dearest Jane! who could have done less for her? But make a virtue of it by all means. My good qualities are under your protection, and you are to exaggerate them as much as possible; and, in return, it belongs to me to find occasions for teasing and quarrelling with you as often as may be; and I shall begin directly, by asking you what made you so unwilling to come to the point at last? What made you so shy of me, when you first called, and afterwards dined here? Why, especially, when you called did you look as if you did not care about me?'

'Because you were grave and silent, and gave me no encouragement.'

'But I was embarrassed.'

'And so was I.'

'You might have talked to me more when you came to dinner.'

'A man who had felt less might.'

'How unlucky that you should have a reasonable answer to give, and that I should be so reasonable as to admit it! But I wonder how long you *would* have gone on, if you had been left to yourself. I wonder when you *would* have spoken if I had not asked you! My resolution of thanking you for your kindness to Lydia had certainly great effect. *Too much* I am afraid; for what becomes of the moral, if our comfort springs from a breach of promise, for I ought not to have mentioned the subject? This will never do.'

'You need not distress yourself. The moral will be perfectly fair. Lady Catherine's unjustifiable endeavours to separate us were the means of removing all my doubts. I am not indebted for my present happiness to your eager desire of expressing your gratitude. I was not in a humour to wait for an opening of yours. My aunt's intelligence had given me hope, and I was determined at once to know everything.'

'Lady Catherine has been of infinite use, which ought to make her happy, for she loves to be of use. But tell me, what did you come down to Netherfield for? Was it merely to ride to Longbourn and be embarrassed? or had you intended any more serious consequences?'

'My real purpose was to see *you*, and to judge, if I could, whether I might ever hope to make you love me. My avowed one, or what I avowed to myself, was to see whether your sister was still partial to Bingley, and if she were, to make the confession to him which I have since made.'

'Shall you ever have courage to announce to Lady Catherine what is to befall her?'

'I am more likely to want time than courage, Elizabeth. But it ought to be done; and if you will give me a sheet of paper it shall be done directly.'

'And if I had not a letter to write myself, I might sit by you, and admire the evenness of your writing, as another young lady once did. But I have an aunt, too, who must not be longer neglected.'

From an unwillingness to confess how much her intimacy with Mr. Darcy had been over-rated, Elizabeth had never yet answered Mrs. Gardiner's long letter; but now, having *that* to communicate which she knew would be most welcome, she was almost ashamed to find that her uncle and aunt had already lost three days of happiness, and immediately wrote as follows:—

'I would have thanked you before, my dear aunt, as I ought to have done, for your long, kind, satisfactory detail of particulars; but, to say the truth, I was too cross to write. You supposed more than really existed. But *now* suppose as much as you choose; give a loose to your fancy, indulge your imagination in every possible flight which the subject will afford, and unless you believe me actually married, you cannot greatly err. You must write again very soon, and praise him a great deal more than you did in your last. I thank you again and again for not going to the Lakes. How could I be so silly as to wish it? Your idea of the ponies is delightful. We will go round the park every day. I am the happiest creature in the world. Perhaps other people have said so before, but no one with such justice. I am happier even than Jane; she only smiles, I laugh. Mr. Darcy sends you all the love in the world that can be spared from me. You are all to come to Pemberley at Christmas. Yours, etc.

Mr. Darcy's letter to Lady Catherine was in a different style, and still different from either was what Mr. Bennet sent to Mr. Collins, in return for his last.

'DEAR SIR—I must trouble you once more for congratulations. Elizabeth will soon be the wife of Mr. Darcy. Console Lady Catherine as well as you can. But, if I were you, I would stand by the nephew. He has more to give.—Yours sincerely,' etc.

Miss Bingley's congratulations to her brother on his approaching marriage were all that was affectionate and insincere. She wrote even to Jane on the occasion, to express her delight, and repeat all her former professions of regard. Jane was not deceived, but she was affected; and though feeling no reliance on her, could not help writing her a much kinder answer than she knew was deserved.

The joy which Miss Darcy expressed on receiving similar information was as sincere as her brother's in sending it. Four sides of paper were insufficient to contain all her delight, and all her earnest desire of being loved by her sister.

Before any answer could arrive from Mr. Collins, or any congratulations to Elizabeth from his wife, the Longbourn family heard that the Collinses were come themselves to Lucas Lodge. The reason of this sudden removal was soon evident. Lady Catherine had been rendered so exceedingly angry by the contents of her nephew's letter, that Charlotte, really rejoicing in the match, was anxious to get away till the storm was blown over. At such a moment the arrival of her friend was a sincere pleasure to Elizabeth, though in the course of their meetings she must sometimes think the pleasure dearly bought, when she saw Mr. Darcy exposed to all the parading and obsequious civility of her husband. He bore it, however, with admirable calmness. He could even listen to Sir William Lucas, when he complimented him on carrying away the brightest jewel of the country, and expressed his hopes of their all meeting frequently at St. James's, with very decent composure. If he did shrug his shoulders, it was not till Sir William was out of sight.

Mrs. Philips's vulgarity was another, and, perhaps, a greater tax on his forbearance; and though Mrs. Philips, as well as her sister, stood in too much awe of him to speak with the familiarity which Bingley's good humour encouraged, yet, whenever she *did* speak, she must be vulgar. Nor was her respect for him, though it made her more quiet, at all likely to make her more elegant. Elizabeth did all she could to shield him from the frequent notice of either, and was ever anxious to keep him to herself, and to those of her family with whom he might converse without mortification; and though the uncomfortable feelings arising from all this took from the season of courtship much of its pleasure, it added to the hope of the future; and she looked forward with delight to the time when they should be removed from society so little pleasing to either, to all the comfort and elegance of their family party at Pemberley.

CHAPTER LXI

HAPPY for all her maternal feelings was the day on which Mrs. Bennet got rid of her two most deserving daughters. With what delighted pride she afterwards visited Mrs. Bingley, and talked of Mrs. Darcy, may be guessed. I wish I could say, for the sake of her family, that the accomplishment of her earnest desire in the establishment of so many of her children produced so happy an effect as to make her a sensible amiable, well-informed woman for the rest of her life; though, perhaps, it was lucky for her husband, who might not have relished domestic felicity in so unusual a form, that she still was occasionally nervous and invariably silly.

Mr. Bennet missed his second daughter exceedingly; his affection for her drew him oftener from home than anything else could do. He delighted in going to Pemberley, especially when he was least expected.

Mr. Bingley and Jane remained at Netherfield only a twelvemonth. So near a vicinity to her mother and Meryton relations was not desirable even to *his* easy temper, or *her* affectionate heart. The darling wish of his sisters was then gratified: he bought an estate in a neighbouring county to Derbyshire; and Jane and Elizabeth, in addition to every other source of happiness, were within thirty miles of each other.

Kitty, to her very material advantage, spent the chief of her time with her two elder sisters. In society so superior to what she had generally known, her improvement was great. She was not of so ungovernable a temper as Lydia; and, removed from the influence of Lydia's example, she became, by proper attention and management, less irritable, less ignorant, and less insipid. From the further disadvantage of Lydia's society she was of course carefully kept; and though Mrs. Wickham frequently invited her to come and stay with her, with the promise of balls and young men, her father would never consent to her going.

Mary was the only daughter who remained at home; and she was necessarily drawn from the pursuit of accomplishments by Mrs. Bennet's being quite unable to sit alone. Mary was obliged to mix more with the world, but she could still moralise over every morning visit; and as she was no longer mortified by comparisons between her sisters' beauty and her own, it was suspected by her father that she submitted to the change without much reluctance.

As for Wickham and Lydia, their characters suffered no revolution from the marriage of her sisters. He bore with philosophy the conviction that Elizabeth must now become acquainted with whatever of his ingratitude and falsehood had before been unknown to her; and, in spite of everything was not wholly without hope that Darcy might yet be prevailed on to make his fortune. The congratulatory letter which Elizabeth received from Lydia on her marriage explained to her that, by his wife at least, if not by himself, such a hope was cherished. The letter was to this effect:—

'MY DEAR LIZZY—I wish you joy. If you love Mr. Darcy half so well as I do my dear Wickham, you must be very happy. It is a great comfort to have you so rich; and when you have nothing else to do, I hope you will think of us. I am sure Wickham would like a place at court very much; and I do not think we shall have quite money enough to live upon without some help. Any place would do of about three or four hundred a year; but, however, do not speak to Mr. Darcy about it, if you had rather not.—Yours,' etc.

As it happened that Elizabeth had much rather not, she endeavoured in her answer to put an end to every entreaty and expectation of the kind. Such relief, however, as it was in her power to afford, by the practice of what might be called economy in her own private expenses, she frequently sent them. It had always been evident to her that such an income as theirs, under the direction of two persons so extravagant in their wants, and heedless of the future, must be very insufficient to their support; and whenever they changed their quarters, either Jane or herself was sure of being applied to for some little assistance towards discharging their bills. Their manner of living, even when the restoration of peace dismissed them to a home, was unsettled in the extreme. They were always moving from place to place in quest of a cheap situation, and always spending more than they ought. His affection for her soon sank into indifference: hers lasted a little longer; and, in spite of her youth and her manners, she retained all the claims to reputation which her marriage had given her.

Though Darcy could never receive *him* at Pemberley, yet, for Elizabeth's sake, he assisted him further in his profession. Lydia was occasionally a visitor there, when her husband was gone to enjoy himself in London or Bath; and with the Bingleys they both of them frequently stayed so long that even Bingley's good humour was overcome, and he proceeded so far as to *talk* of giving them a hint to be gone.

Miss Bingley was very deeply mortified by Darcy's marriage; but as she thought it advisable to retain the right of visiting at Pemberley, she dropt all her resentment; was fonder than ever of Georgiana, almost as attentive to Darcy as heretofore, and paid off every arrear of civility to Elizabeth.

Pemberley was now Georgiana's home; and the attachment of the sisters was exactly what Darcy had hoped to see. They were able to love each other, even as well as they intended. Georgiana had the highest opinion in the world of Elizabeth; though at first she often listened with an astonishment bordering on alarm at her lively, sportive manner of talking to her brother. Him who had always inspired in herself a respect which almost overcame her affection she now saw the object of open pleasantry. Her mind received knowledge, which had never before fallen in her way. By Elizabeth's instructions she began to comprehend that a woman may take liberties with her husband, which a brother will not always allow in a sister more than ten years younger than himself.

Lady Catherine was extremely indignant on the marriage of her nephew; and as she gave way to all the genuine frankness of her character, in her reply to the letter which announced its arrangement, she sent him language so very abusive, especially of Elizabeth, that for some time all intercourse was at an end. But at length, by Elizabeth's persuasion, he was prevailed on to overlook the offence, and seek a reconciliation; and, after a little further resistance on the part of his aunt, her resentment gave way, either to her affection for him, or her curiosity to see how his wife conducted herself; and she condescended to wait on them at Pemberley, in spite of that pollution which its woods had received, not merely from the presence of such a mistress, but visits of her uncle and aunt from the city.

With the Gardiners they were always on the most intimate terms. Darcy, as well as Elizabeth, really loved them; and they were both ever sensible of the warmest gratitude towards the persons who, by bringing her into Derbyshire had been the means of uniting them.